FEARFUL BREAKERS

CHART & COMPASS: BOOK ONE

JANICE SEBRING

ANTIMACASSAR BOOKS

Bible verses from The Holy Bible, English Standard Version. ESV® Text Edition: 2016. Copyright © 2001 by Crossway Bibles, a publishing ministry of Good News Publishers.

Book design and production by Domini Dragoone.

Cover images: "The Capture of Havana, 1762, Taking the Town, 14 August", by Dominic Serres, from WikiMedia Commons. Vintage Papers from TomChalky.com. From 123rf.com: Map, Compass, and Scroll © Andrey Kuzmin; Chisel © Feedough; Hammer © Black Room Studio; back cover Tools © Fong Fong.

Maps by Nat Case, INCase, LLC

Dedicated to my father, Thomas H. Sebring, who loved books and treasure ships. After his death I found his encouraging words penciled on the draft of an early chapter of this book and they buoyed me up throughout the research and writing.

When I was a child, I spoke like a child, I thought like a child, I reasoned like a child. When I became a man, I gave up childish ways. — 1 Corinthians 13: 11

CONTENTS

THE THUNDER OF CANNON

T he sound of cannon came across the waters and took the crew of the *Alejandro* sloop by surprise. British frigates were firing on Spanish vessels. War had found them at last. The conflict had been long anticipated, but somehow they had never expected it to begin now, the 2nd of June, 1762. It had been long expected, yet still they found themselves surprised.

Most of all, he, José Albañez Velázquez, had never thought that the war would find him. He did not belong here, had never wanted to be here, had done all that he could to avoid this moment. Yet, despite all his efforts, he was standing at the bulwark, watching the ships exchange fire, studying the faint puffs of smoke from the guns as if they could reveal the progress of the battle.

He was serving under his uncle, Tío Policarpo, as an ordinary seaman, on the trading sloop *Alejandro*, along with three other crewmen and the mate, Calixto. The *Alejandro*, along with the *Penélope* sloop, had been hired to carry wood from a port up the coast back to the Royal Shipyard in Havana, escorted by three ships belonging to the Spanish navy. On the voyage out they were carrying the families of high-ranking naval officials who sought to escape the pestilential miasmas of Havana by retreating to the hills of Matanzas. It was then, as they prepared to tack for Matanzas, that the British ships had appeared out of nowhere.

His own family had accompanied them. Mamá, accompanied by his sister Magdalena, planned a visit to her parents in Matanzas, the city of his birth. They were on the *Penélope*, along with Señora Morejón and her children, including Marianela, at the age of fifteen just a year younger than José. Marianela, with her soft dark eyes and smooth black hair. Sometimes she lifted up those dark eyes to him and smiled, and his insides gave a somersault. He thought of those dark eyes now and his fear intensified.

Papá was with him on the *Alejandro*. His father did not belong here, was not a member of the crew, did not follow the sea for a living. He had a joiner's shop in Havana, and was here only for his health, to make a restorative visit to Matanzas. He stood by José's side, watching the battle. Both their thoughts were preoccupied with the *Penélope*, now under threat from British gunnery. José thought he could pick up the scent of gunpowder on the wind, but surely they were too far away.

How had it come to this, on what had begun as a perfect day? A brief squall had washed away the salt that encrusted the sails and the lines, and left the sky a clear azure, dotted with soft cumulus clouds. A light breeze cooled their faces and filled the white sails. Rainwater sparkled on the rigging and sunlight danced on the wavelets. The passengers, content after a filling breakfast prepared by Cristóbal, their cook, smiled as they strolled the deck, while the children raced about, laughing. Bernabela, one of the slaves who attended the women, was flirting with Tondo, who was hauling on a staysail sheet, smiling back and displaying his well-muscled arms. The sloop, too, was in perfect form, for Tío Policarpo took pride in a well-run vessel. Her paint shone as the waves splashed off the bow, her rigging was well-tarred and her spars properly oiled. Every line was coiled down, every working sheet suitably belayed. Yet now, here they were, watching warships exchanging shot in a haze of angry smoke.

These thoughts were interrupted as Tío Policarpo gave orders to tack as he set a new course for Matanzas, a course that would also take them closer to the English vessels, beating against the wind, hoping that the English, preoccupied with their prey, would let the sloop reach the city unmolested. The crew trimmed the sails, then trimmed them again, and they saw the green coast slowly, oh so slowly, grow larger on the horizon. Then they saw one of the frigates leave the battle and set a course to overhaul the *Alejandro*.

The next few hours were a blur of slow-moving terror. All about him was fear and desperation as the British frigate pressed on towards them. Tío Policarpo, one eye upon the frigate and its press of sail, shouted orders, and they all raced to obey. Calixto stood grim-faced at the tiller while the rest of the crew hauled with sweaty hands upon lines and studied the sails, willing them to fill with the needed wind. They could not resist taking stealthy glances at the frigate as they worked, and saw its sails and rigging become ever more distinct as it closed the distance between them. José saw Cipriano cross himself, and heard a mumbled prayer for better wind.

Their passengers huddled below decks and in the cabin. Occasional crying from a frightened child came to their ears, followed by the murmurings of its mother. José struggled to do his duty while his thoughts were with the *Penélope*, where Mamá and Magdalena, and Marianela too, were under fire from the English. On shore, in Matanzas, lived the rest of his family. Would the English land forces there? His father stood, supporting himself by the strength of the mast, silently observing it all, his pale face strained.

The crew fought to keep the fear from their faces as they wondered what fate they would meet at the hands of the English. Enslavement was a real threat for most of the crew, who, except for the mate, Calixto, were men of darker skin. José himself was *pardo*, or mixed-race, his lighter skin now made tawny by the sun, and his crewmates ranged from Cipriano's warm brown to the black hues of Tondo, Cristóbal and Tío Policarpo, all men of pure African ancestry. The British were a fierce, piratical race, with a long history of slave-trading, and all the crew feared falling captive to them.

As he worked, rushing to haul on or ease a line, then standing, watching the pursuing vessel narrow the distance between them, José was possessed by anger. He did not want to be at sea, had never wanted to be at sea. All he had ever wanted was to work by Papá's side in the joiner's shop. Becoming a sailor had been the idea of Papá's brother, his uncle Domingo. Tío Domingo had wheedled, cajoled, and manipulated Papá to send him to sea with him, and Papá had agreed, but only as a trial. The childless Domingo, however, had named José as his heir and so inveigled him inextricably into his business. All his life Domingo Albañez had taken risks, pursued wealth by dangerous means, and thought little of the cost to others. He had inserted himself between José and Papá, plotting to draw José into this life, and had succeeded. And now Spain was at war, and all their lives were at risk.

He felt betrayed by the sea, too. The sea, that earlier had sparkled blue in the sunlight, now appeared a vast expanse between the *Alejandro* and safety. The sunlight that had earlier warmed his skin made him sweat in its blaze, and its glare made it difficult for his squinting eyes to make out the progress of the ongoing battle. The tang of the salt spray was now bitter on his tongue, and the once cooling wind blew relentlessly, slowing their progress as they tacked first to starboard, then to larboard, forcing their way against the headwind.

Tío Policarpo ordered another tack, and the crew sprang to the lines. José watched the forestaysail begin to shiver in the wind, and released the starboard sheet. As he watched the sail shift in the wind, watched Cipriano seize the sheet and belay it, he balled up his fists and thought that they must prevail.

They must escape the British frigate that pursued them and protect the women and children now sheltering below in the hold. They must find a way to warn unsuspecting Havana, where almost a hundred ships lay anchored with their unsuspecting crews. And when that was accomplished, José knew he must find a way out of the life his uncle had planned for him and reclaim the life he had planned for himself, working alongside Papá in the joiner's shop. Nothing, he vowed, not the piratical English, his conniving uncle, or the sea itself would stop him. He was José Albañez Velázquez, and he would chart his own course.

2

THE BAY OF SLAUGHTERS

"Papá, Papá!" five-year-old José cried, as he scampered into his parents' room just as the first rays of sun crept through the shutters.

"You must not come in and wake up your mother. She works hard and needs her sleep," Papá scolded. Yet every morning José would scurry in like a sand crab, and every morning Papá would take him up in his arms.

It was not that José did not love his mother. Faustina Velázquez Vuelta was kind, and she smiled and laughed a good deal. She cooked satisfying meals: fried plantains, sweet and salty both, crisp and hot from the oil; sweet preserves from fresh fruit she bought in the market, and, sometimes, *ajiaco*, an ever-surprising stew of available vegetables, fish, and spices. She dressed and bathed José when he was small, mended his clothing when it tore, tended his scrapes when he fell, and gave him many warm kisses. Every Sunday as they walked to Mass, she held his hand in hers. Her plump, golden face with her soft features and wide brown eyes crinkled often with smiles as she listened to him chatter, and her rough, brown curls, so like his own, tickled his face when she hugged him. She was wise, too, understanding that José was, first and foremost, his father's boy. She was glad when his younger sister Magdalena was old enough to toddle behind big brother José and climb up into the bed as well.

They all lived all together in Matanzas, in his grandparents' house, behind the joiner's shop where his father and grandfather worked, a pink house with bright yellow trim, built by his grandfather. In front was a sign that read "La Flor de Caña," the name of the shop, in big black letters, and painted on it the plume-like pink flower of the sugar cane. The house stood near the San Juan River, one of three rivers that flowed through the city.

There, in Matanzas, José was embraced by warmth; his mother's kisses were warm when she tucked him into bed, his father's hand was warm in his when they walked down to the harbor to see the ships, and his whole being was warmed by the penetrating heat of the inescapable Cuban sun. It warmed the bricks and plaster of their home; it warmed the patio of the house where he played with his sister. Its rays filled the streets, reflected off the plastered walls of the houses, sparkled on the blue waters of the sea, and shone between the slats of the shutters and across his bed while José took his siesta. The sun warmed the soil and the seeds; it warmed the soft rain that seemed to fall every afternoon during the summer rainy season, and the sun and rain brought forth the exuberant vegetation that blanketed the hills surrounding the town of Matanzas. It was his constant companion, already abroad when José awoke, and it did not slip beyond the distant hills until José had already slipped into his little cot.

To the elders in his life, however, the warmth that embraced José was a smothering heat that in the midday of summer could fell a hale man; a heat that drove the people into the cool shelter of their homes in the afternoon, where they would nap until had moderated. That same sun blinded his father's eyes when he looked across the sea, watching for the sails of Tío Domingo's sloop. It glared in the face of all the elders, giving their faces almost permanent squints and leaving tiny wrinkles about their eyes.

Everyone knew, however, that it was the sea that ruled Matanzas. Like a benevolent monarch, it used its power, for the most part, for good. It was the sea that had made the bay of Matanzas a deep harbor penetrating far into the land of Cuba's northern coast. The three rivers offered their waters to the bay, and ships sheltered there from the winds. The sea had fed the Taíno Indians who once lived there; it brought the Spanish explorers who first died at the hands of those same Taínos, thus giving the place its name, the "Bay of Slaughters." It brought Dutch pirates to rob the Spanish, and finally it brought Spanish settlers. The sea provided them a livelihood as well, carrying their tobacco harvest to Havana and bringing them slaves to help with that harvest. It provided a livelihood to the fishermen who fed the tobacco farmers, and to the ships that in the coastal trade that carried goods to and from Havana. The sea also provided a livelihood to those ship owners in Matanzas, Tío Domingo among them, who found a way around the inconveniences of the Spanish trade laws.

The sea did not only provide them sustenance. It permeated their entire existence. The breeze off the sea lent a briny tang to the air; the smell of salt seasoned the air they breathed. The salt encrusted itself on Matanzas, on its houses, its wharves, its people. Matanzans breathed the sea, they tasted the sea, they touched the sea every day of their lives. Most of all, they respected the sea. The azure expanse that had brought the town into being over the centuries could, they knew, sweep it away in a few hours. Sometimes, too, men went to sea and did not come home. Matanzans lived ever mindful of the power of the sea and its fierce winds. They kept a sharp eye on the waves, the wind, and the sky, particularly in those months from late summer through the fall when the tropical winds could rise to hurricane force.

It was the sea that had brought his father and his uncle here, from a faraway exotic land, but while his uncle, Domingo, continued to live by the sea, owning, with his partner Anselmo Morejón Acosta, three sloops, his father had settled on the shore, mastering the joiner's trade in the shop of José's grandfather, his abuelo, José Velázquez Pacheco. Abuelo's frame was spare, and when he reached down to pick up José, his hands were hard and brown, like the wood he used in his shop. His words and gestures were spare, like his frame.

Abuelo's stern manner did not invite questions, but occasionally, usually after a long day of work and with a glass of *aguardiente*, the strong drink distilled from sugar cane, Abuelo began to speak of his past.

"My father, too, was a joiner, and I was his fifth son, and the youngest. Our village in Andalusia was small and could not support so many joiners. So, I joined the army of His Catholic Majesty," he began, sitting back in his chair.

"How did you come to Cuba, Abuelo?" José asked.

"My regiment, the Regiment of Sevilla, was stationed here many years ago in Cuba to protect this island from the enemies that would like to steal this rich possession away from Spain. We are surrounded by enemy nations here – the

French, and most piratical of all, the English." Abuelo became fierce as he said
this.

"That was how he met me," interrupted Abuelita.

"Yes, I met the beautiful Catalina Vuelta." Abuelo took control of the narrative
again. "And I found that, having left a land with too many carpenters, I was in one
with too few. When my enlistment expired, I married your Abuelita Catalina and
set up this shop."

"And we had three daughters, Nicolaza, Beatriz, and of course, your mother
Faustina," Abuelita leapt in again.

"And Alejandro," Mamá whispered softly.

With the mention of that name, the sun slipped below the horizon, leaving the
room draped in shadows. José feared to break the silence that had fallen upon
them.

"Tell me about Alejandro," he asked Mamá as she tucked him into his cot.

She sighed. "He was the bright star of the family. He was a fine joiner, and was
meant to take over the shop one day. But a *blanca* woman broke his heart and he
signed onto a privateer."

"Just like Papá!" said José.

"Yes, he was a privateersman, along with your uncles and Señor Morejón. But
they came home, and he did not. And my father, from a family with too many
sons, became a man with no son." She led him in his Paternoster, kissed him on
the forehead, and left the room.

José lay in the dark and thought about that war, the Guerra del Asiento. Papá
said the English called it the War of Jenkins' Ear. It was a silly name, and made José
laugh. How exciting it must have been. He knew Papá and his uncles had fought
bravely during the war and taken many prizes. Mamá had met Papá during that
war, and his aunts Nicolaza and Beatriz had married privateersmen. He wished
he could have met Alejandro. He fell asleep and dreamt of ships, of cannons and
smoke, and brave men with cutlasses slashing their way to glory.

He was awakened in the early morning by a ray of sun tickling his face. His
sister, Magdalena, bare and brown in the morning sun, pattered after José, trying

to imitate him as he did small chores for his mother, feeding the chickens in the courtyard and sweeping the floor. She begged to help with the feeding and then stood, holding the basket of corn, and squealed when the chickens surged about her, almost engulfing her tiny form in their greed. The basket fell from her hands, and she ran back into the shelter of the house. Perched on her fat legs, she looked to José like just one more chicken, and he laughed and called her "*polluela*."

After his chores were done, José and Magdalena played in the courtyard while Mamá and Abuelita did their own chores. Mamá, to drive away the boredom of a task too often repeated, sang one of the songs she had learned from her father, a song from his home in Andalusia. José loved the haunting melodies of these songs, with notes that tumbled and danced like the waves on the beach. José and Magdalena danced to the music, a dance Mamá had taught them, and they waved their arms and stomped their feet about the courtyard until the chickens fled in confusion and they fell down, breathless and laughing, and the two women laughed with them.

In midmorning the family sat down to breakfast, and Abuelita held Magdalena, her favorite, on her lap and she fed her bits of cassava bread. José, his small head just bobbing up above the edge of the table, sat between the upright forms of his father and Abuelo. Mamá gave him a spoon to eat the custardy flesh of the guanábana. The tangy aftertaste made his eyes open wide.

Abuelita, too, had a song she liked to sing, a song she had learned from her grandfather. It was a simple song, with a beat like a pounding heart, and José's grandmother kept the beat with her foot, tap-tap on the floor, and she sang it that morning after breakfast, as she took up her mending.

"What does it mean, Abuelita?" José asked her.

"I don't know myself. The song and its words are African," she replied, and laughed at José's look of surprise.

"How did you learn a song from Africa? Did you go there?" He sat down next to her, anticipating a story.

"Go there? No, *niño*, Africa is far across the ocean. My grandfather was born there. His African name was Achukwo, but in Cuba they gave him the name

Aníbal. He came to Cuba on a big ship. There was a war in his country and he was taken prisoner and sold to be a slave here, far away from his family."

Roberto Albañez rose from the table. "I have much work to do," he said briefly, and he was gone, crossing the courtyard into the shop at the front of the house. José saw that his father's plate was still half full, his fish only half eaten.

Mamá gave a sharp look at Abuelita, the sort she gave to José and Magdalena when they created a disturbance during the meal. "You know that subject touches him too closely."

Abuelita looked down at her plate and pushed her food about with her knife. "I forget sometimes", she said softly, "he has his own story."

After their midday dinner they lay down for their siesta, to escape the worst of the midday heat. Today, however, José could not sleep, for his imagination kept turning relentlessly to the story of the African taken far from his home. Later, while his father was still in the shop, and the warm summer rain beat down on the roof, Abuelita sat mending a shirt for Abuelo. José peppered her with questions about her African grandfather: "Did he ever go home? Did he hear from his family?"

"*Niño*, he could never go home again. Africa is too far away. No letters go to Africa, and no letters come from there. The Africans do not know how to write letters or even to read them." Her needle went in and out of the soft fabric.

"But why didn't he run away? Didn't he want to go home and see his family?" José imagined being taken away from his own family, from Papá, and thought it must be like falling off the edge of the world.

"It is not so easy for a slave to run away. They hunt him down and bring him back. Besides, where would he go? Not back to Africa. It is too far." Abuelita related these tragic facts calmly, still placidly working her needle.

"So he was never free again?" José kept prodding.

"That I did not say. He worked hard and was clever with his hands, and in time he bought his freedom. He worked for a tanner and married his daughter. That daughter was my grandmother." Abuelita smiled and put aside her mending, now completed. She tousled José's hair as she pulled him close to her knees.

"And then they had a baby and he was your father." José continued the story.

She picked up a palm frond and fanned herself. "Yes, he was my father. His name was Jerónimo; Jerónimo Vuelta."

"And did Jerónimo also marry an African?" José hoped not. He had seen Africans slaves, *bozales*, at Mass at the Church of San Carlos. They were very dark, and spoke Spanish poorly, in a strange accent. They would gather on Sundays in their societies, the *cabildos*, and play the drums and sing songs from their lost home, songs that were foreign and different. His mother hinted, frowning, that many of them were not Christian, but sacrificed animals to pagan gods. He did not like to think of such foreignness being part of his family, part of his own being. His father was foreign, it was true, but it was a warm and familiar foreignness. His father was a Catholic, and he told stories of a sad home with brave men and sad songs.

"Oh no, those in my mother's family were all *pardos*, of mixed blood, and have been free-born for generations. They say that very far back, one of our family was a soldier with Columbus, who fell in love with a Taíno princess. Another one, they say, was a French pirate. He took shelter in the harbor of Matanzas and often slipped ashore to visit his beloved, his *enamorada*."

Then Abuelita leaned closer to him and said with quiet intensity, "The Pimienta family was not happy when their daughter wished to marry such a dark *pardo*, the son of an African, a former slave. No, they were not happy at all. In their view, it was an unequal match. But my mother had a violent passion for him."

"Then did your father and mother get married anyways?"

"Yes, he persuaded her to run away with him. Then their families had to agree. Octavia's family could not have born the shame otherwise." Abuelita fanned herself with vehemence.

José noticed his mother quiet in the corner where she had been playing with Magdalena. Tears ran down her cheeks, and she wiped them away with the corner of her kerchief, obscuring her face. Magdalena ran to her and hugged her leg, and Mamá stroked her curls.

"Such a fuss!" exclaimed Abuelita. "This is not a story about you."

"Yes, but it reminds me..." she sobbed. "I just want to pretend it never happened."

"You did nothing wrong," clucked Abuelita.

"Everyone knows I have been a fool," replied Mamá, wiping her eyes with a corner of her kerchief.

"The world is full of fools," said Abuelita. "You are just one more."

José still wanted to hear more of the story. "Did your family want you to marry Abuelo?" José did not ask whether his grandparents wanted their daughter to marry his father; it was impossible that anyone would object to a man so clever, and kind, and good.

Abuelita was relieved by the break in the silence. "My family was very pleased with him; what *pardo* family would not like their daughter to marry a *blanco*, to whiten the blood? And your grandfather is a very fine man, a soldier and very honest. But we had to wait to marry until he retired from his regiment."

"Abuelo is a *blanco*?" It had never occurred to José that his grandfather was not *pardo*; he was swarthy, and had wiry brown hair, and warm brown eyes, like some of the lighter *pardo* men, like José himself.

"Ay, *niño*, all the *peninsulares*, those who come from Spain, are *blancos*. You know, don't you, that your grandfather was born in Andalusia? That is a place in Spain. The Moors conquered Andalusia and held it for many centuries, and they say that if you scratch someone from Andalusia, you will find a Moor. So perhaps your grandfather has some Moorish blood, and that is why he looks *pardo*. But do not say that to him! He is very proud to be a *peninsular*."

"Why didn't he marry a *peninsular*? Couldn't he find one he liked?" José did not stop to think that such a question might be considered an insult by his grandmother. Everyone knew that when a *blanco* married a *parda*, even a *parda* as kind as Abuelita, he lost status.

And his grandmother was not insulted. She, too, understood the rules. "Spain sends many men to Cuba, but it does not send many women. It is difficult for a *peninsular* to find a woman of his own kind to marry, and even difficult, sometimes, to find a white *criolla*, a Cuban-born woman, he can marry. But fortunately, your grandfather found me, and we have been very happy."

José was happy, too. The history of his family was the history of Cuba, and he was part of his island, and the island was part of him. Spanish conquistadors, soldiers, French pirates, Africans, and Taíno princesses, all came together in his island, and in him. He was the end of many chains of people, all leading to one place and one person: José Albañez Velázquez.

Many a time José would ask Abuelita to tell him again the stories about her family, and she obliged, repeating over and over these same tales, until they became a part of him.

In the afternoon José went to the front of house to spend time with Papá and Abuelo in the joiner's shop, Magdalena close on his heels. He loved the smell of the fresh-cut wood, and the feel of the sawdust in his hands. The two children ran their hands through the soft sawdust, and took curls of yellow wood, planed from the boards, and put them behind their ears. Papá put José to work sweeping and fetching tools, then putting them carefully back in their places. He nodded approvingly as he named off each saw, chisel, and drill.

Another day Papá taught him to sand the wood, smoothing away the splinters and tool marks until the surface was as smooth as a china plate. Papá caressed the satiny wood with satisfaction. "You will make a good joiner someday. The two of us will work side by side, here in the shop, then." And José glowed with delight at the thought.

Many members of the family worked in the shop. Abuelo was the master, and when men entered the shop to arrange for work it was to him they spoke. Papá, too, was a skilled joiner, and assisted him. José's cousin, Jacinto, Tía Beatriz's son, and Gonzalo, Tía Nicolaza's son, were apprentices, learning the skills of the trade. In the shop they did many kinds of work; they made doors and windows, built shutters, made simple tables and chairs, and carried out every sort of repair. Everywhere José walked about Matanzas he could see the work of their hands, painted bright colors of blue, pink, and green, gleaming bright in the sunlight, and he felt proud.

Far too often, they also built coffins. Coffins for those who had died of fever, coffins for women who had died in childbirth, for babies that did not thrive but wasted away in their mother's arms, for Matanzans who had drowned in the great bay or one of the city's three rivers, for those who died in a work accident. Coffins, too, for those who simply faded away, old, and loved, and surrounded by family. Death came in many forms, and the Velázquez joinery shop was prepared for them all, there under the sign of the pink cane flower.

Sometimes older men, retired from the military, came in to talk with Abuelo, and sometimes they came to visit on Holy days, as well, and there were many of those, and they would all sit and smoke cigars and drink *aguardiente*, the strong drink made from fermented sugar cane. They gossiped of old comrades and life in the army, and on occasion they told stories of their service during the war, the war that had brought his father and uncle to Cuba. Abuelita did not like to hear these stories, for they reminded her of the son she had lost, but Abuelo did not mind. Although he had left the army before the war, he was proud of his service, and continued to think of himself as a soldier.

Once José asked him, "I saw Abuelita cry when Mamá mentioned Tío Alejandro. Why don't you cry?"

"Soldiers do not cry. I miss Alejandro, it is true, but I do not cry for him. He died a man, and of that I am proud. He was not a soldier, it is true, only a privateersman, but still, he died in the service of his king." Abuelo sat a little more erect when he said this, and his face, wrinkled and brown like the olives of his native Andalusia, looked more taut than usual. His dark eyes looked beyond José, into the distance.

"My father served the king," said José proudly.

"Your father served two kings," Abuelo said gravely.

"That was long ago, and best forgotten," said his father briefly, without looking up from the lathe where he was working. José, however, never forgot the two kings.

One day a man came into the shop to talk to Papá. Many men came to seek his counsel, and he replied, in careful, quiet tones, and they nodded and thanked him. This man had a paper for Papá to read. Roberto Albañez pored over them, squinting, and read out the most important passages.

"The offer is a good one, you think?" Señor Mederos asked.

"Yes," was the verdict of Papá, and the man smiled in relief. José knew that Papá had studied from books, and knew languages. Papá also kept all the books for La Flor de Caña, and was teaching Jacinto to keep the accounts, as well.

José was happiest when there were no outsiders in the shop, and Papá would talk to him while he worked. Often he spoke Gaelic, their secret language, for Papá came from a land called Scotland, far away, where they did not speak Spanish. José thought that Gaelic sounded like the warbling of birds and imagined that Papá had flown to Matanzas from his faraway land where seals disguised themselves as women and lived among the people, where brownies lived in the woods and worked magic, where the king who had stolen his throne waged cruel war upon its people. In Cuba they did not warble, they clucked in Spanish like the chickens that lived in their patio. Papá had flown to Matanzas, the land where flowers bloomed, trees bore sweet fruit, and the chickens clucked merrily together, and here he was happy with his chickens, safe from the cruel king. Papá told stories of this faraway land, fierce, tragic stories, most of them, and it was this, José imagined, that made his father often seem sad when he told them. It was good that his father had left such a sad land and come to be happy here in Cuba, with Mamá and José and Magdalena.

After the work of the long afternoon, and after the fierce afternoon showers had washed the dust from the air and left puddles in the muddy streets, the last lingering rays of light disappeared from the western sky and the family gathered together before bedtime. The door was open, to catch any cooling breeze from the bay, and they talked quietly, tired from the day's labors.

It was that time that José most relished. Then, while his mother and Abuelita sat and sewed, and Abuelo sat in the corner smoking a cigar and drinking *aguardiente*, José sat on his father's knee and listened to his stories. He played with his father's red curls, tied in a simple queue, and marveled at their softness. He wondered if the faint reddish tint in his own curls came from his father, although his own hair was rougher and dark brown. He marveled too at the impossible whiteness of his father's skin peeping out occasionally in places where it had not been burned and reddened by the sun. His mother's skin, in contrast, was the softest tan, like the wood of the pine.

Magdalena pleaded to join José in Papá's lap, and José grew stiff and angry as Papá lifted her up, placed her on one of his knees, and said, "God has given me two knees, one for each of my children." She soon tired of this, however, and slipped down, trotting off to join Mamá and Abuelita. Then José relaxed again, and burrowed closer into his father's arms and listened to a story, a story from his father's lost homeland, told in his native tongue.

His favorite story was the story of the special name, the name he shared with Papá and Tío Domingo. "A long time ago, the great Somerled was Lord of the Isles, ruling over all the many islands on the west coast of Scotland. He wished the hand in marriage of Ragnhild, the daughter of Olaf the Red, the King of Mann. Olaf, however, refused to allow Ragnhild to marry Somerled." His father stopped to take a swallow of his *aguardiente*.

"Then what, Papá?" José knew, of course, but loved to hear it told again.

"Then Macarill, the nephew of Somerled, devised a scheme to help his uncle. He arranged to go out with Olaf in his galley, but before they set sail, he drilled holes in the hull, and filled them with wax. When they were far out on the sea, the wax melted, and the ship began to take on water and to founder."

"Then what, Papá?" The best part was about to come.

"Macarill promised to save the vessel, on one condition; that Olaf give his daughter to Somerled in marriage. Olaf agreed, and Macarill produced the wooden pegs he had previously made to plug the holes. After that Macarill was called 'the carpenter,' and his sons were called 'Mac an t-Saior,' son of the carpenter."

"And are we sons of the carpenter?" José always asked.

And his father always answered, "Yes, lad, we are. We are McIntyres, you, and I, and your uncle."

One night José found the courage to ask a question that had begun to trouble him. "Abuelo says it is important not to lose your good name. Did you lose your good name? Is that why we call ourselves Albañez?" He looked up into his father's face with worried eyes.

His father was silent a moment, and then his rare smile flashed across his face, his smile that always reminded José of the sun breaking out from behind clouds.

"I did not lose it, lad, I but put it aside. It is still there, and I will die with it. Albañez is a name of convenience, because MacIntyre is too odd a name for a Spanish tongue." His father put down his glass in a manner that said he was finished with both the drink and the discussion.

José, however, was not finished. "Who was the first Albañez? And what does the name mean?"

His father considered his words, and then continued. "The first Albañez was my brother Donnie, your Tío Domingo. It was he who chose the name, who did not care any longer to use his own name carried by his family from the time of Somerled. Albañez means simply son of Scotland. It is an honest name, at least. When I joined your uncle I used the name he had chosen." He stood up with an air that said that story time was truly over. "Time it is, now, for both you and your sister to go to bed." Stories that began to touch on his father's life before he came to Cuba usually ended abruptly. José's eyes were already closing as his father carried him to his cot and tucked him in and pulled close the light curtains that sheltered him from the mosquitos.

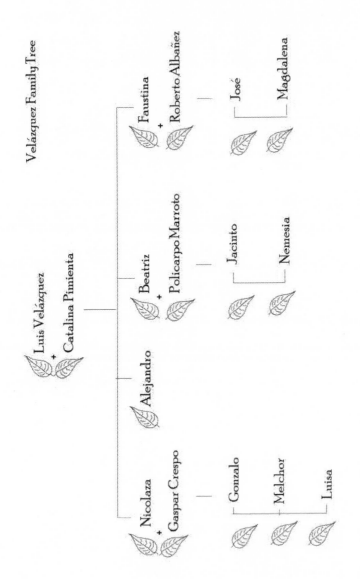

3

A LIFE AT SEA

"When will Domingo return?" José heard Abuelita ask. "He is overdue."

"Domingo is the master of many things," replied Papá, "but no man commands the wind."

José knew that the wind was something to be feared. He also knew that both Tío Domingo and Tío Policarpo were engaged in dangerous trade, but he did not understand why. They carried valuable cargoes to places where they were needed and wanted, yet there were ships abroad that sought to stop them. Tío Gaspar engaged in coastal trade, so his business was less risky, yet still the weather was an ever-present danger for he had heard his aunts and cousins whisper of the dangers at sea. Most of all they feared a hurricane, the "storm of water and all winds."

"Hurricane season is upon us," Abuelo said, shaking his head. José knew, as did everyone in the Caribbean, that with the beginning of June came the risk of hurricanes. Those dangerous storms were at their fiercest from September through October, and now, September had already begun, and he had attended the Mass just a few weeks ago in which the people of Matanzas had prayed for divine mercy and protection from the coming season of storms.

Papá went down to the bay every day to scan for sails, taking José with him. They watched the movement of the clouds, and how the trees and bushes fluttered and bent in a strong breeze. Papá also spent the time at the bay teaching José to identify the different vessels: schooners, sloops, the rare visiting square-rigged ship. The *Orfeo* would not drop anchor in Matanzas harbor, at least not upon arrival, for her business required a more secluded mooring. Still, Papá hoped that another vessel would bring word of the sloop.

Then one day Señor Parreño burst into the shop crying, "Don Roberto, the *Orfeo* has been seen to the east!"

Cheers filled the shop.

The whole family fathered at the house that night: Tío Gaspar and Tía Nicolaza, with their three children; and Tío Policarpo and Tía Beatriz, with two of their own. The Morejón family also joined them. Anselmo Morejón was Tío Domingo's business partner. Together they owned three sloops: Tío Domingo was captain of the *Orfeo*, Tío Gaspar of the *Penélope*, and Tío Policarpo of the *Alejandro*. Señor Morejón did not go to sea; he managed the partnership's affairs on land. He kept the books, purchased the supplies and trade goods, and disposed of the cargoes they brought back. Tonight, he had brought his guitar to play for them. The men smoked their cigars, and the women, too, smoked cigars and fanned themselves quietly, expectantly.

Then Tío Domingo entered the room, like a fresh wind from the north. Voices became louder, laughter rang out, children ran up to Tío Domingo to be tossed into the air, squealing. Noise and turmoil crowded the room, filled it to overflowing, until José felt as if he were drowning. He stood back from the hubbub. Then Tío Domingo's arms reached down and swung him up, out of the confusion and on to his broad shoulders. It was exhilarating, to ride high above the others, but frightening, too. He whimpered, and Tío Domingo held him tight, which frightened him all the more.

"Today you see the world from my shoulders; one day from the masthead," Tío Domingo said.

José thought it would be splendid to gaze upon the world from the very top of the mast. Papá could point out all the sights to him. Now, however, he begged to be put down.

Tío Domingo swung José back to the ground and called out, "Does no one have something to quench the thirst of a sailor just home from the sea?" Abuelo passed him a glass of *aguardiente*. Tío Domingo took his drink, and Mamá pulled José close to her.

Then Abuelita passed around sweets, and plates of sliced fruit, oranges, sapotas, pineapple, and mamey, the latter's red flesh surrounding its great black pit. Mamá poured wine for the aunts, and sweet-tangy lemonade for the children. The men filled their glasses, and Tío Gaspar lit a cigar for Tío Domingo and passed it to him.

"Where did you go this time, Tío Domingo?" asked Jacinto.

"I have been where the drink is strong, the women are beautiful, and the *guarda costas* are scarce," said Tío Domingo, winking.

"Then you have been to Matanzas!" laughed Tío Gaspar, putting his arm around Tía Nicolaza and taking a long draft of his *aguardiente*. Tía Nicolaza gave a tired smile.

"Ah, where I have been, there were also merchants who appreciate fine tobacco, sold at a reasonable price." Tío Domingo winked again.

All the adults laughed at this, and the children laughed too, José among them. He did not know why he laughed, only that the others did so.

The women, especially, enjoyed the attentions of Tío Domingo. He brought them trifling presents, and paid them exorbitant compliments. He even kissed Tía Nicolaza's hands and said, "You have grown more beautiful since last I saw you," which made her blush.

Only Mamá stood back from the merriment, and to her Tío Domingo only bowed in respect as she gazed upon him, unsmiling.

Once upon a time Señor Morejón had gone to sea; he and all the uncles, and Papá, and the late Alejandro had served together on a privateer during the war. Tonight he toasted Tío Domingo, "To my brother-in-arms, Domingo Albañez!" he cried. All raised their glasses and cheered. Then Tío Domingo spoke. "And to Alejandro, who will never be forgotten." The glasses were raised again, and José saw a tear in Abuelita's eye.

"They were indeed like so many brothers," sighed Tía Nicolaza. "If Alejandro had lived, he, too, would own ships now."

"Alejandro is a ship," said Tía Beatriz. The children laughed, not entirely kindly, to think that their late uncle was a ship. Tía Beatriz was taken gravely ill after her brother's death, and now her words did not always make sense.

"*Alejandro* is my ship, and I will always take good care of him, *mi flor*," said Tío Policarpo, very kindly, and her round frame was enveloped by his great black arms. He was always gentle with her, even when she spoke foolishly.

"If Gaspar didn't gamble, he, too, would own ships now," he heard Abuelita say quietly.

"Shhh! Nicolaza will hear you!" warned Mamá.

"She already knows what I think," said Abuelita, unrepentant. "Of all my three girls, Faustina, you have done the best. Roberto takes good care of you and the children."

"You cannot say that Policarpo is not a good husband," replied Mamá.

"Oh, he gives his money away to every stray dog. If anything happened to him I don't know what would become of Beatriz. She can hardly take care of herself, let alone the two children." Abuelita drew on her cigar. "Roberto is a good, steady man. He is an excellent worker, and he does not waste his money."

Mamá only sighed.

"The other doesn't matter, *cariño*," said Abuelita, patting her daughter's arm.

The women had loaded the table with *ajiaco*, rice and beans, fried plantains and every good thing. Sometimes, on other days, food was scant, but on this occasion every family had found something special in their larder. They all ate until they could eat no more, a rare treat. Tío Domingo sat at one end of the table, telling tales of evading the *guarda costas*. The men and cousins listened and added details, for they knew these stories well. The women sat, eyes glowing with admiration. Mamá was quiet at the other end of the table, with Papá and Tía Beatriz. Tío Policarpo was telling stories about the strange ways of the French, for he had been born in Saint-Domingue.

José sat with Rafael, the son of Señor Morejón, and a year older than José. Magdalena was with Marianela, Rafael's sister. She was pretty and quiet, and José liked it when she visited their house. Rafael whispered to José of the pranks they would pull on the girls, who overheard and stuck out their tongues at them.

Then Señor Morejón brought out his guitar, and everyone danced. Tío Domingo made sure to twirl every member of the gentle sex across the floor, even the little girls. The women laughed, and the girls squealed with delight. Only Mamá refused a turn, taking Papá by the arm instead and leading him in a dance.

All was music and laughter, and in the confusion, Rafael seized José's arm and pulled him across the patio in the direction of the shop. "Come with me, I have something to share with you," he whispered, barely audible amid the sound of music and laughter. José followed willingly, for Rafael always found marvelous ways for the boys to amuse themselves.

They slipped through the door of the shop, and entered the dusty dark, half-lit by the glow of a lantern that Rafael carried.

"What is it?" José asked. Rafael's air of mystery suggested that his secret was one of which their elders would not approve.

"I have two things, in truth. First, these." And Rafael pulled two cigars from inside his loose shirt, which was curiously distended. José laughed in admiration, took one, and lit it from the lantern. Cigars were a rare treat. Some boys he knew smoked them every day, but Abuelo was frugal and believed that a good cigar was wasted on the young. The two boys sat and smoked their cigars contentedly.

"What is the second thing?" asked José, eyeing the bulky mass that remained under Rafael's shirt.

"That is my great surprise. Look!" And Rafael reached in his shirt and pulled out a bottle, the tawny glint of *aguardiente* just visible through the distorting waves of the bottle's green glass. It winked at them as if inviting them to adventure.

"What are we going to do with that?" José asked, astounded by his friend's daring.

"Ay, *Dios mío*, we drink it! Just like my papá! I slipped it in my shirt while they were telling their stories," said Rafael, and he put the bottle to his lips and took a great swig. His eyes opened wide in astonishment. He choked a bit, then regained his self-command and handed the bottle to José.

"What will he say if he finds you drinking it?" asked José, wondering, too, what Papá would think of boys drinking *aguardiente*.

"He told me I needed to start acting like a man. So, you see, that is what I am doing!" Rafael urged the bottle on José, who took it, not wishing to appear a milksop.

"Perhaps that is not what he meant," José replied, not wishing to disagree outright with his friend. He took a sip. The liquid burned his mouth like fire, and he gasped.

"That is not the right way. Take a big swallow," said Rafael, suiting his actions to his words. He choked a bit, then pounded his chest and handed the bottle back to José. "It takes practice. Soon we will master it."

José obediently took another drink, putting his head back this time and closing his eyes, eager to prove to Rafael that he, too, was a man like their fathers. Again the liquid burned as it went down, but now he began to feel a pleasant warm sensation emanating from his tummy. The world began to appear brighter. They smoked their cigars and continued to drink, passing the bottle back and forth. José continued to throw his head back to show Rafael that he was really drinking, but he kept the swallows small, just enough to keep up the warm feeling that suffused his being.

Then Rafael stood up, swaying slightly. "*Dios mío*, I am done for!" whispered Rafael. His eyes were fixed on a spot somewhere behind his friend. José turned and he too felt the grip of fear. He remembered that Tío Domingo had more than once described Señora Morejón Valdes as a man-of-war, solid in all her timbers and a terror to her enemies. She now appeared out of the dark and the smoke, bearing down upon the boys with sails crowded and a single purpose; to seize Rafael like a prize and carry him off to face his punishment. She wrested the bottle from his fingers and led him away, one ear firmly grasped between her strong fingers.

Behind Señora Morejón was a sight more terrifying to José. Papá stood looking down upon him, grave and silent.

"Rafael said..." José appealed.

"I am not interested in Rafael. I am only interested in the conduct of José. And he has disobeyed me." Papá stood, still looking down at José. At last he spoke. "I have told you what I think about boys and drink."

"Yes, Papá." José could not meet his father's eyes.

"And yet you disobeyed me." Papá's voice was low and hard.

"Yes, Papá." José watched as his father found a leather strap and turned to him.

"Bend over." José obeyed, his insides tight and his face warm with shame, as his father delivered ten strokes with the strap. They were painful, but less painful than his sense of disgrace.

"I do not enjoy doing this, lad, but you must learn your duty. Unless you learn duty, you will make a poor sort of a man."

Then José was ill, and emptied his stomach. His mother appeared, and her look of shock struck José to the heart. She began, wordlessly, to clean up the mess, and his father picked him up in his arms and carried him to bed, tucking him in with gentle hands. As he lay there, the bed seemed to rock like a ship, and his stomach rocked too, but worse still was the sting he still felt in his backside and the ache in his heart.

José awoke next morning with a pounding head and a thick tongue. He was listless and ate little, his stomach protesting at the odor of Mamá's fried fish. Abuelita gave him a little plain rice, and a banana, and that was good. He slept little during his siesta, his head full of the memory of Papá's angry voice and disappointed face. As he rose from his cot, his father came in from the shop, sawdust and the smell of fresh-cut wood clinging to his clothes.

He sat down on the cot next to José. "Did you boys think that you would be men, drinking spirits?"

"Yes, Papá." José wondered how Papá was able to see into his soul.

"It is no mark of manliness to overindulge in liquor. You can see such worthless wretches in any town. They enjoy the comradeship of other men, but never their respect." Papá spoke with great seriousness. "In my youth I knew a young man who drank too much and too often. It led him into foolish scrapes, and almost cost him his life. I would not want you to follow a similar path."

"Oh no, Papá!" José replied.

"All men drink, José, but a wise man does not allow the drink to command him. He remains in possession of his senses and his faculties. When you are old enough to be such a man, then it will be time to take a drink. Until then, you must keep to wine, well-watered, and learn the lessons of obedience and duty. When you can master yourself, then you can master spirits as well."

"Yes, Papá!" José replied again. His body still felt sluggish, but his spirits soared. His father had confided in him as if he were grown, and he wanted nothing more than to become that man Papá had described, strong and in command of himself, a man very like his father. He was exceptionally obedient the rest of the day, helping Abuelita with small tasks and teaching Magdalena how to pick up the chickens in her arms without upsetting them. Papá smiled at him as he wrapped carefully closed the thin curtains about his cot, and José enjoyed the sleep of the virtuous.

The next morning he awoke just as the sun was beginning to creep through their long windows, before the heat slowed the blood. To his surprise, Tío Domingo, who always stayed with the Moncalvo family when he was in Matanzas, was sitting with the family, a plate of cassava bread and fish before him as he brandished a glass of wine.

"Well, *niño*, how would you like to spend the day with me and see the *Orfeo*?" Tío Domingo said, with an air that said no boy would wish to miss such an opportunity.

"May Papá come? Or Rafael?" José asked. He dearly wished to visit the sloop, but he did want to be alone with Tío Domingo. He was frightened by the way his uncle filled a room when he entered, his loud voice overwhelming all others. His uncle often took command of him as well, as if he were his own possession. He noticed, too, that Mamá did not like some of the things that Tío Domingo said.

"I must help your grandfather in the shop. You will be fine without me for a few hours. But when you are on the *Orfeo*, lad, you may hear vulgar language. Men sometimes use rough words, but you should not. Remember to behave well, be obedient, and do not do anything to bring shame to your mother." Papá's voice was serious, but kind.

"I will be good, Papá," said José humbly, aware that he had already caused his mother shame and determined to be good today.

José took a few bites of cassava bread, his stomach still tender, and then he was walking towards the bay, the ground patterned with long shadows made by the rising sun. His uncle's callused, sunburned hand seized José's and held it tight, even when José tried to pull it away.

The *Orfeo* had already discharged her cargo elsewhere, and was now anchored in the bay of Matanzas. The city had no wharves, so the *Orfeo* and other vessels all rode at anchor in the bay. They met up with Isidro, one of the *Orfeo*'s crew, where the sloop's boat was pulled up on the shore.

"*Buenos días*, José!" he called out.

"*Buenos días*!" he replied.

The two men pushed the boat out into the waters of the bay, splashing in the shallow waves as it reached the water. Tío Domingo picked up José and placed him into the boat. José was startled as the boat moved under his feet, and he fell over the thwart, to the laughter of Isidro. A sharp word from Tío Domingo, and he picked up an oar and the two rowed them out to the waiting sloop.

There was a fair breeze from the north, and faint wisps of cloud could be seen against the faded blue of the sky. Gulls wheeled overhead or waded along the sands, and their cries filled José's ears. A faint fishy smell hung over the shore. The white sunlight glinted off the waves, bright against the clear blue of the bay, a blue that grew darker as they approached the deep waters at the western end of the bay, where the *Orfeo* was anchored. Tío Domingo pointed out other vessels at anchor, including the *Alejandro* and the *Penélope*.

Isidro boarded the sloop first, then reached down his arms for José. José went slowly up the Jacob's ladder, his small hands clinging to the man ropes as he lifted each small foot to the next batten.

Tío Domingo laughed. "You'll get the hang of it soon enough, and be scampering up and down like an old salt." But José noticed that he stayed close behind, watching his every step, until Isidro's strong arms seized him and lifted him over the gunwale.

It felt good on the deck of the ship. The sea breeze cooled the deck, and the smell of the ocean was brisk and clean, sweeping away the land smells of onions and sweat, manure and waste that permeated the streets of the town. José watched with interest as Isidro applied a chisel to a deck board forward of the mast. Tío Domingo explained that he was mending a gouge in the deck.

His uncle was like a boy, laughing and joking with Isidro, beaming with delight as he showed José about the sloop. They peeked through the grating into the hold, where José could see coils of line and empty casks.

Isidro dropped a hammer on his foot and burst out with a string of words unfamiliar to José. He suspected that these were the rough words that he must not repeat. He wanted to ask Tío Domingo what they meant, but he knew that he must be good.

They went up on the quarterdeck, and his uncle showed him the compass in the binnacle that could always tell them where north lay, north where heretics and pirates lived in the English colonies. He let him tug at the great tiller that steered the sloop, but José could barely move it, even with both hands.

Then they entered the cabin, located below the quarterdeck, filled with sunlight from the windows in the transom. A hammock hung on the starboard side, and along the larboard side were a few empty crates and a sack that looked to have once held provisions. A table stood in the center of the cabin, and on it he could see a large chart and several books.

Tío Domingo brought out a box containing a shining brass instrument he called a sextant, and showed José how it was used to take a sighting of the sun, and then, using one of the books on the table, to plot the sloop's position at sea.

"Soon you will go to school, José, where you will study arithmetic. You must work very hard at it, so that someday you can navigate a ship," said Tío Domingo.

José looked at the black squiggles in the book, the indecipherable, unknowable numbers crowding the page, and felt that such a small boy as himself could never prize out their secrets.

"I don't need to go to school, Tío Domingo. I will work with Papá in Abuelo's shop," he replied.

Tío Domingo was silent for a moment. José sensed that his answer had displeased him. Then Tío Domingo sat José down on one of the crates and knelt down in front of him, bending his tall frame until his green eyes looked straight into José's brown ones. He put his hands on José's shoulders and spoke to him in a grave tone.

"José, you know that I have no children. Someday I will be too old to sail, to look after my business. You are my family, José, and I want you to be my heir, to take over my business when I grow old." Tío Domingo's voice was intense, and this frightened José.

"When you are older, you will go to sea with me. I will teach you seamanship, navigation, the art of commerce. You will see the world, as I have done. You will be free, and call no man master. You will not serve a shop or a nation or a king. It is for this reason I wanted you to see the *Orfeo*." Tío Domingo began to gesticulate excitedly. José felt an increasing dismay and even panic. To sail away and leave Papá! He did not want to go to sea. He wanted to sit by the side of Papá, helping him to cut and shape wood into beautiful and useful things for the people of Matanzas.

He sat silent in the boat as Tío Domingo rowed them back to shore. He did not hear as his uncle talked on, describing some of the interesting places he had visited, for his mind was overcome with panic. How could he leave Papá? And Mamá, his grandparents, aunts, uncles, cousins, even Magdalena and the chickens?

"What's all this? Come now!" Tío Domingo cried out as José began to cry, great tears running down his face, and then began to sob uncontrollably.

4

ENGLISH PIRATES

Tío Domingo yanked José out of the boat and placed him unceremoniously upon the shore, then pulled the boat up above the tide line. José had exhausted himself with crying, and now struggled to keep up with his uncle's angry steps as they hurried home for the midday dinner, with only an occasional whimper or hiccup remaining of the earlier storm of tears. A soft, warm rain began to fall and cooled their skin and washed the stench of animals and waste from the streets, and José's clothes were sodden by the time they reached the pink house. Papá invited Tío Domingo to join them for dinner. The family peppered him with questions about the sloop, but he replied in monosyllables as he pushed his rice and beans about his plate, and Tío Domingo, too, had little to say.

"Ay, *pobrecito*, he is all done in! He should lie down right now for his siesta," advised Abuelita.

As Papá tucked him in, the words finally burst out of José. "Papá, I don't want to go to sea with Tío Domingo! I want to stay at home and work in the shop with you and Abuelo." Unmanly tears once again filled his eyes.

Papá's hand stroked José's hair, and his father's firm touch reassured him. Still the tears flowed. "Who then has said that you must go to sea with Donnie?" Donnie was his father's name for Tío Domingo, a name from their old life. No one else used it, not even Tío Domingo himself.

Then the story of José's day poured out, the sun and the waves, the sloop with its big tiller, Isidro's strong language, the numbers and the sextant, all jumbled together and mixed with José's tears.

Papá held him close. "Donnie was wrong to speak to you of this matter. I will talk to him." With those words he tucked José into his cot. José lay awake and restless, still tearful, as he listened to the sounds from the next room. He could hear the voices of his father and Tío Domingo, speaking in Gaelic. José knew that they must be arguing, for his uncle did not care to speak Gaelic, and used it only when he and his brother wished to keep their discussions from others.

"So, Donnie, you must go and tell the lad of your plan to take him to sea," he heard his father begin, in the tone that always made José sit up very straight.

Tío Domingo's own voice came quick and strained. "We made an agreement, Robbie." Robbie was Papá's old name.

"Aye, we made an agreement. But José is only six – too small to think of such things," Papá replied.

"He must know someday. Why not today?" Tío Domingo's voice was defiant.

"We made that agreement earlier, when our passions ran high. Think on it. It is a risky life you lead. There is always the danger of being stopped by a *guarda costa*, or the vessels of foreign navies. You could be killed, or put to hard labor at the very least."

"Such an eventuality is unlikely if you spread enough favors about, and I do," replied Tío Domingo.

"And there are the storms. Many a vessel has left Matanzas, never to return. It is a hard life, one that devours men and leaves them old before their time. Why should he take it up when he can follow a trade on shore?" Papá continued.

"There can be a great future for the boy in commerce, Robbie. He can see the world. I tell you there is money, riches to be made all over these islands, for a man who is bold and clever. My business grows every year. And you would have him become a mere carpenter." Tío Domingo's voice was becoming warm indeed.

"I am inclined to think that the Lord looks with some favor upon the lowly carpenter," replied José's father, with equal warmth.

"You may have your jest, Robbie, but think of the boy's future." Tío Domingo was insistent.

"I do not jest, Donnie. Señor Armonio Póveda has prospered very well at the carpenter's trade. He has two houses, half a dozen slaves, and is well-regarded by everyone in Matanzas, and he a *pardo* at that. José could have a similar future." José could tell that his father was growing impatient.

"And I have half shares in three sloops, and plans to acquire more. Albañez y Morejón is a thriving trading house, and will only grow richer." Tío Domingo was insistent.

"To succeed in life one must take risks," he continued. "That is your problem, Robbie, you were never willing to take a chance. You could have done much. Father McDougal said so. Everyone said so. And you gave it all up." Tío Domingo's voice was increasingly animated.

Papá remained stubbornly calm. "I had my duty."

"Was it duty, or were you simply afraid? Afraid to continue on in the city and fail?" Tío Domingo's voice slashed, bright with anger.

Still Papá remained calm. "Do we not have some duty to his grandfather? He hopes to have José join him in the shop someday. He has already lost Alejandro. Should he lose José, as well?"

"Alejandro? What are they saying about Alejandro?" José heard Abuelo's voice suddenly interject in Spanish.

"It is nothing, Papá," said José's mother soothingly, as if she had understood all that was said. "You look tired. You must take your siesta." And José heard his grandfather's feet move slowly towards his cot, the tired shuffle of a man with no son.

"Duty," Tío Domingo continued. "It is always duty with you. You would crucify the lad on your cross of duty. You did your duty and look what it cost you."

"You scorned your duty, and look what it cost *you*," Papá's voice thrust back, hard and angry.

There was a long silence. This was how their arguments often went.

At last Papá spoke. "That was not kind. I must beg your forgiveness, Donnie."

"And I yours. I should never have reminded you." Tío Domingo's voice was barely audible now.

Mamá's voice intervened. "This is about the boy, yes? His visit to the *Orfeo*?"

"Of all people you know that I want nothing but the best for him, Faustina…" began Tío Domingo, now speaking in Spanish.

"Are you truly thinking of the boy, or of yourself? You both speak of a promise made between you, but José never agreed to that bargain. Perhaps you should leave it to him to decide his own fate. He is a good boy and he will not make bad choices. The Virgin will look after him." Mamá's voice was unusually sharp.

"I think the two of you have decided this already between yourselves. Very well. Let the boy choose." There was bitterness in Tío Domingo's voice. "But he must choose with open eyes."

"And he will. I will honor my promise. When he is old enough, ten, let us say, he will go to sea with you for a year. And then he will spend another year with me. And so he shall do every year until he is old enough to choose for himself." Papá's voice had a note of finality.

The voices continued, but José no longer attended to them, because the discussion had turned to a different subject, a subject that was not him. His mind was calm now, and he began to drift off to sleep. He knew how he would choose. He would spend his days working at his father's side. For a time he would have to go to sea with Tío Domingo, but not until he was ten, and he was only five now, and ten was many years away, too many to imagine.

It was one month later, towards the end of October, and José had forgotten the promise Papá had made to Tío Domingo. Life had resumed its usual rhythm. His uncles spent their days carrying out repairs to their vessels, replacing rotted wood and canvas, running new rigging, tarring line and oiling spars. The *Penélope* was careened on the beach so that her hull could be cleaned. Papá took him to watch and explained it all, but José soon lost interest, and then they looked for seashells along the beach. Señor Morejón met with many important men, well-dressed merchants, impecunious junior officers, and even the mayor, and pursued the affairs of Morejón y Albañez. Abuelo kept everyone in La Flor de

Caña busy making Matanzas the most beautiful city in Cuba. And every day, the sun shone upon Matanzas, upon the Velázquez family, and upon José, until the day no one in Matanzas would forget.

José awoke on the 25th of October damp with sweat. The morning heat was stifling, and no breeze stirred the curtains of his cot. After breakfast Mamá and Abuelita sat on the patio fanning themselves, watching the pale blue sky for some sign of wind or rain to bring relief, but saw only a few wisps of cloud in the distance.

"More drought," complained Abuelita. "We will need to water the garden. My arms weary of it."

José and Magdalena fed the chickens, who pecked lethargically at the corn.

The sound of voices, many voices, came from the shop, and the women slowly made their way towards them, seeking relief from their contemplation of the sky.

"That is Policarpo's voice, and I hear Gaspar, as well," said Abuelita. "What are those fellows up to?"

They found the men in animated debate.

"I know the signs, I tell you," Tío Gaspar said, pointing towards the sea. "I know that foul, sulphurous stench. It means a hurricane."

Tío Policarpo spoke. "Always, before the hurricane, there is the sky, red like the bricks. Do you see such a sky?"

The men, meanwhile, conversed in quiet intensity. "Did you see the birds?" asked Abuelo. "They are flying inland."

Then Abuelita burst out, "It was cloudy on the day of San Vicente, with great thunderheads. You know what they say, 'When San Vicente is dark, of bread there will be none.'"

At last Tío Domingo weighed in. "I have been watching the fish. They are behaving oddly. And have you noticed the waves? Long, heavy swells, and yet there is nary a breath of wind. I do not like it. I would stand out to sea, but there is no wind."

"If you stay, you will find yourselves at the bottom of the bay – or on the shore..." said Tío Gaspar, shaking his head.

"What else can we do?" asked Tío Policarpo, raising his palms.

"We can watch the sky, and sail on the first wind. If Gaspar is right, there will be wind enough soon," said Tío Domingo.

"I will go with you," said Tío Gaspar. "With as many of my men as are willing. You will need many hands."

"I will join you," said Papá, his face grim.

"No," said Tío Domingo quickly, turning to him. "We need someone on shore to watch over the women and children." He paused, then added softly, "José needs you."

Tío Policarpo and Tío Gaspar nodded their ascent, and Tío Policarpo added, putting his arm around Papá's shoulder, "Watch over my dear Beatriz."

"I will go, too, then, if it comes to it," said Señor Morejón. "I have not forgotten how to reef a sail."

J osé woke from his siesta to find a fitful breeze stirring the curtains around his cot. In the kitchen, Señora Morejón was visiting with Mamá.

"We have been talking, Anselmo and I, about making our home in Havana," Señora Morejón was saying. "Domingo suggested it. Albañez y Morejón is now bringing in more goods all the time, and the market in Matanzas is limited. The business will grow in Havana. And Anselmo will be ideally located to make the connections they need to avoid troubles with the officials."

"Does he think to carry on his business right under the eyes of the Captain-General?" came the voice of Abuelo.

"The Captain-General can provide licenses to trade legally," Señora Morejón replied.

"Will Domingo go with you?" Mamá asked.

"Of course," answered Señora Morejón. "He keeps his home with us. I think perhaps he would like to avail himself of the entertainments a larger city can offer."

"I think it will be a most satisfactory arrangement." Mamá smiled, and then blew a ladylike ring of tobacco smoke.

"We hope to find a school for Rafael to attend," Señora Morejón continued. "He is a clever boy."

"Of course," agreed Mamá without enthusiasm, for she had heard much on this topic before.

José went out onto the patio in search of Rafael, who was sure to be near. The girls were chasing the chickens about.

"Come play with us!" called Marianela, pulling on José's arm.

"What do we want with your foolish games?" jeered Rafael, and pulled José by the other arm out into the street. He pulled an orange out of his shirt, and the two shared it, popping the sweet segments into their mouths and spitting out the seeds, as the juice ran down their chins. A sudden gust of wind tousled their shirts, and José saw a dry palm frond blow down the street.

"Rafael! José!" they heard voices call out. There, under the banyan tree at the end of the street, were the neighborhood boys, flocking together like the turkey vultures that roosted in the great gnarled branches above them. They were taking turns riding on Pepe, a donkey that belonged to Fermín's father, Señor Guelvenzo. He was a drayman and he and Pepe delivered goods all over Matanzas. Sometimes they brought lumber to La Flor de Caña. Fermín was making a great show of giving the boys turns on the donkey and leading it about on a rope through the street. Now it was the turn of Leocadio, the tailor's son. José hoped that he could soon have a turn.

Suddenly Señor Guelvenzo stepped out of his house. "That's enough, Fermín. Leave the poor creature be. He's a work animal, not a plaything for boys," he growled. He was unshaven, and José thought he caught a scent of *aguardiente*.

"But it's a holy day, Papá!" protested Fermín.

"Then let him have his day of rest as well. And do not argue with me, or I will whip you worse than I whip Pepe." Señor Guelvenzo went inside, and Fermín stood there, red-faced with shame.

"Let's play another game," suggested cousin Melchor, the son of Tío Gaspar. "What should we play, Rafael?" Melchor was a year older than Rafael, but more inclined to muscle than imagination.

"I say that we play...well...privateer!" This was a new game, inspired no doubt by the stories Rafael often heard from his father. The idea was greeted by cries of approval from the other boys. Only Fermín remained skeptical.

"Just how is this game played?" he asked.

"We will choose sides, the Spanish and the English," Rafael began to explain. "Each side will chase the other and attempt to take them prisoner."

"We will have bases where the prisoners are kept, and then we will arm ourselves with mud balls. If you are struck, you must go to the enemy base. We will know who has been hit!" cried José, warming to the game. This was how it usually went; Rafael came up with the idea, and José built upon it.

"La Flor de Caña will be one base!" cried Melchor.

"La Estrella will be the other," announced Leocadio, naming his father's shop. The sign above it featured a bright star in yellow paint.

"Now we must choose sides..." Rafael began.

"I will be the captain of the Spanish!" announced Fermín, stepping forward.

"I want to be the Spanish captain!" The shoemaker's son, Prudencio, disputed Fermín for the title.

"I let you ride our donkey. Now I ought to be captain," said Fermín, his arms crossed and feet spread wide, as if he were indeed a captain, ready to take on the British fleet. The mutiny was put down.

"Rafael should be the English captain. The game is his idea," suggested Melchor, perhaps to forestall another attempt by the unpopular Prudencio.

"Yes, yes!" called out many voices in affirmation, and the captains began to select their crews.

"I am El Draque, the most fearsome of all English pirates, and I choose José for my crew," cried Rafael.

José was paralyzed for a moment. In his enthusiasm it had not occurred to him that he might find himself on the English side. He knew that his father hated the English, hated them with a fire within that burned fierce and hot. They had treated his father's country most cruelly, and it was because of the English that his father had found himself in Cuba. How could he betray his father and serve with the hated enemy?

"Come on, José! We must plan our attack, and you will be my first mate," called Rafael, and José ran to join him, his qualms forgotten. First mate! This would be a fine game.

It was. They ran through the streets, dodging passers-by, hiding behind hogsheads and carts, and leaping out from behind corners, shrieking and laughing as they flung handfuls of dirt at each other. The groups of dirty prisoners in front of La Flor de Caña and La Estrella grew.

At last Rafael tagged the last remaining member of the Spanish crew, its captain, Fermín, and led the sulky officer back to La Flor de Caña.

"Now you are our prisoners, and we will sell you all as slaves!" cried José triumphantly.

"Slaves? You cannot make slaves of your prisoners," protested Flavio, Fermín's brother.

"That's what those dirty heretics do. They sell their prisoners to the sugar plantations in Jamaica," said José with authority. He had heard many times about the terrible deeds of the English.

"It is true. I have heard my father tell of it," affirmed Rafael.

"I am *blanco*, and you cannot make me a slave, you filthy *pardo*," said Fermín, and he stepped menacingly towards José, fists clenched. Flavio was close behind.

It did not bother José to be called *pardo*; that is what he, and most of his family and friends, were. The addition of the word "filthy," however, made this an insult, and José felt his own fists begin to clench. He might have backed down, before, but now it was a matter of honor not to yield.

"That is what the English do," he said, more belligerently now. "If you do not like it, you should have become the English captain, and not the Spanish."

"That is right. We English are merciless devils. You must submit to your fate, Spanish dogs!" cried Rafael, lost in his passion for the game.

"Yes, submit, Spanish dogs!" cried his crew, caught up in his enthusiasm.

"You vile bastard!" shouted Fermín, but his insult was not directed at Rafael, but at José, and he began to swing wildly at him. José launched himself into the older boy's midriff. They both fell to the ground, fists flailing, as the rest of the Spanish and English crews also fell to blows.

The noise of the melee brought mothers running from out of the doors.

"Ay, *niños*, what is going on here?" they cried. The fathers remained indoors, for they knew that boys fight. They, too, had once been boys.

Señora Guelvenzo pulled Fermín from the ground. Blood ran from his nose and mixed with the mud of the unpaved street, mud that now covered him from his head to his feet. José was pleased when he saw his handiwork.

"What are you doing, rolling about in the muck like a hog? You are coming with me," she said, taking him firmly by the ear and dragging him towards their house.

Nose bloodied and honor even more gravely wounded, Fermín fired his parting shot. "You filthy *pardo* bastard! Your mother is a whore! Everyone knows about your father! He is..." There was a final shriek as his mother yanked him within the door of the house.

José sat, face and knuckles bruised and bleeding, and realized that his mother was standing there. Tears were running down her face.

The sky had grown darker, and José could hear the wind bang a loose shutter down the street. A squealing pig ran down the street looking for shelter. The boys dispersed to their homes, shuffling dispiritedly as they mourned the ruin of what had been, for a time, a glorious game. Mamá, her tears now mixed with rain, took his hand and led him inside the house.

Señora Morejón examined Rafael. "Well, you may have one black eye, but that other boy has two," she said with satisfaction, and sailed off majestically, a proud Rafael in tow, followed by Marianela, carrying the baby, and an awestruck Gabriel.

Mamá paid no heed to her departure, but sat, sobbing. "Ay, Mamá," she wailed softly. "Everyone here knows. I am so ashamed."

"Quiet, *mi hija*. This is nothing new. Why should you cry over the angry words of a rude little *blanco*? His family is nothing. You live as many women live. That is nothing to cry over. A priest is not necessary if you love each other," murmured Abuelita, stroking Mamá's hair.

"It is not that. It is the other...Father Gastón says..." Mamá sobbed, and again Abuelita comforted her.

"Foolish child, everyone knows Father Gastón has a mistress and three children. Who minds what he says? You have a good man, content yourself with that. Many women do not have as much." Mamá grew quieter as she sat, her head on Abuelita's shoulder, and Abuelita continued to murmur comforting words.

José examined his wounds and felt that he was the cause of all Mamá's distress. He began to wonder about the reasons for her grief. Surely it was not because Fermín had called them *pardos*. Fermín had called his mother a whore, a bad woman. And he had called José a bastard. But he was not a bastard. He had a father, not like Régulo, the son of the *morena*, or black, fruit vendor Varinia. She had several children but had never been married. In Matanzas there were many women like her, unmarried women with children, many of them *pardas* or *morenas*.

Now Abuelita was looking down at José. "Ay, *niño*, what a fright you look! Let me wash you up, and see what that *blanco* boy has done to you. He is no good, just like his father. I hope you struck a few blows for your family's honor. You are a brave boy, to fight a great lout like him." So saying, she washed the dirt and blood from his face with a rag.

As she stripped off his dusty clothing, José got up the nerve to ask the question that had been troubling him. "Abuelita, why did Fermín call Mamá a whore? Why did he call me a bastard? I have a father."

"Yes, *niño*, you do, but your father and mother are not married," she replied, dunking his muddy clothes up and down in a bucket of water, not meeting José's eyes. "Here, put these back on. They will dry in the heat."

José stood silent. Papá and Mamá not married? Not man and wife in the eyes of the church? This startling information gnawed at him the rest of the day. He spoke roughly to Magdalena when she wished to play a game with him, was sullen in his replies to his elders, and was silent during the evening meal. Mamá did not notice, for she sat there, still red-eyed and silent.

They had a light supper, a few tostones and some fruit. José peeled a banana and ate it while he listened to Papá and his grandparents discussing the weather. The wind whistled through the slats of the shutters, and Papá checked them to make sure they were secure, then checked them again an hour later. More than once Abuelo went out onto the patio to look at the sky, and then a burst of wind would come through the door and startle them all.

"Domingo has taken his vessels out to sea," said Papá. "There is a southwest wind now, enough to take him far from shore."

"May the Virgin watch over them," cried Abuelita, crossing herself, and Mamá followed her example.

"You think Gaspar is right?" asked Abuelo. "We have had only a blue sky, and a few gusts are nothing new."

"It is the frogs that worry me," said Papá. "Do you hear them?"

José listened very hard, but could hear only the whistling of the wind.

"I can't hear the frogs," he said.

"It is that which worries me," answered Papá.

Abuelo went outside to hammer the shutters closed, and Mamá brought the chickens into the kitchen. Magdalena squealed with delight and ran to hug each one in turn.

That night Papá and Mamá decided to take José and Magdalena into their bed. Magdalena fell instantly asleep, but questions still gnawed away at José.

"Why aren't you and Mamá married?" he asked. "Don't you love her? Don't you want to obey God and go to heaven?"

"Lad, of course I love your mother, and you, and Magdalena. I will always do my duty to you," Papá replied, sitting down on the bed with him under the curtains and holding his hand.

"But why don't you marry Mamá? It makes her cry to be unmarried," José continued.

His father was silent for a time. Then he spoke. "It's not that I do not want to marry your mother. But I cannot under the laws of the church. It's a long story, and perhaps one day you shall hear it, when you are grown."

"Is it because you are not Spanish? Does the Church not like foreigners?" José asked.

His father laughed. "No, lad, no one is a foreigner to the Church. And His Catholic Majesty welcomes any Catholic, like myself, who seeks refuge from persecution. It is a different matter altogether."

"Are you a great sinner, Papá? Are you doomed to perdition, like the English heretics?" José asked worriedly.

"I hope not, lad. I do not wish to spend eternity with a great mob of Englishmen. If a man does his duty, then I believe God's mercies are great enough to cover his remaining sins. That for me is the church." Papá was speaking very earnestly now, as if he were addressing an equal, and José attended every word as best he could.

And then, as he was about to leave the room, Papá turned to José and asked, "Your grandmother says that you gave that Fermín a great bloody nose. Is that true, then?"

José hesistated, then replied shamefacedly, "Yes, Papá."

"Good for you, lad," said his father, and he was gone.

Later, José could hear Papá and Mamá removing their outer clothing in the dark and then he felt their great warm forms about him in the bed. Mamá's soft kisses dampened his cheek, many kisses, and she hugged him as if she meant to keep the wind from whisking him away.

"Do not worry, *mi hijo*," she whispered. And then José did worry, until the irresistible force of slumber closed his eyes.

5
STORM OF WATER AND ALL WINDS

José awoke to find Papá and Mamá already up. The room was dark despite the morning hour, and he could hear the wind tugging at the shutters. Small gusts made their way through the slats and stirred the bedclothes. He shook Magdalena awake and they went in search of breakfast.

On the patio, Abuelita was making corncakes, while Mamá fed the brazier with pieces of dried sugar cane. She gave José and Magdalena each one.

"Look, how beautiful!" cried Magdalena, pointing up at the sky.

Thick clouds now stretched to the horizon, shimmering with hues of pink and violet. Mamá and Abuelita expressed no admiration, however, but only grimaced and continued baking corncakes, more corncakes than even José's large family could consume that morning.

Tía Beatriz and her children had joined them. Her son Jacinto, 12, was finishing his breakfast of corncakes. He gave his mother a kiss on the cheek and followed Abuelo into the shop.

"Take care of Mamá," he said to his nine-year-old sister, Nemesia, and she stood close to her mother and took her hand.

Tía Nicolaza entered with her own children in tow. Gonzalo, the eldest, was 11. He put down the crate of foodstuffs he was carrying. "I should be with him, Mamá! I am eleven and almost a man."

"Your father needs you to look after your family," Abuelo scolded.

José was glad to see cousin Melchor, and Rafael soon had the three of them chasing about the room.

"Do we not have enough to worry about without you boys underfoot?" scolded Tía Nicolaza, brushing a stray strand of hair from her drawn face. "See Luisa, how quiet she is, and such a help."

Luisa, 9, smirked at them as she gathered the dishes to be cleaned.

Heavy drops of rain rattled the palm frond roof and drove Mamá and Abuelita in from the patio, Mamá bending her body over the basket of corncakes to protect them from the rain. Papá and Abuelo, accompanied by Jacinto, came in from the shop. The adults huddled in close conversation.

"The sky tells the story," said Abuelo.

"I have lived here all my life. If the sea begins to rise, we must find higher ground," warned Abuelita.

Papá looked doubtful. "Will we not be at the mercy of the winds, then?"

"There are caves in the hills, although I have never been there," said Abuelita. "I do not know if I could find them."

"Alejandro knows," said Tía Beatriz.

"Hush, foolish child," said Abuelita.

"We will find them if we must," said Abuelo. "If the water rises, God willing it does not."

"If we last that long, "was Tía Nicolaza's caustic comment. "I would leave now."

José tugged at Papá's hand. "Are we leaving Matanzas?"

"Our rivers will swallow us if this storm does not abate," Papá explained. "It is not without cause that a hurricane is called 'the storm of water and all winds.'"

"Hush!" said Abuelita, for several of his cousins heard his question and had begun to whimper.

"I will let nothing happen to my dear ones," said Papá, and swept José up into his arms.

The fat drops of rain became a downpour, the wind driving water through the slats of the shutters until the floor was all puddles and mud. Over the sound of the rain they could hear the roar of the surf, several blocks to the north. The wind rattled the shutters, clawing to break in. The crowded house grew darker.

Papá and Abuelo made forays into the street to see if the water was rising. The women stirred about, making preparations for an eventuality they hoped would not come. The younger children sat quietly until boredom led to squabbles. The older cousins helped their parents and strutted about, feeling their importance.

Suddenly, there was a bang as something struck the wall of the house, and Tía Beatriz seized a bottle of holy water and fluttered about the room, sprinkling them all and praying. In the distance they could hear the sound of the church bell.

"Loud noises break up the wind, they say," commented Tía Nicolaza.

"It is true. Perhaps the military will fire their artillery," suggested Abuelo, and sure enough, they soon heard the boom of a heavy gun.

It was midmorning when a great boom startled them all and rain suddenly poured down upon them. José looked up and saw, through the curtain of rain, dark clouds swirling above their heads and felt the fierce assault of the wind. Magdalena screamed for Mamá, and other voices soon joined hers.

Tía Nicolaza dove under the table, clutching the bag of corncakes they had baked just a few hours earlier, the youngest ones huddled about her as rain poured down through the vast emptiness where the roof of palm fronds had once been.

"The roof is gone. How long before the walls, too?" cried Mamá over the wind.

"I thank the saints I had the foresight to wrap my tools in oilcloth yesterday," said Abuelo.

Abuelita spoke. "I am happy for your chisels and saws. And what about us?" She was already thoroughly drenched.

"We must go," shouted Papá, and no one disagreed.

Tía Nicolaza used a coverlet to carry the precious bundle of corncakes on her back, and the others wrapped themselves up in bedclothes as well as they set off for the hills to the south of the city. The water was beginning to fill the street and creep in doors, and soon José could feel its clammy grip on his ankles. They pushed forward, but the wind, now from the southeast, bore down upon them, almost knocked José off his feet. Then Papá reached down and swung him up upon his shoulders. Around them others, too, were heading towards higher ground.

The mayor, Don Felipe, appeared, splashing through the water, calling out, "You must leave Matanzas now! The sea is rising!"

"You must tell that to Sergeant Espinoza. He refuses to leave," shouted back Señor Barrera.

Sergeant Espinoza's grizzled head appeared in his doorway. "This is my home. I must protect it."

Don Felipe splashed over to Sergeant Espinoza's house. "Do not be a clod, man, the sea is stronger than any of us."

"I will not leave my home," the sergeant said, the lines of his face set like stone.

"Then send the children away, dear fellow," Don Felipe pleaded.

"They will be safe with me," replied Sergeant Espinoza, and José could see Señora Espinoza's fearful face behind him. "It is in God's hands."

"That is what I fear," mumbled Papá as they moved on, leaving Don Felipe still pleading with the sergeant.

"Roberto!" Mamá scolded, stopping in her tracks, rain streaming down her face. "God and his angels are watching over us." It was then José noticed that Mamá was clutching her rosary tightly in her fist while her other arm balanced Magdalena on her hip.

"The chickens!" cried Magdalena, reaching back towards the house. "What about the chickens?"

"The chickens must fend for themselves," said Abuelita.

They saw Señor Guelvenzo pass them on his cart, his donkey struggling to find footing in the mud that lay beneath the swirling waters. Fermín's head appeared above the side.

"Ha!" he jeered. "I am riding and the *pardo* bastard is walking." He stood up to crow his triumph, but the wind tore a branch from a nearby banyan tree and flung it through the air. It struck Fermín on the head and he collapsed into the cart. His head slowly appeared above the side, blood running down his forehead, and his mother slapped him.

"Sit down, you ninny," she scolded.

Ahead they saw Señora Morejón with her children, leading a mule laden with leather bags. They joined up, and trudged forward, struggling in the mud. The children began to tire. They passed the Guelvenzos' cart, mired in mud, and soon the Morejóns' mule could go no longer. The adults shifted the beast's burden on to their own shoulders, and Señora Morejón gave the mule a slap on his hindquarters to send him off into the undergrowth that surrounded the narrow cart path.

"He is on his own, now," she said.

"I'm tired! Can't we stop?" wailed Manuel, Rafael's little brother, and soon the other children echoed his cry.

"We must go on," said Abuelo, and the mothers used their coverlets to carry the youngest on their backs, and pull the others along by their hands.

Under a royal palm they saw a glimpse of white, and as they approached they saw that it was the body of a small girl, propped up against the trunk. Blood and grime mixed with the rain that ran down her face of unearthly whiteness onto her dress. The mothers pulled their children closer, the complaining ceased for a time, and they all walked on with firmer steps, the grim spectacle unremarked but vivid in every mind. At last, as the dim light was fading from the sky, they approached the cave.

They had lost all sense of time, for the thick clouds and lashing rain had created an unending twilight. José thought they had been walking for hours. The children had wearied of complaining.

"How much farther?" asked Abuelita, in a voice faint with exhaustion and despair.

"I know there is a cave here, but I can recognize nothing in this rain," said Jacinto, who had spent many a day in the hills exploring. He stood, looking about in confusion.

"Alejandro knows," said Tía Beatriz, striding ahead with certainty.

"Do not get lost. You have birds in your head, you silly girl," said Abuelita.

"Alejandro knows," repeated Tía Beatriz, and they all began to follow her for lack of another option.

She pushed through bushes, picked her way along paths invisible to others, oblivious to rain and wind. Jacinto tried to restrain his mother.

"Alejandro knows," she said again, and clambered over several rocks and behind a tree. They followed.

"Here, here!" came a man's voice, and a dripping figure appeared out of the gloom to gesture them behind a bush and through a crevice in the rocks. They found themselves in a dark space, illuminated only by the light from the crevice; deeper inside it continued on into utter blackness. José could hear voices and the sounds of movement

: other Matanzans who had found refuge in the cave, and huddled against the cool limestone walls.

They rested their wearied limbs, then Tía Nicolaza took charge and began passing out some of the corncakes they had prepared. They offered some to the earlier arrivals, who in turn shared some plantain chips and fruit. They did not dry off within the cave, but they did not grow wetter, and that was enough for the moment.

José sat in the dark, listening to the roar of the wind outside the cave. There was nothing in the world now, only the cave, and his family, and the wind. Tears began to run down his face.

"We are in God's hands now," whispered Mamá, as if she could read his mind.

He fell asleep with his arms around Magdalena, nestled between Papá and Mamá.

José awoke to the sound of movement and animated voices in the cave. He heard Rafael's voice in the dark. "The hurricane is gone!"

He moved towards the sound, and felt his friend grab his hand. Rafael pulled him towards a faint grey light that marked the mouth of the cave, and soon they were stepping out into a light drizzle. Several Matanzans were already there, gazing down upon their city in silence.

They had a clear view, even in the soft rain, for the greenery that had covered the hill was gone, and all that remained were the shattered remnants of trees and bushes, stripped of leaves and blasted black by the salt water flung from the sea.

"It is gone," said Abuelo in quiet horror, for he had followed behind them.

It was true. As they looked down upon Matanzas, all they could see was the steeple of the church, rising above the receding waters of the bay. The bridges that crossed the three rivers were gone, and only a few broken walls and the odd house rose above the water. A dismasted sloop lay across Matanzas's main street, and the remains of other vessels could be seen scattered across the cityscape.

"*Dios mío!*" said Rafael in awe.

They breakfasted on the last crumbled corncakes, then left the cave to return to the city. They could see patches of blue in the sky, and a ray of sunlight warmed José's cheek.

"The storm has gone west. It will be in Havana by now," said Papá.

They picked their way through the wreckage, down the hillside to Matanzas. Everywhere was destruction. Ruined tobacco fields, only half harvested, blackened plantain walks, and rubble where houses had stood. As they entered the city they saw a women's corpse floating down the river to the sea, and more bodies caught in the scattered wreckage that had once been their city. The carcasses of cows and donkeys, pigs, and chickens lay in puddles in the streets. José saw a pig caught in the cleft of a banyan tree, as if it had been caught trying to fly away from the storm.

At last they came to their street, the street where La Flor de Caña could be found.

They stood staring. The walls were no longer pink, and the roof was gone, but there before them stood the battered walls of the house. Abuelo had built in stone, rather than the wattle and daub of most of the city, and his handiwork stood in muddy triumph amid the detritus of its neighbors.

"God and all his saints have indeed watched over us," Mamá said loudly, for the benefit of Papá.

"My tools!" cried Abuelo, and rushed into the shop.

The workbench where he had placed the bundle of tools lay smashed against the back wall. His shaving horse was in splinters nearby. Abuelo ran to the wreckage and began scrabbling at it with his gnarled hands, clawing away the mud and debris. There, at last, he found the precious bundle.

He unwrapped it and they gazed upon the contents. The water had forced its way within and there they lay, the chisels and planes, saws and augers, in a puddle of water.

"Come, give me a hand," said Abuelo, as he began removing each tool and placing it on a broken timber where it could catch the sun. José picked up a chisel and realized that each one had been heavily coated with tallow, safe from damp and rust. Beneath the thick film, the metal still shone.

"We will have great need of these now," said Abuelo. He and Papá set to work clearing the debris out of the house and using what they could to rig some shelter until they could add a new roof.

Señora Morejón appeared. "Gone," she said, shaking her head. "All gone. If the *Orfeo* and the *Alejandro* do not return..." The terrible thought hung in the air.

"But where is Alejandro?" cried Tía Beatriz.

"Hush, foolish girl. Policarpo is well. He is sturdy as a palm tree and cannot be broke," said Tía Nicolaza, who knew the right words, and Tía Beatriz smiled brightly. The others looked about them at the blasted stumps of what had been palm trees and were not reassured.

The aunts and their children moved into the stone house and the women set about feeding them. The corncakes had all been consumed, but the winds had knocked all of the fruit from the trees, and it lay spread across the ground for the taking. José helped Mamá gather up frutabombas, guanábanas, grapefruit, pawpaws, and bananas into a coverlet and carry them home. Then Abuelita sent him and his cousins to gather bits of wood for the stove. Tía Nicolaza spread the kindling out in the sun to dry.

"Luisa found one of the chickens, drowned on the patio. We will boil him up into soup," Abuelita said. "Beatriz, make yourself of use and dig us up a few onions."

"You boys go and see what you can find," said Abuelo, interrupting his discussions with the neighbor men about rebuilding. "I need wood."

With a cry the boys ran off into the streets. José, panting to keep up, found Rafael out on the same task. They spent a long day in the sunshine. The barren landscape became a garden of treasure, and they dug with glee in the mud. When they tired of this, they stuffed themselves on fallen fruit until the juice ran down their chins and their stomachs ached. Older boys pelted them with mud, and they flung fistfuls of it back, screaming with the glory of battle.

"I am king of Matanzas!" Rafael cried, climbing atop a dory capsized in the middle of the street, until flying mud drove him off.

Rafael set off for home bearing a bedraggled felt hat, and José returned in triumph lugging behind him a heavy barrel hoop.

"Hmm," said Abuelo, examining his prize. "I thought I sent you for wood. I have no use for this myself, but I am sure I can trade it to Señor Palomino, the cooper, for something we need." He gave José a pat on the head.

Don Felipe stopped in. He clapped Abuelo on the back. "It is good indeed to see you, Señor Luis, and your family."

"Did you ever persuade Sergeant Espinoza to leave?" asked Mamá. "Their home is gone without a trace, and I have not seen them."

Don Felipe shook his head. "No one has." He raised his palms helplessly. "I pleaded with them, but the sergeant would not listen. I tried..." He shook his head again, shoulders slumped.

"You did your best," said Papá. "We all saw that."

Abuelo and Papá accompanied Don Felipe to the church, where many men were gathered to discuss the rebuilding of Matanzas. When they returned, they looked grim.

"Don Felipe is sending to the Captain-General in Havana for assistance," Abuelo said.

"If the hurricane has not blown him away," said Papá. This was the sort of occasion when he would bring out a bottle of *aguardiente*, but now there was none.

"Surely the king will not forget us," said Mamá.

"The king is far away and it will be long before he knows of our plight," replied Abuelo.

"If only Alejandro were here!" wailed Tía Beatriz.

"If only," said Abuelo, and no one knew if he meant the vessel or his long-dead son.

T he first few days home had been a giddy time for José. He ran in the streets with his friends, dug in the mud, stuffed himself with fruit, and played games into the night with his cousins. At other times he helped Abuelo and Papá with their building, fetching tools and passing wooden pegs to them, and felt very important. Soon, however, the air of adventure dissipated, leaving behind a house crowded with dirty, quarrelsome family.

"I'm tired of bananas!" whined Luisa at dinner.

"Well, you have your wish, for that is the last of them," snapped Tía Nicolaza. "The rest have rotted."

"What will we eat now?" asked Gonzalo.

"Señor Guelvenzo has gone into the countryside to see if food can be obtained there," replied Abuelo calmly, but his face was taut.

"We need to throw away all that rotting fruit," said Tía Nicolaza, brushing away a cloud of insects from her face. "They are drawing pests and beginning to smell."

"You know that odor does not come from the fruit," said Abuelita sharply.

They knew, they all knew, that the foul, sweetish stench that permeated Matanzas came from the bloated carcasses of the livestock that filled the city. Every day the sun rose, steam rose from the filthy streets, and the bodies swelled until they at last burst. Swarms of flies preyed upon the dead animals and feasted on the rotting fruit. Armies of mosquitos rose up from stagnant pools and roamed the city, seeking victims.

"This foul miasma will sicken us all," said Mamá.

Such was the conversation at every meal now, as the people of Matanzas waited, despaired, and prayed for relief from Havana, and their food supplies grew ever scarcer.

Two weeks had passed since the hurricane. Abuelo had built simple shelters for Tía Nicolaza and Tía Beatriz's families, and they departed, all smiles, the petty quarrels of recent days forgiven and forgotten. The Captain-General had ordered rural residents to clear the roads so that the cities could be resupplied, and Señor Guelvenzo had returned from the countryside with a cartload of yucca, and promised to fetch more soon.

The Matanzans had begun to dump the animal carcasses in the rivers, but their efforts were retarded by the wave of disease that now swept over the city. Abuelita had fallen sick with a bilious fever, and then Mamá, too, was stricken. They were both still weak. Several of the cousins had come down with fevers as well. Flavio Guelvenzo, Fermín's younger brother, died. Ordinarily the Velázquez family would have attended his burial, and wept with the family, but now there was no time for funerals, and there were no tears left for Flavio.

Don Felipe was everywhere in the city, conferring, advising, encouraging, cajoling. One day he said, "While repairing the bridge they found a little girl's body." He hesitated. "The water had done its work, but Señor Massó said he recognized the dress. It was little Teresa Espinoza." Once they would have cried, but now Teresa's was just another death, and they were relieved to know at last the fate of the Espinoza family.

A fresh breeze sprang up that afternoon.

"Ah! Just what we need to blow the stink off this city," said Abuelita.

By morning, however, the sky was a rich pink. Soon the fresh breeze became a fierce wind that brought a dark mass of thunderclouds and driving rain with it. When the wind shifted from the southeast to east, Papá ordered them to head for the caves again. They trudged the long way up into the hills, surrounded by their neighbors. Some, weakened by fever, dropped by the way. Papá urged the family along, helping Mamá and Abuelita when their steps began to falter.

"I want to go home," José heard himself wail, but a sharp word from Abuelo silenced him.

They waited out the hurricane in the caves, the routine numbingly familiar now. Hunger gnawed at them and children whimpered, for there was nothing to eat. When the storm subsided, they issued from the cave. The landscape before them looked little changed, for the previous storm had already devoured everything.

"Two hurricanes in one month. People will speak of this for years to come," said Papá.

"No one will forget the storms of 1752," agreed Abuelo.

"If there is anyone left to tell the tale," replied Papá.

They returned to Matanzas to find much of the rebuilding undone. There were bodies in the street, too, for the sickest had been unable to flee.

Mamá knelt down in the mud and began to cry. "Has God forgotten us?" she murmured between sobs.

Papá knelt down beside her and put his arms about her. "He has not forgotten us, only turned his face away for a moment." His own face was weary and drawn, and José thought he saw a tear slip down his cheek.

Papá was their rock, their anchor. He judged childish sins and administered chastisement, he provided comfort during crises. He was a strong arm to Abuelo and a wise head for the men of Matanzas. If he despaired, what hope was left? Terror flooded José's soul, and he began to wail. Magdalena's voice joined his. Their cries filled the air, and they would not be comforted.

They awoke the next day to a bleak scene, and faced the day with battered hearts. Señor Guelvenzo arrived with another cartload of yucca, which only took the edge off their hunger pangs, for Abuelita was determined to make it last as long as possible.

"I do not know if I will be able to bring back more," warned Señor Guelvenzo. "The earth is sodden, and the crops are rotting in the fields."

No word had come of the *Orfeo* or *Alejandro*, and they had ceased to speak of them, for it only brought dark thoughts.

Papá and Abuelo wondered whether rats made good eating.

"They are fat enough," said Abuelo. "They have gorged on the dead for days now."

"But how to catch them?" asked Papá.

Mamá looked at them in horror; Abuelita, with hope.

José thought to join Rafael and play by the river, but Mamá became frantic. "No, you musn't! Only yesterday a boy drowned while floating sticks in the San Juan River, and Régulo cut his foot playing about and now mortification has set in and he is near death."

José stayed home and drew pictures in the mud with a stick. He drew a chicken and wished it were real.

A cry came from the street, the voice of Don Felipe. "Sails, there are sails on the horizon!"

"Help from Havana?" suggested Abuelo.

"No, they come from the east," reported Don Felipe.

"Santiago, then?" was Papá's thought. No one wished to get their hopes up.

Still, hope fought its way to the surface. As Don Felipe went on to spread the word, they rushed to the bay, where they found the aunts and cousins, as well as the rest of Matanzas.

Señora Morejón stood, staring at the white shapes, shading her eyes from the sun.

A few minutes later she cried, "They are sloops. It is...yes, it is the *Orfeo*! I know that mainsail. And behind her, yes, I am sure of it, it is the *Alejandro*!" She stood taller then, proud and happy. The children began to jump up and down and cheer, although they were not entirely sure why.

"Alejandro, at last!" wept Tía Beatriz, and Jacinto put his arm around his mother, for she looked ready to faint, smiling and crying in turn.

They watched as the sloops dropped anchor, lowered their sails, and eased their boats into the bay. How slowly it all seemed to go, as if they intended the anticipation on shore to build. As they approached, José could see Tío Policarpo and Tío Gaspar in the lead boat, Tío Domingo and Señor Morejón in the one following. They feigned a casual but dignified air, as if their arrival were a matter of routine, but José could see smiles creep across their faces as they heard the joyful cries from shore. They looked smart, their healthy forms filling out their clean white shirts, a striking contrast to the grimy, wan figures awaiting them.

As soon as his boat touched the beach, Tío Policarpo leapt out, leaving Tío Gaspar and the others to pull it up on shore and stow the oars. He ran to Tía Beatriz and enveloped her in his arms.

"*Mi tesoro!* How I have missed you!" he murmured as she collapsed in his embrace.

Tío Gaspar sidled up to Tía Nicolaza. "So, my little anchor, did you fear for me while I was gone?"

"What poppycock! The sea cannot be bothered with such as you," she replied, but then she took his face in her hands and planted a kiss on his stubbled cheek.

All eyes, however, were on Tío Domingo as he slowly, deliberately directed his men as they pulled the *Orfeo*'s boat up onto the sand and carefully stowed each oar in its place. Only then did he turn and saunter up to Don Felipe.

"I hope you have a lighter ready, for I have two sloops with holds filled with hogsheads of flour," he said. His neatly combed hair glinted red in the sun, his cocked hat sat at a jaunty angle, and sunlight was reflected from the silver buttons on his blue coat.

"How handsome he is!" José heard the women whisper.

"And dashing!" added another.

"May the Virgin bless you," said Don Felipe, taking Tío Domingo's arm and pumping it with enthusiasm. Soon the sound of oars splashing in the waves was heard as eager volunteers rowed a lighter out to the *Orfeo*. The mayor and Señor

Morejón, meanwhile, were organizing storage for the hogsheads on shore, and determine how the flour would be distributed.

"Viva Don Domingo!" came the voices of men in the crowd, and soon everyone was echoing the cheer.

A lighter was found, and a fishing boat, and soon the boats were heading up the San Juan River, followed by a boisterous crowd on shore. The men of Matanzas helped unload the boats and transfer the hogsheads onto carts to be taken to the city hall, still standing, for storage.

"Where did Tío Domingo get the flour, Papá?" José asked in wonderment.

"I suspect that he had it stashed in some distant cave, awaiting sale. I also suspect that he took his vessels into some isolated, shallow cove to wait out the storm. This is between the two of us, lad," replied Papá in Gaelic.

Mamá took Magdalena home, but Papá remained to help, and José begged to stay and watch. He and Rafael watched the boats go back and forth, then competed to see who could throw rocks farther into the water.

They heard voices and followed them to find the men no longer working, but crowded around a man wearing a blue coat over a bright red waistcoat. The insignia on the coat identified him as a captain. José admired the sword hanging by his side.

"Lieutenant, seize this contraband. Don Felipe, show me the men responsible so that I may have them arrested. The audacity, to bring foreign flour to Matanzas under my very nose," said the captain, one Don Carlos Rosique. "I will have all these illegal goods gathered up and destroyed."

A gasp of horror arose from the crowd.

"Don Carlos, the people of Matanzas are on the verge of starvation," Don Felipe said, in a sharp tone. "You know this well, for we have discussed it more than once already."

"The hurricane may have swept away the bridges; it did not, however, invalidate the orders of His Catholic Majesty," Don Carlos replied, in a strained voice, as his eyes surveyed the crowd.

There was a buzz of angry voices, and the men began to move towards the officer. Papá was at José's side and took him by the shoulder and drew him back, away from the red faces and clenched fists.

Soldiers appeared with José's uncles and Señor Morejón. Only yesterday José had admired the infantrymen, marching proudly in their blue coats, but now a fiery hatred suffused his body.

"My dear captain," said Tío Domingo, smiling. "We wished only to bring aid and comfort to the people of..."

"Quiet yourself," said Don Carlos. "For shame, Don Felipe, this man is a foreigner, to boot. You have been trafficking with foreign smugglers. I should arrest you as well. The Captain-General in Havana will hear of this."

"This man is a Spanish citizen and he, all of them, served on privateers against His Majesty's enemies in the late war. They desire..." Don Felipe's face was red and angry now.

"Privateersmen are little better than pirates, and we see the proof of that before us." The captain turned to go.

"Don Carlos." Suddenly Señor Morejón was before him, bowing and doffing his hat. "With your permission, I would like to speak." His voice was calm, his smile warm but not presumptuous. He did not speak in his usual common Spanish, redolent of the *vega* where he had grown up, but had adopted a refined tone that gave him, despite his straw hat and flood-stained clothes, the air of a gentleman.

The captain softened. "You may. I warn you not to waste my time."

"Don Carlos, I am Anselmo Morejón, the partner of Domingo Albañez, this man who stands before you." He gestured in the direction of Tío Domingo. "We wish only to assist you in your duty of ensuring the well-being of this city. Surely it has never been the wish of His Catholic Majesty to see his people starve. Surely he, and the Captain-General in Havana, will look with favor upon those wise officers who protect his most valuable colony, the Pearl of the Antilles, lest it weaken and fall into the hands of the English."

The captain paused as he pondered those words. Emboldened, Señor Morejón continued. "Our trading house would like to suggest that we reserve a portion of this flour to send to Havana to relieve the hunger there. I have heard word, as I am sure you have, that Havana, too, has suffered cruelly in these storms. I am certain that the Captain-General will be most appreciative when he learns that you have thought of him in his hour of distress and will be inclined to overlook any local irregularities."

Don Carlos was smiling now as he imagined what form the Captain-General's gratitude might take. "There will be no arrests – not today, at least. Don Felipe, see that the flour reaches the hungry families of Matanzas and that a worthy portion goes on to Havana."

Cheers convulsed the crowd, and men slapped José's uncles on the back in congratulation.

Don Carlos smiled, but looked somewhat discomfited by the unaccustomed adulation.

"With your permission, Don Carlos," Señor Morejón spoke again. "I have a request."

"Anything – within reason," Don Carlos said in a magnanimous tone.

"The flour will not last forever, and it will be some time before more register ships arrive. I would like to request papers allowing these vessels, once they have discharged their cargoes, to travel to any port necessary to purchase more," Señor Morejón continued, bowing slightly to acknowledge the boldness of his petition.

For a moment Don Carlos looked thunderstruck. "The Captain-General must provide such papers."

The crowd murmured. Don Carlos looked about at the thin, desperate faces of the Matanzans, and added, "But I will send him a letter recommending that he so do."

Now the crowd cheered.

Señor Morejón acquired the desired licenses to sail to the nearest Spanish port for flour. That failing, they might then seek out "any port necessary." The *Orfeo* and the *Alejandro* returned in record time. Some suspected that they had not bothered to investigate Spanish ports, but gone straight to Kingston or Cap-François. Tío Domingo, however, denied this.

"The winds favored us. God must truly love Matanzas," he said with a wink.

Forever after the hurricanes of 1752 Domingo Albáñez, Policarpo Marroto, Gaspar Crespo, and Anselmo Morejón, too, were heroes in Matanzas. The church held a *Te Deum* Mass to thank God for saving them from the storms, and Father Gastón called them forward for a special blessing. Men slapped their backs, offered them *aguardiente*, and boasted of their friendship. Women smiled at them, and children pointed to them and followed them down the street. A local poet wrote a ballad saluting "The Saviors of Matanzas." José was proud to be the nephew of such men. The Velázquez women, however, kept them humble.

"If you are such a great man, why are there patches on my skirt?" asked Tía Nicolaza.

"Behind every great man is a thrifty woman," Tío Gaspar responded. "And in truth, what adornment could be worthy of you?"

Tía Nicolaza laughed in spite of herself.

Abuelita scoffed at Señor Morejón. "So, now your *pulperia* by the river is a trading house?"

"And why not? In a few months we will be in Havana. Who knows what may be possible there?" he replied.

It was true, in the spring the Morejón family, accompanied by Tío Domingo, would take up residence in Havana, although they would still do business in Matanzas as well, where many *vegueros* needed a market for their tobacco. And too, some endeavors were better undertaken far from the eyes of the Captain-General.

Tío Domingo, too, was excited by the possibilities of Havana. "Imagine it. The navy, the troops, officers great and small. Not to mention tradesmen and sailors, in the market for goods of all types. Anselmo has already made many friends there who can prove helpful."

When he returned from his quest for foreign flour, he stopped by to share a glass of *aguardiente* with Papá.

"I have bought you a joiner's shop, Robbie," he said in Gaelic, as the two sat sipping their drinks after a meager supper. "The man who owned it died from a fever after the hurricane. The apprentices have all gone to the shipyard, but the shop stands empty, with all its tools." He sat back with a pleased expression. "You may pay me back at your leisure."

Papá met this announcement with a stony expression. "I never..."

"We have spoken of this before, Robbie," Tío Domingo continued. "There are great opportunities in Havana, and Faustina will no longer be subject to gossip. And how would José get any schooling, now that Sergeant Espinoza is dead?"

"How would you like to go to school in Havana?" Tío Domingo asked José, pulling him close, but José pushed away and fled to Papá's knee.

"The old man needs me here. There is much work left to do to rebuild Matanzas," protested Papá.

"He already has Jacinto, and Gonzalo, too. Imagine it, to be paid with silver and not an elderly hen or a few onions," urged Tío Domingo.

José could still hear them arguing as he fell asleep.

In the morning, he arose and stumbled into breakfast, still rubbing his eyes. He looked about the room, and saw the grave faces of Abuelo and Abuelita, and he knew that the decision had been made. They were leaving Matanzas. Havana would be his new home.

6

THE KEY TO THE NEW WORLD

They left Matanzas with the Morejón family, a few days after Easter. There were generous rains that spring, the *vegas* surrounding Matanzas were green with newly transplanted tobacco, and Matanzans were gratified to see that a few of the blackened trees had recovered and offered up a few fruits. The last few months had passed in a golden haze. There were many visits with friends and family, the elders talking late into the night, and bidding farewell with long hugs. Abuelita made their favorite dishes, and often slipped the children sweetmeats. Rafael and José visited all their favorite haunts and played spirited games with the boys of the neighborhood.

Abuelo found time to sit with José, peeling an orange for him and telling him stories of his boyhood in faraway Andalusia.

"So, you are going to Havana. That will be quite an adventure," he said, on the day before their departure.

"I don't want to go, Abuelo! I want to stay home with you and Abuelita and Tía Beatriz and..." A storm of tears drowned the rest of his words.

Abuelo waited for the tears to subside. Then he said, "These tears do not become a man. You must dry your eyes and think of your duty. Your father needs you to be strong and to help him."

José wiped his eyes with the back of his hand, and his grandfather continued, "That is better. I once felt as you do. Long ago, when I left home to join the regiment, and we were sent far across the ocean to this island, I did not know if I would ever see my family again."

"But you didn't cry," said José, anticipating the moral of the story. Abuelo was too stern and strong ever to show such weakness.

"No, I did not show any tears. But I cried inside, to leave my mother and brothers. And I was afraid."

"Afraid!" José had never imagined that his grandfather, once a soldier in the army of His Catholic Majesty, King Felipe V, could ever have known fear.

"Yes, afraid. Afraid that I would never see my family again, afraid of what strange things I might encounter in distant lands. But I did not cry, and I did not show my fear," said Abuelo.

He took José's hand. "Jesus and his holy Virgin Mother were watching over me. Here I found your grandmother, the shop, and then my little José, so many blessings. So you see, my fears were foolish."

"Did you ever see your family again?" asked José.

"No, I never did. But I light candles for them in the church, and I know that far away, in Almogía, they are lighting candles for me."

José did not find the ending of the story as satisfactory as Abuelo may have supposed, but he found comfort in the reassuring tone in which it was delivered.

It was a perfect time, a time that could be wrapped up and put away in the memory to be treasured forever. The sun warmed their skin, the breeze from the sea caressed their cheeks, and the afternoon rain was soft as it washed their faces. José was in Matanzas, and Matanzas was in him, and it seemed impossible that they could ever be parted. Each day blossomed like a flower, bright with promise, and like a flower each day faded away until the happy days in Matanzas were no more, and the day of departure arrived.

The *Orfeo* left early in the morning, to catch the tide. They were accompanied by Gonzalo, now a venerable twelve years of age, who would help Papá in the shop, continuing to learn the joiner's trade. It took at least two men to do the work of a carpenter, and José was still far too small to handle the tools and long boards used in the shop. The whole family, with the exception of Tío Gaspar and Tío Policarpo, who were at sea, had gone to bid them farewell. Their trunks and boxes were already stowed aboard. Aunts and cousins swarmed about them, almost smothering them with hugs, kisses, and good wishes.

"You are a lucky boy, Gonzalo. Tío Roberto will teach you to be a master joiner," said Tía Nicolaza, who stood straight and proud, her eyes fixed on the vessel in the bay, avoiding the face of her son, who appeared to be fighting off tears. "Remember my words, *mi hijo*. Havana is full of temptations. Listen to Tío Roberto, go to Mass with Tía Faustina, and avoid wicked people and evil pursuits. Do not make me sorry that I trusted you," she scolded, her eyes still avoiding his face. "Your papá will see you whenever he comes to Havana," she added, more softly.

Gonzalo could bear it no longer. He buried his face in her warm shoulder, and she clutched him fiercely to her. It is possible that he sobbed, but if any present heard such a sound, they pretended not to notice.

"The sea takes everyone, it took Alejandro, and it takes Policarpo and Gaspar, and now it takes Faustina and José..." said Tía Beatriz, tears running down her plump face.

"Hush, foolish girl, they are only going to Havana. You would think they were leaving for Peru," fussed Abuelita, dabbing at her eyes with a handkerchief and pulling José close to her, smothering him in her skirt.

Tía Beatriz took Magdalena in her arms and the ladies clustered about the little girl, kissing her fat cheeks and caressing her beautiful brown curls.

Abuelita held Mamá in her arms for a long time, then Abuelo took her by the shoulders and looked into her eyes. "Take good care of Roberto and the children," he said. Nicolaza gave her a quick hug, then turned away, and Beatriz took her hands and kissed them.

Then it was time to clamber into the boat and push off for the *Orfeo*, amid cries of farewell, tears, and waving handkerchieves. The tide began to recede, and Tío Domingo shouted orders to his crew. A light wind filled the sails of the *Orfeo* and she stood out from the bay of Matanzas for the open sea. Abuelo and Abuelita were still on shore, watching, Abuelita waving her handkerchief, Abuelo with his hand on her shoulder. Tía Nicolaza stood ramrod straight, by their side, her worn face taut. José fixed his eyes fixed on them until their figures could no longer be seen in the increasing glare of the sun.

It was a day's trip to Havana, and the *Orfeo*, on this occasion, carried many passengers. There was an awning stretched out amidships to protect them from the sun, a hogshead of water for the thirsty, and several hammocks hung in the cabin should any be in need of rest. José watched the women with small children gathered together under the awning, gossiping and fussing over their little ones. Several men strolled the decks, making idle chatter about the weather, and Gonzalo had draped himself over the bulwark, gazing aimlessly at the passing green shore as he sang a ditty to himself.

There was a curtained area on deck where the passengers could perform private functions. The crew had a platform off the bowsprit for such necessities, and José and Rafael were thrilled to see Fabian, one of the sailors, climb up on the bow and let forth a great stream of water into the sea. The women politely turned away and made their daughters do so as well. Rafael, however, ran towards the bow and grabbed at the belaying pins to haul himself up that he might imitate the performance.

"Get down from there, you monkey, lest Don Domingo see you. You will fall into the sea and be devoured by sharks," scolded Señor Parreño, a neighbor from Matanzas, who was traveling to Havana on business.

Papá was watching the boys from nearby. Next to him stood a tall *blanco*, another of the paying passengers, and by his side, a boy, a trifle older than José. The man was pale with dark hair tied in a neat queue, with silver buckles on his shoes and breeches. His buttons, too, shone, with silver. José wished he dared touch their brightness.

"*Pardos*," sniffed the man through his long, aquiline nose, his accent marking him as a *peninsular*. "*Blanco* boys know how to behave with dignity."

"Better a high-spirited boy than a dainty fop," said Papá, putting an arm about José to claim him. José saw the pale boy flinch.

Señor Parreño had moved to the quarterdeck to speak with Señor Morejón, and Rafael now attempted to climb the shrouds. One bare foot after another went up the ratlines. The *blanco* boy watched him, glanced for a hopeful moment up at his father's face, then sighed, shoulders slumping.

Rafael was now many feet above the deck, shouting with triumph. A sturdy form appeared below him, a dark face looked up, unsmiling. His victorious whoop died on his lips and he made his way down to face the judgment of Señora Morejón.

Señor Morejón rescued his son, promising his wife that he would keep the boys out of trouble with a lesson in seamanship.

"That, *niños*, is the boom," he began, pointing out the great spar that extended over the quarterdeck and beyond. Tío Domingo stood below it, on the quarterdeck, at the helm.

The *blanco* boy crept closer, listening surreptitiously, one eye on his father.

Señor Morejón observed the boy's interest. "Señor, I would be honored if your son should wish to join these boys in their lesson."

Señor Morejón's carefully crafted invitation permitted the possibility of a polite refusal, but the plea of the *blanco* boy did not.

"Please, Papá! May I?" His pale face and thin form suggested that his opportunities for boyish fun were few, and the yearning in his voice hinted that this was not of his choice.

"*Mi hijo*, how could I refuse such a gracious invitation? You have my consent. I thank you, sir," he added with a slightest of nods to Señor Morejón.

The *blanco* boy shyly stepped into the circle of Señor Morejón's attention. He smiled and became more animated as the boys learned the difference between sheets and stays, boom and bowsprit, mast and yards. Tío Domingo came to join them for a time, testing the boys on their nautical knowledge. He pointed above, to the spar that carried the mainsail.

"The gaff!" cried Rafael.

He pointed forward, to the long spar that reached far out beyond the bow.

"The jibboom!" Sebastián, for that was the name of the *blanco* boy, hurried to answer.

"José, are you attending? What is this called?" and Tío Domingo pointed to one of the lines supporting the mast.

But José, while he enjoyed the funny sounds of the words, was more interested in the people on deck, and studying the face of the new boy. Tío Domingo frowned as José missed one answer after another, and returned to the quarterdeck. José was relieved to be spared his presence.

It was not long before the three boys were fast friends. They rushed from larboard to starboard, stem to stern, eager not to miss any of the sights on their day's voyage.

"That is a village, there beyond that cay. See the fishing boats!" said José, scanning the green coastline on the larboard side, although he needed to climb on a cask to see over the bulwark.

"A sail! Do you see it? I think it is a brigantine," called Rafael from starboard, although it was impossible to identify the faint smudge of white on the horizon.

Sebastián laughed with joy as he stood on the companionway to the quarterdeck and pointed at the sparkling blue water. "Porpoises! My father says those fish are called porpoises!"

Tío Domingo came down to see the excitement, but the boys were too engrossed in the sights to notice, and he once again returned to his duties.

They gathered about Isidro, one of the crew, who was catching a fish for their dinner. He let them each hold the line for a few minutes, but they were disappointed when he had a tug on the line and insisted on hauling in the fish himself, a big sea bass.

"Here you go boys!" said Isidro. "Here is a task for your idle hands." He handed them each a knife and showed them how to clean the fish.

"Be careful!" Mamá called out.

Sebastián stripped off his fine coat, and they laughed as they saw each other smeared with fish scales. They helped Fabian fry up the fish over a brazier on deck and boil a great pot of rice and beans to accompany it.

The families gathered below decks to enjoy their dinner, perched on their chests and boxes. The air below was already becoming stifling as the sun beat down on the deck above, and they soon moved back on deck. Some took their siesta in the cabin, while others sat under the awning on deck and closed their eyes for a few winks. The boys proclaimed that they were not tired, but their elders insisted, and soon their eyes closed and they slept. They rose not long after, however, refreshed for further adventure.

Don Martín de Ayala, the tall *blanco* man, laughed as he watched little Magdalena and Marianela. "*Un barco chiquito,*" they sang, again and again, as they scampered about the deck. Mamá and Señora Morejón looked on contentedly. The *blanco* man became less proud, and discussed the affairs of the day with Papá and Señor Morejón.

"What business brought you to Matanzas?" Papá asked Don Martín.

"No business, señor. My brother-in-law, Don Patricio Cordovés, has a *vega* outside of Matanzas, and I brought my son to spend a few weeks in the fresh air."

"He seems a good lad," said Papá, his eyes on the three boys.

The proud lines of Don Martín's face softened. "He is a dear boy," he said softly. "His mother died when he was born, and I almost lost the child as well. His health remains delicate. I would spend more time in the country but my position requires my presence in Havana, and I cannot bear to be parted from him. And there is no schooling to be found on a tobacco plantation."

"Your position? You are employed by the government?" asked Señor Morejón, his dark eyes suddenly alert. José noticed that he had assumed his gentleman's diction, his consonants crisp, a shadow of Don Martín's careful Castilian.

"I have been on the staff of the treasury for ten years, ever since my arrival on this blighted island," Don Martín replied, sighing.

"How you must miss Spain!" commented Señor Morejón, agreeably. "In truth, Cuba lacks many amenities."

"Everything must be imported! And it is so expensive. I have searched in vain for a porcelain chocolate set for my sister. And I have not tasted a fine vintage in years..." Don Martín sighed.

"It is sometimes possible to obtain such items, even in Cuba..." said Señor Morejón, in a quiet, intimate tone.

"There she is, José, the key to the New World!" said Papá, his hand on José's shoulder, as they watched the Castillo del Morro, the great fortress that guarded the entrance to Havana's harbor, grow ever larger in the distance. Tío Domingo shouted orders as a *guadaño*, or pilot boat, directed their course through the narrow channel leading into the harbor.

Havana sprawled before them, greedily stretching out across the bay and into the countryside, drawing its resources – cattle, tobacco, wood, fruit, and fresh water – into the city to be consumed or exported. Havana drew to her also the ships of Spain's American empire, from Vera Cruz in Mexico, Cartagena on the Spanish Main, and Portobelo in Central America. From all the ports of the Spanish colonies they came, filled with treasure and goods destined for Spain. They stopped there, in Havana harbor, like great white-winged birds, and then took off for the final leg of their journey to the port of Cádiz in Spain, bearing the riches of the New World. And Havana was the first port of call for ships arriving from Cádiz, where they could replenish their stores and make repairs at the Royal Shipyard.

The ships were safe in Havana harbor, for the city's muscular arms also sheltered them from all foreign threats, from the fleets of the British, the French, the Dutch and the Danish, from privateers and the occasional pirates that still troubled the waters of the Caribbean. Watchtowers along the coast cast a protective gaze over ships approaching the city. At the northwest end of the bay, at the very extreme of the harbor across from the city itself, stood El Morro. On the south point, directly opposite, stood the Castillo de la Punta. Within the harbor, the Castillo de la Real Fuerza sat hunched overlooking the wharves and their ships. Throughout all these fortifications swarmed soldiers: regiments from Spain stationed permanently on the island, reinforcing troops on temporary duty, and occasionally, local militias in which were represented all of Cuba's free citizens, *blancos*, *pardos*, and *morenos*.

The *Orfeo* reduced sail and the *guadaño* guided her through the many vessels that crowded the harbor. They approached the Muelle de la Contaduría, where ships from overseas docked and passed through customs and coastal sloops could unload their cargoes, where they might be purchased locally or shipped out again to other ports.

Just visible in the distance was the Muelle de la Luz, the wharf at the far end of the harbor where the vessels that ferried foodstuffs from the villages across the bay docked. Flocks of sloops and small craft crowded the wharf, jostling for space.

Next to the Muelle de la Contaduría was the Muelle de la Factoría. Cargo ships from Spain lined the dock. A crane was swinging hogsheads from the wharf into the hold of one of the vessels.

"See the barrels fly!" Magdalena cried out, pointing.

"That is where the royal tobacco monopoly ships its goods back to Spain. Bales of tobacco, casks of snuff, all destined for the pipes and the noses of Spain. The finest snuff comes from our own Matanzas," commented Señor Morejón.

José felt a sudden pang of longing, for he remembered that Abuelo was from Spain. What was Abuelo doing now? Was he thinking of the little family now in Havana?

Gonzalo stared fascinated at the men working on shore as scraps of work songs floated to them across the water. Rafael, meanwhile, grew increasingly excited, running from one end of the ship to the other, trying to get the best view of all the sights. "Look, José, look, a frigate!" cried Rafael, pointing to a long, sleek three-masted vessel by the dock. Its blue paint sparkled in the late afternoon sun, and its sides were slotted with ports for its many guns.

"This is the home port for the Spanish fleet in the Indies, *niños*. You will see many frigates, men-of-war, and ships-of-the-line here," said Señor Morejón. "They protect our shipping as it travels to and from Cádiz."

"Do our ships ever go to Cádiz?" asked Rafael.

"No, our vessels are only coastal sloops. Only Spanish-owned bottoms can be used for shipping to and from Cádiz. One needs a license even to trade with another Spanish colony, and trade with foreign colonies is, of course, illegal," explained his father.

"Sometimes, however," he continued, "the Captain-General provides licenses for such trade. Albañez y Morejón has received such licenses, as you know."

One of the ships docked there did not fly any of the various flags used by the Spanish navy or merchant ships, but a different flag, crossed with slashes of blood red and white against a cold blue background.

"What ship is that?" José asked, pointing.

"The flag that ship flies is the flag of Great Britain," replied Tío Domingo. "That was once our flag."

"That was never my flag," spat Papá. "The white cross in the field of blue is the cross of St. Andrew, Scotland's cross. For the rest I do not give a damn," he muttered in Gaelic.

"I care not what flag I fly under," replied Tío Domingo. "My loyalties lie with Spanish silver."

"But if only Spanish ships may come to Cuba, why is this British ship here?" asked José.

"Because the British, perfidious race that they are, have no respect for the law. They sometimes come here, claiming to need repairs, and trade their goods on the sly. A thousand curses upon them!" his father replied.

Tío Domingo said irritatedly in Gaelic. "Why do you cling to the past? If I were you, I would count my blessings in the present."

"Aye, I have many blessings." Papá's grip on José's hand tightened, and he reached out to stroke Magdalena's curls, as she clung to Mamá's skirt while her large, dark eyes took in the many sights.

Tío Domingo gave the order to drop anchor in the bay.

Soon a lighter pulled up alongside to take the passengers to the dock. The adults clambered down the Jacob's ladder into the boat, then the older children, and finally the youngest ones were carefully handed down into waiting arms.

As they approached the pier, José clung to his father's hand and studied the activity on shore. Crowds of men with faces of many hues, a few white, more of various shades of brown, many black. The ships were moored stern end to the pier, planks laid from the stern to the dock, allowing the men to remove the cargo. A gang of men, bare-chested and sweating in the heat, carried bundles of hides from a weather-beaten schooner to their right. On another, the crew was using a line slung from a lower yard to sway crates up from their hold and onto a waiting cart.

Mamá's face, which had been anxiously fixed on Papá's, relaxed, and she called out loudly, "We are here, *niños*, Gonzalo. Soon we will be in our new home."

They waited on the wharf while Tío Domingo and Señor Morejón arranged for carts to carry the passengers' baggage to their lodgings. Tío Domingo called for a *volante* to take Señor Parreño and Don Martín to their destinations. As the gentleman settled themselves between the two large wheels of the open carriage drawn by a prancing black horse, Magdalena fussed in Mamá's arms, and Señora Morejón was busy keeping her two youngest boys close to her skirts. José and Rafael bid farewell to Sebastián before he climbed into the *volante* next to his father. José saw him look back and give a shy wave as the *volante* turned the corner and disappeared from sight.

Now it was time for the Albañez and Morejón families to make their way to their new homes. For a moment it appeared that they had lost Gonzalo; then Papá spotted him in a crowd surrounding a fruit vendor, who was hawking her wares in the most alluring of terms. Papá seized him by the arm and the two families plunged into the crowd, the little ones in the arms of their parents, José and Rafael clinging tightly to their fathers' hands. They were lost in a sea of sailors, dockhands in broad straw hats and checked shirts, blue-clad soldiers, and street vendors with bright kerchieves. The air was filled with the sounds of men shouting orders, wood banging against wood, wheels turning, and above it all, street vendors singing the praises of their goods. Strange smells crowded in on them as well, the sharp briny scent of the sea and a faint undercurrent of rotting fish at the docks, and, as they walked deeper into the city, the powerful stench of the slaughterhouses just outside of the city walls. José felt very small in this great crowd, in this sprawling city that spilled outside its walls into the countryside and across the Almendares River.

At last, after treading down many streets and turning many corners, they arrived at their new homes. They had passed a vast assortment of buildings on the way, some still under repair from the hurricanes almost a year ago. The houses in Havana were of brick, with tile roofs, unlike those in Matanzas. There were buildings of great magnificence, too, but José had long ago stopped looking up to stare. He only wanted to see this, their new house. It was on the Calle Aguacate, the street of the avocado. The house was yellow, bright in the shadows of the street, like sunlight on the blue waves, and the wooden trim was light blue, like the sky above the harbor of Matanzas. Some of the wood was broken in places, and the paint was peeling; Papá would soon fix that. The front of the house was to be the joiner's shop, and Papá would soon make a sign bearing the name "Zum-Zum" with a bright-colored hummingbird painted on it. It would hang it in front, like the sign in front of Abuelo's shop.

Just around the corner, on the Calle Sumidero was the Morejóns' new home. Sumidero meant sewer, but the bright colors of the houses there reminded José instead of a garden. The Morejóns' house was a warm rosy pink, like the hibiscus that had bloomed in the courtyard of their home in Matanzas, and the trim on the doors and windows was green like leaves. Señora Morejón stood in the street, surveying the house, arms akimbo, while Señor Morejón watched her. She gave a nod of approval, and Señor Morejón glowed with pride.

The two houses were laid out in a similar fashion. In the front of the building was a large room, dedicated to business. Long, shuttered windows stretched almost from the eaves to the ground, shutters open to allow the sea breezes to cool the house, with only a wooden grating to separate passers-by from the scene within. Through the windows passers-by on the Calle Aguacate could watch the tradesmen at their craft, a kind of daily street theatre. The front room of the Albañez house would soon be filled with sawdust and the smell of fresh-cut wood.

José and Rafael would spend much of their time in the spaces behind the front room. In the center of the house, behind the shop, was the patio, which allowed cool breezes to sweep through the rooms that surrounded it and dissipated the hot fumes from the brazier that resided there. On one side was located the kitchen where the family would gather and eat, on the other, two small bedrooms. One would house José's parents, the other, José and Gonzalo. Magdalena, still small, slept in their parents' room. In the back was a room that had been used for storage and was now filled with broken furniture and refuse.

"Soon we will need to put a bed in here for Magdalena," said Papá.

Magdalena clung to Mamá's skirt, and Mamá patted her curls and said gently, "There will not be room for four in our room." Papá squeezed Mamá and gave her a quick kiss.

That night, as José tried to fall asleep in his new bed, under its cotton curtains, he heard the strange new sounds of the city. Horses' hooves clopped in the street as they carried revelers to evening entertainments. In the distance the church bells called Habaneros to prayer. Dogs barked, and were silenced by rocks from sleepy neighbors. Gonzalo tossed and turned in the next bed. The voices of José's parents and Tío Domingo drifted across the patio as the adults shared a celebratory bottle of Spanish wine. José missed the voices of Abuelo and Abuelita.

He heard his father's voice, speaking in Gaelic with unusual warmth, "Thank you, Donnie, for all that you are doing for us. I swear to you that I will repay you as business begins to prosper."

Tío Domingo was gruff in his reply. "I know well enough how much I owe you. I have not forgotten, whatever you may think."

"Still, I wish that there had been another way. I meant to work side-by-side with the old man, always." José could hear the pain in his father's voice.

Tío Domingo protested, "He still has Jacinto, and he is an able lad. Señor Luis encouraged the move."

"Aye, it is the best thing for Faustina," his father murmured. "And for the boy."

José ceased to listen to their conversation as tears filled his eyes. It was because of him that they had left Abuelo and Abuelita and all the uncles and aunts and cousins! He thought of Abuelo, grey and grizzled, working in his shop without the steady, capable hands of his son-in-law. If Abuelo were with him now, he would tell José a story to ease his sadness, but Abuelo was back in Matanzas, and so José cried quiet tears as he drifted off to sleep, alone in his bed in the strange new house, in the big, crowded city of Havana.

In Matanzas, José had awakened to the sound of the vultures in the banyan tree outside the house. Today he awoke to the rattle of wheels and the cries of street vendors, advertising their goods to the housewives who were just beginning their morning routines. Crusty bread, pineapple, fragrant bananas, jars of cool water drawn fresh from the pump, these and many other good things could be purchased from women, mostly *morenas* or *pardas*, dressed in bright skirts and kerchieves.

The family breakfasted quietly on cassava bread and bananas purchased from two of these vendors, and then began the long morning's work of transporting their goods from the *Orfeo* to the new house on the Calle Aguacate. Their household goods were few; the house came already furnished, and what they lacked Papá could make. They had brought their few clothes and personal items with them the day before, and the linens, pots, and utensils they had brought from Abuelo's house all fit into another crate they would fetch today. Other goods they might need could be purchased here, in Havana. No, the focus of their efforts were the many boxes and bundles stowed in the forward end of the hold in the *Orfeo*. They had been covered with a tarpaulin during the trip to keep them from the curious eyes of the passengers. They contained the trade goods to be stored in Señor Morejón's house around the corner, which would serve as a warehouse for the goods of Albañez y Morejón. Bottles of wine, rich fabrics, pungent spices, jars of delicacies from distant lands; José knew that these were the sort of things that Señor Morejón would offer to the right buyers in Havana, but he also knew that they did not speak freely of this trade to others. Papá helped Señor Morejón move these goods into the front room of the pink house. As he returned home from the pink house, dark eyes watched him from between the balustrades of the windows next door. At last a short, sturdy woman with greying hair held back tightly by two combs emerged from the door of the lime-green house.

"My name is Señora Peña. I own this house," she announced, gesturing to the building behind her. "So, you are the one who has purchased this shop," she said, eyeing Papá up and down. "Now Señor Casales ran a very prosperous business, patrons coming and going all day, some of them from the best families in Havana." She seemed to suggest that Papá was an unlikely successor to such an enterprising tradesman.

"Well, Señora, my name is Roberto Albañez, and from this day forward this will be my shop," said Papá bluntly.

"We are certain to find success in such a fortunate location," added Mamá in a propitiatory tone.

"You do not sound like a *criollo*, nor do you sound like any *peninsular* that I have ever met," said Señora Peña, looking Papá straight in the eye.

"No, I do not," replied Papá brusquely. "Come, Faustina, we have a great deal of work to do."

"Roberto, you might have spoken to her more graciously," Mamá scolded when they were behind the blue door.

"She wanted to ferret out everything she could, the nosy old biddy," replied Papá. "She lives next door; she will learn all about us soon enough."

Once inside the shop, Papá gazed about at the tools that lay on shelves under a thick layer of dust, then looked down at the drifts of sawdust that still lay on the floor. He then addressed Gonzalo. "We have a great opportunity, you and I. You must pay careful attention and work hard. You are the oldest and your mother is counting on you to make her proud. Now, let us clean up this sty so that we can open for business tomorrow."

José watched sadly as Gonzalo helped his father with this important task, but his face brightened when Papá gave him some scrapers to clean. "Someday, José, when you are big as Gonzalo, big enough to reach the workbench you will come and work in the shop with me and learn to use all of the tools. But that will be many years yet." And José glowed with pleasure to think of himself working side by side with Papá. Then Papá would not need Gonzalo there. His cousin could be sent packing back to Matanzas.

Mamá and Magdalena were finishing preparations for dinner, and the menfolk were just sweeping up the last of the sawdust when there was a knock on the door. It was a loud, important knock, as befitted the first knock on their new door.

Papá opened the door to find a tall, lean man in a smart blue uniform with red facing, bearing the insignia of an ensign. José stared in admiration at the long sword in a scabbard the ensign wore at his side. Behind him stood two soldiers, dusty and sweating in the growing heat of the day.

"I am looking for the man who calls himself Roberto Albañez," said the lieutenant in a formal tone, his face impassive.

"I am Roberto Albañez," said Papá. He waited, cautiously observing the officer.

"You have been ordered to report to the office of the Captain-General. I am here to make sure that you do so," the ensign announced. The soldiers behind him stood straighter.

Mamá hurried for Papá's coat and hat and gave him a worried kiss.

José watched from the door as Papá was marched off between the two soldiers, watched until they disappeared among the crowd of strangers on the Calle Aguacate.

7

LOST

They had their noonday dinner without Papá, they took their afternoon siesta without Papá, and the light began to fade from the sky without Papá. Gonzalo, without Papá to direct him, disappeared from the shop, and Mamá had not the spirit to stop him. It was quiet in the house. Mamá moved a chair up close to the window and sat silently, watching through the grating, fingering her rosary. José and Magdalena played listlessly nearby. The tools had lost their luster in the dusk, and the weak breeze made only fitful efforts to stir the air in the room. Magdalena and José's eyelids began to flutter.

At last Mamá arose. "Time to go to bed, *niños*. There is no use in all of us waiting up."

As she chivied the children to the back rooms, the sound of laughter and sturdy boots was heard outside the door, which flew open to reveal Papá and Tío Domingo. Tío Domingo was holding up Papá, or perhaps it was Papá who was supporting Tío Domingo.

Mamá flew to Papá and threw her arms around him. "I was so worried! So were we all!" she cried as José and Magdalena shouted, "Papá! Papá!" in voices that were no longer sleepy.

"Faustina, you did not worry about us, did you?" asked Papá in an indistinct voice.

Mamá stood back, arms akimbo, and fixed him with a look. José knew that look, for he had often seen it, not under the best of circumstances, but never before directed at Papá.

"Faustina, it was nothing..." Tío Domingo said cajolingly, putting his arm around her shoulder, but Mamá struck it away.

"Come, Roberto, we will sit and drink some punch and I will explain every-thing. It is all fine, no, it is better than fine. We have news...news for you, José!" And Tío Domingo lifted José on his shoulder and they all trooped into the kitchen, Mamá yielding with a rueful smile.

As he spoke, Tío Domingo began the ritual of making punch. Papá brought out several of their precious limes and began slicing them. Mamá threw up her arms, but, after a flurry of protest, went to heat the sugar and water in a small pan over the remnants of the coals in the brazier in the courtyard. Soon the hot sugar mixture was mixed with *aguardiente* and Tío Domingo squeezed the limes to add their juice to the mixture. Mamá squeezed some lime juice into sweetened water for José and Magdalena.

Tío Domingo began the story. "It was all a misunderstanding, as we explained to the lieutenant, the misguided diligence of a minor functionary. You remember old Señora Peña? She came yesterday to investigate her new neighbors, you met her then. She heard our accents, thought us to be British spies, and reported this to one of the sergeants who boards with her. She probably hoped for some sort of reward, the nosy biddy. There is nothing remarkable about our presence. Half the time Havana is awash in French and Irish seaman waiting for their ships to sail for Spain."

"Those men do not reside here. Señora Peña is a loyal servant of His Majesty King Fernando, protecting her home from those who would do it harm." Papá waved the trouble away.

"Of course she is. And I am Robert the Bruce. We explained it all to the lieutenant, that we are both good Catholics..." explained Tío Domingo as he handed Papá a glass of punch.

"I am a good Catholic. You are an apostate," grumbled Papá, but accepted the proffered drink.

"I have been seen at Mass on more than one occasion," replied Tío Domingo, with an upright but unsteady air. "We explained that as devout Catholics, hound-ed by the perfidious forces of that notorious and heretical monarch George II, we

had been granted permission to reside in the dominions of His Catholic Majesty."
Tío Domingo poured himself a glass and sat down.

"I was hounded out. You ran like a dog," muttered Papá, now slurring his
words.

"And we must thank the Virgin that you both found your way to Cuba,"
Mamá said soothingly.

"And so we showed him our papers, signed by Captain-General Cajigal de la
Vega himself, giving us permission to live on this island in return for all of our
services to the crown in the late war," explained Papá.

"I hinted that it was good that his superiors did not know of the grave mistake
he was making," interrupted Tío Domingo. "And then we praised His Majesty
profusely for his beneficent treatment for poor persecuted Catholics, and all was
well. More than well..."

There was a loud knocking on the door, and Señor Morejón and Señora
Morejón joined them.

"Where are the children?" asked Mamá, about to take Magdalena, already
asleep, off to bed.

"We have found a girl to help around the house. Dionisia is watching them,"
said Señor Morejón, proud that he could take such good care of his family.

"You must have the second sense, Anselmo, to know that we had returned,"
said Tío Domingo. And to know that I had made punch," he added, handing
him a glass.

"It did not take second sense to hear the racket you two made as you passed the
house," noted Señora Morejón tartly.

"We did not come here to berate them, *mi cariño*," Señor Morejón quieted his
wife. "But in all truth, this is not unexpected. The Spanish government is very
careful about whom it permits to reside on this island. It is, after all, the home of
the Spanish fleet in the New World. If you had not provided such valuable service
during the war...so when I received your most urgent message requesting that I
immediately send a suitably generous gift to the lieutenant, I of course chose a

few bottles of the finest Madeira. And I have been anxiously waiting to learn how the gift was received."

"Well, now I understand everything," laughed Mamá.

Tío Domingo gesticulated dramatically as he described the scene.

"He was delighted. He opened a bottle immediately. We all shared a glass while I described to him our service to the crown, how we had both served on a privateer, many times making prizes of ships belonging to our former monarch, facing death as traitors should we have been captured."

"That German was never our monarch. I owe loyalty only to King James, God bless him," burst out Papá.

"Lieutenant Sifontes was impressed by this sign of our loyalty," continued Tío Domingo. "We further shared with him several tales of our encounters with the enemy, and he was most appreciative. He shared a few adventures of his own."

"And a bottle of our best Madeira," noted Señor Morejón wryly.

"And that most excellent Madeira," laughed Tío Domingo. "He enjoyed as well Roberto's description of the Battle of Prestopans."

"On that day the English received the drubbing they so deserved. They fell like oat stalks," said Papá with satisfaction.

José's eyes were great with admiration. He wished he had been there to hear these stories, for his father never spoke to his family of his service in either war. How glorious it must have been!

"Then we drank to the many Scots who have served the Spanish crown. We raised a glass to the Earl of Argyll, who served the crown so bravely in West Flanders. We saluted General Wauschope of Niddrie-Marishcal, who died serving the King in Catalonia. Again we raised a glass to Colonel James Keith, who fought at the siege of Gibraltar. Another to Commodore Don Pedro Stuart y Portugal of the Spanish Navy. And we concluded with a toast to the Black Douglas, who carried the heart of Robert the Bruce into battle in Spain against the Moors." As Tío Domingo finished, he and Papá raised their glasses again to these great heroes.

"It is good you had several bottles of Madeira for so many toasts," noted Señora Morejón wryly.

Tío Domingo was not to be shamed. "Are we to blame that Scottish swords are valued everywhere in the world? There are Scottish soldiers in Spain, in France, in Russia, Poland, wherever brave men are needed..."

"There are Scottish swords everywhere but in Scotland," Papá said morosely. "In Scotland men must bury their claymores to hide them from the English tyrant."

"But you said that you had news for José," said Mamá, who had heard these complaints many times before.

"Yes, how could I neglect to mention it? In the end, Lieutenant Sifontes declared us to be fine fellows, adornments to His Majesty's colony, and sent us on our way," continued Tío Domingo. "But not before he had provided us with some very useful advice. He gave us the name of a teacher who runs a small school on the Calle Villegas. He is an old lieutenant from the Army, obliged to retire from His Majesty's service after he lost an arm at Casteldelfino. He originally came to Cuba as a minor functionary and now has turned schoolteacher. He drills young boys in their letters and sums until they are prepared to enter the best of schools."

"We have been looking for such a school for Rafael," interjected Señora Morejón.

"I do not care about the best of schools," said Papá. "But a good knowledge of arithmetic and books will prepare him to run the shop someday."

Mamá looked worried. "But what of the cost?" she asked quietly, looking at Papá.

"I will pay for the boy's schooling," announced Tío Domingo. "Do not worry about the money."

Mamá turned to Papá. "Perhaps we should not..."

"I can easily afford it," said Tío Domingo. "It is nothing."

"Reading and mathematics will be good for the boy," said Papá, patting Mamá reassuringly on the shoulder. "And Domingo wishes it."

"So, José," said Tío Domingo, pulling the boy towards him, "What do you think of that? You will be going off to school soon!"

José pulled away and looked at Papá.

"An education is a fine thing," said Papá reassuringly, picking up José and putting him on his lap.

"I think I will like it," replied José, burying his face in Papá's shoulder and breathing in the enticing perfume of wine and mahogany.

"It will prepare him to do many things," said Tío Domingo firmly. "It is all arranged. Another bottle of Anselmo's excellent Madeira and a visit to Lieutenant Galeano has served to procure a place in the school. He starts on Monday. We shared a drink to seal the agreement. The lieutenant is an excellent character, I think, if somewhat deaf. A drawback of life in the artillery."

"Oh, so that explains all this merriment," Señor Morejón observed.

"*Dios mío*, my little boy is going off to school all by himself so soon!" cried Mamá.

"Not alone," Señora Morejón commanded. "Not alone. Rafael will go with him. You will arrange it tomorrow, Anselmo. My son will learn to read and cipher and hold up his head with the best of them." She sat there, head high.

"As you wish, *mi cariño*," replied Señor Morejón. As Mamá swept the children off to bed, the Morejóns rose to leave.

"Isn't she magnificent?" José heard Señor Morejón whisper to Papá, nodding his head slightly towards his wife.

Papá came to tuck José in. Gonzalo was already in his bed, fast asleep. He had slipped in at some point, unnoticed.

"Papá, someday will you tell me about the battles you were in?" José asked, fighting to keep his eyes open.

There was a silence, and José struggled to see if his father were still in the dark room.

At last his father spoke. "There are some things I no longer wish to remember."

"Not ever?" José asked pleadingly.

"Not ever," was his father's reply.

Monday had come at last, and it was time for José and Rafael to begin school. Tío Domingo had bought José his own slate and slate pencil. The slate was heavy, a dull back square framed by varnished wood. José clutched it in his left hand, his right in Rafael's as the two strode proudly off to school, parents smiling and waving. Magdalena waved too, and so did Marianela, surrounded by her little brothers. José waved at her, and she smiled back at him. Mamá looked heavy and tired, dark circles under her eyes, and Papá hurried her back into the house to rest.

Old Señora Peña looked out of her front window, attracted by the noise. "Going to school, is he? Good boy!" she exclaimed, and she waved, too.

Rafael pulled at José's hand, leading him along, for Rafael knew the way. While José had been helping his father in the shop, Rafael had been exploring the streets of the city.

Lieutenant Galeano held school in the front room of his house on Calle Villegas. Three rows of small boys sat at small desks, facing the front of the room. Many were *blancos*, but José was relieved to see that there were *pardos* as well, and one big *moreno* boy sitting in the back row. In the front stood Lieutenant Galeano, straight as a ramrod, dressed in a neat but faded blue jacket fastened with pewter buttons. One blue sleeve held his right arm, which brandished a ferrule, and the other hung empty by his side.

Lieutenant Galeano assigned José and Rafael to seats in the front row.

"Attention, students. I introduce to you José and Rafael, our new scholars," he barked out, in a hoarse voice.

There was a murmur among the other boys.

"Silence!" shouted Lieutenant Galeano, as he banged his ferrule on the desk in front of José, who started in his seat. "You will review your lessons until I am ready to hear them."

Their teacher then examined José and Rafael to determine the extent of their education. Both boys could count to one hundred, and José had learned a few letters from Papá, but that was the sum of their knowledge.

Lieutenant Galeano began with the alphabet, showing them the letters printed neatly on the first page of their catechism books, making the sounds, barking out the words till their ears rang, and listening and nodding as the boys repeated after him. The teacher's deafness suggested a prank to Rafael.

"Jota!" boomed the voice of Lieutenant Galeano, pointing to the letter J. "Jarra!" and José pictured the large red jar for water in their house.

"Jarra," repeated José.

"Gato!" said Rafael softly, and meowed, and then winced as the ferrule cracked across his knuckles. Lieutenant Galeano was not without some hearing and had lost none of his powers of observation.

He then set them to copy the letters on their slates.

Rafael scratched away diligently. José enjoyed the feel of the slate pencil, firm in his hand, and heard it squeak as it made a coarse white line on the dull black of the slate. His letters appeared clean and straight. What fine fellows these letters were! The A, with his legs splayed wide, like a sailor trying to get his land legs after a long voyage. And the "B," a butcher waddling to Mass on Sunday. But he needed a hat, and boots...and it was done. So José worked his way through the alphabet, his pencil moving rapidly across the slate. A shadow fell over his work, and José looked up. Lieutenant Galeano looked down to see José's latest work, a fat fish flopping on the hook that was the "J."

"José Albañez Velázquez, put out your hands," barked the lieutenant.

José put them forward, palms up, and felt the sting of the ferrule. He pulled his reddened palms back, and remembered what Abuelo had told him: men do not cry. He scrunched his eyes tight, but his eyes did not know that he was a man, and two tears trickled down his nose and on to the guilty slate, half-melting his drawing.

The rest of the school day passed in a blur until, suddenly, class had ended and the students rushed to the door to return home for noonday dinner. José followed Rafael, imagining the disappointed faces of Papá and Mamá when he confessed his sin.

He felt Rafael tug at his hand to lead him across the street, but suddenly a *volante* rushed in front of them. He leapt back as the horse reared and a well-dressed matron accompanying a pretty, black-haired young woman looked down from her leather cushions and clucked, "*Madre de Dios*! Those *pardo* boys..." and then the driver, a slightly built *moreno* in tall leather boots and a green striped waistcoat made a show of flicking his whip and called out encouragement to the horse. José watched as the *volante* sped away. His eyes were fixed on the buttery yellow of the girl's shawl accented against her soft blue dress, and the deeper blue of her companion's attire. Then they disappeared around the corner, and José found himself standing alone. He tried to peer through the passers-by, tall figures who jostled past him, obscuring his view, and the carts and *volantes* that crowded the narrow street. Where was Rafael? He began to panic. Rafael knew the way home – how had they come that morning? What landmarks could he find to guide him home?

He remembered an emaciated cat, orange and black, dashing out of a weathered red door. He remembered two soldiers, with jackets of royal blue and gleaming swords. He remembered a fat, laughing *parda* woman in a red kerchief. But he did not remember the way home.

Perhaps if he returned to the school and began again? He looked up and down the street, but nothing seemed familiar. Perhaps around this corner? It, too, was unfamiliar. Was he closer to the school now, or farther away?

He thought now of his parents, and how worried they would be. He thought of the warm dinner Mamá was no doubt preparing, and the sweet orange he would have with it. He thought of the siesta he would have afterwards, in the little bedroom with the afternoon breeze from the patio cooling him as his tired head rested from the long, hard morning in the classroom. He resolved to find his way home somehow. He would march down this street, and he would look carefully, on one side and then the other, for the yellow house with the blue door.

He began to walk but soon he felt hunger gnawing at his innards. He began to feel empty inside, for it was dinner time and he thought of his mother's fried plantains, hot from the oil, with a salty crisp. The sun was overhead, and he felt its rays hot on his head, and his eyes squinted in the brightness. He felt clammy in the steamy air, the sweat running down his face and chest. He remembered the cool rainwater his mother drew from the cistern in the patio. His feet were sore in their small wooden clogs.

Still he walked. There were fewer people in the streets now, as most had retired to their dinner and a siesta. A pig, fattened on the refuse of the streets, turned its malignant eyes on him as it waddled past. Several dogs barked at him and leapt towards him. He backed into a pile of rubble that had once been a house as they continued to bark, closing in on him, leaping at him. He held up his slate as a shield, but they barked still louder. A rat dashed out from behind him, and the dogs set off in pursuit.

He resumed walking. He saw a small crowd of boys ahead of him, older than he was, barefoot, dressed in ragged shirts. Two were *morenos*, the other two, with their dirty, sun-browned faces and unkempt locks, were of an indeterminate race. He felt uneasily that he should avoid them. Perhaps he could turn the next corner...

And suddenly they were upon him. "What a pretty little thing he is!" cried the tallest boy, as he snatched the ribbon that tied José's curly brown hair in a queue.

"Where are you going, little girl?" taunted another, grabbing his new slate.

A third pushed José so that he fell in the mud of the street and his clean checked muslin shirt was smeared with dirt. He stood up, but one of the boys pushed him again, but this time he kept his balance. More boys joined the group, and formed a circle around him. He saw their faces all around him, smiling cruelly, towering over him like the horses in the street.

Again one pushed him on the chest and he tottered backwards, and felt another pair of hands on his back, pushing him forward. The boys circled around, pushing him back and forth like an inflated pig's bladder, a toy for their amusement. Tears mixed with the mud on his face, and every tear seemed to make them laugh harder.

At that moment a tall *moreno* man carrying a basket of pineapples came around the corner.

"What are you doing, you ruffians!" he shouted, putting down his basket, and the boys scattered, jeering as they ran, and José ran too, as fast as his legs would take him, down one street after another. He lost his clogs, and his feet hurt, but still he ran, his long hair flying behind him. At last he slowed, and looked around him. He did not like this neighborhood. The siesta was ending, and the streets were filling with people. Small groups of naked children clustered near doorways. Loud cries came from a tavern. Two unshaven *blanco* sailors nearly ran down José as they noisily exited the establishment in a haze of stale tobacco and *aguardiente*. He hurried on, past a house with peeling pink paint. Two *morena* women idled by the door, dressed in torn garments. One had bare arms and shoulders; the other wore nothing at all above the waist. One of them called out and reached her arms towards José, but he rushed past, evading her grimy hands.

At last, too tired to run anymore, he stopped, and found himself in the shadow of a great church, with worn grey stones mottled and stained by many years by the sea. Its tall bell tower loomed over the street, and only three small windows squinted out of its fortress-like bulk. José found himself dwarfed by the great archway of the door, its wide wooden planks studded with heavy nail heads. Two smaller doors were set in the larger ones, and these were open to the street.

José was too tired now to walk any farther. His feet were sore and bleeding. He sat down in the protective shadow of the great stone walls to rest. A shadow fell over him, and looking up, he saw a short, barrel-chested man in a black robe. His long-nosed face was shaded by a wide-brimmed black hat, and a large cross shone bright against his black robes.

"What is your name, *mi hijo*?" he asked kindly. He had the accent of a *peninsular*.

"José," the boy replied, and then the tears began, first a few trickling down his nose, then many as great sobs shook his tired frame.

"José, *mi hijo*, you must tell me what is troubling you," the priest asked, kneeling before him and looking in his tear-streaked face.

And José poured out his stories, between gulping sobs, how he became lost on the way home from school, and ran from the boys who stole his slate, and how he had lost his shoes.

"I want Papá," he sobbed in conclusion.

"Do you not know that your Father has been with you all along?" said Father Borrero gently, for that was the priest's name. "Your heavenly father cares for you always. But now, *mi hijo*, I think we must get you home to your earthly father. First, however, we will go inside the church of Espíritu Santo and clean you up a bit." And with that the priest hoisted José on his shoulders and carried him off to a small room, where he and another priest wiped the dust and tears from José's face and washed his torn, bruised feet.

"You must be thirsty," said the other priest, who was named Father Aquila, and scurried to bring José a dipper of cool water and a piece of bread, which José ate slowly at first, then more quickly as his stomach remembered its hunger.

"And now I will take you home to the Calle Aguacate," pronounced Father Borrero, "but I will give your poor sore feet a rest." And at that he lifted the boy onto his shoulders, and José waved good-bye to Father Aquila. He felt safe, high above the crowds. Ahead of him he could see a river of straw hats and kerchieves, as well as the occasional basket carried high by strong arms. He could see the heads of the mules bobbing as they drew their empty carts back to their villages after selling their goods in the city. He felt a kinship with the *caliseros* who drove the *volantes*, perched on their horses high above the street, clad in fine livery and tall black boots.

"Now tell me about this school, José. If we know where the school is, we shall soon be able to find your house. I know most of the schools in Havana, for I work in a school myself," said Father Borrero, as his sturdy legs took them purposefully back the way José had come.

And José described Lieutenant Galeano and his little school.

"Ah, I know that school well, on the Calle Villegas! I think we shall soon find your home." Father Borrero's words made José's heart soar higher than the tall hats of the *volante* drivers.

"The lieutenant is a good teacher. One of my current students began his studies with him," said Father Borrero conversationally, as if José were a good friend of his.

"I do not like school very much. Perhaps I will not go for very long. I would rather help my father in his shop," said José. How he longed to be in the shop at that moment, learning to use his father's tools amid the fragrance of the sawdust.

"And what has led you to this conclusion, after only half a day of school?" asked the priest, still in his conversational tone.

José told Father Borrero how the lieutenant had shouted at them, and struck them with his ferrule, and then, in a quieter voice, he confessed the sin of the J that became a fishhook with a fine fat fish on it.

"A fish! What an imagination! Not many boys would have thought of it. I know I never would have. So that is why the lieutenant punished you," said Father Borrero.

"That is why I do not want to go back to school." His offense did not seem so great, now that he had told it to Father Borrero.

"'There is a time to be born, and a time to die; a time to sow, and a time to reap...and there is a time to put fish on our letters, and a time to refrain from doing so. One reason we go to school, José, is to learn when it is such a time, to learn the art of self-discipline. That is a skill that will stand you in good stead in life." José was not sure he entirely understood what the priest was telling him, but he liked that Father Borrero believed that he could, and was entrusting him with his words. "Remember that Lieutenant Galeano is a military man, a man of discipline and honor. He has fought for his country with valor, and given an arm in her service. He wishes you boys to grow up to be men of honor as well, and so he is teaching you the art of obedience. It is a hard lesson, but a valuable one. My first teacher was very much the same. I learned a great deal from him."

"Did your teacher also strike you when you did wrong?" asked José in astonishment. He could not imagine that Father Borrero, a priest in a long black robe, had ever been a naughty boy.

"Oh my, yes. More times than I can count. I think my palms still sting to this day," laughed Father Borrero ruefully.

And then José saw it. The yellow house with the blue door. And there was Papá, running down the street and calling his name, heedless of the passers-by as he jostled past them. Then Father Borrero swung him down and into Papá's arms and his face was crushed in Papá's thick red hair.

"Thank you, Father, for finding our boy," Papá said to the priest. His voice was hoarse and his appearance disheveled. "His mother has been frantic when he did not come home. A small boy, lost in a big city...and now..."

"I was happy to be of service," replied Father Borrero, bowing slightly.

"Father, please, will you come in and see her? I am so afraid...the strain of the worry...she has collapsed." Papá clutched at Father Borrero's arm.

"Is she in need of the sacrament?" Father Borrero asked softly.

"I don't know...perhaps...the baby came too soon..." Papá was almost in tears now.

"A baptism, certainly," said Father Borrero, moving more quickly.

"No, it is too late for that. But please, you must see Faustina." The two of them moved into the room shared by Papá and Mamá.

Mamá might die! José knew that the church provided extreme unction to the dying. In Matanzas, he had seen the procession making its way from the church to the home of the sick person, the priest carrying the host, preparing to offer a final communion, to hear confession, and to provide the last rites to ensure that the ill one would go to Heaven to be with God and all his angels. But José did not want Mamá to go to Heaven, not now, not when he and Papá and Magdalena needed her so much in this strange city.

He forgot that he was still hungry, that he was tired. He sat in the little kitchen and could think only of Mamá, lying sick in her bed. And that it was his fault, for losing his way. Magdalena came in and ran into his arms. She began to cry, and José clutched her, and said a little prayer to God to please, please let Mamá not die. He felt very alone. Why would God listen to the prayer of a boy who had brought such danger to his mother?

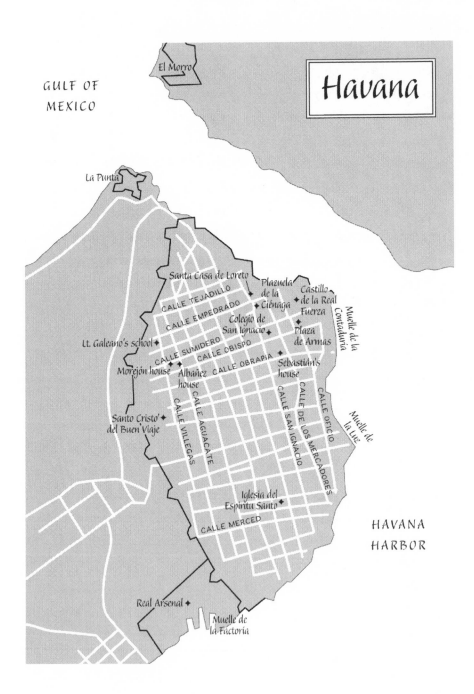

GULF OF
MEXICO

El Morro

Havana

La Punta

Santa Casa de Loreto

CALLE TEJADILLO

Plazuela
de la
Ciénaga

Castillo
de la Real
Fuerza

CALLE EMPEDRADO

Colegio de
San Ignacio

Plaza
de Armas

Lt. Galeano's school

CALLE SUMIDERO

CALLE OBISPO

Muelle de la
Contaduría

Morejón house

Albañez
house

CALLE OBRAPÍA

Sebastián's
house

Santo Cristo'
del Buen Viaje

CALLE VILLEGAS

CALLE AGUACATE

CALLE SAN IGNACIO

CALLE DE LOS MERCADORES

CALLE OFICIO

Muelle de
la Luz

Iglesia del
Espíritu Santo

HAVANA

CALLE MERCED

HARBOR

Real Arsenal

Muelle de
la Factoría

8

IN THE EYES OF GOD

In the end Mamá did not die. Perhaps it was the prayers of Father Borrero, perhaps it was the tender care of Papá, or perhaps it was her own robust spirit, but she rallied and grew stronger. Old Señora Peña came about, wanting to know what the fuss was next door, and soon she had arranged for José and Magdalena to stay with the Morejóns and she herself set to nursing Mamá back to health. Papá no longer called her "that nosy old biddy," but "our good neighbor." Ordinarily José would have been happy to spend more time with Rafael, but now it was as if a shadow had fallen over his heart. Rafael proposed many fine games, but José refused them all. Even bright-spirited Magdalena was subdued. His father visited them every day, and seeing their sad faces, told them they must be brave for a few days yet. Señora Morejón saw the children's sadness, and her voice was less stern when she spoke to them. Instead, she gave Rafael several extra wallops when he misbehaved, to show them that she had not relaxed her standards. For this reason Rafael was relieved to see José and Magdalena return home in a few days.

The house was unnaturally quiet when they entered. Even the chickens seemed downcast by Mamá's illness, scratching listlessly at the oyster shells in the court-yard. As they entered his parents' room, José noticed that the cradle that Papá had made for the baby was no longer there.

Mamá was sitting up in bed when they arrived home, her shawl about her shoulders. "Mamá! Mamá!" José and Magdalena leapt onto the bed and into her open arms.

"Do not spring on your mother like wild dogs!" cried Papá. "She is not well yet."

"Nonsense, Roberto," said Mamá. "I want to fill my arms with my children. God may have given you two knees, one for each child, but he has given me two arms." And she wrapped them tightly to herself, and José buried his face in her warm, plump shoulder, and felt her rough, cooper-colored curls, bright as the late afternoon sun, tickle his face. He heard Magdalena squeal, wriggling with delight.

"So, my little José remembers that he has a mother after all," exclaimed Mamá, stroking his brown curls.

José remembered how many times he had refused his mother's hand and taken his father's instead, how many times he had run to his father and ignored his mother's outstretched arms. He remembered also how his mother had sung him to sleep when he was very small, and how, when a nightmare had caused him to cry out in the night, his mother had soothed him back to sleep with her soft voice. He remembered, too, how she had brought him sweet coconut milk to drink when he was burning up with fever and fed him the soft meat of the coconut with a spoon.

His eyes became warm and moist, and soon a salty tear slipped down his nose, and then another. Soon he was bawling like a baby. He was tired of being brave. And what was the use of all his bravery? Bravery would not bring back the lost baby, and bravery would not make Mamá well, and bravery would not ease the terrible knowledge that his thoughtlessness had caused it all. All of this he blurted out between his great gulping sobs.

"*Ay, mi pobrecito!*" cried Mamá. "Do not cry. How could you think that this was your fault? In truth, I had been feeling very poorly for several days already when...oh, *mi pobrecito*! I thank God nothing bad happened to you and pray nothing will." And now Mamá was crying, and Magdalena cried too, because she did not want to be left out, and Papá laughed to see them so, and soon they were all laughing, laughing and crying, and everything was happy, as it had been before.

T hat night, Papá tucked José into his cot and wrapped the curtains tight around it. "Tomorrow, José, I myself will walk you to school and make sure that you know every landmark along the way. And later we will walk about the city together, and you will learn all the streets. There are many good people in this city, but there are also bad ones, and you must always be able to find your way home."

José's heart was still troubled, however. "Why did God let Mamá lose the baby, Papá? Why did God let her get sick?"

"I do not know, José. The world is full of great sorrows, it is awash in them, and I do not know why God stands by and allows it to happen. I wonder sometimes if he is too far away to hear our prayers." Papá's face suddenly looked very tired as the faint moonlight from the window made deep shadows upon it.

This was not the answer that José had expected. "Don't you believe in God, Papá?" he asked anxiously. He knew that Mamá did. She had a beautiful print of the Virgin Mary in the kitchen, and José loved to look at the soft blue robes of the Holy Mother as she looked down fondly on his family. And Mamá often said her Rosary, and every Sunday in Matanzas she had taken José and Magdalena to Mass. It is true, Papá seldom went with them, only on holy days, like Christmas, but most men did not attend Mass. And Papá always seemed pleased when they went. He had strong words, too, for the enemies of the Church, like the English, calling them "damnable heretics." Surely Papá believed in God.

"I always have, José and I always will. And I have always tried to do my duty to him, and always will. But I wonder, sometimes, if he is even watching or how he can abide the things he sees." And with that Papá turned and left the room. And José was not comforted.

J osé returned to the school of Lieutenant Galeano. Papá set Gonzalo to his chores in the shop, and then walked José to school, and later, back home, and taught him to note the landmarks on the way. They left the yellow house with the blue door on the Calle Aguacate, then turned left on the Calle Sumidoro, near the Morejón house with its pink hibiscus door, to the corner of the Calle Villegas. They walked three long blocks along the Calle Villegas: on one block there was a tobacconist with a sign showing the bright yellow sun; on the next block a house painted a deep sea-blue, with beautifully carved balustrades; and on the third block, the house of Lieutenant Galeano, its door freshly painted green like a parrot. Soon José could find the way on his own, and over the following months and years, José and Rafael came to know all the corners of Havana.

José learned to like school. He enjoyed being with Rafael and soon came to know many new boys from around the neighborhood. On holy days, of which there were many in Cuba, and on Sundays, they would gather for games and for talk. He also enjoyed learning to read. He liked drawing the letters and making their sounds, and soon he could piece out many of the familiar words in his catechism, and learned many new ones as well. He found no magic in arithmetic. His mind wandered when Lieutenant Galeano began to drone on about addition and subtraction, and then he felt the sharp rap of the ferrule across his knuckles. Rafael, however, loved the numbers, and his pencil danced across his slate when he did his sums, and his quick mind always found the correct answer.

The highlight of the school day came at its close. Many times, when the school day was winding to an end, and the boys were becoming restless, Lieutenant Galeano would end the lesson and begin to read from one of the tattered volumes he kept at his desk. Sometimes it was the story of El Cid, the brave and honorable warrior who fought the Moors. Sometimes it was the adventures of Don Quixote, the imagined knight of La Mancha. On other occasions he read of Lazarillo de Tormes, the struggling beggar boy. The stories came alive in his rasping voice, which miraculously changed with every character, and no longer seemed to belong to him. Sometimes, too, he read from a history of Spain, adding many details and comments of his own, to make sure that the boys understood that Spain was a country of brave and honorable Catholics, and that when they grew to be men, they, too, must uphold the glory of Spain. His empty sleeve reminded them that Lieutenant Galeano was also one of those honorable men. Always their teacher's stories would quiet the most restless of the boys. Their eyes followed the gestures of his remaining arm and all ears attended his words in the dusty warmth of the little classroom.

And in the months that followed Mamá's illness, Father Teodoro Borrero became a regular part of their lives. Several days after that terrible night, he had stopped in to see how Mamá was faring, and Papá had invited him to stay for a glass of wine, and so a friendship had begun. Father Borrero would drop by to visit Papá in the evening, after the labors of the day were finished, as the sun was slipping towards the horizon and cooling breezes came up from the harbor. Sometimes they played a game of chess, but often they simply enjoyed their wine and talked together in low voices.

The whole family enjoyed his visits. "And how are you today, good lady?" he would ask Mamá, in a cultivated Castilian accent, and he would take her brown hand, rough from her labors, and give it a kiss. Mamá would stand a little straighter then, and hum as she bustled about her chores.

Father Borrero would also ask José about his schoolwork, and listen attentively to his answer. "Well, done, young man," he would say when José had a success to relate.

"And the blessing of our Lord upon you, child of God," he would say to Magdalena, and she would smile shyly and cross herself as if she were in church.

"Once again I saw you at the chapel for our Saturday concert. It is good to see a young man so interested in church festivities," he once said to Gonzalo. José's cousin appeared discomfited, and Papá and Mamá's faces bore looks of surprise. Is this where Gonzalo disappeared to?

Mamá especially was happy to have him visit because Papá laughed and flashed his rare smile, his smile that brightened his face like the sunshine that poured in when a door is opened.

"They understand each other. They have both known great sadness," explained Mamá to Señora Morejón one day, as they shared a lemonade and gossiped together in the Morejóns' patio.

"What sorrow?" asked José, who had accompanied his mother on the visit.

"Go find Rafael," said his mother. "I am sure he is anxious to see you."

Only Señora Peña found anything amiss in the priest's visits.

"Everywhere I go in Havana, Father, I find you. Chatting with the vendors in the Plaza Nueva, making social calls on the Calle de la Obra Pía, playing checkers with an old man by the Muelle de la Luz, drinking wine with Lieutenant Galeano. I think you are everywhere in this city but in your church."

"My dear lady," Father Borrero protested with a smile. "I am simply following the command our good Lord gave to St. Peter. 'Feed my sheep!' And those sheep are not to be found only within the walls of the church."

Señora Peña snorted. "Feed my sheep! I think the sheep are feeding you!" And she poked his thick midriff.

Mamá began taking the family sometimes to the great stone shell that was the Jesuit church, still under construction, where services were held in Santa Casa de Loreto, the chapel. Properly they should have attended Santo Cristo del Buen Viaje, which was their parish church and was closer.

"Father Borrero is there, and so I know that God cannot be far away," she said. "Perhaps Papá will come with us one day."

Sometimes when he visited, Father Borrero would gently chide Papá because he did not accompany the family to church. "Perhaps I will see you at Mass on Sunday," he would remark.

"Very likely you will not," was Papá's reply.

"Ah, the men of Cuba. Never to be found at church except for baptisms, funerals, or perhaps a concert," Father Borrero would sigh.

"I do my duty. I do my work, I support my family, and I do no man harm. If God should wish to find me He knows where I am," Papá would reply.

"But do you know where to find God?" Father Borrero once asked. And Papá was silent.

José enjoyed listening to Father Borrero's stories about his life in Castile. His family had money, and an ancient lineage. He had gone to university and enjoyed the pleasures that money provided. He had entered the law, enjoyed success in his career, and held an important position in the town government. José sat quietly in a corner, listening as he practiced his sums or drew on his slate. Soon, however, he would be sent to bed, and he could still hear their voices, the voices of Papá and Father Borrero, talking softly as he lay in his cot.

One night, after he was safely in bed, he realized that he had left his slate in the kitchen. He pushed aside the curtains around his cot and padded quietly on his bare feet towards the kitchen to fetch it. The voices became clearer, and he stopped suddenly in the dark, checked by the passion in their voices.

"...yet the wicked seem happy enough," Papá was saying. "Why does God not smite the English devils for all their wickedness? There's a Scot or two would gladly lend their claymores to such a project," Papá added roughly.

"I hear confessions. Do not think that the wicked sleep easily at night," said Father Borrero.

"Nor do I, for spirits of my lost ones haunt my dreams," said Papá. "Do your loved ones not come to you in your sleep?"

"Sometimes," said Father Borrero. "But in the morning I remember them before the smallpox came, and I go about my day."

"I cannot forget so easily. I see the blood..." Papá's voice was barely audible. José was tense in the darkness that enveloped him outside the light from the kitchen. He could hear in the distance the barking of a dog, alarmed by a passing stranger.

"Oh, do not think that the pain is gone!" continued Father Borrero. "It is not as sharp as it was. Now it is more like the dull throb of a soldier's old wound. The children help me forget. I did not even realize it until one day it came to me as if I were Archimedes in his bath. In truth, I did not even intend to become a teacher. I set out to be a missionary to one of the unreached tribes deep in South America, but I fell ill and was left behind in Havana. When I had recovered sufficiently, I began to assist the fathers here by teaching Latin at the *colegio*. The work was repetitive, and there were days when it seemed no knowledge could penetrate the hard heads of my pupils. Then one day I heard that one of my pupils had died suddenly, struck down by a runaway *volante*. His father asked me to conduct the funeral Mass."

"'My son loved the school, Father. What a blessing it was to him!' he said to me as he made the request. 'His presence was a blessing to us,' I replied perfunctorily, and then I realized with a start that it was so. He was an unremarkable student, but diligent. He put his best effort into his work, and he was not among those who required frequent discipline. I took pleasure every day in seeing his amiable face before me, ready to learn. I realized that my life was full of many such blessings, my students, my fellow priests, even the gift of an orange from a parishioner."

"More wine?" Papá asked, already refilling the priest's glass.

"Please," replied Father Borrero. He continued, "I began to live by the words of Ecclesiastes. 'I perceived that there is nothing better for them than to be joyful and to do good as long as they live.' It is not the fate of most of us to perform extraordinary works of faith but simply to persevere, every day, in the work to which God has called us."

"Sometimes miseries rain down upon us as they did on Job. But when the clouds break, and God sends healing blessings, we must let them do their work. My friend, allow me to speak frankly. You have been clutching this pain like a nettle. Let go now, and let God heal the wound," Father Borrero pleaded.

José did not hear Papá's response, for he was already running to his room. He felt ashamed to have been listening to a conversation not meant for his ears. He did not fall asleep for some time. He lay in his bed, staring into the dark, listening to the occasional *volante* rattle by in the street, and the sound of dogs barking in the distance. Who were Papá's lost ones? Had there been others in his life he loved more than José, Mamá and Magdalena? Whose blood had the English spilled?

In the morning José looked at Papá, wondering if he was in fact a stranger among them, but Papá seemed no different than on any other day. He bussed Mamá on the cheek, he tousled Magdalena's brown curls, and he commanded José to stand straighter, "like a man and not a beggar from the streets." By Sunday morning, almost a week later, the memory of the strange night's talk had become as hazy as the far hills that shimmered green through the steam of the humid Havana summer. He was Papá, José's Papá, and he had never been anyone else.

That Sunday Papá appeared in his good blue jacket with pewter buttons, and his face shone pink from a fresh shave. "Are we ready, then?" he asked. Mamá beamed as he took her arm.

"Are you coming to Mass, Papá?" asked Magdalena.

"Yes, my dear, I am going. We are all going together," Papá replied, and hoisted her onto his shoulder. He began to move towards the door to the street, the street of the avocado that would, after many blocks, lead to the Calle Empedrado and then to the Plazuela de la Ciénaga where the Jesuit chapel could be found.

"Why, Papá, why?" asked Magdalena, using her favorite phrase. Papá attended church only on high holy days, and this was a day of only ordinary holiness.

"Because it is my duty," said Papá finally. "It is everyone's duty to go to church and give thanks to God."

"Why, Papá, why?" asked Magdalena again.

"Because I have much to be thankful for," José heard him whisper in her ear.

Mamá never asked the reason, either, but she slipped little treats to Father Borrero when he visited, an orange or a little sweetmeat. Father Borrero would thank her graciously and slip the fruit in his pocket, and once José saw him pull just such a piece of fruit out of his pocket and bestow it on a ragged-looking boy.

"For you, child of God," he said.

One day Father Borrero brought Mamá a present, a little woodcut of the Virgin with her infant son.

"I bring you a picture of our Holy Mother, because, like her, you are the best of wives and mothers," he said as he presented it to her.

"A small token of thanks for your generosity to the Church," he said to Papá.

"You are very kind," answered Papá.

Mamá had smiled to receive the little picture, but now a tear ran down her check and she sunk into a chair.

"But what is wrong, good lady?" asked Father Borrero.

"I am not the best of wives," said Mamá, dropping her face into her hands, the tears falling faster now. Father Borrero looked at her in amazement.

"What she means, Father, is that we have not been married by the Church," Papá explained.

"Oh, well, there are many such couples in Cuba. It is a problem that is easily remedied," said Father Borrero, laughing in relief.

"Not so easily, I am afraid," said Papá. "José, take Magdalena and go to the Morejóns. I am certain that Rafael and Marianela are eager for your company."

José did not wish to miss what seemed certain to prove a most interesting story. "But, Papá…"

"That was not a request. Go to the Morejóns. I will fetch you when we are ready."

Señora Morejón said not a word when José and Magdalena appeared among her brood. They were often at the Morejóns, and the Morejón children were equally to be found at the Alabañez home. José and Rafael were immersed in a game of checkers when Papá arrived to call the two children home.

"Why aren't you and Mamá married?" asked José as they walked the short turn around the corner to the house on the Calle Aguacate.

"Perhaps we soon will be, lad," said Papá. "Father Borrero has promised to find a way. He is a good man, and I believe he can work whatever wonders are required."

For weeks to come, Father Borrero would make frequent visits to confer with Papá and Mamá, and there were whisperings, and sometimes papers were signed.

One evening, as the soft blue of the sky deepened to black, and the carts of the tradesmen that filled daytime streets gave way to the *volantes* of evening pleasure-seekers, Father Borrero appeared again. The family was gathered in the kitchen. "I have finally received a reply from the bishop," he began, hesitatingly.

"And he has granted us the dispensation?" asked Papá, as Mamá reached up to clutch his arm.

"No, I am afraid...he has not, my dear lady. I do not understand it. I have seen similar cases before, and he has invariably approved them. I cannot explain it." Father Borrero twisted his hands together in distress.

Mamá wilted. "Is there no chance?" she asked, in a voice that was barely audible.

"None whatsoever, my dear lady," replied Father Borrero. "I pleaded in vain."

"Well, then all will continue as it has. This is all the marriage we need. We do not need a bishop's permission to be happy," Papá announced, putting his hand on Mamá's shoulder.

Mamá paled, and began weeping, gentle, hopeless tears that coursed down her cheeks. She did not bother to wipe them away. Papá pulled out his handkerchief and tried to dry her eyes, but she pushed his hand away.

"All I ever wanted is to love God and to be faithful to him," said Mamá with a sob. "I cannot bear to go on like this. I do not wish to die in sin."

Papá's voice became heated. "Well, then we live in sin. It is the fate of man, to be born in sin and to die in sin."

"God punishes me because I have been foolish," Mamá wailed. "I do not wish to live in sin, but what of my children?"

"Dear lady," said Father Borrero, "you did nothing wrong. And God sees that you wish to avoid sin. You must do what is best for the children above all."

Father Borrero turned to Papá. "Faustina has a penitent heart. But open defiance of God is most assuredly a sin. For all that is holy, do not spit in God's eye."

Papá stood, stony-faced, while Mamá sobbed into her skirt. José and Magdalena watched in bafflement. Father Borrero laid his hand upon their heads, first one, then the other, and then silently let himself out of the door.

9

WE ARE NOT BORN FOR OURSELVES ALONE

José and Rafael spent four years in Lieutenant Galeano's school. They learned to read and write in Spanish, to add and subtract many-columned numbers, and even to multiply and occasionally divide. They could define a personal pronoun, identify the pluperfect, and produce a participle on demand. In short, they had mastered all the subjects taught by Lieutenant Galeano. The lieutenant told their proud fathers that their sons had proven, after some initial stumbles, to be excellent pupils. He did not, of course, tell the boys this, for that would have encouraged complacency and pride.

During that time José and Rafael had also become true natives of Havana. No longer strangers who picked their way tentatively through its narrow, muddy, crowded streets, they joined in games with the other boys of the neighborhood and explored their parish of Buen Viaje. They awakened to the sound of street vendors, calling out their wares to the neighborhood housewives in sing-song falsettos. They became accustomed to the trains of donkeys, tied head to tail, laden with panniers of ripe fruits and vegetables, or squawking chickens hanging by their feet, bringing the produce of the countryside to the city's markets. They relished the sight of so many military uniforms, the bright blues, reds, and whites, and came to recognize the regalia of every unit stationed in Havana. They knew every beggar, blind, crippled, or mad, who frequented their neighborhood. Most of all, they loved Señora Rosarita, who sold fritters on the Calle Obispo and always had a friendly word for them.

In the evenings, José watched Rafael engage with Señor Espada, his elderly neighbor, in a sharply contested game of chess, which Rafael always lost.

"Why do you play him if you cannot win?" asked José one day.

"Because every time I play, I get better. And one day I will beat him, you watch. Won't that be the day!" Rafael vowed fiercely.

"And then what?" asked José.

"Then," answered Rafael, "I shall find new worlds to conquer."

The boys did not forget Matanzas. During the long Christmas holiday, and during the summer, they went with their families to Matanzas on one of the sloops belonging to Albañez y Morejón to visit family and friends there. How happy Abuelo and Abuelita were to see them all! The aunts cooked wonderful stews of chicken or pork, swimming in tomatoes, okra, peppers, plantains, and other good things that filled the house with spicy redolence and warmed their insides, followed by cooling fruits, preserves, and sweetmeats. The cousins took them exploring the white sandy shore and they revisited the caves outside the city. They rowed boats out into the bay and rowed them back again. They learned to swim in the surf, always with a sharp eye out for sharks. In Abuelo's workshop, they crafted small boats and raced them in one of the three rivers.

Abuelita exclaimed proudly over all that José had learned. "Just think! A scholar in our family. You are the first," and she gave him a hug and peeled him an orange. Abuelo sat up a little straighter, and nodded at José, ever so slightly, to signal that he too, approved, but that such achievements were only to be expected from a well-brought-up boy.

Gonzalo strutted before his brothers and cousins, regaling them with tales of his adventures in Havana, tales that were new to the Albañez family. Papá raised an eyebrow when Tía Nicolaza told him of Gonzalo's stories. "Is it true?" she asked. "Does he spend all his time gallivanting about Havana?"

Papá snorted. "He spends most of his time scraping wood and cutting mortises. I think that Gonzalo has the makings of a great storyteller."

Tía Nicolaza breathed a sigh of relief, but Mamá added in a low tone, "It is true that he disappears from the shop on Sundays and every holiday, even sometimes in the evening. He never tells us where he goes." The worry lines around Tía Nicolaza's face grew deeper, for there were many holidays on the church calendar.

"I sent him to Havana to avoid temptation, not to leap in with both feet! He will fall in with bad companions, and they will teach him to drink, and gamble, like his..." Tía Nicolaza didn't finish her sentence. She never criticized Tío Gaspar. Only the taut lines of her face betrayed her worries.

"Do not fret yourself, Nicolaza," Papá reassured her. "If he drank I would see it in his gait and smell it on his breath. And he has nary a peso with which to gamble." Mamá smiled and patted Tía Nicolaza's knee reassuringly.

"The boy has a good heart," Papá continued. "He may have inherited the face of Gaspar, but in temperament he has more in common with Beatriz."

Tía Nicolaza did not look reassured.

José loved his time in Matanzas, surrounded by family, but he missed Havana, his school, his friends, the visits from Father Borrero, and the bustle of the great port city. Yet when he returned home, he thought with a pang of Abuelo and Abuelita, far away in the city with three rivers. He tried to explain it to Papá.

"You're a most fortunate lad to have two homes full of loving kin. Some folk have not even the one," his father commented. And this satisfied José.

F ather Borrero continued to be a regular visitor, but they did not discuss again the issue of marriage. One day, however, the subject came up of a boy who wished to enter the priesthood but could not because of his illegitimacy. Mamá, sewing in the corner under the light of a lamp, put her head down and wiped her eye with the end of her kerchief. José, doing his schoolwork at the table, and Magdalena, sewing by her side, had learned to keep quiet at such times.

"To hell with Spaniards and all their pettifogging priests and canon lawyers," Papá snarled. "In Scotland it is simple – a man and woman plight their troth, and this is enough for man and God."

"Is that so?" asked Father Borrero softly. "And those priests in Scotland, did they perform the sacrament of marriage for these couples when they had a chance?"

"No, why should they have?" answered Papá. "They were already married. 'It's as good as if the Pope himself had done it,' so said Father Cameron to me. So why should we need a priest or bishop here to..."

"And have you and Faustina made such a pledge?" he asked Papá.

"Aye, of course we have. We are pledged before God. In Scotland we had few priests, and I think we did better without them," Papá replied in a combative tone.

José was shocked that Papá could speak so to a priest, but Father Borrero listened without comment. He was quiet for a long time, picking up his glass of wine and swirling the red liquid about, staring at it meditatively. No one dared break the silence.

"I think..." he said at last, speaking slowly and carefully, as if he were still working out his thoughts, "I think that we must rely on the wisdom of Father Cameron. We must yield to his greater understanding. Clearly, our Holy Father in Rome has established a different order of law for the church in Scotland, befitting the circumstances there. And so, Roberto, as a communing member of that church, surely it is the laws of the Scottish church, and not those of the Spanish, that should prevail in this case. The Society of Jesus has learned that it is sometimes necessary to adjust the practice of the church to accommodate local custom. I believe, therefore, that you are already wed under the laws of the Scottish church, and so in the eyes of the Pope and of God himself."

Mamá threw herself into Papá's arms, and he held her tight.

Papá looked quizzically at Father Borrero. "And will you be pressing this argument upon the bishop?"

"I do not think it is necessary to bother the bishop with this. He is a busy man, and in any case, this matter concerns the Scottish church alone," replied Father Borrero, staring again into his glass, avoiding Papá's gaze.

"I thought so," said Papá. "And I thank you from the bottom of my heart," he added, as he held Mamá tightly.

As Father Borrero slipped out the door, José heard him whisper to himself, "Dear God in heaven, I hope that I have done right."

The final day of class with Lieutenant Galeano approached, but José and Rafael did not speak of it among themselves, for it would mean a parting of the ways. Rafael was to attend the Colegio de San Ignacio, the Jesuit school where Father Borrero served as the prefect of studies. Lieutenant Galeano had spoken to Father Borrero in glowing terms of Rafael's abilities, a fact which Señora Morejón had shared with others on more than one occasion. Father Borrero, in turn, had persuaded Señor Morejón to send Rafael to the *colegio*.

"It is an excellent plan," said Señor Morejón. "There he will meet students from influential families, families that may become customers for select merchandise and protect our interests. And the study of rhetoric will give him powers of persuasion that will serve him well in this business." So Anselmo Morejón explained the choice, but everyone knew that the decision had been made by Señora Morejón, who stood a little more erect whenever she spoke of it.

Rafael had his own reasons for wishing to attend, which he shared with José but not with his mother. "I will go and I will excel. I want to show all those toffee-nosed *peninsulares*. I will master all they have to teach, and then I will go to sea and become the master of my own ship." It was Rafael who spoke the words, but in them José heard the voice of Señora Morejón. Rafael had the warm brown skin, wiry build, and easy charm of his father, but José realized that underneath, he had his mother's steel.

There were no plans to send José to the *colegio*. He had heard Father Borrero speak intently with Papá, and knew that his abilities were equal to those of Rafael, but his destiny had already been decided. Tío Domingo had at last laid claim to him, and he was to accompany his uncle on his next voyage on the *Orfeo*, to learn the art of seamanship.

Mamá protested, "He is too young!" but Tío Domingo replied with truth that more than one boy had gone to sea at the age of eleven.

Papá listened in tight-lipped silence, remembering his promise. He knew, however, that José was still too young to reach the bench in the shop and to work with the long, heavy boards and unwieldy tools, but not too small to learn to splice a line or fetch and carry on a sloop. He would have a chance to try his hand at joinery later.

José resented his uncle's claim upon him. He did not understand why Papá and Mamá did not fight harder for him. Why had Papá ever made such a foolish promise, before he was even old enough to speak, old enough to insist upon his own path? Still, he knew that it would not do to argue or disobey. He would count out the time, demonstrate his lack of interest in the sea, and then they would let him join Papá in the shop.

He knew that he was needed there. Papá's business was growing and he needed assistance, but men and boys were difficult to find, for he was known to be gruff, and impatient with the incompetent. And Papá still needed to pay off the debt he had taken on in acquiring the shop. Some of that was owed to Tío Domingo, who offered to forgive it, but Papá insisted that he would pay every last *maravedí*. Albañez y Morejón, in contrast, prospered at every turn. They had recovered from the losses during the hurricane of 1752, and had since miraculously evaded both storms and legal difficulties. Tío Domingo wore silver buttons on his best coat, and Señor Morejón, although as a *pardo* was not allowed silver, appeared on formal occasions in a silk waistcoat, regardless of the heat.

Rafael could not understand José's reluctance. "*Dios mío!* I would give every book in Christendom to take your place."

"You may take it," José replied. "I will charge you nothing for it."

Rafael was anticipating the great fiesta Señora Morejón was planning in celebration. José ached inside as he listened to Rafael excitedly describe the new school. He fingered the schoolbook that Señor Morejón had already purchased for his son, Alvarez's *Latin Grammar*, and marveled at the mysterious words within, a spell that waited to be broken. He learned that the students at the school served as altar boys, adorned in magnificent white robes as they assisted the priests. He pictured Rafael making his way to school every day, arm in arm with the new friends he would make at the *colegio*. And José listened in silence, imagining the lonely weeks at sea with Tío Domingo, away from Mamá's soft hugs, the sound of Papá scolding Gonzalo, and the laughter of Magdalena.

The evening of the fiesta arrived. The Morejón house had been wholly dedicated to the celebration – in the store front, the crates of goods had been pushed to the side, covered with cloths, and laid with good things to eat. Señora Morejón had scrimped for weeks to provide a grand feast. A great roast pig enjoyed pride of place, along with various well-spiced vegetables. To complement their tang there was a vast array of fruits: oranges, bananas, pineapples, soursops, and pawpaws. On the other side of the room, there was a punch bowl for the adults, slices of lemon swimming in red claret. For the children, there was *agualoja*, honey-sweet water with a tang of cinnamon. And for a final temptation, a tray heaped with caramels, meringues, and lady fingers awaited. Lanterns lit the courtyard, and in the kitchen, now cleared of furniture, a violin player hired for the occasion began a sprightly tune that made the feet of the guests long to dance.

And there were so many guests! The Albáñez family, of course, and Lieutenant Galeano, and all the boys from school with their families. Many of the neighbors came as well. Old Señora Peña was there, with her two strapping boys who worked at the Royal Shipyard, as well as Señor Espada, the chess player, and Señora Rosarita, the fritter vendor.

Over it all presided Señora Morejón. Usually a forbidding presence, tonight she glowed. She had a smile and a welcoming word for every guest, urging them to fill their plates and have another glass of punch. She consented to take a turn on the dance floor with Señor Morejón, although her solid form moved with more dignity than grace. She was queen of the evening, for all her work and sacrifice were bearing fruit. She stood in the lantern light, the soft green of her dress highlighting her clear dark skin. Her deep brown eyes sparkled with joy.

"Isn't she magnificent?" José heard Señor Morejón whisper to Papá.

Father Borrero arrived and the crowd swirled around him as he congratulated Rafael.

"Soon you will enter the ranks of the scholars at the *colegio*," Father Borrero said to him gravely. "I hope you are prepared to work diligently."

Rafael stood straight and looked the priest boldly in the eye. "I will do whatever is necessary to excel," he said.

"That is all that anyone can ask," Father Borrero replied, smiling.

"And if he does not, Father, just let me know, and I will see to him," added Señora Polonia, as she gave her son a painful squeeze on the shoulder.

"What are you doing, Father Borrero? You will turn this boy into a great swell," Señora Peña scolded the priest. "He will become insufferable, strutting about the city with all those boys from fashionable families. Soon he will want lace on his coat and a walking stick."

Father Borrero reassured her. "Do not worry, good Señora Peña! Rafael will find, as do those fashionable boys, his studies will leave little time for strutting about town. The *colegio* does not seek to turn out coxcombs."

Señor Espada commented, "I thought that the law did not permit *pardos* to attend such schools. And it seems an extravagantly expensive education for a tradesman's boy. Of what use will all that Latin and Greek be to him?"

Father Borrero rounded on him. "Do not wonder at the cost. A Jesuit education is free to all boys of talent and industry."

José heard Señora Peña whisper to Señor Espada, "There are laws, but there are also ways around those laws. Anselmo Morejón knows people of influence."

"And as for the value of such an education, we above all seek to teach virtue, to inculcate in our scholars the habits worthy of a true Christian. Grammar and rhetoric provide discipline for the mind. Our goal is to raise up a man who will be a blessing to his family, his community, and his country. 'We are not born for ourselves alone' we remind them, at every possible occasion."

As he spoke, the light began to leave Rafael's face.

The priest noticed the change. "Let me assure you, young man, the path to learning and virtue need not be a dull one. We learn virtue by the example of the ancients, the great men of Rome and Greece. Have you heard of Cincinnatus, who left his farm to lead Rome in its fight against an invading enemy, and having defeated them, returned to his plow? Or Horatius, who single-handedly stopped an army from crossing a bridge and taking the city? A man of learning knows more than grammar and sums. These things are merely tools that enable us to acquire true wisdom."

Now Rafael was rapt with attention. So too, was José. Who was this Cincinnatus? How did a farmer become a great leader? And did Horatius survive to enjoy the praise and thanks of his fellow citizens, or did he leave behind a grieving family? Was Rome victorious or was his sacrifice wasted? He had so many questions. He wished with all his heart it were he attending the Jesuit school. He would give every sail in Christendom to be one of those boys.

"Rafael, when you go to the *colegio*, you must tell me these stories about the men of virtue. I want to hear them all," he whispered urgently to his friend.

"Of course, *mi amigo*. It would be better, though, if you were there with me. We would have some fine larks! But you will be at sea on the *Orfeo*. What adventures you will have. Perhaps you will meet pirates, or be shipwrecked and forced to build a raft to return home. You will work alongside real men, doing a man's job, while I sit over a book of grammar. How I envy you!" Rafael exclaimed. "Someday I too will go to sea, with or without Latin."

"But you know you are to work with your father in his shop..." José began.

"I will be what I choose to be," said Rafael defiantly.

"And what of you, José? Do you look forward to a life at sea?" the priest inquired, searching his face.

"My father has agreed to it," José replied without enthusiasm, avoiding Father Borrero's gaze. "And I must do my duty."

"That is a noble sentiment," replied Father Borrero.

José had not realized that Mamá was near, listening intently. Now she seized his hands and twirled him about on the waves of the music. The fiesta became merrier, and the gyrations of the dancers became increasingly animated. The room grew warmer, and Magdalena and Marianela had found a corner where they, too, could swing about. They laughed as they spun, and Magdalena's brown curls danced with the music. José felt proud to have such a pretty, lively sister. And then he noticed Marianela. Her dark hair was pulled tightly back, forming a soft cap for her head. Although her arms and legs swung in delight to the music, her face, dark in the shadowy light of the corner, did not reveal the emotions within. Behind her long lashes, however, her brown eyes sparkled. She saw him watching her, and bestowed upon him a quick, shy smile. She was only a girl, however, and he quickly shifted his attentions to the caramels that Rafael had found.

The girls fell into a giggling heap, exhausted by their dancing, and in the Morejóns' bedroom, the youngest children had collapsed into a tired, slumbering heap. Finally the parents gathered up the children and took them home to their own beds. The fiesta had been a glorious success, they all said, as they thanked the Morejóns. They had forgotten the occasion of the festivities, amid all the drinking, and eating, and dancing, but, as they made their way home, they remembered that Señora Morejón had felt joy, and that she had shared that joy with her friends and neighbors.

Soon Tío Domingo would arrive in Havana on the *Orfeo*, and José would leave with him. Every day, whenever José heard the shop door open, he would hold his breath fearing the sound of his uncle's voice, and release it only when he heard the voice of a stranger.

José spent many hours in the shop, helping Papá with small chores. He swept up sawdust, learned to measure and scribe wood for cutting, and wrote down orders in Papá's account book. Gonzalo would hum, and the clop of horses' hooves and the rumbles of the carts and carriages outside the tall, grated windows added a pleasing percussive rhythm. The sea wind blew through the open windows and its cool, salty caress tickled their faces and brought relief from the humid Havana summer.

So one happy day followed another until, one day, over the sound of Gonzalo's humming, they heard the boom of Tío Domingo's voice. Soon he hove in sight, and set a course towards José.

"So, lad, are you looking forward to your first real sea voyage?" he asked in a tone that left no doubt that such an adventure was a thing much to be desired by any right-minded young boy.

"Yes, Tío Domingo," was José's reply. He knew that it was the answer that was expected, the proper answer for a boy of his age, a boy who was too old to wish to stay forever with his papá and mamá.

"He's growing up to be a fine young lad," said Tío Domingo to Papá.

"Aye, he is," was all Papá said.

That night at dinner Tío Domingo was at his most animated, full of stories of strange ports and long-ago battles at sea. At times his stories became spicy, then Mamá gave him a sharp look, and he found a new subject. Papá and Mamá were quiet, and Gonzalo, as usual, ate busily, oblivious to all but Mamá's rice and beans.

As soon as he could slip away, José went around the corner of the Calle Aguacate to Rafael's house. Soon they would be separated by miles of ocean, and he wished to enjoy what few days remained with his friend.

When he returned home, he found his parents and Tío Domingo sitting gravely around the table. A bottle of *aguardiente* sat between the two men. Mamá sat quietly beside Papá.

"Come here, lad," said Papá.

José approached with trepidation.

Tío Domingo looked directly at him. "Is it true you wish to attend this Jesuit school?"

His face flushed and he stuttered, trying to find words that would not offend his uncle. He looked from face to face, his eyes hopeful. Had his uncle released Papá from his promise?

"I see it is true," said Tío Domingo. His shoulders slumped and he reached for his tumbler of *aguardiente*.

"Your mother wishes you to go to Father Borrero's school. She has been forceful on your behalf, and we have not been able to withstand her." Papá put his

hand on Mamá's. "So, if you indeed wish to study at the *colegio*, we will delay your
time at sea."

"Thank you, Mamá!" cried José, flinging his arms around her neck. Now he
would be among the boys wending their way to the *colegio* through the streets of
Havana. He would learn the secret of the magical words he heard in church, don
the pure white robes of the acolyte, open the books there and step in among the
Roman and Greek heroes of old. He would stand with Horatius at the bridge, see
what he saw, feel what he felt, learn those words that inspired him to greatness.
The words "thank you" seemed inadequate to express the joy that surged through
every fiber of his being, but he said them nonetheless.

"This is your doing, Robbie. You always regretted missing your opportunity
in Edinburgh," growled Tío Domingo.

"I never regretted doing my duty," Papá shot back.

"It pained you deeply," Tío Domingo challenged him.

"Aye, that it did," Papá admitted softly.

Tío Domingo took another drink of *aguardiente*. "Well, Anselmo is right.
The school will provide him with good connections that will prove of value in
commerce. And a knowledge of geometry will not come amiss when he begins to
learn navigation. I suppose it is for the best."

He looked at José now. "A man of commerce can go far in this world. I know
a man of far more humble beginnings than my own who began with little more
than a fishing boat, and ended up trading among the islands. He now owns a great
house in Regla across the bay, and is welcome in every fine home in Havana."

He turned to Papá. "He shall go to the Jesuit school for now. But in good time
you must honor your promise to send José to sea with me. There he will learn to
be a man, and that is something no priests' school can teach him."

Suddenly Mamá's voice broke in, with an unexpected sharpness. "The school
will teach him to be a good man, a man who thinks of others rather than himself,
a man like Father Borrero. A man like Roberto."

There was a silence, and then Papá said, "He will go to sea with you, Donnie. But first he will go to the *colegio*. And, in time, he will choose his own path, at sea or in the shop. The choice will be with him."

José retreated to the refuge of his cot to savor the miracle that had just occurred. As he went, he heard his father say, "You knew he was too young to go to sea yet."

And José heard a long sigh from Tío Domingo. "Aye, I did. But I wanted it so badly."

10

SOME KIND OF HERETIC

The first day of school arrived, and morning sunlight warmed José's face as he met Rafael at the corner of the Calle Sumidoro. Mamá and Papá watched proudly from the doorway, waving. Papá stood with his hand on Mamá's shoulder, and Magdalena stood between them, crying, "Good luck, José!" José waved in return, and walked proudly to the corner, with his slate and a copy of Emmanuel's *Latin Grammar* bound with a leather strap and slung across his back. José could hear Magdalena's farewells behind him, but felt himself too old to turn around for a last wave. Then, at the corner, he could contain himself no longer, and turned back to gaze at them again through the crowd on the street. There was Magdalena, still waving.

They were joining the older boys now, and felt themselves on the verge of manhood. José was already eleven years of age, and Rafael was his elder at twelve. They turned down the Calle Sumidoro and set off resolutely on the long walk to the *colegio*. José and Rafael were both adorned in cotton shirts as white as their mothers' laundering could make them. José's hair was tied in a neat queue while Rafael's, too rough and brittle to be combed, was short under his wide-brimmed black hat. Just below their knees, brass buckles shone on the straps of their breeches. Señora Morejón stood on the corner like a fortress, watching Rafael's every step. Her face, under the shadow of a building, glowed. The youngest boys clustered around her skirts and Marianela stood next to her, smiling as she watched the boys. José was aware of her eyes as they set off.

The two walked the long blocks of the Calle Sumidoro and turned left onto the Calle San Ignacio. And there, to the right, the magnificent entrance to the Colegio de San Ignacio soared above their heads. The building itself was two stories, a long wall that ran the length of the block, punctured by long windows to let in the cooling breezes from the nearby harbor. Its stones shone white in the sunlight. At the street level, they were greeted by great black wood doors, topped by a row of carved medallions. Above them a cupola topped with a cross pointed to heaven. José and Rafael were silent as they stepped tentatively through the doors and on into a paved courtyard filled with greenery. A *moreno* porter directed them up a wide stone staircase and into the classroom of the first year Grammar class.

The room had long windows looking out on the Calle San Ignacio, and below the window, José could see the red tile roofs of the houses below. The shutters were open, and sunlight poured in, illuminating every corner of the classroom and every face in it. He stood self-consciously in the entrance. The room was filled with boys their own age, most of them *blancos*. These sat boldly in the front, confident of their right to be in this room. Rafael found a seat in the back. "If I'd wished to sit in the front, I would have," whispered Rafael to José. "But I do not wish to." José knew that such a choice was not available.

A tall man with a thinning grey tonsure entered the room. The black robe of the Jesuit order hung loosely on his thin frame. A beak like a parrot's sat in the middle of his long, deeply lined face. He rapped a ferrule on the edge of his desk and the sharp sound drew every pair of eyes towards him.

The priest waited a long moment, and began, in a Mexican accent, "My name is Father Jiménez, and I am the teacher of the first year class. I have spent twenty years preaching the Gospel to the savage heathens in the darkest jungles of the Americas. I have been shipwrecked, taken prisoner by the heretic English, and seen men beaten and tortured for the Holy Catholic Church. Eleven-year-old boys hold no terrors for me, but if you do not obey in this class, my classroom will hold terrors for you."

A thrill went through the room and every pair of eyes was fixed upon the priest in black. José knew that every boy, like him, trembled within to be in the presence of so awe-inspiring an individual. To think that such a man deigned to teach them the declension of Latin nouns. It would be an honor to be caned by such a man.

He continued: "From this day you begin to study grammar, the first part of the trivium of a scholastic education. Each day one of you will be chosen to lead us in prayer. I will explain the lesson and we will recite our exercises in class. At midday we will attend Mass, and you will return to your homes for dinner and the siesta. We will resume at the 4 o'clock hour for an additional two hours of lessons. You will have written work each night which we will review in class the next day. Every week we will attend the sermon together, and you will memorize and recite a portion of Christian doctrine.

"Do not think that I will allow this schedule to become monotonous. You will engage in competition, both as individuals and in groups. You will recite poetry, and, in time, your own compositions. You will perform dramas.

"Most important, I will train you not only in the use of your mind, but in the care of your soul. I will encourage you in prayer, lead you in the Rosary, and teach you to examine your conscience daily that you may lead a life dedicated to the glory and service of God."

A voice arose from the front, carefully enunciated words in the lisping accent of Castile. "Why do we study the languages and writers of antiquity, and not modern subjects such as mathematics and science?" The tone was not confrontational, but neither was it deferential.

Every boy froze in his seat. They waited, breathlessly, for the inevitable wrath to descend, for the crash of the ferrule. But there was no crack, only the inquiring voice of Father Jiménez. "What is your name, young man?"

"My name is Sebastián de Ayala Cordovés, Father." Still the boy showed no fear.

"Well, Sebastián de Ayala Cordovés, the first thing you will learn in this class is that you must not speak out of turn. This time, however, I will answer your question, because every good question deserves an answer.

"We study the works of antiquity because the ancients have provided the building blocks for all our modern learning. They gave us science and mathematics, and to study these subjects you must first learn Latin or their doors will remain closed to you. In this class we will master Latin; if you continue to the higher classes you will get a taste of mathematics and the sciences as well."

Rafael groaned softly, "I do not want to have to wait that long!" he whispered.

After prayer, they opened their copies of *Emmanuel* and the class began. José, however, heard only fragments of what was said. In his mind flickered the name of Sebastián de Ayala. Then images began to flash in his mind. Bright sunlight glinting off of blue water. A pallid, serious face, warmed by a shy smile. Laughter on a sunbaked deck. The *blanco* boy on the *Orfeo*. He remembered him now, the sickly boy without a mother going to live with his father in Havana.

At last class was dismissed so that the many day students could return home for their midday meal, while those few who boarded ate in the hall. Many of the boys rushed to the door, calling out each other's names, and it was clear that they already knew each other. José thought that they must have attended the primary school that was attached to the *colegio*. José and Rafael were the last to make their way out the great black doors, through the patio, and into the Calle San Ignacio. Dark clouds hung over the street, and a few drops of rain hit their faces.

José grabbed Rafael's arm and whispered, "Sebastián! He's the boy from the *Orfeo*!" Rafael looked baffled for a moment, then his eyes widened in recognition, and he searched for the *blanco* boy. There he was, standing a few feet away, a swarm of boys buzzing about him, as the rain splashed in the street, soaking them all.

"He thinks he knows more than the teacher!" cried the boy named Miguel Cordero, a tall, solidly built fellow. In class he had been all graces and charm. Now that charm was utterly absent as he loomed threateningly over the frail-looking Sebastián.

"Perhaps he is not even Catholic!" joined in Vidal Pedroso, balling up his fists in imitation of Miguel.

A third boy, who was called Francisco Xavier del Valle, waved a fist encircled by a lace-trimmed cuff and shouted, glancing at Miguel, "Perhaps he is some kind of heretic! Let us teach him a different sort of lesson!"

Miguel's fist shot forward into Sebastián's startled face. Then, in an instant, Rafael had raced towards the cluster of boys and leapt onto Miguel's back, pounding him with his fists. More fists began to fly, battering Rafael, and now José threw himself into the melee. Soon all the boys had leapt in, fists flailing. The rainwater was swirling about their ankles now, and soon they were all rolling in the muddy waters. Suddenly strong hands began pulling them apart, and then they were standing there, red-faced, clothes sodden and muddy, facing the glare of Father Jiménez. José saw that Rafael's nose had been bloodied, and Sebastian's fist looked raw. José's right eye ached savagely. Their opponents were in a similar state.

"Fighting at school is a most serious infraction," said the Father, with the grimmest of expressions. "You will accompany me to the office of the rector. He will have something to say to you."

The boys trailed behind him, silent, shoulders slumped, to the rector's office as Father Jiménez sent the porter to fetch the rector from his dinner. The two priests entered the office together, and Father Alvarado looked none too pleased to have his noonday meal interrupted by a handful of unruly boys.

Father Jiménez began to explain, but Father Alvarado held up his hand to stop him. "It is clear to me what has happened. Our new grammar students have been fighting among themselves. The punishment for such behavior is a whipping." He sat silently, letting the gravity of their punishment sink in.

José felt a pain far sharper than the ache in his swelling eye. What would Papá and Mamá think when he came home the first day having received a whipping? And oh, how he would sink in his sister's esteem. He thought of their proud smiles as they had seen him off just that morning, and the disgrace seemed more than he could bear.

After a pause that seemed to last a century, the rector spoke again. "It is the first day of school, however, and so I believe that mercy is in order. You will not be whipped – this time. Tonight, however, I want you all to begin the practice of spiritual exercise outlined by our founder, St. Ignatius. Examine yourselves to determine in what way you are guilty in this affair."

He had escaped a whipping. His heart soared, until he remembered that he had in fact deserved one.

The rector spoke again, looking first at the big *blanco* boys to his left. "I also want you to ask yourselves, have I behaved like a bully? Have I preyed upon the weak? If so, you must repent and vow to do better."

He looked then at José, Rafael, and Sebastián. "We must turn our own cheek, but to stand by while others are abused is the act of a coward. If you have been defending the weak, then you have nothing to repent. If, however, you simply enjoyed a bout of fisticuffs, then you must ask our Savior for forgiveness. Only you and God know the truth. Now, go home to your dinners. I hope that mine is not yet cold."

By the time José had arrived home for dinner, his eye was purple. He hesitated before he entered the shop, but his father had already seen him approach through the open shutters and met him with a stony face. Gonzalo stopped mid-tune, gape-mouthed, a plane in his hand.

Papá seized José by the collar, which was no longer so white as it had been when he had left for school that morning, and marched him to the back of the house where Mamá was chopping onions. Gonzalo followed to enjoy the sight.

Mamá cried out when she saw her scholar.

"Explain to your mother how you ended up brawling like a street ruffian on your first day at the school where she sent you to learn to be a good Catholic," demanded Papá.

The words tumbled over themselves as José explained about meeting Sebastián again, and how the big *blanco* boys had fallen upon him, and how Rafael had come to Sebastián's aid, and how he, José, had helped his friend. Magdalena listened, wide-eyed.

"You must stay away from those terrible boys!" clucked Mamá as she bathed his face with a cloth dipped in cool water that Magdalena had hurried to bring.

Papá turned to go back to the shop, followed by Gonzalo. José heard him say, too softly for Mamá to hear, "And to think that Donnie said that the Jesuit school would not make a man of him."

That night, as he lay in his cot, the rector's words came to José's mind. Had he been at fault, he wondered? He remembered the joy of combat that he felt as he piled into the bigger boys, and did indeed feel a pang of guilt. Then he remembered Miguel's fist landing on Sebastián's thin face, and the guilt vanished. No, he would do it again. But next time he would remember not to enjoy it so much.

The following day, they arrived at school several minutes early, stopping a moment in the patio. José's eye was as black as a ripe olive, and Rafael's cheek looked raw and bruised. Sebastián appeared through an archway. His face, too, was red and battered.

"What did your father say when you arrived home like that?" asked Rafael, imagining the shock of the proud *blanco* official when his son came home from the Jesuit school looking like a ruffian from the streets.

"He wanted to withdraw me from school immediately and consign me to another tutor," replied Sebastián. "But then I told him that it was the greatest day of my life!" An enormous grin lit up his whole face. "My father soon gave up that notion," he laughed.

The other boys passed them on the way to class, bearing similar marks of combat. There were no jibes or sneers today, however; a truce had been established. The bells of the city rang the 9 o'clock hour, and the threesome hurried up the stairs, anxious to avoid being scolded for tardiness.

The routine of school began. Father Jiménez blessed himself, led them in prayer, and then began intensive lessons in grammar with a speed that left José dazed. The other boys had already covered Emmanuel's grammar in their elementary classes and sailed through what was for them a review. Sebastián, too, was already well-versed in the basics of Latin grammar. José struggled manfully to keep up, taking pleasure in the sounds and poetry of the language so familiar from church. Rafael, however, was floundering.

Later they joined the other classes at a brief Mass in the chapel of Santa Casa de Loreto which adjoined the *colegio*. The priests took turns conducting the services, each in their own style. Father Jiménez's strong voice rang out to the very rafters, demanding the attention of every boy. Father Rodelo of the 2nd grammar class shambled about the altar, speaking the words of institution, then turning at unexpected moments as if to catch inattentive students unawares. Ancient Father de la Cruz of the 3rd grammar class moved slowly, his soft voice barely audible, but when he lifted the consecrated host with his wrinkled hands, he seemed to be reaching for Heaven itself, a place where, they imagined, he would soon find himself. Father Navarette of the Rhetoric class recited the liturgy in an elevated tone that turned the familiar words into poetry. José loved it best, however, when Father Borrero led the Mass, in warm tones that echoed those of Christ himself, calling them to share in his body and blood, sacrifice and redemption. It was all a far cry from the perfunctory mumblings of his parish priest. It was a shock to exit the cool, quiet refuge of the chapel into the hot glare and bustle of the Havana streets.

At noon, students returned home for dinner and the siesta and returned for what would be a tidal wave of new grammar. José could barely keep his head above water, but Rafael seemed caught in the undertow. He, who had instantly mastered every mathematical problem in the class of Lieutenant Galeano, now looked dazed and beaten. And Rafael knew that he was beaten, and this anguished José. So did the subtle looks of contempt from Miguel, Vidal, and Francisco, the trio with whom they had scuffled that first day.

On Fridays they recited Christian doctrine, and then attended confession. José examined his conscience, as St. Ignatius had taught, and found much to regret. Thus, a month into their time at the *colegio*, José stood miserably waiting his turn outside the dark confessional booth.

"Don't let Diego go first!" cried Mauricio, but Diego O'Sullivan sprinted behind the black curtain, and all the boys groaned. "This will take forever!" wailed Mauricio.

"I do not understand," grumbled Pedro. "Why does he wish to become a priest if he has so many sins?"

After what seemed an interminable time, Diego emerged, smiling angelically, blissfully indifferent to the glares of his classmates.

Almost unnoticed, Antonio slipped into the box.

"Do you think he will actually say his confession," asked Mauricio, "or just hang his head like an old donkey?" He made a clownish face so like Antonio's in its glumness that a titter arose from the waiting boys.

José wondered what Mauricio was saying about him as he took his place in the confessional. He had so much to repent. He had teased Magdalena until she cried, spoken back to his father, shrugged away Mamá's kisses, put salt in Gonzalo's lemonade, and then laughed at his silly surprised face. He was shocked that such a litany of sin merited only a Paternoster. His heart felt pure and clean again when he left, as he had known it would, and yet still he had not wanted to confess. He vowed to live a pure life this week, and not to pile up such a great mountain of sin again.

"I am happy that is done," said José to his friends as it was Miguel's turn to enter the booth.

"Why do you not do what I do?" asked Sebastián. "Simply make something up!" He laughed at José's shocked face. "My sins are not the business of the priest," he explained.

Rafael interjected, "I just make sure that I do one bad thing every week. That way I always have something to confess. This week I pinched my sister and made her squeal."

José was not sure that this was how confession was meant to work. "But surely there are more things that trouble you," he queried.

"No," replied Rafael, as he turned towards the confessional.

"What will Rafael confess, that he is the stupidest boy in class?" Mauricio's voice echoed through the chapel and found the ears of Rafael. José saw his friend stop where he was.

Father Rodelo's voice arose from behind the baptismal font. "The tongue is a fire, a world of iniquity...it is an unruly evil, full of deadly poison."

Mauricio looked stricken as he realized that he had gone too far. "I'm sorry," he called to Rafael, who walked on as if he hadn't heard, stiffly, shoulders straight, head held high.

José knew what angry thoughts must be convulsing his friend's heart, and he thought that Rafael would now have much to confess indeed. Then he realized the great restraint that it must have required for his friend to walk away from that insult, and he thought that such endurance must expiate a great deal of sin.

After confession the students were dismissed to go their separate ways home. As the three friends left, they heard a faint voice from down the street, a voice they recognized to be that of Miguel, "I doubt that boy will be with us much longer," and they knew he referred to Rafael. They stood silent amidst the noise of the street, and the brisk breeze from the sea could never be enough to cool the two hot tears that forced their way from Rafael's eyes.

"I can help you, Rafael," said Sebastián, but Rafael stood wordless.

Sebastián was pleading now. "Please, I do not want to lose you. Please let me help you. Come to my house and I will teach you how to show up Miguel and those others."

Still Rafael was silent.

"Please, let him help," José added his own pleas.

And, finally, wordlessly, with the slightest nod of his head, Rafael assented.

They set off to Sebastián's house. His home was on the Calle Obrapía, in the fashionable neighborhood near the harbor, where the houses had a second story to catch the cooling sea breezes. Plodding donkeys and carts gave way to the dashing *volantes* with their handsomely liveried *caleseros* riding astride gaily caparisoned horses, the cries of beggars and the boisterous music of street musicians was supplanted by the animated tones of well-dressed men hurrying to concerts and dances, and the pervasive odor that wafted from the slaughterhouses at the edge of the city was swept away by the salty air blowing in from the harbor. There, basking in the cooling breezes of the sea were the houses of the city's most prosperous and influential citizens, close to the official edifices where power was wielded. Sebastián's house was not as imposing as some of its neighbors, but was far grander than the little blue house on the Calle Aguacate. A tobacconist occupied the ground floor, and next to it there was a pair of enormous dark, carved doors, studded with nails, large enough to let a *volante* through. Set inside one of these doors was a smaller, people-sized door that opened into the *zaguan*, the vestibule that led to the rest of the house.

They entered a small patio, paved with tiles, and edged by an abundance of potted greenery. At the back of the patio José could see what appeared to be a warehouse, and a muddy passage with traces of manure that suggested that it led to the stable. Sebastián led his friends up a staircase to the second floor, where a narrow, arcaded gallery encircled the patio. On the other side, through a tall, narrow window, José could see a *morena* woman bustling about. From a doorway issued a tiny, white-haired *blanco* woman dressed in a black silk dress that heightened the pallor of her skin. Her face was dominated by a beak-like nose, and the sharp black eyes in her wrinkled face narrowed upon seeing that Sebastián had brought company.

With a gesture towards his friends, Sebastián announced, "Tía Isabela, let me introduce my good friends from school, José Albañez and Rafael Morejón. And this," he said, waving in turn at his diminutive aunt, "is my aunt, Doña Isabela Cordovés."

"You are very welcome in our house," said Doña Isabela, with a smile at José.

There was a pause, and then she added, "As are you, Rafael," in a tone that carried no enthusiasm.

Rafael looked uncomfortable in the awkward silence that followed. Sebastián, with an annoyed look at his aunt, led them though several rooms into his bedroom, where they sat, Sebastián perched on the bed, Rafael sitting astride the desk chair, and José sitting sprawled on the floor, his back against the wall.

"Your aunt does not like me," Rafael stated with truth.

"She is a *peninsular*, and does not care for free *pardos*. She says that while it may be permissible to associate with them in public, it is not appropriate to entertain them socially," Sebastián explained. There was an uncomfortable silence.

"She likes José," Rafael pointed out.

"She thinks he is *blanco*," Sebastián replied, and they all laughed, José the hardest.

José then began to imagine what it would be like to be *blanco*, just like his father. He imagined himself with red hair, strong and wise. He could carry a musket, even without belonging to the militia, and wear silver buttons. Then he thought about the soft golden brown of his mother's face, her tawny curls, and Abuelita's warm embraces. They were a part of him, and he would not be himself without them. He was José Albañez Velázquez, and he would not want to be anyone else.

While José meditated on this, Sebastián began to reveal the secrets to mastering Latin grammar.

"My father says that learning a language is like arithmetic. Learn the rules, and you can solve any problem, parse any sentence."

"If I knew the rules, I would not be here," moaned Rafael.

Sebastián began to review the grammar with Rafael. He had a gift for explaining everything in a clear and simple fashion, and for making Rafael laugh at his own mistakes. José saw his friend become more relaxed and gradually more confident. Sebastián grew increasingly animated, clearly delighted to have a friend with whom he could share his studies. José enjoyed the review as well, particularly when Sebastián pulled out a well-thumbed copy of Phaedrus's fables.

After a time he began to look around and examine the room in detail. The furniture – a bed, a desk and chair, and a wardrobe – were made of expensive woods and boasted the fine finish and details only a master cabinetmaker could provide, someone with skills far beyond those of Papá and Abuelo. On the desk a row of books was arrayed, bound in fine leather but well-worn. José picked one up and found it was *Don Quixote*, and he saw that the other volumes consisted of equally enticing books. He wondered what it would be like to live in such a fine house, with all those story books to read, and a tutor to initiate one into the mysteries of Latin and Greek, far from the sneering faces of the other boys.

At last, Rafael and Sebastián sat down, and Sebastián left the room to return with an intricately carved chess set.

"Do you play?" he asked, and Rafael nodded eagerly.

"And you, do you play as well?" Sebastián asked José politely as he and Rafael set up the pieces.

"No, I do not like the game," replied José. He saw little purpose in pushing bits of wood about on a board. There was a second reason, one he could never admit to his friends. He felt sorry for the pawns, forever doomed to be the victims of the more powerful pieces.

"Do you miss having a tutor?" he asked Sebastián idly.

"No, never," replied Sebastián, in a low, fierce voice, and he bent his head over the board, so that a lock of hair that had escaped his queue fell over his face and hid his eyes.

José was surprised. Then he looked about the pure white room, and heard the silence. Only the faintest sounds of the street penetrated to the back of the house where the bedroom was located. Slaves toiled nearby, but the sound of their voices did not reach across the patio. José no longer wondered why Sebastián preferred the *colegio*.

Eventually it was time to go home, and as José and Rafael made their way down the stairs, they were followed by the frosty gaze of Doña Isabela.

Rafael did not transmogrify into a great scholar. He still struggled in class with new material, making mistakes when called upon, and lagging in class competitions. He listened attentively, however, and his mistakes became fewer than in the past.

They continued to meet sometimes during the week to study, but no longer at the home of Sebastián. Rafael, remembering the disapproval of Doña Isabela, invited them to study at his house.

Señora Morejón beamed as she welcomed the *blanco* boy to her home, and plied them all with freshly made *tostones*. The little ones swarmed about Sebastián until Marianela shooed them away. She smiled shyly at Rafael's new friend.

Sebastián stood looking at her. "Your sister is nice, Rafael," he commented. "And pretty, too."

"I suppose so," answered Rafael. "José's sister is also pretty." José had never thought of Magdalena as beautiful. She played games, sometimes annoyed him, and laughed a lot. He knew that Marianela was pretty. He supposed that Magdalena might also be thought attractive, if one bothered to think about it, which he did not.

Sometimes they met at the Albañez home. Mamá smiled upon them, delighted to host such erudition in her kitchen, and Papá glanced in occasionally, and nodded with approval. This reminded José that it was Gonzalo, and not him, who was working in the shop with Papá, but then he looked about him at his friends, and was content. When he finished the *colegio*, he would go to work with Papá, and they would make the shop under the sign of the Zum-Zum the greatest joiner's establishment in Havana, with many workers, and he would live in a big house like Sebastián.

Their studies would end when a *volante* would appear to fetch Sebastián, for it was many blocks to his house from the Calle Aguacate. Señora Peña would come out to see the sight, and as the *volante* disappeared around the corner, would cluck, "Well, we have become very grand," but she smiled as she said this. She liked Sebastián, for he always bowed to her gravely and said, *"Buenas tardes*, Señora Peña," in a tone of exquisite politeness.

One afternoon Father Jiménez announced a new competition. They would form two sides that would compete in their knowledge of Latin vocabulary.

"The side that loses," proclaimed Father Jiménez, "will have four extra exercises to complete tonight."

The class groaned.

"What will the winners get?" asked Miguel.

"Glory," replied Father Jiménez. "The eternal glory of mastering the language of Cicero."

Glory is a very fine thing, avoiding four extra exercises is an even finer thing, and defeating the other boys would be the finest thing of all, and so they all threw themselves into the competition.

Miguel was named captain of the first side. Then Father Jiménez caused a murmur of amazement in the class when he added, "Rafael, you may form the other side. Captains, you may take turns selecting the members of your side."

Miguel quickly chose his closest comrades, Francisco and Vidal. Rafael in turn chose José and Sebastián. Rafael then chose Diego, who was, in addition to being pious, bright and studious. Rafael hesitated over Mauricio, remembering his insult during confession.

"He is clever," urged José in a low voice, and Rafael added Mauricio to their side. Mauricio grinned broadly at being chosen, and Rafael grinned back.

Rafael struggled over the last choices. "Pick Anastasio!" whispered José.

"He is always looking out the window or doodling on his slate," objected Rafael.

José persisted. "He is nice. And perhaps he is doodling in Latin."

Rafael called Anastasio's name.

That left only two boys remaining. Pedro Gúzman, the son of a prosperous merchant, was remarkable only for his blandness. He did what was expected, no more, no less, scurrying through life like a banana rat, indistinguishable from the others.

Antonio Alférez was an enigma. He spoke only when called upon, and then only sparingly. He slipped silently in and out of school like a shadow. José had once seen a bruise on his arm, and he wondered how such a passive boy could have come by it.

"Choose Antonio!" whispered José, and now Antonio joined their side. A smile might have flit across Antonio's face, but José could not be sure.

The competition was intense. Students who gave wrong answers were eliminated, and soon Vidal, Pedro, and Francisco were gone, and one by one, others as well. José was taken out by an irregular verb, and Sebastián confused two similar words. And then, there were only two left, and those two were Miguel and Rafael.

"*Quaeso*," challenged Father Jiménez.

"Cheese," answered Miguel.

"Rafael?" said Father Jiménez.

"I beseech," responded Rafael, "It means 'I beseech," and José remembered that Sebastián had taught him that word from Phaedrus's "The Wolf and the Lamb."

It was over, Rafael was the victor, and the boys broke out in cheers. Even Father Jiménez smiled.

As they filed out into the patio to go home, boys pounded Rafael on the back in congratulation.

Miguel, flanked by Francisco and Vidal, walked past him silently.

"*Veni, vedi, vici*," Rafael called after them. "I think that I will be in this school a while longer."

II

EL SANTÍSIMO

José and Rafael settled into a comfortable routine at the Colegio de San Ignacio. They, along with Sebastián, became part of a circle of friends which included Diego, Anastasio, Antonio, and Mauricio. They gathered on school holidays, the many holy days that filled the church calendar of Cuba, and they explored all that the city had to entice boys. They went to the shore outside the Puerta de la Punta to chase the sand crabs and turtles that swarmed ashore. They watched the daily washing of the horses, as bare-shirted men led the animals prancing into the surf, and then the boys kicked off their shoes and dove into the water, splashing each other and laughing. They went to the Plaza de las Armas to see the soldiers parade in royal blue uniforms, sunlight glinting on their bayonets, and thrilled to the sound of the fife and drum. They spent time at the wharves watching the ships come in. They visited the Plaza Nueva, where, in the stench of manure and rotting produce, country vendors hawked farm-raised vegetables and squawking chickens, and fishermen sold glistening fish straight from their nets. They roamed the Calle de Mercaderes and admired the fine goods that the merchants put on display beneath the awnings of their stores.

"My father sells better," Rafael would sniff. "Someday Albañez y Morejón will have a shop right here, on the Calle de Mercaderes."

The friends maintained an uneasy rivalry with the boys who surrounded Miguel. Never again did they come to blows with them on the grounds of the school, but instead the two factions resorted to jibes, grimaces, and the occasional shove when the Father's attention was elsewhere. Occasionally, when they met outside of school, they engaged in fisticuffs, but both groups of boys gave as good as they got. Their rivalry found expression, too, in their academic work. Father

Jiménez continued the competitions in class. He paired each boy with a "friendly rival," and they corrected each other's work and strove to be the best. José was paired with Rafael, for they both still had to work hard to keep up. Sebastián was first teamed with Miguel, but proud, angry words erupted from their desks, and soon Miguel's new rival was Virgilio, a *pardo* boy known to all to be the bastard son of a very high official. Sparks again flew, and this time Miguel's new competitor, the slavish Vidal, proved more congenial, while Sebastián worked harmoniously with the saintly Diego.

The true competition, however, was for the position of class officers. Once a month they would each submit a written composition in Latin, and the author of the paper judged best by Father Jiménez would be chosen as class consul. The rest, which invariably included José and Rafael, had to content themselves with the rank of humble plebeian.

The holders of these honors assisted Father Jiménez with sundry classroom chores. José longed to hold one of these posts. He imagined himself hearing recitations and keeping tally of the students' successes and deficiencies in the big ledger on the priest's desk. Several times Sebastián became consul, but seemed to put little store by the honor. At other times it was Mauricio, or Diego, or Virgilio. He dreaded those months, however, when Miguel presided over them. Miguel was harsh in judging recitations – except when it was one of his coterie of friends. José suspected, too, that the marks he made in the ledger were more favorable to some and unduly harsh for others. He suspected as well that Father Jiménez eventually corrected any errors that had crept into his records. As they read and reread the speeches of Cicero, the master of Latin prose, José began to think of Miguel as Cataline, the treacherous Roman whose malign plotting was exposed and defeated by Cicero, as the great orator was at pains to point out. Among themselves he and his friends began to refer to Miguel by the name of that famous traitor.

The rivalry continued as they began the 2nd grammar class the following year with fat Father Rodelo. He waddled about the class, sweating in the midday heat, his wrinkled black robe askew. The boys often thought that he had fallen asleep at his desk, but he was instantly awake should any of them begin to cause trouble. Once Mauricio thought to play a prank on him and placed a sand crab in the drawer where he kept his quills. The boys erupted in giggles when Father Rodelo opened the drawer, Mauricio loudest of all. Father Rodelo raised his thick eyebrows, silently extracted the crab, and dropped it into the lap of the startled Mauricio. The abashed offender was sent to release it in the Plazuela de la Ciénaga whence it had no doubt come. Father Rodelo continued the lesson without comment. The prank had disappointed, but Sebastián was inspired to attempt the same trick on his aunt, Doña Isabela, with much greater effect. He recounted the tale many times for them.

José and Rafael began to feel like true scholars and could hold limited conversations in Latin. They loved to show off before their families, and tease their sisters by looking pointedly at them and whispering loudly in Latin.

"*Agere considerate pluris est quam cogitare prudenter,*" Rafael might say, quoting Cicero's adage that itt is of more consequence to act considerately than to think sagely

And José would nod in agreement and reply with more Ciceronian wisdom, "*Accipere quam facere praestat injuriam,*" (It is better to receive than to do an injury.)

The girls would make faces at them and run away. This would make Mamá and Señora Morejón frown. Sebastián never teased the girls, however. He would smile and call them "*señoritas*" and they would giggle and smile back at him.

Somewhere, between lessons and friends, José also found time to work in the shop with Papá, adding to his skills, listening to Papá's stories, and preparing himself for the time, one day, when he would work by Papá's side as a master joiner.

A year flew by, and they were in the 3rd year grammar class with Father De la Cruz. They began the study of Greek, and wrote and read aloud their compositions in Latin. They memorized speeches by Cicero and declaimed them before the class. José especially enjoyed reading Livy's *History of Rome*.

They also began to study Euclid's *Geometry*. Rafael began to shine, his star finally ascendant. Neither José nor Sebastián, however, found it easy, and now Papá became their tutor. When he taught them, all became clear, and they wondered why they had struggled so. Papá took exceptional pleasure in this work, and more than once he borrowed José's book and sat up, thumbing through it with a rapt look and almost the shadow of a smile.

"Why do you enjoy geometry so?" José once asked him, for he himself preferred Latin.

"Geometry provides order in a disordered world," his father replied. "It is a window into the perfection that is God."

José had not expected such a philosophical answer. They sat in silence for a time. Then his father added, "Once I had intended to go to Edinburgh to study mathematics. My father died, and I was needed at home. Family always comes first, remember that." They continued on in silence, each with his books and his thoughts.

Tío Domingo was also a keen advocate of geometry. "Finally the priests are teaching you something useful. It will stand you in good stead when you learn navigation."

Such praise caused Rafael to redouble his efforts. "Someday I will be the captain of my own ship," he said.

Christmas in Matanzas with the Velázquez family provided a welcomed relief from their studies. In Cuba Christmas was an exuberant two-week celebration, and the *colegio* was closed from *Noche Buena*, Christmas Eve, through Epiphany, the *Día de los Reyes*. Habaneros who owned estates in the country also traveled there during this time. José knew, for example, that Miguel and his family would go to their *estancia*, cattle ranch, on the plains south of Havana. This year the Morejón family would also come to Matanzas, for Señor Morejón had many matters of business to attend to there. All his uncles would be there, too, for they liked to delay their departure on new voyages until after the Christmas season.

How happy the Velázquez family was to see them all. Abuelo, looking thinner and greyer, looked José and Magdalena up and down.

"You have grown so," was all he said, but his eyes shone with approval.

Abuelita and the aunts squeezed them and pinched their cheeks. "How well you both look!" exclaimed Abuelita, and Tía Beatriz gave them an extra hug.

Tía Nicolaza held Gonzalo closely to her, and he threw his arms about her and did not let go for a long time.

The women and girls poured themselves into preparations for the great feast they would have on *Noche Buena*. While good things were sometimes scarce at other times of the year, everyone saved the best for this special time. Abuelita had already begun marinating a pig in a fragrant sauce, and José's mouth began to water as the odor of bitter orange, onion, and garlic filled the pink house. Now Tío Gaspar and Tío Policarpo would roast it in a big pit behind the house. They worked shirtless as they tenderly arranged the pig on the glowing charcoal, and José could see the knotted scars that crossed Tío Policarpo's dark back. Remembering stories that his uncle had once been a slave on a French sugar plantation and had experienced great cruelty, he shivered for a moment. He forgot this sad history, however, as he listened to his uncles argue over the proper way to cook the pig. The two laughed and exchanged playful insults as they struggled for dominance in that manly endeavor.

The whole Velázquez family, joined by the Morejóns, gathered together in Abuelo's house for the *Noche Buena* feast. They dragged in tables and benches from the shop, and crowded together, elbow to elbow. The roast pork fell apart in tender pieces on the plate, savory with Abuelita's spicy marinade. There was plenty for everyone. Tía Nicolaza passed around the bowl of sauce in which to dip the fried plantains, and Tía Beatriz heaped everyone's plate with rice and beans. José wanted to eat till he burst, but he remembered what came next.

When the plates were cleaned, and sighs of contentment could be heard about the table, the girls brought out the sweets: rum cake, with its bittersweet tang, soft flan that melted in the mouth, and the sharp crisp of sugar cookies. José and Rafael sampled it all. José glowed within both from the satisfying fullness of the meal and the joy of being with the vast Velázquez family.

Contented sighs were heard as the sated diners sat back. The odor of cigar smoke filled the room.

Tía Nicolaza was quietly pressing Papá, once again trying to learn about Gonzalo's life in Havana. "How does he do in the shop? Is he learning the trade?"

"He is a capable enough joiner, but I am not sure that he will ever be a great one," replied Papá with honesty.

"Well, as long as he does his work. What does he do with the rest of his time?" she probed.

"He is seventeen, I do not follow him about like a mother sheep. He does his work, he does not stay out all hours, and he does not come home reeking of strong drink. What he does in his free time is up to him," Papá replied with finality.

Abuelita whispered to Mamá, "Nicolaza does not want him to grow up like that irresponsible Gaspar."

"And yet that is why she fell in love with Gaspar – he laughed, and was carefree, and gave her many presents," Abuelita whispered back.

Mamá reassured Tía Nicolaza. "He is a great help to Roberto. The business does well. They can hardly keep up with the work!"

Papá nodded in assent. "When José is big enough to handle the work of a joiner, the shop Zum-Zum can become the busiest in the city. Every great house in Havana will come to us for their wooden trim."

José felt warm inside at those words, as well as from all the well-watered wine he had consumed, until he heard Tío Domingo join in.

"Carpentry will put food on the table. But trade offers the path to true riches," he said as he puffed on a cigar.

"But at what danger?" asked Tía Nicolaza in a low voice. "Everything may be lost in a moment," she added as she took a long drag from her own cigar.

"Like Alejandro!" wailed Tía Beatriz.

"Never will I leave my Beatriz," said Tío Policarpo, and patted her plump hand, and she smiled back at him.

"As if he could control the wind – or the *guarda costa*," sniffed Abuelita.

Later they, with the rest of Matanzas, went to the church to see the priest place the carved figure of the Christ child in the manger, part of a large, brightly painted *nacimiento*, the nativity scene that stood in the square outside of the church. At home they had their own *nacimiento*, carved by Abuelo, and tomorrow they would place their own Christ child in the manger and surround the scene with lighted candles. After this ceremony they attended the *misa del gallo*, the midnight mass. The church was transformed as the flickering lights of the candles highlighted the bright colors of the women's finery and the ornate embroidery that adorned the priests' Christmas vestments, and the voices of the parishioners singing the old, familiar carols filled the great space. They were enveloped by magic, a reminder that God could work miracles, that He had once sent his son upon the earth in the form of a tiny baby to reconcile sinners to Him. Afterwards they returned home to have hot cocoa prepared with the special chocolate set that Tío Domingo had brought from Curaçao.

As the family walked home in the brisk December air, Magdalena began singing a *villancico*, "Ya viena la vieja," and soon all voices joined in its rolling cadences. Gradually one tenor voice rose above them all, and soon the other voices fell silent as they stopped to listen to the singer's achingly sweet tone change a simple children's carol into a poem that touched every heart in the darkness. José looked, and saw that the voice belonged to Gonzalo, whose face shone in the starlight with an untroubled joy.

"Gonzalo is an angel!" whispered Tía Beatriz.

"Hush! He is just a boy," Tía Nicolaza whispered back, but her face shone, too.

Kings of Orient riding

Guided by the starlight

Bringing to the baby

Gifts of love this night

How beautiful those words were as sung by Gonzalo. José looked up and rejoiced at the sight of the many stars shining in the black sky, the stars that had guided the men of the family safely home from the sea. And he remembered the special star that had guided the three kings to the stable long ago, those same kings who would soon visit Matanzas bringing presents for all the children.

It was a joyous two weeks in Matanzas, basking in the adoring attentions of Abuelo and Abuelita, and roaming the city with his cousins and Rafael. José wondered if Matanzas grew smaller every time they visited, or did Havana grow larger? Sometimes he and Papá walked the city together. Papá admired the workmanship, much of it from Abuelo's shop, now largely under the guidance of Jacinto, on display on the new houses that had replaced the city destroyed by the hurricane.

One day Tío Domingo walked with him down to the bay to see the many ships riding at anchor.

"In a few years you will join me on the *Orfeo*," his uncle said, pointing to her black hull, rocking gently on the blue waves.

"There, boy, lies the path to wealth and position. Many a fortune has been built on trade," he added expansively.

"Tío Gaspar and Tío Policarpo have not become wealthy," noted José, not caring that he sounded insolent.

"They do not own their own vessels. Anselmo and I have invested in this and other vessels, and we have done well. We think to add another one to our fleet soon. I will have to find a captain for it, and a crew. Someday you can be captain of your own sloop, and when I am gone, become the Albañez half of Albañez y Morejón. It is good you and Rafael get on so well." Although his uncle liked to speak of his passing, it was hard to imagine him in his grave, for he was only thirty-five, and his long red hair showed no sign of grey.

He added more brightly, "The connections you are making in the priests' school will help you do more than Anselmo and I ever could. This business requires friends in high places."

"Do you not fear the storms?" José asked.

"All men fear them," replied Tío Domingo. "The wise man keeps a weather eye out at all times."

José said little as they returned to the pink house, but he thought how different were his uncle's views on education from those of Father Borrero.

T hey returned to Havana after the *Día de los Reyes*, the children's presents from the three kings packed in their trunk. The kings had brought Magdalena a carved wooden comb, like Mamá's, to hold back her cascade of brown curls.

"Ah, the kings know that you are growing up!" exclaimed Mamá.

José had received a copy, in Latin, of *The Lives of the Saints*.

"It seems the kings know that you are doing well in your studies," observed Papá.

Mamá, however, received the best gift of all, not from the kings, but from the wiry hands of Abuelo. He presented her with her own *nacimiento* set, which he had lovingly carved and painted himself.

"So you may remember me when I am long gone," he said. Mamá threw her arms around him, dropping wet tears on his shoulders.

T he Christmas holidays restored everyone's spirits. The friendly competitions at school became more intense, study sessions at the Albañez home more animated, the girls teased the boys with more spirit, Mamá's cooking still more savory, and even Papá could be heard humming a piper's tune as he finished another order. And no one could forget the magic notes of Gonzalo's singing, rising through the dark night to the stars above.

"He is like an angel," whispered Mamá. "They say that fools are closer to God."

"Then he has one foot in Heaven," replied Papá, "for he spoiled two pieces of good lumber today."

Then came a March day that would not be easily forgotten by any of them.

José was poring over his copy of Virgil's *Aeneid*, daunted by the new vocabulary but thrilled by the story of Aeneid's escape to Latium with the refugees of the fallen Troy. The tricky conjugations were interrupted by the sound of loud cries emanating from the shop. He rushed to find Papá and Gonzalo, the latter moaning and clutching his right arm, which hung oddly in his bloodied shirtsleeve. Mamá, entering, assessed the situation and sent Magdalena for a pan of water and a clean cloth to bathe Gonzalo's wound.

"We were fastening the new balustrades at the Jáurequi house on Lamparilla and the fool fell straight down into the street. He was too busy watching a passing funeral cortege to remember his own safety. It's lucky he wasn't killed." Papá's words were fierce with anger, but his face was worried.

José knew Gonzalo's injury was serious, for after Mamá and Papá had examined it closely, they sent him to fetch Señor Machado, the surgeon.

"This is beyond the skills of Señora Peña," said Papá tersely, in a low voice so that Gonzalo could not hear. "I have seen such injuries in war. This is bad, very bad."

Señor Machado arrived quickly. He was renowned for his skill with the saw, a skill acquired during long years as a ship's surgeon. He was not known for being overly solicitous of his patients' feelings, preferring the company of his gamecocks.

The surgeon, too, looked grim after examining the grey-faced Gonzalo.

"His arm must come off," he pronounced loudly. "When the broken bone protrudes from the skin, as it does here, the injury invariably results in morbid putrefaction. Even with amputation his life is not assured."

Gonzalo's eyes filled with terror, and Magdalena, sitting by his side, squeezed his good hand as her own eyes filled with tears of sympathy.

"He cannot work as a carpenter with only one arm," said Papá.

"He cannot work at all if he is in his grave," replied Señor Machado.

The room was silent, for there was no reply to such wisdom. Gonzalo whimpered, and Magdalena bathed his forehead with water.

They began preparations for the operation. The surgeon had Gonzalo sit on the shop's workbench while Mamá brought a bucket of fresh water and began tearing up a sheet to make bandages. Papá fetched a bottle of *aguardiente* from the kitchen.

"Drink up, lad, do not spare the bottle," he ordered.

Gonzalo took the bottle with his left hand and held it to his mouth, taking in a great swig of liquor. He grimaced as the burning liquid flooded his gullet.

"Keep drinking. It will dull the pain," Papá urged, and Gonzalo forced down another swallow.

When the bottle was half empty, and Gonzalo had begun to sway slightly, Papá took back the bottle.

"We want you dead to the pain, not dead to all worldly cares," he said.

Now Gonzalo lay back on the workbench, his eyes pools of terror in his sweating face.

"I need you both to hold him down, with all your strength," said the surgeon, pointing to Papá and José. Papá nodded his assent, but José stood there, a queasy feeling in the pit of his stomach.

"Come on, lad, your cousin needs you to be a man now," growled Papá, and José clenched his jaw and grabbed Gonzalo's feet. Papá held down Gonzalo's shoulder with both his strong hands. The surgeon placed a strip of wood in the patient's mouth for him to bite down upon.

"Time for the womenfolk to clear out," said the surgeon. "I do not think they want to witness this."

Mamá moved quickly towards the door, but Magdalena lingered.

"I want to help Gonzalo, Papá," she said pleaded softly.

"She would only be in the way," said the surgeon firmly.

"Please let her stay," Gonzalo moaned.

The surgeon shook his head no, but Papá considered a moment, and then nodded his assent. Magdalena stood by Gonzalo's side, and held his good hand. Papá pushed her head down so that she could not witness the surgeon's work.

Suddenly the shop was filled with Gonzalo's screams as the surgeon's saw bit into his arm above the elbow. Blood splattered from the cut, and José could feel drops of it on his face but dared not let go of Gonzalo's struggling feet. They could hear the grinding of the saw on bone as the surgeon severed the arm in a few swift, fierce cuts. Then Gonzalo's shattered arm was in a bucket on the floor, and the surgeon was binding the bleeding stump with lint and swathes of bandages.

José saw that Magdalena had raised her head to watch the operation, her wide eyes full of tears of sympathy for Gonzalo. Now she was stroking his hand and murmuring, "It is all over now, *pobrecito*, I will look after you and Mamá and I will pray to St. Anthony for your healing." Was this the silly girl who teased him and did not know how to read or write?

They moved Gonzalo into the cot in his room, and moved José temporarily into Magdalena's room. Gonzalo slept for many long hours after his ordeal. Mamá and Magdalena maintained a careful vigil, checking often to make sure that he had not developed a fever. Señor Machado came the next day to check his handiwork and to teach Mamá how to change the bandages. He did not like what he saw.

"His wound manifests too much inflammation, and I perceive the beginnings of a fever. I fear that, despite my efforts, he may yet develop morbid putrefaction."

Such scientific language impressed Mamá, and she and Magdalena redoubled their attentions to Gonzalo. Gonzalo was indeed developing a fever. He tossed and turned during the night, soaking the sheets with sweat, although the worst of the summer heat was not yet upon them. Mamá washed his sheets and bandages daily, and Magdalena bathed his forehead with *aguardiente* and brought him good things to eat: healing broths, fruit, and soothing flan.

"You must eat and grow well," she would say, urging him to take one more bite. She told him stories to make him laugh, and sang him songs, which also made him laugh weakly because she was not always in tune.

Papá found a boy to help him in the shop, but his work was constantly interrupted by the flow of visitors calling upon the ailing Gonzalo. The Albañez family was amazed by the variety of his acquaintance. There was a multitude of musicians, for they learned to their astonishment that Gonzalo had been spending his free hours performing at dances and concerts. Father Aquila of Espíritu Santo came to pray with him every day. He was grateful, he told Papá, for Gonzalo's assistance in the choir. Many admirers also came, too, to express their enjoyment of his singing at the many dances where he had performed, and brought flowers and fruit. A well-dressed *blanco* lady pulled up in a *volante* in front of the shop under the sign of the Zum-Zum and her *calisero*, liveried in blue and gold, stepped down to bring a basket of delicacies for the patient.

The old woman lifted her black veil. "Such a sweet young man! With a voice that puts the birds to shame!" she called out to a startled Papá.

Diego O'Sullivan and his father came as well, for it seems they had met him at Espíritu Santo. Patricio O'Sullivan had served in the Hibernia Regiment and was now on the staff of the Captain-General. Lieutenant O'Sullivan and Papá attempted to exchange pleasantries, each in their own variety of Gaelic, but the languages were too different, and finally they resorted to Spanish and enjoyed a glass of Madeira together while José and Diego entertained Gonzalo.

Papá did not think that so many visitors were good for Gonzalo in his condition, but Mamá invited them all in. "It cheers him so! How he smiles to see them. I am sure he would already have left us if not for their encouragement," Mamá argued. And Gonzalo did smile to see his visitors, but that smile grew ever more wan and he spoke little. He continued to worsen.

Mamá added, in a low voice, "He needs their prayers." She would always join the visitors as they knelt by his bedside to pray to St. Anthony, the patron saint of amputees, for healing.

One day Father Aquila announced that it was time. He would bring Gonzalo *el Santísimo*, the last rites, from Espíritu Santo. In preparation, Mamá somberly spread a cloth on a table near Gonzalo's bed to form an altar, and on it she placed two candles, which flickered in the approaching twilight. Soon they heard the bell that signaled Father Aquila's approach. The family rushed to the long windows at the front of the shop and gazed through the wooden grating to see, at a distance, a boy ringing a bell, and behind him Father Aquila in his black robes, holding aloft the holy oils. The neighbors, too, appeared at the sound of the bell, bringing candles to light the way. They knelt on the ground as the priest approached, both in reverence for the sacrament and to offer up their prayers for the ailing boy, for everyone knew it was for Gonzalo that the priest was coming. Señora Peña, flanked by her two great sons, knelt on her fat knees, her wrinkled face squeezed tight to hold back her tears, her lips moving in silent prayer. Señor Espada looked grave as he doffed his broad black hat and lowered his grey head. Around the corner came the Morejón family, down to the smallest, and all knelt in an orderly line is response to Señora Morejón's sharp command. The whole street rustled in prayer for Gonzalo.

The solemn procession arrived at the blue door of the Albañez house, and proceeded to the patient's bedside. The family gathered around, heads lowered, as Father Aquila heard Gonzalo's last confession and anointed his head with holy oil. Gonzalo's face was mottled looking, and his lips barely moved.

After the priest left, Magdalena insisted that she take José's empty cot that night. "I will stay and watch over him," she said, and the slightest of smiles moved across Gonzalo's face.

Mamá ordered Magdalena to call her should anything happen, and they all went to their beds, wondering if Gonzalo would be with them in the morning. The night seemed especially dark, the barking of dogs in the distance carried a new menace, and the evening bells tolled mournfully.

José awoke at dawn with a feeling of dread. They all crept into Gonzalo's room to see how he had fared during the night, and found both Gonzalo and Magdalena deep in restful sleep. Gonzalo's face was cool to the touch, and his breathing was deep and regular. Señor Machado came to check on him that morning and, on removing his bandages, was well pleased.

"The wound has begun to produce laudable pus. He has, I believe, passed through the critical phase and will make a full recovery," he said with authority.

Mamá was delighted at the good news and dazzled by this further display of medical expertise.

"So many people prayed for him, Mamá," explained Magdalena. "I know that God listened."

"You have prayed very faithfully, *mi hija*," replied Mamá. "Jesus and St. Anthony surely heard you."

When Tío Gaspar next arrived in Havana on the *Penélope* sloop, he was aghast to learn of Gonzalo's travails. He wrapped his long arms about his son, and Gonzalo's face shone with happiness, an expression that had been little seen since the accident. Gonzalo returned home with his father, his apprenticeship at an end.

They heard many stories about his new life in Matanzas from Tío Domingo, Tío Policarpo, and of course, from Tío Gaspar. It turned out that Gonzalo had accumulated a not insignificant sum of money from his career as a musician, and now expended it on a cart and a donkey, which he then used to bring fruits and vegetables from the countryside to the city every day. He advertised his wares with songs of his own composition, and housewives, hearing his liquid tenor, poured out of their homes to bargain for fresh oranges and peppers.

"Even the lemons are sweet when Gonzalo sings of them," they were heard to say.

On Saturday evenings and holy days he joined his fellow musicians to perform at concerts and dances. The priests, too, sought him out to perform sacred music at mass. Tía Nicolaza sighed with contentment to see her son in church every Sunday. The young women enjoyed his singing, as well, and everywhere he went, they would smile at him from behind their fans or the gratings of the long windows in the houses. He did not take improper advantage of this, however, and that, too, pleased Tía Nicolaza.

"God has been very good to Gonzalo!" said Mamá.

"Not one sparrow is forgotten by God. And truly he has a special eye for his fools," commented Papá. "I wish that I understood why he sometimes seems to forget some of the rest of us."

12

A PACT WITH THE DEVIL

The Albañez family felt the loss of Gonzalo. They had not realized how much they had enjoyed his easygoing presence and gentle smile, the ever-present humming in the shop. It was Papá, however, who felt his absence most deeply. Gonzalo had become at least a competent joiner, and was the second pair of hands needed to handle the large jobs in the shop.

"You should have had several apprentices!" wailed Mamá, but she, and the rest of the family, knew that Papá's gruff manner drove away many potential assistants, and that he did not let others into his world readily.

Papá had taken on a youth during Gonzalo's illness, but had not obliged his helper to sign indenture papers yet, waiting to see whether he would prove worthy of his trust. Then one day they found that the fellow had been lured away by the *Real Arsenal*, the royal shipyard. The shipyard was a great maw which sucked in everything a carpenter needed: timber, tools, and men. It had also, however, made a Havana a great city, where men built many houses, large and small, and those houses needed windows and doors, shutters and railings. It was Havana's largest employer, and took on hundreds of men, skilled and unskilled. It had built some of the finest ships in the Spanish navy, using the abundant cedar and mahogany of the New World to make vessels that could resist the rot that plagued wooden ships, especially those in the tropics. José remembered going with Papá and Tío Gaspar to watch the launching of the great ship of the line *Asturo*. His heart had swelled with pride as he saw its brass work glint in the sun and imagined its sails, now tightly bound to its yards, unfurled to fill with wind as she left the harbor and entered the open sea. Now, however, the Albañez family was paying a price for the *Real Arsenal*'s success and greed.

Two new apprentices soon joined the shop. Señora Peña knew a likely *blanco* youth, Tomás, son of a woman who was the daughter of their neighbors on the Calle Amargura when she was a girl. Señor Espada, too, recommended his cousin's nephew's friend, Hilario, a *pardo* boy who lived on Calle Villegas. Papá was pleased with them both, and proclaimed them quick learners. Tomás was strong and diligent, and Hilario made the tools fly with his quick hands while he entertained them with stories. One day, however, Tomás did not appear at the shop, and soon they learned that he had been impressed into the navy of His Most Catholic Majesty. Then, a month later, Hilario disappeared. An angry man appeared at the shop, looking for him, for there was trouble about a girl. They found out later from Señor Esposo that Hilario had found a berth on a ship leaving Havana in order to escape the father's wrath.

Papá began to fall behind on his orders. A bill for a large shipment of wood fell due, and he had to turn to Tío Domingo for help in paying it. His shoulders always slumped now, and he grew ever more silent.

José tossed and turned at night, swatting at the occasional mosquito that found its way past the curtains around his bed. In the distance, he could hear the dogs bark and the tomcats' fierce fights for love and dominance. He thought of his school, the glorious hours spent with Rafael, Sebastián, and his other friends. He thought of the encouragement he received from his teachers, and the prize he had won the year before in Greek. He thought of all the books that he had yet to read – works by Ovid, by Virgil, by Homer.

Then he thought of Papá, struggling to find a steady worker for his shop, someone who would learn the trade and take the great weight off of Papá's shoulders. José knew that he could be that helper and work alongside his father until Papá was ready to lay down his tools. Then, in their turn, José's own sons would take them up. He had hoped, however, that he could defer that day until he had finished the *colegio*. He saw clearly that he was the helper his father needed – he was big enough now to handle the long boards used, to safely work the lathe, and manage all the other myriad tasks of a joiner's shop. A tiny voice within whispered that he could also in this way avoid joining Tío Domingo on the *Orfeo*.

The next night, as he was parsing a passage of the *Aeneid*, he put down his quill and spoke to his father. "I am ready to join you in the shop, Papá," he said quietly.

"You must finish your schooling, lad. Your mamá could not bear to see you leave, she takes such pride in all you have learned. And I would not have you give it up as I did," said Papá. "Then when you are done at the *colegio*, you must go to sea with Donnie."

"But why, Papá? I am needed here! You need me, Mamá and Magdalena need me!" cried José. He could not understand why Papá still insisted that he go with Tío Domingo when the need here was so urgent.

"Donnie needs you. And I made a promise to him, long ago, and I will keep it. He is my brother, and I will not fail him. We must always put family before our own desires. I made a promise to your mother, as well. Donnie has already promised to find a remedy."

The *Orfeo* had in fact sailed into Havana harbor the previous day, and Tío Domingo was rooming with Señora Peña. The night before he and Papá could be heard in discussions that ran long into the night.

A few days later, after the *siesta*, Tío Domingo arrived at the shop. He stood in the doorway, his form a black shadow framed by the white-hot blaze of the sun. Another shadow followed behind him, tall and lean, but his blackness did not resolve into the light as he entered the room and the door closed behind him. The stranger stood there, dressed in threadbare clothing, only his eyes moving as he glanced about, trying to take in his surroundings.

"This is Agustín," announced Tío Domingo. "He will be your new assistant."

Papá walked about the stranger, examining all the details of his person. "I asked you for a teachable youth, and this is who you bring me?" replied Papá, now in Gaelic. "He looks to be no more than a beggar! Where did you find this man, in prison?"

Tío Domingo was unperturbed. "He is a slave. He will work for you and learn the joiner's trade, so that José can attend the *colegio*," he replied calmly.

"A slave? After all that has happened, you expect me to hold another man in servitude? Do you not understand how it degrades a man to be bought and sold like cattle?" Papá raged.

"You are far too sentimental," Tío Domingo said, a hard tone entering his voice. "You cannot keep up with your work without assistance, and so you asked me to find you a helper. Other craftsmen use slaves. You can see them all over Havana."

"I had hoped you would find some young sailor looking for a berth on land," Papá replied.

Tío Domingo waved away Papá's objections. "Such men know that there are good wages to be had at the *Real Arsenal*. Agustín will serve your purpose. He is intelligent – I can see that in his eyes – and his hands are strong and nimble."

"Who is he? How can I trust him in my shop?" complained Papá.

"Who knows? All we know is that he is a man like you were once, one who has encountered misfortune. And he is a *bozal*, he is from Africa. You will have to discover the rest for yourself," Tío Domingo replied with indifference.

Papá was silent, defeated. "How much do I owe you?" he asked at last. "And then there is the tax."

"You may repay me as you can. And as for the tax, well..." Tío Domingo waved it away.

"You are smuggling slaves, after your solemn vow to me!" Papá was enraged anew.

"Only this once, as a favor to you, my own brother. I found him in Jamaica. You must believe me, he is better off with you than ground to dust on a sugar plantation there. A fate you yourself barely escaped." Tío Domingo looked a little smug as he said that.

There was no answer to this, and Papá did not attempt one. He retreated to the kitchen to explain everything to Mamá, leaving José with Tío Domingo and the stranger.

Throughout this discussion Agustín's eyes had shifted from one speaker to the next in an apparent effort to read in their faces what he could not discern in their words. José stared at him in fascination. He remembered his ancestor Achukwo, who had come from faraway Africa. Had he looked like this man? Agustín caught his gaze. José, too, retreated to the kitchen, where he found Papá, his head sunk in his hands.

"I can help you, Papá. I can stay home and be your new apprentice," he offered once again.

"No," answered Papá. "I promised your mamá that you would finish the *colegio*, and Tío Domingo that you would go to sea with him. I must keep my promises." His face looked grim and hard. "God help me," he added.

At first Agustín spoke little, even after José had introduced him to the most useful phrases in Spanish. And when Papá had taught him small tasks about the shop, his hands moved listlessly about their work. Papá observed him with increasing irritation.

Agustín's only enthusiasm was for Mamá's cooking. He shoveled food from his plate to his mouth with a silent, steady energy.

"Roberto, this *bozal* will eat all of your profit!" Mamá would scold. Then she would fill Agustín's plate with another serving of rice and beans. Gradually his emaciated frame filled out.

"If that *bozal* does not work, you should sell him," advised Señora Peña.

One evening, after supper, José saw Agustín in animated conversation with another *bozal*. His face was alive in a way that José had not seen it before, hands waving wildly in an attempt to keep pace with the words that poured from his mouth, a river of strange sounds, rounded, bouncing sounds that José knew did not come from Spanish or Latin or any other tongue with which he was familiar. José recognized the *bozal* with whom Agustín was speaking; he belonged to Señor Cabrían, a tailor who lived around the corner on the Calle Compostela.

After that, José frequently saw Agustín in the evenings with that same *bozal,* and with them were other Africans. Papá's new assistant now stood taller, his eyes shone brighter, and he began to tackle his work with greater attention and a growing skill. Soon he could mark, cut, plane, and square a board as well as Papá. He continued to meet with the other *bozales* in the dusk, their dark faces disappearing into the fading light.

Mamá remarked upon it. "What do those *bozales* get up to every night?" she asked.

"They go to find the music of the mother-tongue; to speak with those who have trod their native soil," said Papá, but in Gaelic, words meant only for himself. He then poured himself a glass of *aguardiente*. José had never heard his father speak such poetry. He then realized that, except for Tío Domingo, his father had no fellow countrymen in Cuba. He wondered if Papá longed to see Scotland again, and if, in his dreams, he still walked there and spoke with people unknown to them.

Early one late summer evening, Anselmo and Polonia Morejón were gathered in the kitchen with Papá and Mamá. The men drank *aguardiente* and the women sipped *café au lait*, which Mamá served proudly in new porcelain teacups Tío Domingo had brought from Curaçao. It was a drink new to them, and Mamá and Señora Morejón argued over the recipe. José and Rafael labored over their Greek at the table, and Magdalena and Marianela giggled and whispered girlish secrets to one another as they flitted in and out of the room. José looked up once from his work and Marianela caught his eye and smiled shyly. He quickly looked down again at his Greek. Agustín was in the shop, sweeping up, for he was very tidy. At the Morejón house, Dionisia was putting the younger ones to bed.

Then they heard the pounding of the heavy iron knocker on the door of the shop. They did not find it unusual to look up and see Father Borrero entering the room, for the priest often stopped in to see Papá when his business brought him to that part of the city, and Papá quickly arose to offer his guest his customary glass of Madeira.

Father Borrero accepted the drink with thanks and said, in a tone that required an answer, "You have a new member of your household, Roberto."

"Domingo found me a *bozal* to assist me in the shop so that José can attend the *colegio*," answered Papá, with an unnatural carelessness.

"He is not simply a *bozal*, is he? He is a slave. You have purchased a slave," said Father Borrero.

"Domingo found him. I could not find a suitable assistant anywhere in Havana," replied Papá.

"Do you not know under what conditions these poor wretches are brought here?" Father Borrero's voice rose.

Papá tone became heated. "And we have saved him from all that. We have given him a decent set of clothes, fed him amply – he already looks more like a man and less like a bag of bones." He pointed to Agustín. It was true. Agustín's tall, dark figure had become that of a healthy, muscular man in his prime.

"The Albañez family has purchased a man, a man would still be free if not for the slave dealers who demand to be fed with the lives of others. A man with feelings, with dignity, with pride. You have taken everything from him so that you may bend him to your will," said Father Borrero sternly, as if he were speaking to a disobedient child.

"Do you not think I know what that is like? To be torn from family and home? What can I do? Every man must do what is best for his own family, and everyone else look out for themselves." Papá's eyes had become harsh and angry.

Father Borrero looked at Papá's angry face, and said softly, "Those are your brother's words. I know you do not truly believe them, my friend." Then all fell silent, and the priest's face looked older in the shadows of the kitchen.

Then suddenly Señora Morejón spoke, her voice loud and angry. "It is the way of the world, Father. People are bought, and people are sold. In Jamaica, in Florida, in Saint Domingue, and in Africa itself. It is in the Bible. There has always been slavery, and there always will be. Nothing we do can ever change that." José remembered that the Morejóns' girl, Dionisia, was a slave.

"We do not have to be a part of that sinful trade, dear woman," replied Father Borrero.

"Surely they are better off in a Catholic country?" asked Mamá in distress.

"How many have died in the Middle Passage, unbaptized? How many souls are thus lost to the Church?" Father Borrero replied.

Mamá's face twisted in distress, but Señora Morejón spoke again, still angry. "We have nothing to do with that. The British bring the *bozales* here to sell, and we buy them."

Father Borrero looked straight at her. "I am surprised that you, of all people, would defend slavery, since you have been a slave yourself," he said.

There it was. Father Borrero had mentioned the thing that was never spoken. He had heard Mamá hint at it, and Rafael had told him the truth of it, but no one ever spoke of it to the formidable Señora Morejón. Indeed, José found it hard to imagine Señora Morejón at the beck and call of any individual, even a *blanco*.

Father Borrero was unrelenting. "And you own a slave yourself, now," he continued.

The room fell silent. Señora Morejón fought back like a wounded animal. "We pay Dionisia a wage and she is buying her freedom from her owner under the *coartación*. The court set her price, and she has already paid thirty percent of that. In time, she will have purchased her freedom, just as I once purchased mine."

"Yes, all over Havana there are families and businesses eager to hire slaves under the *coartación*, or buy them outright. And that makes them valuable, and so the slave ships, legal and illegal, continue to bring them, these valuable workers," argued Father Borrero unrelentingly.

"Who are you to pronounce judgement?" Señora Morejón spat. "I know that there are slaves at the *colegio*. And that the free education there is paid for by the *ingenios* that it owns. Everyone knows the brutality needed to produce sugar from cane." With these words she gestured for Rafael and Marianela to accompany her, and left the house under full sail.

The room fell into a silence still deeper. One did not speak so to a priest, not even a bad one, and Father Borrero was one of the best. One might gossip about a certain priest, or laugh at his vanity or hypocrisies, but never to his face.

Señor Morejón had remained. There was an awkward silence, as everyone stirred uncomfortably in their seats and shifted their gaze. Then Señor Morejón rose and spoke to Father Borrero. "Perhaps you think that I should apologize for my wife, and perhaps you are right. But I will not.

"I can never apologize for my Polonia. I know how others see her. They dread her tongue and fear her presence. But she is my rock. You know, Roberto, what I was before I met her." Tears moistened Señor Morejón's eyes.

"How often I begged her to marry me! I offered to buy her freedom myself. But she refused me, every time, until she had paid the last *real* of the *coartación* herself. And then, as a free woman, she at last offered me her hand. 'I wanted you to know that I married you freely, with all my heart,' she said. *Dios mío*, she is magnificent! Never will I apologize for such a woman." Then wiping a tear from his eyes with his handkerchief, he left.

They were silent again, and then Papá asked, "Is it true that the *colegio* is supported by the income from *ingenios*?"

"Yes, my friend, I am ashamed to admit, it is true. We have made a pact with the devil, all of us. I fear that in time we will pay a stiff price for it."

Father Borrero departed into the deepening twilight. They heard him bid good night to Agustín as he left.

13

EL DÍA DE LOS REYES

In time, they grew accustomed to Agustín's presence as they had grown accustomed to Gonzalo's. Mamá marveled at his strange ways.

"He washes before every meal, like a cat!" she exclaimed. "Who does such a thing?"

It was true. Agustín washed his hands meticulously and sometimes, too, the rest of his body. José watched these rituals with fascination. Such fastidiousness seemed unnecessary when the frequent rains washed the city, its people, and its animals. Agustín performed other odd rituals around mealtime. Sometimes he poured a bit of tamarind water on the ground in the courtyard. At other times he placed a morsel of yam or fruit before Mamá's picture of the Virgin.

"Some sort of heathen foolishness," Papá would growl.

"No, it is that he has a pious heart," Mamá would insist.

Agustín was a great help to Papá in the shop, and it was this that José resented. He wanted to be there, by Papá's side, sharing in every task, hearing his praise, even accepting his rebukes. Instead this stranger, a slave and an African, was in his place, occupying the place that should have been his. Yet he could not but admit to himself that he was glad he had not needed to leave the *colegio*.

Agustín was learning to speak a stumbling sort of Spanish, able to converse about his work in the shop, and ask for second helpings of Mamá's good cooking. Still, he organized his words strangely, as if he had tossed them together in a shaker and cast them out to land where they would. Magdalena found Agustín's fractured Spanish a source of infinite amusement, going into gales of laughter at his grammatical atrocities. Then Agustín would smile broadly, and join in the laughter.

Sometimes Mamá called her aside. "Do not laugh at the poor man. He is just a *bozal* and does not know any better," she would scold.

But still Magdalena laughed, and Agustín smiled. He choked on her name, with its many syllables and consonants, till it simply became "Lena" in his mouth.

Most annoying, perhaps, was Agustín's fascination with the Albañez children, especially José. He would peer over José's shoulder as he parsed his Latin poetry, and say in his halting Spanish, "What talk word paper, *niño*?"

How that word *niño* galled José. He certainly did not think of himself as a little boy, for he had achieved the advanced age of fourteen. , He, along with Rafael and Sebastián, were now cocky fourth-year scholars who looked down upon the fresh-faced children in Father Jiménez's first year grammar class, flaunting their status as students in the class of Rhetoric. Father Navarette – tall, emaciated, and impossibly old – taught them the Latin poets and Greek fathers in a reedy and refined Castilian accent. Every word and every move was made with exquisite deliberation, and it was thus he held their attention.

He also taught them astronomy; how to find the planets, the movements of the stars in the night sky, and the names of the constellations. It is true, Tío Policarpo had once shown José how to find the North Star, but now the soft darkness of the night twinkled with stories of mythology.

One clear night in late October Father Navarette invited all the fathers to bring the boys to observe the stars from the Plazuela de la Ciénaga. Papá and Señor Morejón, carrying lanterns, carefully walked their sons through the dark, quiet, streets, alert to the presence of thieves who might lurk in the shadows. They were relieved to see only a few dogs and an occasional *volante*, taking its occupant to some nighttime entertainment. In the plaza they doused their lanterns and stood, avoiding the puddles.

They spotted Sebastián and his father, Don Martín. "*Buenas noches!*" said Papá and Señor Morejón, in friendly salutation.

"*Buenas noches,*" replied Don Martín, with a polite smile, remaining where he stood.

While they waited for all the boys to gather, Señor Morejón moved about, making sure to greet all of the adults. Some were already customers. Soon all the students were gathered, excited to be out in the mystery of the dark night and to share the experience with their fathers.

"There's the North Star!" said Señor Morejón, eager to show off his nautical expertise.

"The North Star is the last star in the tail of Ursa Minor, the Little Bear," added Papá, who had his own store of knowledge.

Father Navarette beamed and commented, "Strabo tells us that the Phoenicians used Ursa Minor to guide their ships centuries before the birth of Our Lord." He pointed. "That bright light to the right of the moon is the planet Jupiter."

"The moon is waning crescent." Lt. O'Sullivan added his own observation, keen to demonstrate that the infantry could also read the skies.

"I believe it is waxing crescent," disagreed Señor Pedroso, Vidal's father, an official at the shipyard. "It was a moonless night just a few days ago."

"It is indeed a waxing moon," affirmed Father Navarette.

Then Mauricio's father, Commander Castellón, a naval officer stationed in Havana, said quietly, "There, near Jupiter, we can see the constellation Sagittarius, the archer." He showed all the boys how to discern the outline of the mounted rider and his bow.

"Near Sagittarius we have Scorpio. Notice the bright reddish star in his heart. That is the star Antares." The commander continued to reveal the secrets of the skies to the boys as Father Navarette stood and smiled with delight at their enthusiasm.

Not all of the boys had fathers in attendance. Anastasio had come with Diego O'Sullivan. Everyone knew his own father was a priest and could hardly make an appearance. Antonio's father was deceased, and so he had come with Mauricio and Commander Castellón. Sebastián, who somehow knew everything about everyone, whispered that Antonio's stepfather had probably already consumed a bottle of *aguardiente* and so was unable to stagger the few blocks to the plaza.

They crowded around Father Navarette as he pointed out constellations and told them the myths that lay behind them. In all the excited jostling, Miguel bumped roughly against Rafael.

"Stop shoving!" whispered Rafael loudly.

"And who will make me?" asked Miguel, even more loudly.

"Your father should thrash you well – if you even have a father," replied Rafael, still more loudly.

A silence fell upon the group. Miguel gave Rafael a hard push, on purpose this time.

"It is grown late, and time to return home, I think," said Vidal's father, and it was then that José realized that Miguel had come with Vidal and Señor Pedroso. Miguel's father was not in attendance. Was he visiting his *estancia*?

The boys had been proud to be seen with their fathers, but out of their company they sometimes slipped the traces of parental authority. After school the boys gathered in the square and smoked cigars, Rafael among them. José did not have the pocket money for such extravagance, for Papá did not smoke and did not allow Mamá to do so either. Only when she was with her sisters did she have a chance to indulge.

"Yours is the only family on the island of Cuba that does not smoke cigars," Rafael observed.

"Papá says that they are a waste of money, no better than throwing coins into the sea," explained José. "I think that he prefers to spend his money on Madeira."

Sebastián began to defy the chilly glare of Doña Isabela and sometimes brought his friends home after school. There they looked through Don Martín's books in Latin, searching for the full text of the expurgated love poems that they had read in class. They found all the forbidden lines and poems in Ovid and Horace, and read Suetonius's description of the shocking private lives of the Roman emperors. Their dictionary lacked the words to translate the worst of Catullus. José had seen dogs engage in sexual congress in the streets, and heard his uncles make ribald jokes, but this literature both shocked and fascinated him in its erotic detail. Lurid descriptions of men and women coupling, and even men with other men, caused the boys to first snigger, then wonder if this was indeed how grown men behaved. José thought that he would not like to be married if this was what it meant. He was certain that Papá and Mamá had never done anything so shameless; other people's parents, perhaps, but never his own. He had thought that he longed to be a man – but perhaps he was not in such a hurry after all.

Christmas of 1759 arrived, but this year the Albañez family did not go to Matanzas. At the last minute Mamá fell ill with a fever, and Tío Gaspar sailed without them. Señora Peña was back and forth, tending to Mamá. Magdalena followed at her heels, eager to learn the art of nursing. She tried to take Mamá's place in the kitchen, and the family praised her cooking, even when the rice was dry or she forgot to salt the plantains. Sometimes Señora Morejón sent Marianela over with a dish from her kitchen, which was always met with enthusiasm.

They observed the feast of *Noche Buena* with the Morejón family, and attended the *Noche Buena* Mass at the chapel attached to the *colegio*. The Mass was even more magnificent than in Matanzas, and José saw many classmates there, but he missed his family in the city of the three rivers. He missed the warm if annoying attentions of his aunts, the rough jesting of his uncles and the wisdom of Abuelo and Abuelita. He especially missed his cousins, even Gonzalo. Things were changing in Matanzas, and he was not there to hear about it. Jacinto had married, and was more and more recognized as the master of Abuelo's shop.

One afternoon he and Rafael and Sebastián were playing dominoes in the courtyard of the Albañez house. Magdalena passed through carrying a basket of vegetables peelings and other kitchen waste to toss in the street for the roaming pigs to devour. "Someday I will marry Magdalena," remarked Rafael when she had gone.

"Why?" asked José, startled.

"The girls have decided it. I will marry Magdalena, and you will marry my sister. It is a fine idea! It means that we will always be together." He drew three tiles from the boneyard, and at last found one to match José's, and put it down.

That did sound like a splendid idea. He and Rafael would be like brothers, forever. And when he was grown, he would need someone to cook, sew, and to keep the house tidy. He thought for a moment about the forbidden Latin literature, and knew that he did not want to engage in such improprieties. He was sure, however, that a nice girl like Marianela would never want to do such things. He also remembered Marianela's black eyes and sideways smiles, and his heart beat a little faster to think of having her always about.

"It would be nice to marry Marianela," said Sebastián. "I would wed her."

Rafael laughed. "You cannot. You are a *blanco*."

"*Blancos* can marry *pardos*. Señor Albañez is a *blanco*," Sebastián replied defensively.

"*Blancos* who own *volantes* do not marry *pardos*. Your father would not permit it. And the government would not allow you to marry without your family's permission," Rafael stated plainly.

There no sound but the click of the dominoes for a time. Then Sebastián asked, "Will Agustín take part in the *Día de los Reyes* processions?" He casually placed another tile.

On the Day of the Three Kings, all the slaves enjoyed a holiday. The festivities revolved around the *cabildos*, the lodges to which many *morenos* and even *pardos*, enslaved and free, belonged. They were both social clubs and religious centers, and sometimes helped slaves arrange to buy their freedom. Mamá had no interest in such societies, for her African roots were barely a memory, and Señora Morejón did not care to have her family belong to what she called "clubs for those without proper homes or decent Spanish." The *cabildos* organized a procession down the

Calle Oficios to the Castillo de la Real Fuerza. José realized that the upcoming holy day explained Agustín's recent excitement.

"We should go and see the procession. Mauricio says it is the most amazing spectacle!" urged Sebastián.

"We should!" Rafael assented. "I saw it when I was small. It is tremendous!"

José demurred. "Papá does not approve of the *Día de los Reyes*. He says it is just so much heathen mummery."

Rafael snorted.

"Well, you do not need to tell your father that we are going. Just find an excuse to slip away," Sebastián suggested.

José did not like the idea of deceiving Papá. He thought of the excitement of the crowds and the procession, however, and how much he wished to join his friends, and found himself agreeing.

On the 6th of December, the Day of the Three Kings, they met up after the siesta on the Calle Oficios near the corner of the Calle Lamparilla. The street was packed with people of all colors, men, women, and children, jostling and calling out to their friends, as they waited to see the processions. Food vendors roamed the street, touting their wares. The boys inserted themselves among the crowd and waited for the procession to reach them.

"How did you persuade Doña Isabela to allow you to come?" José asked Sebastián. He received no reply, which was in itself an answer.

They stood waiting in the bright afternoon sunshine. The sky was a clear, brilliant blue and a light breeze from the harbor freshened the air. From down the street they could hear a raucous sound growing ever louder, shouts, and songs, and the deep pounding of many drums. At last they could see the procession growing closer, and then it was before them.

The first group was led by the king and queen of the *cabildo*, dressed in the most magnificent of finery. The king wore an elegant velvet coat trimmed with lace, a feather hat upon his head. His queen promenaded grandly in a purple dress with a train held by a small girl, and her hair was adorned with bright red flowers. Gaily clad attendants bowed, curtsied, and waited upon their royal personages.

Behind the royal court came dancers. One wore a skirt of palm fronds, a necklace of copper beads, and a headdress of peacock feathers. Other dancers wore animal skins, and their scanty costumes exposed expanses of black skin, glistening with sweat in the hot, crowded street. They bobbed and swayed, and shook themselves in a wild ecstasy in time to the music provided by men with drums, rattles, and cow horns.

The beat of the music stirred the blood of those watching. Crowds of watching *morenos* swayed and shook with the rhythm. The *blancos* observed quietly, but José saw more than a few feet tap to the beat. His own heart beat faster, and he felt a wildness within that longed to escape, that called to him to join the dancers, but he remembered that he was José Albañez Velázquez, a student at the Colegio de San Ignacio and so only his toes joined in. *Cabildo* after *cabildo* followed, each louder and more boisterous than the last, shimmying their way to the Plaza de Armas, where they would receive gifts of coin from the Captain-General of Cuba.

"Does Agustín belong to a *cabildo*?" asked Sebastián.

Rafael was also curious. "Each tribe has its own *cabildo*. To which tribe does he belong?"

José realized that he did not know the answer to either of these questions, and that he knew almost nothing about the tall, dark presence who filled their home and shared their meals.

Suddenly, there he was, Agustín, among the dancers of one of the *cabildos*. He saw José, too, and rushed over to him with a great grin upon his face.

"*Niño!* With two *niño!* Come, with Agustín!" He seized their arms and dragged them into the procession with him.

Then they were alongside him, swept along with the crowd of dancers and merrymakers. Rafael and Sebastián shouted with abandon, and José hurried to keep up. Suddenly, in front of them, at the edge of the harbor, was the Castillo de Real Fuerza, the ancient fort that loomed over the harbor and the Plaza de Armas. It housed the Captain-General, governor of Cuba. Great limestone walls spread out in a star-shape, their sloping walls reflected in the deep moat that surrounded the fort. The yellow limestone blocks stood unadorned by stucco or decorative stonework and, in their simplicity, spoke of raw power. The fort's only concession to beauty was a simple watchtower adorned by a weathervane capped by a statue of a woman, La Giraldilla, who surveyed the harbor protectively. The crowd became calmer now, as if overawed by this symbol of Spain's might. The boys watched as the king of Agustín's *cabildo* went up to be greeted by the Captain-General Francisco Antonio Caxigal de la Vega and receive his gift of coins. The crowd cheered and the drums pounded the beat.

"I recognize this *cabildo*," said Rafael loudly, trying to be heard over the cries of the crowd. "It is Yoruba, the Tem Changó *cabildo*." José marveled at Rafael's seemingly limitless knowledge of the city.

"Come, *niño*! Come to *cabildo*!" Agustín cried, with a gesture that included them all.

"Let's go!" urged Sebastián, his eyes bright with excitement.

José hesitated. Several hours had passed, and his parents did not know where he had gone. A deep disquietude whispered that Papá would not wish him to visit a *cabildo*, no doubt a place where heathen mummery abounded.

"Come on!" said Rafael. "We may never get a chance like this again!"

So José found himself trailing Agustín through the streets to the crowded Jesús Maria neighborhood near the dock called Muelle de la Luz. There, on the Calle Merced, they entered a small house that already seemed to tremble with the sound of drumbeats. They stuck close to Agustín as he waded into the large crowd. José became acutely conscious that he, the lightest of *pardos*, and Sebastián, were attracting glances. Agustín's long arm embraced the two as he shouted something in his liquid tongue to the others, who smiled broadly and shouted in response. Agustín strode through the gathered people, tall and confident. Then they entered a patio, where men and women gyrated wildly to the rhythm of drums and rattles, accompanied by the singing of several men in raffia skirts and animal skins. The light from torches flickered on their ecstatic faces as the dancers swirled in a frenzied mass of bright reds and blues. There was something sensual in their movements, the thrusting, shaking, and writhing of their bodies, the seductive way in which the women's hips and bosoms moved to the music, their curves barely concealed by low-cut dresses. José remembered uncomfortably the forbidden Latin poems. The other boys unleashed the wildness in their hearts and swayed to the beat of the drums. Rafael shouted with joy, and Sebastián's eyes glittered feverishly. José hung back from the madness, thinking again that they should not have come.

Suddenly Agustín gestured for them to follow him into a small room, lit by a lantern and the flicker of torchlight through the open window and door. At the far end of the room was a small statue of a man in rags. Before him were placed a pair of crutches and many small offerings of food. In the corner, a small dog, chained to the wall, growled half-heartedly at them.

"Babalú-Ayé!" cried Agustín, pointing at the statue. "Babalú-Ayé! We pray to him, Señora Fausta be well." With these words, Agustín pulled a handful of beans from his pocket, and placed them, one by one, before the statue. José counted seventeen. Agustín began to chant loudly in his own tongue. Rafael and Sebastián crossed themselves and began to pray.

José poked Rafael and whispered loudly, "We musn't! It is a pagan idol!"

Rafael poked him back. "You are crazy! It is Saint Lazarus, the patron saint of the sick. I recognize him."

José looked and saw that it was indeed the statue of Saint Lazarus, the saint whom Jesus had raised from the dead, yet strangely out of place here. There was a feeling of evil in this room and in this house. He thought that something dark and malign was trying to steal his soul. The music and the drums, the torchlight and the swaying bodies, were pounding on the walls of his soul and breaking them down, trying to burst through and destroy all that was good within him. His heart beat too fast in his chest and there was a pounding of blood in his head. He felt as if he could not breathe. He was overwhelmed by the powerful odors of sweating bodies and the rotting smells of the docks and streets.

Agustín led them outside to a long table spread with an assortment of food-stuffs. He recognized baked yams and cassava bread, but he also detected the odor of alien seasonings wafting from a large pot resting at the end of the table. Agustín hurried to dish them each out a bowl of stew. José stirred it about with his spoon, and saw that it was full of meaty bones in a swirl of strange green leaves. He took a taste, and it left a greasy aftertaste. Rafael and Sebastián wolfed theirs down.

Agustín head disappeared into the crowd of black forms. José thought he saw him swaying among the dancers. The torchlights flickered weirdly about, and then he lost sight of him. Suddenly he felt nauseous, and leaned up against a wall. He leaned over, afraid he might be sick.

Agustín appeared before him. "*Niño* sick?" he asked. His tone was no longer ebullient, but carried a note of worry.

"I want to go home!" José cried out. He knew he sounded like a child. In truth, he felt like a one. He was no longer the young man he had pictured himself when he had slipped out that day without telling Papá, but a boy who needed to be home, safe in Mamá's kitchen, away from the flickering torchlight and alien chants.

"Papá is wondering where I am now," he added weakly.

Rafael suddenly came to himself. "My mother will have my hide."

Reluctantly, the boys made motions to leave. Agustín grew serious, and led them out of the *cabildo* and towards the Calle Aguacate. Had he not been there, they might never have found their way home, for the streets appeared unrecognizable in the deep shade of night, and were full of noisy individuals of dubious mien who leered at them as they passed. Wild laughter rang out from behind shadowy corners.

Agustín walked with a firm and rapid step. He was silent now, lost in his own thoughts. When a particularly raucous figure made as if to approach them, he warned them off with a fierce look, waving his arm over them in a gesture that told others that they were under his protection. A door suddenly opened and light poured out, revealing worried lines on his face.

José was enveloped in thought as they wended their way home. He thought of how foolish he had been to disobey Papá, how greatly he had sinned, he, a Catholic and a student of the Colegio de San Ignacio. He wished only to throw himself on his knees and repent in long and tearful prayer. First, however, he must face the wrath of Papá.

When they arrived at the Albañez home, they were startled to see a *volante* in the narrow street, attended by its *calisero*, dressed in the familiar livery of the De Ayala family.

"Your father is waiting inside," said Justo, the *calisaro* to Sebastián. "He is out of his mind with worry."

As they approached the door, Justo said loudly, "Because of this I am here and not at my *cabildo*."

Reluctantly, José opened the great door, loath to enter and face Papá. At the first creak of the hinges, however, they were surrounded by parents – Papá, Mamá, Señor Morejón, and Don Martín. Papá seized José by the collar and dragged him inside, and Señor Morejón cuffed Rafael on the ear. Mamá was almost weeping with relief.

Don Martín, arms akimbo, looked upon them all with imposing dignity as Sebastián hung his head.

"Doña Isabela said that you were keeping bad company, and I see now that she was right," he intoned.

Sebastián faced his father boldly. "It was my idea to see the *Día de los Reyes* procession. And it was I who urged the others to go to the *cabildo*."

"Your honesty, at least, is commendable," replied his father, and with those words he seized Sebastián by the ear and hauled him out to the *volante*.

"Your mother will have much to say about this," Señor Morejón said, as he hustled Rafael out the door.

Papá turned to José. "I thought that you were too old to thrash, but I was wrong."

Tears sprang to José's eyes as he said, "I am sorry, Papá. I disobeyed you and went to the procession and to a *cabildo*. You are right, they are full of heathen mummery!" The dam then burst and the tears streamed from his eyes.

Papá turned now to Agustín. "You have drawn my son into the wickedness of these pagan performances. I want you to steer clear of my children. I have not yet decided whether you remain in my house or I will sell you off to some other master."

Tears ran down Agustín's face. "I love *niño*!" he cried as he reached out his arms towards José and Magdalena. "Like my *niño*, I no see more."

José was startled. Agustín, a father? He had never thought that the man might have left a family back in Africa. He had always been simply the *bozal* in the workshop.

"I see him no more, wife, *niño*. No more, no more!" Agustín wept quietly for a time, and then reached out his arms to Papá in supplication. "Please, Don Roberto. No more! No more!" Again, he wept, head bowed and body shaking.

A silence fell upon them all. The flickering light in the lantern cast eerie shadows and distorted the faces of those in the room. No one spoke. At long last they saw Agustín, through the screen that had been created by his broken Spanish. They saw a man who had been manhandled, starved, and sold like a stick of furniture. They saw a man, created by the hand of God, but who had not found love among the people of His church. And each of them felt the sting of this, silently, in his or her own heart, as Agustín quietly wept. At last Magdalena went to him and knelt by his side, putting her soft arm around his neck.

Papá left the shop without a word.

"*Dios mío, pobrecito!*" said Mamá and sent Agustín to his bed. Magdalena gave him a parting pat on his hand.

They found Papá sitting in the kitchen, his head in his hands. "God forgive me," he said in Gaelic. "How do I redeem this sin?"

14

PUTTING AWAY CHILDISH THINGS

After that night, everything changed for Agustín in the Albañez household, and yet everything remained the same. Papá arranged with Father Borrero to have himeceive religious instruction. Father Borrero also spoke with Father Aquila at Espíritu Santo, who promised to make regular visits to the Tem Changó *cabildo* to ensure that all its members were instructed in the faith and received the sacraments.

One evening Mamá sat up with Agustín and, through much effort and many tears, prized out more of his story, helping him over the stumbling block of his limited Spanish. Later, she related the sad details to the rest of the family.

First Agustín had related the saga of his courtship. For weeks he had seen in the marketplace the woman who would become his wife. There were many girls there, sent by their parents to sell produce and handiwork and to look for suitors, but he saw only Adaoma. One day she noticed him as well, and gave him a smile. Then he found the courage to ask his parents if he might seek her hand in marriage. His father approached her family's elder and asked if his son might court their family's beautiful flower. The elder chose a wife from Agustín's family to act as a go-between. She would investigate Adaoma's family and determine whether a daughter from such a family would make a suitable wife for Agustín. Iboronke was a wise woman, and took her time in learning about Adaoma's family. She explored every rumor, spoke to many people, and visited them many times. Her report was reassuring: they were a hard-working family, sober in their habits, and respectful to their elders. And Adaoma was worthy of her name: she was indeed a virtuous girl, the finest flower on their tree. Agustín's family consulted the gods, and the omens, too, were favorable.

Then began the prescribed six months of visits by Agustín and his uncle to Adaoma's family. After many lengthy marks of respect, he was allowed to meet with her under his uncle's watchful eye. For the first few visits, only he was allowed to speak. He told of his great love for her, her beauty, and of his diligence as a farmer. She smiled often, and each time his heart melted within him. Finally she, too, was allowed to speak, and they smiled and laughed at every meeting. He could no longer recall her words, for they were not of importance – only the gazes that they exchanged in the twilight. Finally, the elders of his family visited Adaoma's family to request that the couple be engaged to marry. The elder of her family, surrounded by the other relatives, pronounced his approval. In truth, the outcome was understood and expected, yet still his heart had fluttered anxiously as he awaited the return of the elders. Later, his family brought the required gifts to her family that would bless their future. He barely remembered the marriage celebration that followed in time. He only remembered the joy that he felt when at last he took his beloved in his arms. First came their son, Banjoko, and then, three years later, a daughter, Yejide.

All his family loved Adaoma. His younger half-brother, Ige, often expressed his admiration of her, and Agustín glowed with pride in his wife. Ige's mother, Kehinde, would often ask her son, "Why can you not find a worthy girl such as Adaoma?" and yet Ige remained stubbornly single, to the astonishment of the family, the sorrow of his mother, and the derision of his friends. Then came the day when Agustín and Ige were sent to trade in a much larger town, several days travel from their home. They conducted their business and settled down for the night, planning to leave for home in the morning. During the night, Agustín awoke in confusion and then terror to find himself bound by strange men. He learned that he had been sold to the men by Ige, who had already disappeared in the dark with his blood money. Over the next several weeks, Agustín was transported over many miles and finally sold to *blanco* men on a ship. His sufferings on that ship were great, but none so great as the pain in his heart at the loss of Adaoma and their children. He imagined how his father would weep, his aunts and uncles mourn, and his elders say prayers to the gods. And then they would assign his wife to another member of the family, and he knew with every bitter fiber of his being that her new husband would be the malignant Ige. It was Ige who would now embrace his wife, Ige who would teach his son to be a man, who would help choose a husband for his daughter.

Mamá wept as she related the details to the rest of the family. Magdalena hid her face in her arms. And Papá, a glass of *aguardiente* in his hand, took refuge in the shop. Mamá never introduced the subject again, nor did Agustín himself mention it. Never again was there talk of selling Agustín.

Papá's demeanor towards him, which had always been scrupulously fair, remained unchanged. He made a point, though, of explaining to Agustín that in seven years he would be eligible for the *coartación*. He could work for himself in his free time and earn his own money, even save it to buy his freedom. In the meantime, however, Papá would allow him to begin working and saving informally for the day when he became eligible. He began to set the day's tasks for him, and allow him to pursue his own interests after they were completed. In private, however, he spoke to Mamá of granting Agustín his freedom now.

"You cannot restore what has been taken from him. A piece of paper would change nothing," Mamá dissented. "Where would he go but here? In seven years he will be able to buy his freedom in any case. And of course, if he wished to marry, we would have to arrange that. In the meantime, you need him. If he were free, perhaps he would leave, he might follow the others to the *Real Arsenal*."

Papá sighed his assent and took another pull from his glass of *aguardiente*.

Agustín took full advantage of his new arrangements. He completed all of his tasks quickly and well, and then disappeared to places unknown. They learned from Father Borrero that Agustín had made him his banker and entrusted him with his savings, and that his little sum was growing weekly. Papá was pleased with his newfound industriousness.

Mamá made no more disparaging remarks about "those *bozales*." Magdalena would smile at him and ask after his welfare. Agustín rewarded her attentions by carving her little figures from scraps of wood from the shop, which Mamá would show to Father Borrero to ensure that they were not the heathen mummery of which Papá warned them. The priest assured her that they were harmless trinkets and that Agustín was progressing well with his studies. He would soon be ready for baptism.

Agustín continued to dog José with his attentions and call him "*niño.*" How could he know Agustín's story and continue to resent the man's clumsy effort to fill the hole in his fatherly heart? Yet he did. Papá and Agustín seemed even closer now, and José was jealous of his place in the shop and in his papá's trust. At night he would examine his conscience and ask himself why could he not master his envious heart? Well, it was a reliable subject for his weekly confession, and freed him from the necessity of digging deeper into the darkness of his soul. So he told himself as he dutifully repeated the Paternosters he earned for penance.

Sometimes, though, he lay awake at night in his cot, imagining the pain of losing family, friends, and country. He remembered what Abuelita had said about his ancestor Achukwo, that Africa was far, far away and that he could never return or even send a letter there. He knew that Agustín would never see or hear from his own family again, would never again walk the fields of his native home. He tried to imagine what it would be like to never see Papá, Mamá, or Magdalena again, to know he could not see the faces of Abuelo and Abuelita and all his aunts and uncles and cousins, to never walk the streets of Havana or Matanzas. These people and places made up his warp and woof, and to lose them would be to lose the foundation of his being.

When Tío Policarpo and Tío Gaspar made port in Havana, they always stayed with the Albañez family. Papá and Mamá enjoyed the quiet and steady presence of Policarpo, but the children relished the arrival of Tío Gaspar. It was a Saturday in late January when his perpetually whiskered face, a face that always reminded José of a cat, appeared in the doorway as they were about to sit down for their midday dinner.

"*Hola*, Santa Fausta!" cried Tío Gaspar, for he had nicknames for everyone. "And how is my *polluela*, my favorite little chick?" he queried as he chucked his niece under the chin.

The kitchen was filled with sunlight and all shadows were banished as Tío Gaspar regaled them through dinner with funny stories of people in Matanzas. Gonzalo had serenaded a pretty young miss outside her window until her mother had pelted him with his own fruit. Jacinto and his bride had had their first fight when he discovered that his demure young wife had smoked the last of his cigars. The young couple had named their new baby Alejandro, and Tía Beatriz was in their home three times a day to check on his welfare and tickle his tiny toes.

Finally, he pushed his chair back from the table and sighed with contentment, having swallowed his last mouthful of sweet potato, washed down with well-watered wine. Then, reconsidering, he helped himself to a slice of pineapple from a plate Magdalena had brought to the table.

"I must get back to the *Penélope*," he said, finishing off the pineapple with a smack of his lips. "The casks do not discharge themselves."

Before he left, he turned to Papá. "So, Capitán Rojo, I am taking Rafael to the cockfights tomorrow. Maybe the young scholar would like to get away from his books for a few hours and see the entertainment. What do you say, Sabio?" he asked, looking at José.

"What will Nicolaza think?" chided Mamá.

"She will think nothing if you do not tell her," replied Tío Gaspar, blowing her a kiss.

José looked hopefully at Papá. He had never seen a cockfight, although they took place weekly in every city and town on the island of Cuba. "Please, Papá?"

"I do not know which is more foolish, the destruction of perfectly good poultry in such sport, or the money thrown away on wagers. I have seen enough bloodshed for a lifetime, but if the lad wishes to go, I will permit it. See for yourself, José, how foolishly men spend their hard-earned pesos."

So it was agreed. Tomorrow José and Rafael would accompany Tío Gaspar to the cockpit.

T ío Gaspar and José rose from their siesta and were soon turning the corner to collect Rafael from the residence of the Morejón family.

"Eh, Toro, are you ready to go?" Tío Gaspar asked Rafael as they entered the kitchen. "And you, Capitán Preso, it is not too late to throw in your lot with us."

Señor Morejón began to rise from his chair, but Señora Morejón fixed him with her gaze. "Aurelio is struggling with his arithmetic and needs help, and you have promised to mend that broken chair."

Señor Morejón sank back into his seat.

The streets of Havana were quieter without the carts of farmers bringing goods in from the countryside. Well-dressed gentleman strolled to afternoon diversions, and occasional *volantes* rushed ladies in veils to social calls, leaving a cloud of dust as they passed. Others, dressed in cheaper but gaudier attire, were, like them, on their way to less uplifting destinations. Many small shops were open, their awnings out and their wares displayed on tables outside to tempt passers-by.

They passed through the Gates of Monserrate at the end of the Calle Sumidoro, one of several breaks in the thick grey stone walls that protected Havana from potential invaders. At 9 o'clock at night a gun at the fortress of La Cabaña at the mouth of the harbor fired to signal the closing of the gates and all movement into the city ended until morning. During the day, however, the gates were open, allowing Habaneros to visit the city's suburbs and its outer denizens to flow in and sample of its delights. José gazed upon the great walls and thought about how safe they all were, nestled in the great city, embraced by the powerful arms of His Most Catholic Majesty's forces, on land and at sea.

Tío Gaspar led them through narrow streets and around corners until they came to the great cockpit. The building rose above the surrounding houses. Crowds were gathered around the adjoining pens, where the cockfighters displayed their gamebirds. Occasionally one would take the bird out, and holding it underneath the breast with one arm and cradling the neck with the other, to avoid its savage beak and claws, he would boast of the cock's prowess in previous matches and point out his superior features. Tío Gaspar, followed by the boys, waded into the crowd to make his assessment of each gamecock before the fights began.

The first man was showing off a bird he called "Pepito," a solid gamecock with dirty white feathers, bald in patches. One eye was missing.

"Pepito has won eight matches!" boasted his owner, who looked as battered as his bird.

Tío Gaspar admired Pepito. "See how straight his legs are!" he observed. Pepito tried to stretch out his long neck and peck at him. "And he is game!"

They moved on, examining bird after bird. Tío Gaspar asked after their histories, and had a comment on each one.

"See how low the black's spurs are," he noted of one. "He will be a good slasher."

"That one is too fat," he said about a sturdy cock with mottled black and white feathers. "He will be slow and lazy."

At last they came to a tall gamecock that stood out from the others. While the heads of the other birds had been plucked bald, this one sported a rich mane of golden plumes that shone against the deep red of his saddle feathers. The black stub that remained of his tail feathers flashed iridescent in the sunlight as he strutted proudly in the dust.

"See how handsome he is! He struts like a winner! El Conde has won two matches already!" proclaimed his owner loudly.

Tío Gaspar eyed him skeptically. "Perhaps he was fighting brood hens," he whispered loudly to the boys.

"No one is asking you to bet on my bird!" retorted the man angrily.

"I do not think even he will bet on El Conde," commented Tío Gaspar as they walked away. He paid the entrance fee and they entered the shadows of the cockpit.

They took their places in the second of the three arcaded tiers of seats. Below them they could see the round cockpit with its low wooden walls surrounding a dirt floor scattered with sawdust. José gazed about at the variety of people who had come to see the sport. There were sailors from the docks, notable for their rolling gaits, who had been paid off from their ship and were hoping to multiply their earnings, or enjoy the losing of them. There were other rough men, of all colors, jostling for seats. There were women, too, in bright skirts and kerchieves, chattering as they waited for the first match to begin. In the first tier, the seats with the best view, there were *blanco* gentleman in coats adorned with silver buttons, and *pardo* men whose coats bore pewter buttons. José observed one gentleman take a pinch of snuff and sneeze genteelly into a lawn handkerchief. There were even a few ladies, accompanied by their husbands, their faces hidden demurely behind fluttering fans.

"Look!" said Raphael. "That man in the blue coat, with the *parda* woman. That is Señor Cordero, Catiline's father."

José looked, and saw that the gentleman was paying many attentions to his female companion, helping her find a comfortable seat and settle herself. A young boy, also *pardo*, stood next to her and Señor Cordero took him on his knees and pointed to something in the pit as he whispered in his ear.

"Who is the woman?" José asked, for he knew that Miguel was not a *pardo*.

"That is his mistress, and the child is his son. They say that Señor Cordero and his wife are on the coldest of terms. He ignores his legitimate children and gives all his affection to his *pardo* family. That child is hers. He is in the lower school at San Ignacio."

How sad to be virtually estranged from one's father. He remembered that Señor Cordero had not attended the star-gazing evening. Who provided Miguel with approbation, with advice, who taught him what was expected of a man? Then he was distracted by the sight of Father Aquila in the crowd on the third tier, laughing and gesturing with men who undoubtedly belonged to his parish of Espíritu Santo in the dockside district of Campeche.

Tío Gaspar gave each boy a half *real* coin. "You may each wager on a match. If you win, you will return the coin to me and keep the winnings."

"And if I lose?" asked Rafael.

"Well, we will figure that out later," said Tío Gaspar with a wink.

José clutched his small silver coin in his hand. It had been crudely stamped in Bolivia with the coat of arms of King Carlos III, but it was of silver and held value, despite its crude appearance. His heart beat faster now, as he estimated his chances.

The crowd waited as the pitmaster weighed each bird and assigned matches between cocks of comparable size. At last he announced that the first match was to be between the black slasher and the fat, speckled bird. Immediately, men and women began shouting and gesticulating, making bets on the winner. Neither José nor Rafael made a wager, waiting to understand the sport better.

Tío Gaspar bet one silver *dollar* on the black, accepting odds of three to one in favor of his bird from a fat man sweating in a dirty white cotton shirt. "Like favors like," Tío Gaspar whispered. "The fat bird will lose."

The boys watched enthralled as the battle ritual began.

"They have agreed to short heels," explained Tío Gaspar. "See how they are attaching the gaffs, the sharp metal blades, to their legs? They use a leather thong to tie them on the stump where their spurs once were." It was true, the long curved claws every male developed on his legs were missing.

"Why don't they look like our rooster at home?" asked José. "Where are their wattles? And their neck feathers?"

"Their owners cut off the combs, wattles and ears to prepare them to fight," Tío Gaspar continued. "Otherwise the other bird would sink his beak into them and tear them away. They cut off their tails, and pluck all the feathers from their necks. Then everyday they rub the neck with *aguardiente* to toughen it up so they feel no pain there. El Conde's owner will be sorry that he did not do so."

They saw the owner of the fat bird inhale a great lungful of cigar smoke and blow it in his bird's face. "The smoke will make the cock angry and more combative," said Tío Gaspar. "It is unlikely to help that overfed creature, though."

On command, the two owners, cradling their birds in their arms, presented them, bill to bill. A few pecks were exchanged, and the men pulled them back. They did this two more times, until the cocks were angry and eager to fight.

Placing the birds on the floor of the pit, the handlers held the tails of the straining birds until they heard the pitmaster call "Pit!" and they released the cocks. The black arose in a flurry of feathers and the fat bird spread his own wings and left the ground, the two crashing in mid-air. They fell to the ground, righted themselves, and circled, each seeking advantage. First one lunged, then the other, striking with beaks and claws. Both birds were marked with blood now, and yet still each sought to savage the other. The ringing of a church bell announced that the battle had been going on for over an hour, and yet the birds seemed untiring. Suddenly the black struck the fat bird, seizing him with his claws and slashing with his steel blade. The blade stuck in the fat bird's wing and the two flailed helplessly, locked together.

"Handle!" cried the pitmaster, and the two owners disentangled the cocks. They took their birds aside to rest for a minute. A red patch began to spread on the breast of the fat bird.

Again the owners held the two birds by their tail stubs, then, with a whirr of wings the fat bird struck the black. The crowd rose to its feet. Tío Gaspar looked nervous.

The fat bird had sunk his claws into the black. He shuffled his feet on his opponent's back, pounding and dominating him with every blow of his sharp toes, as the ever-weakening bird sank to the ground. Unmoving, the black lay there, feathers torn and bloodied, until his owner removed his body. The fat one strutted and gave a crow of victory.

"That fat one has game!" admitted Tío Gaspar ruefully as he paid off the sweaty man. "You know how to pick a winner."

"That bird belongs to my cousin," replied the other. "His sire was a great champion."

José felt a sense of excitement when he heard that the next match would be between Pepito and El Conde.

"I am betting my half *real* on Pepito," Rafael announced decisively.

"I will bet on El Conde," replied José quickly.

The two friends agreed, and shook on it. He could see El Conde down in the pit, strutting about like a general, and José was feeling confident in his choice.

The battle began like the other. On the command to "Bill!" the two birds pecked angrily at each other. José admired the noble lines of El Conde's golden neck as he craned to reach the bedraggled Pepito. His excitement rose as he saw his favorite's red wings rise as he strained forward to reach his opponent while they awaited the command to fight.

And with that word "Pit!" they were released. Shouts arose from the crowd. José and Rafael rose to their feet, crying out with the rest. The two birds flapped their wings and rose in the air, each trying to find advantage. Pepito struck first, trying to slash El Conde's neck, but the handsome bird flew at him and landed a blade in Pepito's breast. José cheered.

"Handle!" cried the pitmaster, and the two cocks were separated.

"He is more game than I expected," Tío Gaspar remarked.

Again the mad fluttering of wings as the birds circled and struck, again and again, Pepito bloodied but undeterred. José felt faint, whether from anxiety for his favorite, or the powerful stench of cigars that wafted through the seats, he did not know. He clenched his fist tight. Then it was Pepito who struck El Conde a blow deep in his breast.

"Handle!" came the cry.

José could see El Conde's handler rubbing the bird's chest, warming his head in his own mouth, and spitting down his beak, as if to infuse the bird with his own life force.

Once again the cocks were released. Pepito propelled himself at El Conde, who turned the stub of his black tail to him and fled, looking for an escape from the pit. He cowered by the pit wall as the white bird fell upon him, claws and blades tearing at the long, beautiful neck. Soon El Conde's handsome body lay oozing blood in the sawdust of the pit, and Pepito strutted back and forth, savoring his triumph. El Conde's owner picked up his bird's lifeless body, still beautiful in its plumage, and cradled it in his arms. As he did so, the gamecock's blood spread in a great stain across his shirt and streaks of it appeared on his face.

José felt sick in the pit of his stomach. He sat down, silent, while Rafael and Tío Gaspar continued to cheer the following battles. The shouting and cries enveloped him, but all he could think of was the broken, bloody body of El Conde.

Afterwards, José gave his coin to Rafael, who in turn gave it to Tío Gaspar.

He was quiet on the walk home, until at last he exclaimed, "It was a shame to see so many beautiful gamecocks killed. It is a cruel death." He was now ashamed that at first he had cheered on the sport.

"It is the way of the world," observed Rafael. "The strong defeat the weak. The Greeks defeated the Trojans, the Romans the Carthaginians, the Barbarians the Romans, and so it has always gone."

"Eh, Sabio, the cocks are born to fight. It is their destiny. Put two roosters together and there will be a fight. We are simply onlookers," argued Tío Gaspar.

"It is a shame," José repeated stubbornly. "To see such a beautiful creature die so ignominious a death."

"Listen, Sabio, don't put your faith in beautiful things, neither birds nor women. Find the one with game and put your money on that one," advised his uncle.

José wondered if that was the reason Tío Gaspar had chosen Tía Nicolaza. Did she have game? He thought of the deep lines in her face, worn there by years of worry for her family.

When they arrived home, Tío Gaspar said, "You still owe me a half *real*, José."

"You did not encourage him to gamble, did you?" asked Papá in annoyance.

"I lent each of them a half *real*, and they made a bet. José chose to wager it on a showy bird that lacked pluck, and lost it," shrugged Tío Gaspar. "He can work off the debt by spending next Saturday cleaning the hold of the *Penélope*."

"That seems more than fair," agreed Papá, laughing. "You are more clever than you look, Gaspar. No matter which way the fight went, you gained a helper. While they gambled, you had a certain win. Still, I believe that you are paying too much for labor."

"Do not fret, I will get my money's worth," replied Tío Gaspar.

"But Rafael gets the winnings, and I get the work!" cried José in protest.

"You have not come out a loser, either, for you have learned a valuable lesson about the folly of gambling," replied Papá.

That night Papá came in to bid him good night.

"You are right, Papá, so many beautiful birds killed for no reason," José said, struggling to stay awake one moment longer.

"It is the same with men. We are but so many birds subject to the will of kings and nobles," Papá observed bitterly as José's eyes closed for the night.

The following Saturday José spent the rest of the afternoon swabbing out the hold, now emptied of Tío Gaspar's cargo of tobacco leaf. Under the supervision of Ventura, one of the *Penélope*'s crew, he swept out the tobacco dust, scrubbed away the accumulated filth of more than one voyage, and flushed out the fetid water in the bilge. Then he finished by rinsing it all out with strong vinegar. Ventura sat comfortably on the deck, splicing a line, and occasionally poked his head through the hatch to provide advice, pointing out places that did not yet meet his standards. José arrived home just as the sun disappeared behind the roofs of the houses, tired, ravenous, and aching in every muscle. After supper he collapsed exhausted into his cot.

There was great excitement in the *colegio* as Easter approached. Not only because of the long holiday, and the various masses in which the students would participate as altar boys and choristers, but because of the public declamation to take place during Lent. All the boys in the upper classes were preparing essays, and would read their works in the Plazuela de Ciénagas. Family and friends were certain to be present, but anyone might attend.

Each student would write on a topic of his own choosing, with Father Navarette advising them. José labored mightily on his, in between his other lessons, and spent dusty hours in the small school library after class. He wished his parents to be proud of him. It would be nice, as well, to catch an admiring glance from Marianela.

José was so wrapped up in this task that he paid little attention to Tío Domingo's most recent visit. As was his custom, Tío Domingo spent his nights at the Morejón home but sometimes took his meals with the Albañez family. During this visit he was up late, speaking in low tones with Papá. José heard only the murmur of their voices until, bleary-eyed, he fell asleep in his cot as the guns of la Cabaña boomed out over the city.

One evening after a light supper, Papá sat him down to talk.

"What is it, Papá?" asked José, noting the somber look on his father's face. Perhaps Mamá was sick again?

"It is time, José," replied his father.

"Time? For what is it time, Papá?" José asked, more frightened now.

"Time to go to sea with Donnie. You have sprouted up over the last year and are big enough to be of some use on a ship. I must keep my promise, and so must you." Papá's voice was firm.

"But I have another year yet at the *colegio*!" protested José.

"You have learned enough. Your mother is delighted with your devotion to the church, and the mathematics and astronomy you have learned will prove of great value if you choose a life at sea."

"But I want to work with you in the shop and become a joiner!" protested José.

"You do not need Latin and Greek for that. You can calculate measurements, write up work orders, and keep the books. And you now know families from all over Havana who will gladly patronize the shop. I have already seen our work increase because of this. If you wish to become a joiner, you may, but first you must go with Donnie. He needs you now. Isidro has met with an unfortunate death. We owe Donnie everything, and a man must always honor his debts."

José knew that Tío Domingo had made the move to Havana possible and kept the shop afloat after Gonzalo's injury. He knew, too, from his father's tone that the decision had been made and that he must obey. He made even greater exertions over his speech. He would not return to school after the Easter holiday, and this speech would be his swan song. He intended to leave them with a magnificent display of oratory.

T he speeches completed, each student submitted a fair copy to Father Navarette. They would then deliver them to the class on Saturday as practice before the declamation in the *plazuela* on the morrow.

Diego was eager to be the first, and Father Navarette, knowing he would set a good standard, motioned him to begin. With passion and sincerity, he spoke on the topic "There is no salvation outside of the Roman Church."

"Very sound," said Father Navarette, nodding with satisfaction. "If you indeed choose to take a vocation, you will do well."

Diego glowed, for his greatest wish was to become a priest.

Mauricio now wished to speak, and announced his theme as "The wisdom of Christ is the foolishness of the world," delivering his address with many gestures and dramatic pauses.

"I can think of no one better suited to speak on the topic of foolishness than you," observed Father Navarette dryly, for he had already been the victim of several of Mauricio's pranks.

Father Navarette began to call boys up to speak. Francisco's theme was "The virtue of poverty." The priest arched an eyebrow as he no doubt noted the lace on Francisco's shirt cuff, but said nothing. José's head began to nod as Pedro droned on about the importance of obedience to the Pope. He fought to keep his eyes open as Vidal described the difference between venal and mortal sins. He was almost asleep when Virgilio began upon "Monarchy as the best form of government."

Tomás then swaggered before them. He was a handsome boy and knew it, and enjoyed the attention he received for it. José's eyes snapped open as he heard Tomás begin "This is the story of the terrifying martyrdom of St. Lawrence." He related, in simple but moving sentences, how the Emperor Valerian commanded

Lawrence to bring him the wealth of the church. The saint gathered together the poor and the crippled, the beggars and the sick and brought them before the emperor. "These are the riches of the church," he announced. In anger, the emperor had Lawrence roasted alive. Tomás paused dramatically, and ended, "St. Lawrence's last defiant words were, 'Turn me over, I am not done yet!'"

The class roared in approbation. Tomás bowed and took his seat, beaming.

Father Navarette said, smiling, "There is much that is wrong with this speech grammatically and thematically. I am too delighted, however, to mind."

José pitied Catiline, who had to follow this riveting performance. Miguel spoke with a quiet intensity on St. Thomas Aquinas's belief that justice is the highest virtue, that justice is what one man owes another. José himself thought that Miguel would not recognize justice if it slapped him in the face, and he wished with all his heart that it would.

"Remember, Miguel," said Father Navarette, "that for a Christian, what we owe others is more important than what we ourselves are owed." Then he added, "And woe betide us if God ever dealt out to any of us what we truly deserved."

Antonio was called up. He walked slowly to the front of the class, head down, and José noticed that his clothes were in need of soap and a needle. Antonio stood looking straight ahead, and spoke in an almost inaudible tone. His voice become stronger as he warmed to his theme, "What is a hero?"

"A hero", concluded Antonio, "is the one who does what is necessary, whatever the risk." He bowed his head again, and returned to his seat.

Anastasio was next. His topic was "Miracles," and José thought to himself that it would be a miracle if he had anything to say, as Anastasio was more often than not seen gazing out of the window, and he often made careless mistakes in his work or left it incomplete. He began by describing the miracles in the Bible, but by the end he had wandered far afield. "Life itself is a miracle! Look at the birds, how they fly! Look at the many tiny parts of the flower! Every work of God is a miracle!" he cried excitedly, waving his arms wildly. Then, astonished by his own enthusiasm, he sat down.

Sebastián's topic was "The harmony between faith and reason." His diction was clear, his voice steady, and his gestures perfectly suited to his words. Father Navarette looked at him quizzically and said, "You speak with Ciceronian perfection, your theme is admirable, and your words most true. I only wish I were sure that you believed all that you wrote."

Now it was José's turn. He wished that Tomás had not chosen a martyr for his subject, for that was also his topic. He began with the example of St. Policarpo, who in his eighties, had been burned and stabbed for refusing to deny Christ. His stalwart example brought others to the faith. José spoke of the need to do what was right, no matter the cost, to take the difficult path rather than the easy one. He concluded by cautioning his audience that "we must all be ready to accept martyrdom should it find us, and every day we must prepare ourselves for such a fate."

"Commendable sentiments. I wonder if you perhaps make martyrdom sound too easy. Nonetheless, your grammar is perfect and your arguments flow well," commented Father Navarette.

José breathed a sigh of relief.

At last it was Rafael's turn. He strode to the front and launched into a speech on patriotism. He spoke in bold tones of love for Spain, for Cuba, for Havana, and for King Carlos. He called upon all patriots to defend His Most Catholic Majesty and the Spanish empire against its enemies, most especially those dreaded heretics, the English. "*Anglia delenda est!* England must be destroyed!" he concluded.

The whole class rose and cheered. "What you lack in style you make up for in passion," said Father Navarette. "If ever the navy seeks a recruiting officer, I shall give them your name."

The class filed out to go home, giddy with excitement about the next day's declamation.

"Hey, Anastasio, show me a miracle!" teased Vidal, giving Anastasio a shove.

"Here is a miracle for you," intervened Rafael. "It is a miracle that I have not punched your fat face," and he shoved Vidal back.

How he would miss this, thought José.

José was restless with anticipation during Mass that Sunday, eager for success and yet fearful of failure. He barely tasted his rice and beans, and tossed restlessly during the siesta. Papá, Mamá, and Magdalena accompanied him to the *plazuela*. Even Agustín gave up his activities at the *cabildo* to join them. When they arrived, José joined the boys chattering with excitement around Father Navarette. The day was perfect, the sky a bright blue, while a mild breeze swept away the worst of the city's stench. The *plazuela* was only slightly muddy, as it was not yet the rainy season, which so often turned the area into a small lake. In years past José had attended declamations by the older classes, but now it was his turn. He scanned the crowd and saw his family. He saw the Morejón family, too. Señora Morejón was struggling to keep her young children in order. Marianela lifted her eyes to gaze at the boys, and José felt as if she were looking directly at him.

Each boy spoke in turn, first in Latin, then giving a translation into Spanish. Father Navarette led off with Anastasio's animated speech. As the last words, "Every work of God is a miracle!" rang out over the *plazuela*, ragged cheers broke out through the crowd, and Anastasio smiled, flushed with elation. So it went boy after boy. Small children became restless, and mothers could be seen chasing them through the crowd.

When José's turn came to speak, he stood dry-mouthed, afraid he would forget all his carefully chosen words. He could not look at the crowd, but stared beyond them. Then the words came, just as he had practiced them, in careful, measured tones. The cheers were few, for his theme was not one that made the blood rise, and the listeners were growing fatigued. He looked out at Papá and Mamá. Papá was nodding in approbation, and Mamá was wiping her eyes with the corner of her kerchief. He saw Marianela lift up her dark eyes and smile at him. He had succeeded. He could leave the *colegio*, head held high.

The declamation concluded with Rafael's fiery exhortation to patriotism. Passers-by stopped to listen, restless children were transfixed by the power of his voice, and the assembled relatives stood fixed in place, all eyes upon him as he spoke. After his last rousing cry of "England must be destroyed!" a great cheer swept across the *plazuela*, with cries of "Bravo, young man!" José could see Señora Morejón standing ramrod straight among the crowd. She did not lower her dignity with a smile or a cheer. Instead, she glowed like a hot coal with pride in her eldest son.

The boys left, one by one, in the company of their proud families. Miguel was accompanied only by his mother, a tall, spare, unsmiling woman.

Catiline fell behind for a moment to spit words at José. "The *colegio* will be better without such *pardo* trash as you. You can go chop wood with your father."

Anger flared through every fiber of José's being. Just when he had reconciled himself to leaving the school, Miguel's words exposed the wound again. What was worse he had insulted Papá, and truth be told, Mamá as well. Such insults could not stand.

"At least I have a father," he spat back. Even before the words left his mouth he regretted them, and he rued them even more as he saw pain contort Miguel's face. The words could never be recalled, however, and now they had penetrated his enemy's soul like poisoned splinters.

José heard someone gasp behind him, and then saw Mamá's sorrowful face.

"Oh, José, how could you?" she asked. Her words cut through José like a cold blade, and all the joy of the day was gone.

15

A VENTURE

José regarded the upcoming voyage with resignation. His elders had long conspired to force him on this journey, and so he would go for the promised year. He would never embrace this life, however, and he already knew what his decision would be when the year was over. He would join Papá in the shop Zum-Zum. Mamá and Papá set about acquiring the necessary rig, purchased with an advance on his meager pay of a ship's boy.

"I shall have nothing left when we are done!" he protested as Mamá laid out several pesos for heavy linen fabric for his new shirts.

"So says every boy going to sea for the first time," commented Papá.

Mamá sewed up the shirts for him, and she and Magdalena made him several pairs of thick woolen stockings. This was his sister's first effort at knitting, and it showed, but Mamá made José thank her as if the stockings had been made of spun gold. José was glad of his dissembling, for Magdalena glowed with pleasure at his words.

José was also fitted out with two pairs of heavy loose-legged slops of duck to cover his breeches, and a broad canvas hat, daubed with black paint to protect him from sun and rain. A sturdy blue jacket with wooden buttons lay in his new chest, ready for days when brisk night winds from the Atlantic chilled the air. Papá had lovingly built the chest of cedar, and Agustín had burned the initials "JAV" into the lid after Papá had traced them out for him. A red kerchief tied jauntily around his neck completed his gear.

His frame of mind improved considerably when Papá bought him a clasp knife, with a long, sharp blade in a hard wooden handle. With such a knife he felt himself a real man, ready to take on the world.

"Every seaman must have his knife," said Papá. "It will prove your best friend in many a task."

José donned his new kit to show Mamá and Magdalena.

"Do not swagger quite so much," said Papá, one eyebrow arched. "You might trip and hurt yourself."

While he awaited the return of the *Orfeo*, José was put to work assisting Rafael's father in his shop so that he would better understand trade. Although Señor Morejón called it his shop, it more closely resembled a warehouse. Casks of olive oil and of flour were piled high along one wall, plainly visible as one entered. Piled behind them, more discreetly, were crates of wine, of textiles, and of fine dishware gently cradled in straw. There were also bundles of fashionable clothing and millinery, and sturdier wear for purchasers of more humble means. A small box contained lace, dainty fans, and combs to hold back a woman's hair. Another crate held a fine clock nestled in sawdust, along with mirrors of divers sizes. Several held muskets and pistols. While in the other buildings in the city the long, grated windows that faced the street were open so that passers-by could see their wares, visit with the occupants, or gaze upon their flirtatious daughters, the windows of Albañez y Morejón were curtained by a fine cotton fabric that allowed some of the precious breeze through but obscured the contents of the shop from curious eyes. In one corner by the windows stood Señor Morejón's ink-stained desk, positioned to catch the light. Several large ledgers lay upon it, accompanied by an inkwell and a sharp quill. In the other corner could be found a simple table and several chairs, built of a warm mahogany that glowed when warmed by stray rays of sunshine from the window. They seemed to invite company. Above the table hung a faded engraving of a schooner, as if to advertise the reach of the company's business.

The shop was not open to the general public, but individuals known to Señor Morejón came to purchase goods or examine the selection. Sometimes they came to fetch items they had commissioned beforehand. Many shopkeepers came to procure wares for their stores, or to ask for his help in acquiring certain goods. Government officials also called upon him. Señor Morejón would serve his visitors chocolate and sit with them to discuss business and the affairs of the day. José became adept at preparing the drink to Señor Morejón's exacting taste.

"Remember, José, every sip of chocolate is an advertisement for our wares. It must be of the highest quality, a drink that will linger on the palate and in the memory, and remind the customer that there are no finer goods than those sold by Albañez y Morejón." And chocolate and cacao did seem to be popular items with customers, as were the finely made ceramic chocolate sets of Dutch manufacture.

One day a gentleman in a handsomely tailored naval uniform with gilt buttons came to call. José recognized him as Commander Ramón Castellón, the father of Mauricio. José listened to their discussions as he broke off a piece of hardened chocolate paste and added it to the water that was heating in the enameled chocolate pot on a small coal brazier.

After exchanging pleasantries, Señor Morejón gestured to his guest to take a seat. "What news of the war?" he asked. He spoke in the refined tones that he assumed in genteel company.

"You have surely heard that the French surrendered Montreal to the British in September. If they cannot dislodge the British, they will have lost Canada. If the British are able to dominate North America, in time they may cast their eyes upon Florida," said Don Ramón with the authority that came with access to inside information.

José broke a small piece from a cone of sugar and added it to the brewing chocolate. He listened intently to the conversation, trying hard to add just the right dash of cinnamon without missing a single word. He finished with a sprinkle of achiote to add a slight tang, and whisked the concoction with the wooden *molinillo* until it frothed, flecks of cinnamon winking enticingly on the foam. The two men barely noticed as he served it to them in delicate porcelain cups, so engrossed were they in their discussion.

"The English fleet harasses the French ships here in the Caribbean and grows bolder by the day. They have already taken Guadeloupe and almost gained Martinique. They surely have their eyes upon Saint-Domingue as well. How they would love to add the riches of its sugar plantations to those of Jamaica." The commander sipped his chocolate and his eyes closed in appreciation.

"But what of the French? Have they no fleet? Are they not men?" asked Señor Morejón, the foaming drink before him forgotten.

Commander Castellón took another languorous sip of chocolate. "Their fleet has slipped the British blockade at Brest. They are preoccupied, I think, with the attempt to preserve their North American empire. Their privateers, however, raid the British where they can. They have made several sorties against Jamaica and made away with some of their slaves."

Now Señor Morejón leaned forward and looked the officer in the eye. "And they harass our shipping at all turns under the pretext that we are supplying their enemy. When then, Don Ramón, do we begin to defend our interests?"

The commander leaned in and asked in a low voice, "And do you not supply the French?"

"We are a neutral nation. We may sail where we will," protested Señor Morejón, then added quickly, "As the Captain-General permits."

"The Admiralty shares your outrage, as does, I think, our king. For now we sit and watch the British and French pick each other apart. I do not think His Catholic Majesty will wish to see the British dominate the West Indies. If they vanquish the French, in time they will inevitably cast their eyes upon our own possessions. Nor do I think that the king will wish to see his Bourbon cousin humiliated in war." He finished his chocolate with a sigh of satisfaction.

Señor Morejón swirled his drink about in the cup, took a swallow, and then gazed into the depths as if hoping to find answers there. "And should we enter the war, how much danger would we face here in Havana?" he asked at last.

"Very little, I should imagine. Surely the British would prefer to add to their North American colonies by seizing Florida. It is true, they have long gazed upon Havana the way an amorous youth looks upon a voluptuous woman, but this city's virtue is too well guarded. We have been steadily adding to our fleet here, and in any case, we would spy their fleet coming before it had passed the Isla de Pinos," Don Ramón asserted. "We maintain a regular patrol of the south coast."

"Suppose, however, they came by the north?" asked Señor Morejón.

"Impossible," replied Commander Castellón, waving away the possibility. "They would have to follow the Old Bahama Channel. That would be impossible without pilots who knew the passage well. They would lose half their ships before they arrived."

Señor Morejón cocked his head and replied carefully, "Such pilots exist."

"You think like an old privateersman. We have such pilots; the British do not. I assure you as a naval man, they would never attempt it." Don Ramón rose to leave. He pulled some papers from his inside his jacket and handed them to his host. "I nearly forgot. This is the license for the *Orfeo* sloop to trade in Caracas, as well as a letter of passage should she be stopped by the *guarda costa* or the British. Not that the British show much respect for our neutrality."

"I am most grateful," replied Señor Morejón. "I will have José bring to you a token of my appreciation."

"The English would never dare to attack Havana," commented José, as soon as the commander had departed. "Our fleet and our soldiers would make them pay dearly for their insolence. So, too, would our militia," he added, remembering that Señor Morejón served in the *pardo* militia. There was also a *blanco* militia, in which many of the fathers of his friends served, and even a *moreno* militia, which included free members of the *cabildo* to which Agustín belonged.

Señor Morejón sighed ruefully, and replied, now speaking once again in his accustomed Havana vernacular, "Have you ever seen our militia drill?"

Within the hour José found himself delivering a neatly wrapped package of processed chocolate to the home of Commander Castellón, located near the customs building. When he returned he found Señor Morejón at his desk, his quill dancing about as he entered figures in a ledger.

"Señor Morejón," he inquired. "Why is Tío Domingo now trading with Caracas? I thought..."

"Shhh!" replied the merchant, putting his finger to his lips. "The authorities have few objections to trade with other Spanish colonies. And if other ports along the way prove more profitable? They do not need to know." With a wink, he returned to his accounts.

One day Señor Morejón showed José the small warehouse he leased on the ground floor of a great house near the wharves for goods, such as hides, tallow, and salt beef, of a thoroughly respectable provenance. The sloops of Albañez y Morejón cruised the coasts of Cuba and brought back the products of the island's agriculture for sale in Havana or shipment aboard vessels sailing to Cádiz in Spain. When the crown-authorized monopolies sometimes failed to purchase some of these goods, however, Albañez y Morejón made sure that they found buyers elsewhere. Register vessels from Spain – those with licenses to trade with the colonies – brought goods in high demand, foodstuffs and manufactures, from both Spain and other European countries, but it was seldom that these goods made their way from Havana to settlements such as Trinidad on the southern coast. Here too, Albañez y Morejón offered its services.

Sometimes Señor Morejón took José along as he visited the shops along the Calle de Mercaderes. He examined the wares arrayed on small tables outside the shops, and went in to survey the goods bursting from crates and shelves. He inquired about the prices of everything, fingered textiles, judged the lightness of the porcelain, and breathed in the aroma of the foodstuffs. No detail escaped his eye, and every merchant had a friendly greeting for him.

Outside the shop Luna he whispered to José: "That lace is coarse yet it is priced higher than the Belgian lace in the shop Pegaso. I think I could fob off almost anything on Señor Prieto and still get a good price."

Señor Morejón had a keen eye for fashion, as well. "Notice that lady outside in the *volante*, examining the green silk? Dressed in the pale blue robe *a la Anglois*?

I assure you, every lady in Havana will soon wish to be so attired. Albañez y Morejón will make sure that they are."

Señor Morejón also introduced José to his bookkeeping system. He opened one of the great ledgers and taught him to enter the many transactions conducted by Morejón y Albañez, with dates and prices, calculating profit for each item. There was another ledger for debts, monies owed and owing, going back years. Señor Morejón showed him, too, great bundles of paper, tied up with string, containing bills of lading, receipts for customs duties, reflecting years' worth of trading in the products of Cuba – tobacco, snuff, beef, hides, tallow, onions, and wood. José found that he enjoyed tracing the movement of goods, from unseen farmers and tradesmen around the world into the holds of the company's ships and thence into the hands of eager customers. At home, he began assisting his father with the books for the shop, and received a nod of gratitude.

"What are you taking as your venture?" Señor Morejón asked him one day as José was sweeping up the shop.

José sneezed as his broom sent dust flying into the air. "The advance on my pay has all gone for clothing. Tío Domingo says that when I am paid off I will have something left for a venture on another trip."

"We must amend that! Every sailor has the right to carry some goods of his own to trade. You must not waste the opportunity. Let us say I loan you the money for a small venture, and you repay me from the profits – along with the usual interest – on your return. Shall we call it a bargain?" Señor Morejón's tone assumed assent.

"But what if I should fail to make a profit?" José asked, taken aback. He had not pictured himself bargaining like a huckster in every port. Suppose that his venture was ruined in the hold, or he was cheated by some hard-nosed merchant? "Is it not something like gambling?"

"Ah, still stung by your outing with Gaspar. You will make a profit. You have the makings of a man of trade, I have seen that already. You are worthy of the risk." And so it was settled.

José signed a marker for the loan of a princely Spanish *dollar*, and the debt was entered into the ledger. Then came the weighty decision of what goods to purchase for that sum.

"May I make a suggestion?" Señor Morejón perceived his hesitation. "Perhaps a keg of rice. They raise cattle in Trinidad and often lack for other victuals. Rice always sells there. With the profits you make in Trinidad, you can then purchase other goods to sell in Jamaica. I would suggest limes. They, too, carry well, and they are always eager for foodstuffs in Jamaica. That island is rich in sugar and poor in provisions."

Jamaica. That was the first time he heard anyone mention their destination. He felt a nervous tingle as he wondered how they would slip past the British navy, now on high alert after the French raids on their coast. Limes, he thought. I hope the English like limes.

When not helping Señor Morejón, José spent as much time as he could in the shop with Papá, learning what he could of the joiner's trade. Too soon the *Orfeo* arrived in Havana from Matanzas, where the crew had spent time with their families and carried out repairs. One day, late in Lent, Tío Domingo burst into the yellow house like a summer squall. Papá and José were in the shop with Agustín, where Papá was teaching José to use a spoke shave on wood that would one day become a spindle.

"So, José, I hope you are ready for your first sea voyage," he said, clapping José on the back. "That is the way to become a man – not cracking your skull over ancient languages all day.

"In a few years, you won't know him!" he laughed, speaking to Papá. "Soon he will be drinking and wenching with the best of them."

Behind him Mamá, who had quietly entered the shop from the patio, froze.

"I jest, Faustina, I jest. José is a good boy," he reassured her.

There was much to do before the *Orfeo* sloop could leave port. Tío Domingo put José to work helping the crew discharge the cargo. The sloop had warped up to the *Muelle de la Real Contaduría*, the dock for all ships arriving in Havana, and had been granted permission to discharge its cargo. José found himself laboring side by side with his new crewmates. They were already familiar to him from previous trips on the *Orfeo*, but then they had simply been friendly deckhands working in the background as he enjoyed the passage with his family to Matanzas. Now he was at their command. The deck was stacked with rough wooden boards harvested from the forests near Matanzas and hewn into boards by the local carpenter. All the wood on the island belonged to the crown monopoly, but Tío Domingo had licenses for his cargo. It was possible, José thought, that some of them might even have been legitimate. Using tackles affixed to the crowjack, they swayed bundles of boards into a cart waiting for them on the pier, to be stored later in the company warehouse near the wharves. Soon Señor Morejón would sell it to woodworkers throughout the city, some to joiners like Papá, and others to cabinetmakers in the more fashionable part of Havana.

Belowdecks, the hold was filled with hogsheads of snuff from Matanza's mills. After the lumber had been sent on its way, small boats towed the *Orfeo* over to the Muelle de la Factoría, dedicated to the use of the royal monopoly for tobacco. The *Factoría* contracted with Albañez y Morejón to bring the snuff to Havana. Once at the wharf, they attached a hogshead sling to each container in turn, and a great wooden crane, one of the marvels of Havana's harbor, would raise each one out of the hold and onto the quay.

They labored for the better part of a week. The sun beat down upon them and they stopped frequently for a ladle of water or to splash themselves from a bucket. Señor Morejón often came down to the wharf to supervise, indicating where the various cargo items should be directed. Vicente, the mate, however, had direct charge of the work and gave José little time to rest. He was still a young man, although he appeared a very greybeard to José's eyes. His squinting eyes darted everywhere, and his narrow lips seemed perpetually pursed as he observed their work. His tall, spare frame was as erect and unyielding as the mast before which he often stood, calling out, "Steady there!" "Watch yourself!" When José was not swift enough, he felt the sting of a rope's end. By evening of the first day his hands were already sore, his whole body ached, and he nursed an abiding hatred of Vicente.

By the end of Maundy Thursday the hold had been emptied of all but the ship's stores. José was put to work cleaning it out, while Osorio pumped out the bilge. The smell of fetid bilge water mixed with that of tobacco filled José's nostrils and he made a face.

"When the bilge is full of stagnant water, that means she does not leak much! It is a smell much to be desired," declared Osorio, smiling as he inhaled deeply.

The next day was Good Friday, and Renzo, one of the crew members, wished to see the great procession that was to take place from the church of Espíritu Santo, but Señor Morejón insisted that they begin filling the hold. "There is no better time to work when the wharves are half deserted," he said with a wink.

The work began as the first rays of dawn appeared over the harbor. Usually a vessel spent weeks in harbor, seeking out buyers for its goods and negotiating for a new cargo, but because Señor Morejón handled all these matters for Albañez y Morejón, the *Orfeo* was able to manage a quick turnaround. José helped Señor Morejón fill the cart he had hired with goods for the *Orfeo*. First went a number of large bundles of hides, tied with palm fiber. José found the bales light in comparison to the lumber, but awkward to handle. He was surprised at the sudden heft of several of them. Then followed crates, casks, and bags, filled with goods of local manufacture or imported from nearby Spanish colonies. José recognized a bolt of fabric from a Mexican workshop, and a cask of nails made in Havana.

After they had filled the cart for the final time, the driver waited while Señor Morejón added the last lines to a document on his desk. He handed it to José, then gave a second sheet to him. "This one goes only to Domingo. You understand?"

José understood very well. The first paper was the cargo manifest, with a list of goods of local provenance. José had seen them go onto the cart. The second list contained items from distant countries and colonies. He realized now the reason for the heft of some of the bales of hides. He put them both in his shirt for safekeeping.

Señor Morejón opened a small mahogany chest where he kept his writing supplies – quills, ink bottles, stationery, sealing wax, and odd bits of ribbon and string, and emptied it of its contents. Then he reached in and carefully shifted the wooden bottom until it lifted up in his hands. Under the false bottom José saw another folio volume, identical to the one on the desk.

"This cunningly made chest is the handiwork of your father," commented Señor Morejón. "He is very clever with his hands, and with numbers. It is he who taught me bookkeeping."

He opened the ledger to reveal pages of numbers and curious symbols. "It is a code of my own devising," he said.

"Here are listed all the goods that are not contained in the official accounting. And here," he added, turning to the last page of the book, "are all those individuals who have proven helpful to us and the remuneration which they have received." José saw a list of initials, accompanied by sums of differing values.

"Someday I will teach you the code," Señor Morejón said, as he began entering the new wares in the secret ledger. "And should anything ever happen to me, God forfend, Rafael has it by heart."

José was astonished that Rafael had never breathed a word of such secrets to him. He marveled at his discretion but also wondered, too, that his friend should speak so scornfully of his father's work in the shop. Señor Morejón sat at the center of the Caribbean world, managing the flow of goods across empires. He kept men employed, businesses solvent, and merchants' shops filled with wares to satisfy the needs and delight the tastes of purchasers, great and small, throughout the island. The goods of several continents passed through his hands and yet he seldom traveled more than a few blocks from his home. Some of that trade took place in direct contravention of the laws of Spain. Señor Anselmo lived a life of daring without even leaving his shop.

José climbed up next to the driver of the cart and they rattled through the streets to the wharf. He rejoiced that at last he was the one looking down upon the people in the streets, watching children, pigs, and dogs scurrying out of the way.

They spent two long days stowing the goods that Señor Morejón had acquired for them, ending their work late on Holy Saturday. José discovered that stowage was an art. On this voyage they carried pig iron from the Havana foundry, intended for the blacksmiths of Trinidad. It would go at the bottom, near the keel. They then laid down a bed of staves to keep the cargo well above the bilge. Several cases of wine were stowed in the forepeak, bung up, and braced with wooden quoins so that they could not rub against each other. Then a good number of hogsheads of cornmeal from Vera Cruz were swayed in and down into the hold, to be braced like the wine casks. Somewhere behind the hogsheads were the leather-wrapped bundles, hidden from the view of anyone entering the hold. Someone who wished to inspect the cargo would need to go to some lengths to find them there. Finally, in the wings, the crews stowed their small ventures. As he wedged a chock below one of the hogsheads, José thought he heard a rustling and saw a flash of something move under the staves. A quick glance found nothing, and he forgot about it.

The final step was to load the provisions for their voyage and two barrels of fresh water. Tío Domingo appeared, having spent the day filing paperwork with the customs office and paying the taxes. He took José into the cabin and placed a paper before him. It was the ship's articles, declaring that he, José Albañez Velázquez, would serve as a ship's boy on the *Orfeo* until she returned to Havana. He dipped the quill in ink and signed his name in careful, beautifully shaped letters such as would bring pride to his teachers. He contemplated his name with satisfaction. Albañez from Papá, Velázquez from Mamá. A name that tied him to his family and to his home. He would serve Tío Domingo for a year, and then he would return to the people who had given him that name, and he would never leave them again.

José said a quick prayer that night and collapsed into bed. His last thought before falling asleep was to wonder how many of His Catholic Majesty's laws he had broken that day. He would have much to confess tomorrow at church.

E aster Sunday was José's last glorious day of freedom in his city. Havana was on its best behavior. The sky was a bright azure, the breeze from the sea was brisk and reached even the narrow streets far from the wharves, and the air was noticeably fresher, for the slaughterhouse had been closed for several days.

The Albañez family, along with many people in their neighborhood, attended the early morning Mass at the church of Santo Cristo del Buen Viaje. The family skipped breakfast in order to take advantage of this rare occasion to take communion, and walked the two blocks south on the Calle Aguacate to the church, Mamá with her head covered piously in a shawl, and Papá in his broad-brimmed black hat. Magdalena clung to José's arm as if she were afraid to lose him forever. Outside the church stood young men dressed in their Sunday plumage, smiling and bowing as they offered amorous compliments to the young women being carefully chaperoned inside.

The church's tall, ornate, white towers seemed to welcome him across the small square and beyond them its red tile roof glowed warmly. On Easter, this most holy of days, the church was unaccustomedly crowded. Towards the front José could see a few women of good family in silk dresses, hair held tightly on their heads with tortoiseshell combs, heads draped in black lace mantillas. *Morena* companions, no doubt their slaves, lay down small carpets on which they then knelt to protect their fine dresses from the dust of the floor. The Albañez family knelt in the middle section, and José recognized many neighbors there: Señora Peña, Señor Espada, and the families of many of the shopkeepers nearby. Mamá and Señora Peña laid down cotton kerchieves to protect their own skirts. Magdalena took out a green kerchief of her own and laid it on the tiles in dutiful imitation of her mother. The men of the family were above such fopperies. Behind them José could hear the buzz of the poorer congregants, street vendors, slaves, individuals of dubious employment, and the many sailors who frequented the "church of the good voyage" to pray for safe travel. Today the Albañez family was also praying for a safe voyage for José.

The pungent odor of incense filled the air. The flames of the candles and the flowers that adorned the altar seemed to dance to the sprightly waltz played by a violinist who was performing for this special service. Later in the Mass the harmonies of the choir singing the *Agnus Dei* filled the divine space. José lifted his eyes to the dark, carved rafters that floated above the cool white walls of the church, half expecting to see angels hovering there.

Agnus Dei, qui tolis peccata mundi, miserere nobis. Have mercy upon me. He prayed that the Savior would see him, a fifteen-year-old boy on a small vessel in the sea, and keep him safe. He heard his mother whispering a prayer beside him and he prayed, too, that the Savior would keep his family safe while he was gone.

They left the cool of the church and found themselves in the heat of the city streets. The city seemed exceptionally enticing today, whether it was to provide him a merry send-off or to torment him with the thoughts of what he was leaving behind he could not say. Every Habanero's face had a smile and the bright colors of their Sunday finery seemed to glow in the sunlight. Even the pigs grunted joyously as they roamed the streets enjoying the rich leavings from the holiday preparations.

While the womenfolk cooked, Papá and José sat companionably in the shop, enjoying the breeze that swept in through the grating of the long windows and stirred the sawdust on the floor. At times Papá seemed about to speak, then faltered and sat back in his chair, looking tired.

"Donnie says that time at sea will make a man of you," he said at last. "He may be right. Just make sure you do not come home a bad man."

"Why even risk such a thing? You need me in the shop..." he began to protest, knowing all the while that it would be in vain.

Papá cut him short. "You know that I have promised Donnie. And I have Agustín to help me. I am tired of this subject." His face looked pale and strained.

The smell of *ajiaco* wafted into the shop and called them to dinner. Six weeks of Lenten fish made Mamá's dish even more satisfying, and José did not complain when she heaped his plate once and then again. They all made much of him, laughing and teasing him, and José laughed, too, but within his heart was sore. He resented the gaiety of Agustín, whose tall frame seemed ready to fill his empty space in the shop.

He awoke from a restless siesta to find Rafael and Sebastián at the door. They sprawled out in chairs that they had moved into the shade of the patio and admired his new knife, enthusiastically pounding him on the back.

"Classes are not the same without you," related Sebastián. "'Catiline and his mates have been swaggering about more than usual. They imagine they can give us a good thumping now that your departure has diminished our numbers."

"Miguel has been most insulting," added Rafael.

"What has he said?" asked José, moving restlessly in his chair and staring at his feet. He could still see Miguel's anguished face in his mind.

"He says that you slunk away like the cur that you are, knowing that you are no gentleman, and that you are in the place you belong, sweating and grunting like a dirty pig..."

"I take his meaning well enough," José cut him off.

"We should find him and give him a good beating when you return," Rafael answered. "We must not let him get by with such insults."

"Perhaps," replied José, still gazing at his shoes.

"And when you return you must tell us every moment of your adventures! Perhaps you should keep a journal, so that you do not forget a moment of it!" cried Sebastián, his eyes alight in his pale face.

"Someday I, too, will go to sea, I swear it," said Rafael, his words fierce with desire. "And I will become master of my own ship, like your uncles."

José wondered how long Rafael's enthusiasm would last after a day of discharging cargo. "But your father expects you to work in his store. He speaks of it often." One did not disobey fathers.

"I have two little brothers. They can work in his shop. And I will go to sea. I will insist on following you when I finish the *colegio*," Rafael then vowed, pounding his fist on the chair. "If a sea voyage makes a man of one, then I, too, should have a chance at it. Why should I bury myself in dusty tales of Troy and Carthage when I can see the world for myself?"

Suddenly José understood why Rafael so longed to go to sea. He had grown up surrounded by goods that spoke to him of distant lands and climes, of exotic peoples and languages. It was only natural that he should want to see them for himself.

"Hear, hear!" cried Sebastián. "Someday, I, too, will see the world!"

Well, thought José to himself, perhaps I will not see the world, but soon, at least, I will see Trinidad.

16

THROUGH THE TRANSOM

The wind was favorable, and Tío Domingo announced that they would cast off on the ebb tide that afternoon. José was awash in nervous excitement as he sat down for his last dinner with his family before joining the *Orfeo*. José wanted to savor every mouthful of his mother's rice and beans, but they were dry in his mouth and he could barely swallow.

His uncle was ebullient. "Now you will do a man's work, José!" he kept repeating. "You will not be some whey-faced scribe, poring over dry old tomes."

Mamá looked down at her plate, still half full, and pushed it away. "If only you did not carry such risky cargoes, Domingo," she said.

"Do not concern yourself about that," Tío Domingo replied. "Most of my cargoes are under license. Between droughts and hurricanes, the Captain-General must allow some foreign trade or this island would starve. Cuba needs flour and the North Americans have it in abundance."

"Flour is not the only thing you carry, though," Papá intervened. "The king wants trade in contraband stopped and any official who prosecutes it with vigor is likely to see his career prosper. One day your luck will run out. They will confiscate everything you own and exile you to Florida, or worse, sentence you to years of hard labor building fortifications in some fever swamp."

"I do not wish such a fate for José," said Mamá.

"I assure you. I have the best of connections. I provide particular favors for certain officials, and they would not wish to lose my services." Tío Domingo's voice grew louder. "This system of licenses, register ships, and eternal harassment is breaking down. I can feel it cracking about me. One day, His Most High and Mighty Catholic Majesty will see sense and let us trade as we will, and then this island will truly prosper. And when that day comes, Albañez y Morejón will be ready to seize the day."

"Let us hope that when that day comes it does not find you in chains," said Papá dryly.

During the siesta José simply stared at the curtains about his cot and waited for the time to pass. It seemed that Tío Domingo could not sleep, either, for soon he was at the door to rouse the rest of the family from their rest.

Mamá had wanted to go to the wharf to see them off, but Papá forbade it. "The *barrio* de Campeche is full of sailors, drinking and whoring away their silver until their ships depart for Cádiz. I would not have you subjected to their insults and indecencies. We will make our farewells here."

Papá was grave. "Do your duty," he said. "Do not make us ashamed of your conduct."

Mamá kissed him and said, "Remember, *mi hijo*, all that you have learned in Father Borrero's school. Do not forget your prayers." She held him close and whispered in his ear, "Be a man like Papá, do not follow the example of Domingo." Standing back, she added, "Remember that God sees all that you do, even at sea."

She kissed him once more on the forehead, softly. "He sees you in the ports, as well."

Agustín shook his hand and pressed something into it. José shoved it inside his jacket.

Magdalena reached up and kissed him on the cheek. "The chickens will miss you!" she said, then added, "And so will I." José made a face, but realized with a pang that he would miss her, too. "Mind the sharks!" she called out through the grated window of the shop as she watched them depart. As her voice faded into the noise of the street, José heard one last warning, "Beware the French and the English heretic dogs!"

José's sea chest was already aboard. He and Tío Domingo now pushed their way through the crowds of sailors who had just risen for the first time that day after another long night of revelry, as if yesterday had not been Easter. José heard many languages that were not Spanish. He knew that Spain, like sea powers throughout the Atlantic world, wished that its sailors be native sons, but like the rest, it was obliged to hire the willing.

They stopped at the customs office where Tío Domingo presented his bill of lading, license, crew manifest, and other papers. The customs official pored over the documents, shuffled them about, but made no comment. At last he signed and sealed yet another paper giving the *Orfeo*, under the command of master Don Domingo Albañez, clearance to leave port. José realized that he hadn't looked at the object that Agustín had pressed into his hand. He took it out of his jacket. It was a small carving of a lamb, undoubtedly of Agustín's making. He felt a burst of resentment. Was he a child? He did not need a toy to remind him that it was Agustín who would be filling his place beside Papá in the shop. He tossed it off the wharf and into the water, where it bobbed about in stagnant green water alongside a dead fish and a rotting orange peel.

A *guadaño* took them out to the *Orfeo*, now located in the center of the harbor once loading had been completed. Accompanying them was a large crate of chickens, squawking and flapping their wings as their feathers felt the spray from the oars. They were destined to be dinner for the voyage and no doubt resented it.

As the rowers made for the sloop, the helmsman observed, "Seldom have I seen so many ships of war in this harbor," he commented. "They mean to warn off the English should they think to trifle with Spain, once England has done with the French."

It was true. There were eighteen frigates, ships-of-the line, and other warships in the harbor, crowded in among the usual merchant vessels.

"If they want to frighten the British," Tío Domingo replied, "they might wish to bend sails and complete their rigging." It was also true that too many of these vessels rode at anchor under bare poles, their rigging flapping limp and tattered in the breeze.

The long, cigar-shaped *guadaño* boat, propelled by its six banks of rowers, approached the *Orfeo*. José sat under the awning in the stern with Tío Domingo, and the water churned by the oars echoed the disturbance in his stomach. He had never spent a night away from his family, and now he would spend months at sea with only Tío Domingo and the other men.

At last they were at the side of the *Orfeo*. From a distance she seemed tiny among the ships-of-war and merchantmen, but now that he was bobbing in the *guadaño* at her waterline and looking up at her the 59-ton vessel seemed immense. Tío Domingo was proud of every inch of her and described her dimensions to him in detail on his first day of work. Her mast, with the addition of the topmast, soared a full ninety-three feet into the sky, and the truck was barely visible. Many of the ships in the harbor were gaily painted, but the *Orfeo*'s simple lines gave her a serious mien, relieved only by the three transom windows that adorned her stern, below which was painted her name in plain black letters. The hull itself was sixty-one feet in length, and bowsprit and jibboom made her total length one hundred and three feet. She looked snub-nosed at the moment, for the jibboom that extended her bowsprit to a full forty-four feet had been retracted to permit easier maneuvering in the crowded harbor.

Once aboard, they stowed the crate of chickens on the deck amidships, abaft the mast. José went into the cabin to check that his sea chest had indeed been brought aboard. The cabin was crowded with provisions and sea chests, and amidst it all stood a table with a chart spread out upon it. On a chair beside it stood a mahogany chest open to show a jumble of papers and ledgers. The chest was a twin to the one in Señor Morejón's office.

José opened his sea chest to see that all was within. His spare clothing rested on top, including his good breeches. Underneath these he found a Bible and a rosary, all lovingly packed by Mamá. There, too, was the copy of Homer's *Odyssey* he had placed inside, hoping that he would find an opportunity for study. They had barely begun the book in class, and he longed to know more of Odysseus's struggle to make his way home to Ithaca.

With the harbor pilot by his side to guide them, Tío Domingo barked out orders to the crew and suddenly all was motion. Vicente and Renzo cast off the gaskets on the staysail, while Vicente hauled on the halyard and the tall, triangular sail rose up. As the sail filled with wind, the *Orfeo* tugged at her anchors.

José joined Osorio at the winch, and as it turned the long anchor cable came slowly through the hawser hole to starboard. Together, José and Osorio raised the anchor up and they catted and fished it, raising up the flukes and lashing it to the cathead that projected over the gunwale on the starboard bow. They then did the same for the larboard anchor. Osorio did much of the work, patiently instructing José, who followed his guidance uncomprehendingly. The sloop began to gently make way towards the channel that led out to the sea. José watched blankly, at a loss to understand the tangle of rigging that controlled the action of sail and sloop.

"Do not stand there like a lubber," José heard Vicente shout. "Coil down those anchor cables! Neatly, mind you."

The *Orfeo* picked up speed as she moved through the channel and soon they saw the blue-green sea spread before them, the waves a translucent green in the sunlight. José could feel the light breeze on his face, and heard the cries of gulls. As he looked up, he could see them circling the topmast.

"Coil down those halyards!" shouted Vicente. "Keep your mind on your work. Those gulls can see to themselves."

Now clear of the crowded harbor and narrow channel, Renzo and Osorio extended the jibboom through the gammoning iron that fastened it to the bowsprit, and then secured the stays that kept the boom and mast in perfect tension. Osorio and Renzo then bent first the flying jib and then the outer jib to their respective stays, and they took shape in the wind. A *guadaño* boat approached and took off the pilot.

Tío Domingo now ordered the mainsail set. José helped Osorio cast off the gaskets, the plaited cords that stowed the mainsail under the gaff. They moved along the spar, Osorio balancing on the foot ropes rigged under the long boom below, José working his way towards him from the quarterdeck at the stern of the vessel. Then Osorio, standing on the main deck, unlashed the throat halyard that raised the end of the gaff nearest the mast, and José, guided by Vicente, did the same with the peak halyard, used to raise the outer end. On Tío Domingo's command, they hauled away and the gaff began to ascend the mast, jerkily, and Tío Domingo shouted commands to ease up or haul on one halyard or other to bring them up together. Vicente assisted José, making sure that he never lost hold of the halyard and so bring the peak crashing down on deck. Up went the great white mainsail.

"I could wish for more wind," grumbled Tío Domingo. "Still, we can hope the wind may be with us, even if the current is not, until we reach Cabo San Antonio."

José gazed about the vessel that would be his home for the next several months. For so many years he and Rafael had gamboled on the deck, raced up the shrouds, and treated it like a place of amusement. Now he saw it as if for the first time. From the small cabin below the raised quarterdeck at the stern to the bowsprit that seemed to point their way to sea, he realized that it was a great engine of work, a tangle of blocks, tackle, and deadeyes, stays and shrouds, littered with the cables and lines needed to work the vessel. All of it was dominated by the single mast that stood amidships on the main deck, its great boom ready to sweep across the quarterdeck. He and Rafael had taken great pride in knowing the names of all the sails and spars – now he knew that such knowledge was just a drop in the sea, a lubber's view of the vessel. He heard the welter of orders, saw the movements of lines, yards, braces, and boom, and understood none of it. The crew acted, and the ship moved in response, but he did not understand why, nor did he wish to. He longed to be in the familiar shop with his father, where he knew the name and purpose of every tool.

"Do not stand there! Get that ladder up and stowed. You should already have seen to it!" Vicente's voice broke his attention.

Tío Domingo assigned the crew to two watches, alternating every four hours. For now all hands were needed, but the formal watch system would begin at 8 o'clock, after they had eaten a late supper. José was disappointed to find himself in the larboard watch, under the command of Vicente. He was relieved to learn, however, that Osorio, too, would be part of the watch, while Renzo would be under Tío Domingo. He had come to like the man over the last few days, although he had been struck by his homeliness when first they met. Osorio's faced was ravaged by smallpox, for he had barely survived the outbreak that had taken his parents and small sister when he was just a boy. A *pardo* like José, his was cursed with lumpy features and mottled skin. Perhaps resigned to his physiognomy, he made no effort to improve his appearance, and left his rough, copper-colored hair uncombed and untrimmed, restrained only by a red bandana tied indifferently about his head. His chin was ever in want of a shave, and the loose clothing worn by a sailor became shapeless and baggy on his ungainly figure. Yet within the few days he had known him, José had forgotten that Osorio was ugly, and was aware only of the broad smile that seemed a permanent fixture on his face, of his bright brown eyes and of his energetic form, always at the ready to lend a hand.

Tío Domingo disappeared into the cabin to labor over his paperwork and José found himself under the eye of Vicente.

"The deck is in need of a good swabbing down," said Vicente, placing a bucket in José's hands. "Haul up some water and see to it."

It was true. The deck was fouled with the filth of the wharf that had been tracked in during the days of stowing cargo.

"I would have washed down the desk myself, but Vicente advised me to leave it for you." Osorio grinned at him from the helm.

"So this is how sailors live," said José, to no one in particular, as he lowered the bucket over the side.

"Sailor? You are no more a sailor than one of the rats in the hold. For the moment you are only a ship's boy, a very lubber. You will be a sailor, though from stem to stern, when I have finished with you," said Vicente. "You will know every sheet and sail, every knot, and be able to hand, reef, and steer, or you'll have my rope end to answer to."

It was tedious work, using a broom to sweep away the filth and sluice the dirty water off the deck into the scuppers. Whenever he looked up from his work, there was Vicente, pointing out a spot he had missed. Then he would indicate a sail or a piece of rigging and demand to know its name. When at last the wet deck glistened in the sunlight, and he had made sure every line was properly coiled and all the gear stowed away, Vicente sent him below to check for leakage. Again he heard the rustling sound. When he came above, painfully conscious that yet another two hours remained before the end of the watch at eight, he saw Renzo's solid form at the larboard rail. His dark, deep-set eyes, set beneath heavy black brows, were fixed on the coastline barely visible on the horizon, a slice of green in the fading glow of the sun.

José knew from the few words that he had heard Renzo speak that he was Italian, but little else about him. He was a silent man, as quiet as the sea when the wind has dropped off and barely stirs its surface, giving no hint of the pulsing life just below. Thus José was taken aback to hear Renzo address him.

"Come, look, *garzone!*" he called. José joined him at the rail, with a careful glance over his shoulder at Vicente, who stood at the helm and nodded his assent.

"See, there, the fin. That is a dolphin. And also others, just there. And see how the sea stirs around them. I think they find a school of sardines." He opened a locker that stood on deck near the cabin and pulled out an armful of netting. He beckoned José to follow him to the quarterdeck, where they stood at the taffrail.

"Watch how I cast the net." He threw it wide across the water. It sank slowly beneath the water and Renzo watched for a time, then suddenly began to haul it in and up over the side. Several small fish glittered silver within.

"Look, I show you how to clean sardines." Renzo hauled up a bucket of seawater and with his fingers, gently rubbed the scales from one of the fish. He pulled out his clasp knife and, barely looking at his work, with quick gestures gutted it, removed head and tail, and sliced it laterally. He plucked out its backbone with his fingers and dropped the refuse in a bucket. "Now you do the rest. You learn it *bene*."

José sighed as he pulled out his own knife and began gutting the fish. Renzo had cozened him into the most distasteful chore yet. He handed the fish to Osorio.

"Toss those fish guts over the side. See what happens!" called out Renzo, who was again gazing at the shore. José emptied the bucket into the water below. Seagulls swept down to pluck bits out of the water. Then José saw a long, thin, silver fish speed towards the chum and engulf it with its sharp, protruding jaw.

"Barracuda," commented Renzo. "Nasty fish, bad eating."

Osorio added the sardines to a cast iron kettle that was already bubbling over charcoals on a brazier under the awning that was strung up aft of the mast. A thick layer of sand, surrounded by a low barrier of bricks, protected the ship's deck timbers from the heat and sparks of the fire. Osorio stirred the simmering water and added slices of plantain to the onions and tomato already swirling alongside the fish. He added pinches of powders and leaves, stirring then and tasting the broth with a large spoon.

At last he sighed and proclaimed, "It is all I could wish!"

Tío Domingo and Renzo hurried to fill their bowls, for they would soon be on watch. Osorio poured hot black coffee into their tin mugs and they both seized up a piece of cassava bread. José washed away the refuse left in Osorio's wake. Into the chicken crate went peels and unwanted scraps of vegetable, and the chickens squawked and jostled for a chance at the best bits. José leaned on the gunwale and caught a moment of rest.

"Thank the Virgin and all the saints we have a fisherman aboard!" said Osorio. "We will always eat well."

"Why did you give up the fishing trade?" José asked Renzo. "Did it not pay well?"

"They not want me anymore in the Kingdom of Napoli," he replied, between rapid spoonfuls of soup.

"Or perhaps they wanted you too much," laughed Osorio.

"I find a ship to Spain, then I find a ship. The mate, he ask me, 'Where you from?' I look at him, I not want to say, for I know they not want Italians. He say, 'You Basque, yes?' and he wink at me. I wink back and say, 'You think right.' I get to Havana and jump ship. Now I catch sardines in the Florida Straits. A strange thing, the ways of God."

It was already dark when Tío Domingo and Renzo, having scraped the bottoms of their bowls, began their watch. In the moonlight José could see them brush the crumbs of cassava bread on the decking he had just recently rendered spotless. He remembered guiltily the many times he had himself brushed crumbs onto the tile floor at home, the floor that Magdalena swept daily. He joined Vicente and Osorio and filled his own bowl with soup. He tasted it gingerly, and was amazed at how well the salty sardines blended with the vegetables. It required a second helping to fill the ravenous void within him. Among the five of them, they had managed to empty the kettle.

"Well, douse the fire, scrub the pot, and you are done for the time being," said Osorio.

"But I am no longer on watch!" protested José. He felt the sting of the rope's end.

"You do what you are ordered, when you are ordered, whatever tasks are assigned a ship's boy who cannot work a sloop," snapped Vicente.

The sun was below the horizon, and Renzo at the helm, when Tío Domingo approached José. "It is time now for you to learn a little English," he said in Gaelic.

"Why?" asked José, his aching muscles crying out for rest. "With whom would I speak it?"

"With traders in Jamaica and other English colonies. Every man on this ship can speak English, at least a smattering, and some French as well. How else, pray tell, do you intend to market your venture?"

They began with common phrases, and José found he enjoyed it. This, at last, was something he understood. He listened carefully, trying to determine the verbs, the nouns, and the adjectives that modified them. The words jostled in his head as he prepared to turn in, hanging up his hammock and stripping off his slops. He tried to fall asleep as the unfamiliar hammock swung about with the motion of the ship. The air in the cabin was close, and Osorio and Vicente took their bedding out on the deck, leaving him alone with his thoughts. His ears were full of the creak of its timbers. He closed his eyes, but in his mind, Vicente was everywhere, dogging his every step, finding fault with his work. Tío Domingo, meanwhile, said nothing. He had put him on the larboard watch with Vicente, and when his uncle was on deck he seemed not to see the mate's bullying, averting his eyes whenever Vicente gave him the rope's end. Tío Domingo himself was a different man at sea, all shouting and worry, his gracious manners gone. Only when they were together for their English lessons did he resemble the man who so charmed everyone on land.

He wished only to be home in his own cot, listening to the sounds of the Havana streets and the boom of the guns that signaled the closing of the city gates. Home, where he was a scholar and not a ship's boy, pursued by the end of Vicente's rope. He owed Tío Domingo one year, and one year only, and then he would work with Papá and help him make the shop Zum-Zum into the most renowned joiner's shop in all of Havana. He finally gave in to fatigue and fell into a deep sleep.

He was dragged out of his slumber by Osorio. "It is almost midnight. We must go on watch."

José groaned, realizing that he had only gotten three hours of sleep. His body cried out that it wished another five at least.

The night was quiet. The clouds were few, and in the light from the moon and stars the shrouds and sheets were a ghostly grey against the dark sky. The sails, dingy in the sunlight, seemed to glow white in the night, and the waves sparkled magically in the dark as they caught the light. An occasional splash in the distance betrayed the presence of a fish or dolphin. On another occasion José might have enjoyed the sight, but Vicente left him no time for such indulgence.

During the day they had been hugging the shoreline, in order to avoid the stiff eastward current, close enough to see the birds rising from the tangles of mangroves. Now they stood farther out to sea lest they run aground during the night. The *Orfeo* continued on a west-southwest heading, with a light northeast wind on the starboard quarter. Vicente described it, but the words meant nothing to José. The mate showed him how to check their heading using the compass in the binnacle that stood before the helm. While Vicente kept the tiller steady, Osorio trimmed the jib the better to catch the wind. Then came the moment when Vicente let José take control of the tiller.

"Feel the tug of the current. Watch for other vessels and debris. See how the sails move in the wind. You must keep them filled," he said, his eyes scanning every inch of the rigging and sails, then looking towards the dark shape of the land.

José felt nothing, however. The tiller was a solid beam of wood in his hands, still bearing the marks of the saw that had hewn it out of a timber. The sea splashed along the sides of the vessel, but said nothing to him, and the mainsail billowed inscrutably above him.

"Turn her a point to starboard," ordered Vicente.

José hauled the heavy tiller to the starboard side, and saw the *Orfeo* point her bow to larboard.

"*Dios mío!*" cried Vicente, seizing the tiller from José and hauling it back. "To turn the sloop to starboard, you must turn the tiller to larboard." He gave a tired sigh. "That is enough for tonight, I think."

José felt foolish and he was glad to be relieved from further lessons. Osorio flashed him a sympathetic smile, and he felt still worse.

A cloud obscured the brilliant radiance of the full moon, and José strained to see in the sudden gloom. The few stars still visible above provided only faint illumination, and José became acutely aware of the banging of the blocks against the mast, the rustle of the rigging, and the occasional movement of the sails when the wind shifted slightly. He was suddenly startled by a deep groan coming from the cabin.

"No, no! *Prego*, no!" cried the voice.

Osorio rushed to the cabin and shouted, "Go back to sleep, Renzo!" His voice was joined by that of Tío Domingo, and the cries died down.

Osorio spoke to José. "He often has such nightmares. He is haunted by the blood."

José looked startled, and Osorio explained, "Did you not know? He killed a man, his closest friend." Starlight escaped the cloud cover momentarily and its shadows on Osorio's face made his pox marks look cavernous, then the clouds reclaimed the sky, and his face was lost in the darkness.

Vicente broke in from his place at the helm, his voice carrying down from the quarterdeck. "He was no friend. Renzo found him in bed with his wife. No man can stand by and be cuckolded."

"Still," Osorio observed. "It haunts him. He sees the eyes, the dying eyes like a fish. That is why he does not like to clean them, only to catch them. He does not like to see their eyes." And then there were only the sounds of the ship for a long time, until at four, his watch ended and he fell unconscious into his hammock. He was up again at eight to find the sun blazing down, and a wave of orders washing over him. The chickens must be fed and watered and their pen cleaned. Buckets of water needed to be hauled up to soak the deck boards lest they dry and crack in the heat. Vicente taught José how to work the pump, for that would be a daily duty of his. The mate also showed him how to inspect the cargo to be sure it had not shifted, and they checked for seepage that could damage the goods they carried. While they were below, Vicente spied something scurrying behind a hogshead, and then another.

"Rats! Foul little vermin after our cornmeal!" he cried. He examined the cargo more closely. "They smell the meal and think to get at it. I will never permit it!"

As the watch wore to a close, a savory smell drifted across the deck. Osorio was stirring what proved to be a stew of dried beef, plantains, and peppers.

"Osorio, he the best cook afloat," commented Renzo.

"We can be grateful that Don Domingo enjoys his creature comforts," allowed Vicente.

After wolfing down Osorio's dinner, and a siesta, José scanned the deck and found no sign of Vicente. He curled up by the anchor with his copy of *The Odyssey* and was transported into a world of heroes where men fought for honor and glory. It was a far cry from the *Orfeo*, full of the creaking of timbers and rigging, and the sweaty scent of men who worked hard in the full of the sun.

He was torn away from the cave of Calypso by the voice of Osorio. "You are needed on watch now, Sabio."

Sabio. The nickname Tío Gaspar had given him meant scholar, but now it had a hint of mockery to it.

Now Vicente set José to learning knots under the tutelage of Osorio. He sat cross-legged, back against the gunwale, under the awning, while Osorio showed him knot after knot. Osorio seemed always to be circling about him like a seagull, checking on his progress.

"Try it once more, I think," he said, his lips pursed as he squinted at José's first tangled attempt at a bowline.

"Too loose," was the verdict when next he appeared to inspect a sheet bend.

So it went through the watch. José practiced and practiced again. Suddenly the shadow of Vicente fell upon the deck. The mate examined the tangle of line that was supposed to be a carrick bend.

"My abuela could tie a knot better than you," he barked. "Do it again until you get it right. If you master it before dark, you might just make it to mess."

José groaned. He undid the knot and began again, his fingers now raw from the work. Osorio had just given a nod of approval to his last attempt when Vicente, examining the horizon, remarked, "I believe that is a sail two points off the starboard bow. José, go aloft and tell me what flag it flies."

"I will go, too," said Osorio, too quickly.

Vicente nodded his assent. José felt a twinge of resentment as he began to climb the larboard shrouds to the masthead. He and Rafael had often climbed the shrouds on his uncles' ships when traveling to Matanzas, and he did not need a nursemaid.

"Mind you do not fall. I do not want to have to swab your guts off the deck." Vicente's warning followed him up.

José clambered up the larboard shrouds, hurrying to escape the sound of the mate's voice. He stopped below the crosstrees that supported the topmast.

"Do not stop!" called out Osorio, who was climbing up the shrouds on the starboard side.

And José realized that he had still to climb the upper shrouds. While he calculated the best method to ascend, Osorio seized onto the futtock shrouds that ran from the lower mast to the crosstrees that helped support the topmast and climbed the short distance, hanging almost backwards like a monkey, his awkward form remarkably agile. Then he swung himself up on the crosstrees and began climbing the upper shrouds.

"Follow me!" he called down. "Have a care as you go!"

José followed, slowly and gingerly, trying not to imagine his brains splashed on the deck below. At last he joined Osorio at the top. He felt a sudden thrill at surveying the sea from a height of ninety-three feet. In the distance he could see the sail, somewhat closer now. Osorio saw it, too.

"In a few minutes we will know from whence she hails. It is good to get aloft and get the feel of the ship. Vicente will send you up again, and often." His eyes scanned the horizon. "Look, to larboard, see the mountains rising behind the shore? And the small break in the coastline? That is Bahía Honda. She makes a good refuge in a gale. And too, there is good fishing there," said Osorio.

"It all looks very much the same to me," confessed José.

"In time you will recognize every mile of coastline. A navigator knows his landmarks. A good master needs only a compass and his experience," Osorio opined. "In two days at this speed we will round Cabo San Antonio and begin tacking east, to Trinidad."

José was beginning to enjoy the roll of the ship, the quiet far above the deck, with only the creaking of rigging and timber. If only he did not have to go down again to the dreary routine of the ship.

He looked again at the sail. "I can see the flag now on the ship. She is one of ours," he cried. There it was, the jagged white St. Andrew's cross on a field of blue that flew on Spanish merchantmen.

"She is perhaps coming from Vera Cruz or Campeche. You must always tell the captain when you see another ship. Omit no detail. He keeps a careful log of such things," Osorio explained.

José grew accustomed to the routine: washing down the deck, straightening lines, tending to the chickens, and pumping out the bilge. He helped haul on the main and jib sheets, but the rig on a sloop was simple and did not demand excessive attention. The upkeep, however, seemed endless. The tropical sun, salt water, and hard usage took a heavy toil on a vessel's wood and cordage. The monotony was broken by his English lessons with Tío Domingo and fishing with Renzo. Best of all, however, was the time he could steal with Odysseus and his men in their odyssey across the "wine-dark sea." How glorious to face peril with heroes! He thought he would rather do battle with the Cyclops Polyphemus than to spend every day sloshing chicken manure into the scuppers.

Once past Bahía Honda they set a new course west-southwest, and the wind, which had shifted to the east, was now on their larboard quarter. José helped Osorio haul the boom far out to starboard to catch the wind, which had become a goodly breeze. The gusts that sprang up in the afternoon put a smile upon the face of Tío Domingo. Vicente, however, kept a careful eye on the compass and the water off the larboard side, for the northwest end of the island was a dangerous expanse of rocks, reefs, and sandy shallows, hidden among scattered cays.

As the sun rose they passed the western end of the island and stood south to round Cabo San Antonio. Tío Domingo chose the Paso de la Sorda, which took them closer to the land, avoiding the contrary pull of the powerful Florida current. The starboard watch was called up early to help navigate the challenging passage. Renzo stood at the larboard bow, watching carefully for rocks and shoals, and Vicente took the tiller from Tío Domingo. Occasional fierce gusts swept down off the land and rattled the sails. Tío Domingo ordered innumerable changes to the trim of the sails to compensate for the shifting winds. Osorio, with

José's assistance, hurried to obey. José became weary of the constant easing and hauling of the sheets. The gusts increased, and Vicente ordered them to take a reef in the mainsail and to trim the jib. José helped tie the reef knots, then Osorio hauled in the jib sheet. He, however, had breakfast to ready, and ordered José to belay the line and coil it down.

"You have seen me do this many a time by now. You do not need my help anymore," Osorio said with an encouraging smile.

Yes, he had seen Osorio do it, and helped as well, and was weary of the entire business, and exhausted from his shortened sleep. Here was yet another line to coil, and he still had the chickens to feed and the deck to wash. He gave the jib sheet a figure eight loop over the belaying pin, over and under, and left the remainder of the line in a heap on the deck. He would feed the chickens and then return to it. The line was secured, and no one would notice the untidy pile in the meantime.

He had fed the hens and was hauling up a bucket of water to wet the deck, the coil of line on the deck long forgotten. José was sweeping chicken droppings into the scuppers when he heard the sound of canvas flapping, a thump, and cry from forward. The wind had worked the jib sheet loose, and a sudden gust caused the sail to thrash about wildly. Renzo had tried to grab at the sheet as it writhed through the air, but had tripped on the heap on the deck and fallen, hitting his head on the bulwark. He lay there groaning, blood running onto the deck from his head, as Osorio ran to the halyard to lower the errant jib. He reached it too late, for the jib sheet caught on the fluke of the starboard anchor and with a great rending sound, tore in half, and hung flapping from the rigging. Without the balancing force of the jib, the bow began to head into the wind, and they found themselves in irons, the mainsail rattling helplessly in the wind.

José stood aghast as Tío Domingo shouted orders, while Vicente struggled with the tiller to keep the bow from working to leeward and take them onto a nearby cluster of rocks that appeared just above the water. His uncle strode down from the quarterdeck to take command of the situation and soon restored order.

The remnants of the jib were hauled down, Renzo's battered head was bandaged, and the flying jib was set in place of the jib.

José had never seen Vicente so angry. "There is no place for careless boys on a sloop. We need those who follow orders, who understand that lives may depend on the actions they take. Finish with the deck and stay out of my way."

Tío Domingo stood behind him, grim-faced, and Osorio, too, was unaccustomedly silent and unsmiling. Renzo, once his friend, did not look at him but only stood rubbing his aching head. José wished only for this day to end. He stumbled listlessly through the watches of that day, watch on and watch off, acutely aware of the silence of his crewmates. He was relieved when night fell, hiding him in folds of darkness. At eight o'clock his watch ended and he could turn in and lose himself in sleep. As he lay in his hammock, sleepless, he heard the wind in the rigging, making a melody he could not follow, and the waves slapped against the unyielding hull of the ship determined to take him places he did not wish to go. He hated the sea, he hated the *Orfeo*, and at that moment, he hated Tío Domingo and every man aboard. He knew it was a sin and he did not care, a prisoner of his anger.

He heard the low voices of Osorio and Vicente outside the cabin.

"He is just a boy. He will learn," said Osorio in a conciliatory tone.

"He is a spoiled boy, with no more notion of duty and honest labor than those chickens on deck. I have known monkeys that could tie a better knot," was the hoarse reply.

"He is trying..."

"He does not try, and that is the nub of it. His uncle is a partner in the company and wishes his nephew to take his place one day. That useless whelp thinks to come into his position through the transom rather than the forecastle, and so he need not learn the ropes. I despise such people." Vicente almost spat his contempt.

"It is a strange thing, for I hear that his father was a good seaman in his day," mused Osorio.

"They say that the splinter is like the stick. I say many a splinter snaps and breaks. Too many books and not enough thrashings, I will wager," said Vicente as he slung his hammock and climbed in.

José lay stiff in his hammock. He closed his eyes and feigned sleep. Soon the rumble of Osorio's snores filled the cabin. José clenched his fists and squeezed his eyes tight to hold back the tears that crept insistently from the corners of his eyes. Papá! What would Papá think when he learned of his conduct on the *Orfeo*? He had told him to work hard and to do his duty.

The cabin was black and shadowless, for above the ship, clouds obscured the stars and moon and so no light came through the transom. José was enveloped by gloom as he felt the torments of the soul that come only in the darkest hours of the night. This, José knew, was the self-examination which the Jesuit fathers had taught him, and he did not like it, for he saw himself all too clearly.

17

CONTRABAND

On Thursday, having rounded the cape, Tío Domingo set a new course east-southeast to take them past the Isla de Pinos. There was a brisk north-northeast wind on the *Orfeo*'s starboard beam, and periodically fierce gusts would rattle her sails. They no longer kept a lantern at the masthead, for, Tío Domingo said, there were sometimes pirates in this area. At night, the cabin was illuminated only by the reddish light from a calabash filled with fireflies that they fed on sugar water.

When the larboard watch arose at midnight, he had slept little, but, ignoring the fatigue of muscle and mind, he arose with a new will. He moved resolutely, speaking not a word. He tied every line, feeling where each belonged when he could not see. He spent tedious hours watching over the larboard rail, straining to see the foam of water breaking over rock, keeping himself at attention by silently reciting the name of every part of the ship, first in Spanish, then in English, then in Gaelic, till they ran through his brain like a rhyme. And when "rosy-fingered dawn" broke he was already washing down the deck, unbidden, and surprising the chickens with his prompt solicitude. His breakfast had a savor it had lacked before, and after cleaning up he fell into his hammock for the most peaceful slumber he had yet known on board.

On the late afternoon watch he listened attentively as Osorio showed him how to use a great thick needle to stitch the torn canvas of the jib sail. Strapped on to his left hand was a "palm," a leather piece with a metal plate in the center which he used like a thimble to push the needle through the heavy canvas. He worked slowly and carefully. Osorio checked his work often, but not a stitch needed to be picked out and redone. Osorio smiled broadly when the work was finished and Tío Domingo almost smiled.

"Sadly, José Albañez appears to have disappeared overboard. I do not know who this new hand is, but I hope he continues as he has begun," Vicente remarked.

José began to look forward to his work. He took pride in the orderly appearance of the deck, the tidy hold and cabin. He set himself to learn every knot, and Osorio proclaimed that he feared he would soon leave them to become a rigger at the shipyard. Renzo vowed he would teach him all there was to know about fishing, and soon José could identify many of the fish that broke the waves. Osorio had many suggestions on how they might be prepared.

At last he dared to ask Vicente why they must always tack the ship and not sail straight ahead, as they had when standing to the west.

For once Vicente did not bark at him. "We are sailing in the direction of the wind, so we cannot go straight ahead or the wind would push us backwards. If we go on a larboard tack, we can catch the wind sideways and move forward at an angle to our destination. If we continued on that tack, however, in time we would find ourselves in Caracas. So we then switch to a starboard tack and again sail at an angle. It is slow, but we reach our destination in the end."

José was confused. "But if we are going to larboard, then we will land in Cuba."

Vicente snorted. "*Dios mío*! It is called the larboard tack because the wind is to our larboard side. The *Orfeo*, however is headed to starboard. Soon it will all be second nature."

José thought that he might never understand. Everything on a ship seemed deliberately contrary.

Vicente was enjoying himself. "There is nothing better than a sloop for sailing close-hauled to the wind, and the *Orfeo* is an exceptionally weatherly craft.

"Here, you may see for yourself. Take the tiller and steer her into the wind. Just now the wind is from the southeast, so guide her slowly to starboard. Watch the mainsail. When she just begins to luff – to shiver – turn her back to larboard. Gently, now watch the sail."

José moved the tiller with some slight trepidation and soon saw the wind begin to spill from the sails. The mainsail made a rattling sound as it began to flap in the breeze.

"Now back to larboard. Quickly!" cried Vicente. And then, as the sails began to fill again, he added, "*Muy bien.*"

"*Muy bien.*" Two small words, but refreshing to José's ears.

One day, when they were on a starboard tack, they could see off the larboard bow a vast expanse of rocky cays, coral reefs, and sandbars. Seabirds wheeled over groves of palm trees, and he could just see flamingoes wading among the grasses in the shallow waters. In a rare indulgence, Vicente handed José the spyglass so that he could look more closely. He could see smaller waterbirds taking shelter among the knees of mangrove trees and multicolored birds fluttering about their nests in low-growing shrubs. Red rock crabs scuttled along the shore, and a pair of enormous iguanas battled for feminine favors on a rocky outcropping. Ahead, on a distant cay, José could see the bleached and broken ribs of a vessel that had once been very like their own.

"Those are Los Jardines," remarked Vicente. The gardens.

"It is a paradise for fish and birds, but a place of death for any ship that steers too close," continued Vicente. "That is why I will now teach you to take soundings with the lead."

He took a heavy piece of lead strung on a long line marked at intervals with bits of leather and cloth. He showed José how to stand on the channel and swing the lead about his head and cast it as far as possible before the vessel's starboard bow. It proved to be a great heavy thing, and José needed several attempts before he could send it well ahead. Then, when the *Orfeo* approached the point where the line was perpendicular to her side, observed the three bits of leather just above the surface of the water, and sang out "By the mark three!" The *Orfeo* had a draft of eight feet, or significantly more than one fathom, so the news that they were in a good three fathoms of water was reassuring.

As long as they were off Los Jardines, they took turns heaving the lead at fifteen-minute intervals. As night fell, they beat to windward to keep well clear of their hazards. In the dark, José could see a phosphorescent glow illuminating their shores. Los Jardines now resembled a fairy wonderland, albeit one inhabited by so many malicious pixies hoping to draw them ashore.

Beating against the wind made for slow going, for it took nine days to reach their destination of Trinidad Sancti Spíritus. Life on board settled into a routine that was broken only by Sunday, when only the most unavoidable tasks were assigned and there was time to divert themselves.

"I did not think Tío Domingo cared about religious observance," José remarked to Osorio.

"He does not. He does, however, appreciate the need for a man to rest from his labors," Osorio replied. "And Vicente, well, he likes to be correct in all things."

The men smoked cigars, told tales, and exchanged ribald jests. José remembered Mamá's cautions and, armed with his rosary, sat on one of the lockers to perform his devotions. He was surprised to find Renzo beside him. The Italian's lips moved as he began silently to tell the beads of his own Rosary.

"Say a prayer for me," requested Osorio, knocking the ashes from his cigar off the bulwark into the waters below.

"For what you need prayer?" asked Renzo.

"Pray that I find a woman," was the reply.

"You pray that yourself. God, maybe he listen to you," grumbled Renzo.

"I have but I do not think that he listens to me. Perhaps he will listen to José," Osorio suggested, dropping the butt of the cigar into the waters below. He took up his guitar and began a ballad of unrequited love in a voice surprisingly sweet.

José added a prayer for Osorio to his litany. Then, after some consideration, he added a prayer that the woman Osorio found bore no resemblance to those so easily found near the docks of Havana.

A t last, on the morning of the 5th of April, the *Orfeo* stood into the open waters of the Gulf of Xagua. There was no need to heave the lead here, for the waters of the gulf exceeded 60 fathoms. The wind was from the northeast, and they continued to beat across the gulf until suddenly the wind shifted, and a southeast breeze on their starboard quarter sent them flying to their destination. In the afternoon a cloudburst drenched the sails and thoroughly soaked the afternoon watch, and then as suddenly was replaced by a bright sun that made the deck and rigging glisten in its rays. Tío Domingo gave the order to heave to.

José surveyed the landscape before them. He was surprised to see that they were in the shelter of a low rise of land, skirted at the base by a small beach of grey sand. He had thought that they would enter a harbor like that of Havana or Matanzas, encircled by a bustling commercial city.

"Is this Trinidad?" he asked in a doubtful tone.

It was Tío Domingo who replied. "Trinidad is inland. To the east is Puerta Casilda, but we would need a pilot to navigate those treacherous shoals that front that coast. Where it is difficult to enter, it is equally difficult to depart, should we wish to leave in a hurry."

"The *guarda costa* is less likely to find us here," added Vicente. "To cross the bar and enter Boca Guaurabo one must have a vessel of shallow draft, like the *Orfeo*. For this reason local vessels prefer this port."

"And for this reason the *guarda costa* is less likely to visit," added Osorio. "Once up the river they cannot easily see us."

"What would happen should they stop us?" asked José.

"Should they closely examine our cargo? We would be sent to the mines to spend many years at hard labor," Vicente replied without concern.

"*They* would be sent to the mines," Osorio hissed at José, gesturing to indicate Tío Domingo and Vicente. "You and I are *pardos*. We might well be enslaved." He, too, seemed remarkably unperturbed.

José cast a sudden, fearful glance to sea. He saw no sail.

"It has not happened yet," said Tío Domingo with a shrug. "And I take measures to ensure that it does not."

It was almost sunset when the tide reached its peak and Tío Domingo ordered the mainsail raised. He kept a careful hand on the tiller as the sail filled, while Vicente and Osorio stood in the bow and shouted directions back to him, guiding him over the sandbar at the mouth of the river and through a narrow channel into the depths of the River Guaurabo. For one perilous moment the keel caught on the sand, then the rising tide pushed it over and into the river's mouth.

Along the brushy shore of the river stood a long wooden dock. A smaller coastal sloop was tied up alongside the far end, accompanied by several fishing boats. The *Orfeo* gently maneuvered near the wharf as Osorio, Renzo, and José tossed lengths of old cable over the side to serve as fenders and protect the sloop's side. Renzo clambered onto the starboard channel and leapt onto the wharf, where he caught the mooring lines as Osorio and José tossed them ashore.

It was night by the time they had securely tied up at the dock, and Osorio went aloft to hang a blue lantern from the masthead. Tío Domingo signaled to José to join him, and they climbed over the bulwark and leapt down onto the dock. His uncle led the way through a narrow path that led through the mass of trees and brush that grew close to the rocky shore of grey limestone. All about them the trees and bushes glowed with the red phosphorescence of tiny insects, lighting their way. José slapped vainly at the cloud of mosquitos. Through the branches he could see the bright eyes of banana rats and hear their scurryings. Something almost flew in his face and he started.

"It is only a bat," said Tío Domingo, stepping over a large snake that slipped across the muddy path.

Soon they came to a broad wooden house. Light glowed in its windows, and from a nearby ramada came the lowing of cattle, the bleating of goats, and the too familiar smell of chicken manure. Tío Domingo knocked, and a middle-aged *blanco* came to the door.

"Thank the Virgin and all the saints you are here!" he said, waving them in. Tío Domingo introduced him as Señor Bitoria. They sat at his table and the aroma of ground coffee began to fill the room as Señora Bitoria began, unbidden, to prepare the beverage.

The man puzzled José. He owned one of the boats at the wharf, according to Tío Domingo, and the nets in the bottom said that he was a fisherman. If so, then fishing in Boca Guaurabo was most profitable, for he wore a clean white shirt of finely woven cotton, and a gold ring sparkled on his left hand. Señora Bitoria served the coffee on a handsome mahogany table, in delicate porcelain cups that José recognized to be of Dutch manufacture.

"I would offer you wine, but we have long since run out, and we are near the bottom of the flour barrel, as well. And olive oil! Well, never mind about that. It is this war! The English used to bring us so many things, but now they would rather plunder the French," complained Señor Bitoria. In his joy at having a new ear to hear his complaints he seemed to forget that he was giving his visitor a competitive advantage.

"I am delighted that I may be of service," said Tío Domingo, his eyes aglow upon learning of the shortfalls of the English smugglers who usually haunted the southern coast.

There followed a prolonged discussion of the needs of the province, of the cattle market, and of the tobacco crop. Then it was Tío Domingo's turn to describe the goods he had in the hold.

"How marvelous! You are a godsend," exclaimed Señor Bitoria. "Our blacksmith will be most grateful to receive his iron at last, as will our unshod horses. I have already sent my sons to notify the necessary people, in case they do not see your blue light. They will be here in the morning."

Tío Domingo rose to leave. Señor Bitoria touched his arm. "Before you go, what news of the war? Will Spain be drawn in? I fear we cannot bear any more disruption."

"Perhaps it would not be so bad," said Tío Domingo. "The *guarda costa* would find themselves with little time to interfere in commerce. And we would then have the chance to raid the English. Every sloop and schooner in Cuba would turn privateer. Imagine the goods we would bring home!"

"Perhaps," replied Señor Bitoria, stirring his coffee with a silver spoon. "But what if they plunder us instead?"

Far too early in the morning, as the first rays of day appeared over the mountains on which the city of Trinidad was perched, several boats made their way down the river and tied up alongside the *Orfeo*. Men, too, having followed the path towards the river, appeared among the trees and brush. On board, Tío Domingo was ready with samples of his wares. Several were interested in the bolt of sturdy osnaburg fabric from Scotland, others in the saws with well-tempered blades from England, and a box of drill bits from Antwerp. Some went below to see the barrels of flour, casks of olive oil and of wine. Several hung longingly over the dresses, lace, ribbons, and shoes, the discarded fashions of more stylish cities, imagining the delighted cries of wives and daughters should they return with a few of these items.

José listened closely as the men haggled with Tío Domingo. Vicente, Osorio, and Renzo also joined in, enthusiastically touting the goods they had brought as ventures.

"This cornmeal is from Vera Cruz, and is of the finest grind," asserted Osorio. "I will accept nothing less than ten pesos for it." In the end he took seven, and grinned triumphantly.

Renzo hawked a small assortment of hardware, including finely made fishhooks and weights for nets. "They no fail – catch many fish!" he boasted, and his efforts netted him a satisfactory return. He fondled the items longingly, as if he did not wish to part with them, and then, deal concluded, he and his purchaser fell into deep conversation about the pursuit of marine life.

Vicente approached his negotiations like a swordsman, forcefully advocating for his goods with bold strokes and parrying away any dissent. Prices were exchanged, and, instantly upon hearing the price upon which he had long ago decided, he moved in and finished it.

José knew that he must step forward and make his own sale or miss the chance. "I have a keg of rice to sell," he announced at last.

"Yes? What sort of rice?" asked one of the men, not unkindly.

"From Campeche," he said, trying to assume the boldness of Vicente. "It is excellent rice," knowing too little of rice to say more. Up until it had simply appeared on his plate, piping hot, as if by magic.

"Let me see that rice," the man said, with just a hint of a smile, and they went below to pry open the keg. The man ran his fingers through the rice, which shone smooth and white in a ray of sunlight from the grating above.

"Those Mexicans are no farmers," he said, as if he had not just purchased Osorio's cornmeal from Vera Cruz. "I will offer you three pesos for the lot."

Three pesos! That was barely more than he had paid for them! He had hoped to receive six. "Eight pesos at the very least," José said, hoping that he sounded like a man of determination and not a callow youth making his first bargain.

"I suppose I might go as high as four," was the quick response.

"I might be tempted to consider seven," José returned as quickly.

There was a long, anxious pause. "Perhaps I could manage five. Shall we call it a bargain?" the man responded at last.

"I must insist upon six, señor," said José.

The man turned to go.

"Five. You may have them for five," said José quickly, and they shook upon it. His heart soared. He had made his first sale, and made a profit of three pesos, a magnificent sum.

As he ascended the companionway, Vicente whispered to him, "You gave up too early. He would have paid six."

The afternoon was spent hauling goods out of the hold and lowering them into waiting boats. One by one, they attached a pair of can hooks onto each barrel and crate, hoisted it up by a tackle affixed to the top yard, then, using the braces to swing the yard, swayed the load out over the side and lowered it into a waiting boat. As they worked, José cast occasional glances out to sea, alert to any sail that might signal the arrival of the *guarda costa*. He also had time to think about the obvious joy of their customers at obtaining items difficult to procure here on the southern coast. It had felt like the Día de los Reyes, and he was one of the kings bearing gifts. He had not imagined that a saw or fishhook could bring a grown man such joy.

The cargo delivered, Tío Domingo took José into the cabin to instruct him in bookkeeping. Looking in the account book, José saw each transaction listed with its cost and the price received at sale. He marveled at the difference. Quickly calculating in his head, he estimated that Albañez y Morejón had made a generous profit.

"Do you always do so well?" he asked Tío Domingo.

"Almost always, thanks to the shortsighted policies of the crowns of Europe. The more they restrict trade, the greater the profits of those who can get goods to those who need them. God bless those ninnies in Madrid!

"Mind you, that is not all profit, lad," he added. "Remember that wages must still be paid and stores purchased. A vessel is a great hungry creature, ever needing to be fed."

Tío Domingo had already made arrangements with Señor Bitoria to purchase an outgoing cargo. He seemed to know everyone, asking Señor Bitoria which ones had goods to sell and at what price. Vicente now went ashore to inspect several casks of snuff. Osorio and Renzo accompanied him, eager to stretch their legs and fill their lungs with fresh spring air.

"Will you inspect the salt beef and hides?" asked José.

"No, there is no need, for I have known these men for some time. Trade is built upon trust between men," replied Tío Domingo.

"Doesn't Vicente trust them?" asked José in puzzlement.

"Aye, but he takes pride in his expertise regarding tobacco. His father had a *vega*. That is how he knows Anselmo. He is a kind of cousin," answered Tío Domingo.

"How is he not a *veguero* then?" José asked.

"His father lost the *vega*. The crown paid too little and too late and all his work was for naught. And so Vicente went to sea," Tío Domingo concluded, staring at the distant waves as he puffed on a cigar.

They were still sitting there when the rest of the crew returned. Vicente had purchased fresh viands to add to their provisions. José had entrusted his profits to him and he had purchased a sack of limes to serve as José's venture in Jamaica, and the others had acquired similar items for trade. The boat also contained two unexpected purchases. Renzo had with him a wicker cage containing a small bird, green with a white breast and patches of red and yellow. It had a sharp beak and trilled "tocororo!" as it flickered its long tail excitedly.

"Renzo has bought himself a bird," explained Osorio. "Let us hope she is a better companion than his last woman," he added with a laugh.

In a flash Renzo had his knife at Osorio's throat.

Osorio laughed nervously. "It was only a poor jest! I beg your forgiveness, *mi amigo*."

Renzo lowered the knife.

While this transpired, Vicente was climbing carefully over the gunwale, clutching the mouth of a large burlap sack that writhed mysteriously. Once on deck, he whispered inaudibly as he gently placed the bag down and opened it. They waited for what seemed an excessive amount of time, while Vicente stood watching his bag expectantly. At last there emerged a feline, no longer a kitten but not yet a cat, with a torn ear and rough, patchy black fur. He stepped regally out of the bag, tail held high.

"I introduce to you General Scipio Africanus," announced Vicente triumphantly. "He has come to vanquish our legions of rats just as his namesake defeated the Carthaginians in Spain."

Young Scipio disappeared down the companionway, and Vicente declared of him, "A model crew member, already entering upon his duties."

A squeak, a yowl, and a thump from below confirmed Vicente's judgement.

Osorio had brought back a bit of pork and prepared a stew with sweet potato, tomatoes, and peppers. They stuffed themselves, knowing that there would be little time to eat tomorrow, when they stowed their new cargo and prepared to make sail for Jamaica.

"If the *guarda costa* finds us, will we use the cannon?" José asked, for the four-pounder had long fascinated him.

"The captain has other ways of dealing with the *guarda costa*," laughed Vicente.

"We will practice the gun one day," remarked Tío Domingo.

"Will I learn to fire it?" asked José eagerly.

"You will fire the gun when you have earned the privilege," Vicente cut in.

José remembered again that he was only the ship's boy, and fell silent.

After a time, Osorio said kindly. "Sabio, what is that book you have been reading? Is it a good story?"

José had put aside *The Odyssey* for the time being, but he welcomed the chance to enter into conversation.

"It is a story of a hero who wishes to return home to his wife after a war, but the goddess Calypso is holding him captive in her cave."

"Is this goddess beautiful? If so, I would gladly stay in her cave," smiled Osorio, eyes half closed with delight.

"He goes home to keep other men away from his wife," opined Renzo darkly. "Very like she already in bed with one."

"Yes," said José, warming to his subject. "His wife Penelope is besieged by suitors, but she is faithful and refuses all their offers. But they are eating her out of house and home."

"He must go home and stop them, then, or his children will lose their inheritance," interjected Vicente, suddenly interested.

"And for that reason his young son Telemachus has gone in search of his father in order to protect his patrimony," José affirmed.

The somber voice of Tío Domingo interrupted. "He must go home because she is the love of his life, and he can know no joy without her. No other woman can fill her place in his heart. He has seen the world, known many women, and still there is no one like her," he pronounced. With that he ascended to the quarterdeck, where he stood staring out to sea until the setting of the sun left nothing more to be seen.

The next day they brought on board their cargo of salt beef, hides, and tallow candles, stowed carefully in the hold – barrels of salt beef on the bottom, bundles of hides on top, carefully, and the few boxes of candles stowed about the edges. Behind all of this were hidden the casks of snuff from Matanzas. José saw a rat scurry out from under one of the planks supporting the barrels, and General Scipio gave chase.

An outburst of bleating heralded the arrival of one of the final items of cargo, eight young goats ferried over by Renzo. Each one protested loudly as a strap was hitched under its belly and it was swayed aboard. José helped Osorio build a crude pen for them before the mast, and learned that the care of the animals would become another of his tasks. The goats glared at him as he herded the last one into the pen, and he glared back, thinking that he had never foreseen that his time on the *Orfeo* might involve as much animal husbandry as seamanship.

They lost little time in setting sail and raising anchor, for they had a favorable southeast wind on their stern that would give them an easy sail to Jamaica, and Tío Domingo did not wish to lose a minute of such a gift. The mainsail was set, the staysail filled with wind, and José was cheerily coiling the lines as the rocky perils off Puerta Cabilda disappeared off the larboard side.

Suddenly he heard Osorio cry, "Sail ho!"

There, ahead of them to larboard, appeared a schooner, still at a distance, but rapidly closing on them. The vessel's approach had been obscured by the cliff to larboard, but now it was clearly visible, as was its flag. A puff of smoke appeared on the vessel's bow, they heard a boom, and then there was a splash in the water ahead of them. José dropped the line he held as, with a sickening feeling in the pit of his stomach, he recognized the schooner to be a *guarda costa*. While the flag of the Spanish merchant marine flew on the stern, the half-dozen four-pounders on the deck told him that this was no coasting vessel. The several dozen men visible on deck exceeded by far the number necessary to handle its sails. As the schooner approached José could see the men more clearly. They were rough and ragged, armed with an assortment of muskets, pistols, and cutlasses.

The schooner soon crossed their hawse, and Tío Domingo gave the order to heave to. As they did so, the schooner lowered its boat, which carried to their side a tall *blanco* man sweating in a faded blue coat with dingy white facings whose shouted orders could be heard over the splashing of the oars. One hand was clapped on his head to secure his tricorn hat, which threatened to fly off in every gust. The man mounted the ladder Renzo threw down the side, followed by a burly, dark-haired man whose muscles almost burst out of his shirt.

"*Dios mío!*" said Tío Domingo under his breath. "I do not know this man." He looked pale.

"Try to keep up, man!" shouted the thin man, now climbing the ladder with the other close upon his heels.

"They are a hungry looking lot," whispered Vicente to Osorio, as Tío Domingo hurried to greet the visitors.

"They long to feed upon the *Orfeo*," replied Osorio.

"They feed upon hard-working farmers, merchants, and sailors, taking what they have not earned," spat Vicente.

"Do they not pay the sailors of the *guarda costa*?" asked José, who knew little of them except that they were the enemy.

"Pay them!" snorted Vicente. "They receive no pay whatsoever, only a share of whatever vessels they seize. And more if they meet with resistance. They have been known to slaughter an entire crew just to increase their take."

"They are pirates!" whispered José.

"You may call them pirates. I have worse names for them." Vicente then shared several epithets that did not bring credit to the *guarda costas* or their mothers.

Once on deck the *guarda costa* captain stood up to his full height and barked in the tones of a *peninsula*r, "I am Captain Don Nicolás Marroto de Carques of the schooner *Potencia*." He opened his coat and tapped a document that peeked out of an inner pocket. "I hold a commission from Don Julián de Arriaga y Ribera, Minister of the Navy and the Indies to patrol the coast of Cuba. I insist upon seeing the papers of this vessel." His sharp nose lifted in the wind as if hoping to sniff out contraband goods.

Tío Domingo responded graciously, "And I am Captain Don Domingo Albañez. I welcome you to the sloop *Orfe*o. Come into the cabin and you will see that all is at it should be." He motioned to José to follow.

As José entered the cabin, he could see out of the corner of his eye a man on the *Potencia* strutting about, his nose in the air, in mimicry of his captain. The others stood about, laughing at his antics. Tío Domingo ordered José to bring out his best bottle of Madeira and pour a glass for the two men. Don Nicolás took his without a word and began poring over the documents Tío Domingo put before him. He read each bill of lading carefully, then read it again. His lips moved silently as he ran his finger under each line.

"Perhaps, Don Domingo, you have been accustomed to an indifferent style of enforcement on this coast, when the *Potencia* was under the command of Captain Don Ignacio Arranda. Unfortunately for Don Ignacio, he seized a French packet and manhandled the diplomatic envoy it carried. My cousin, the Vizconde Catasparra, has heard that the court was most distressed by his gross insult to a country allied by blood with His Catholic Majesty King Carlos. He has heard, too, that the king is eager to see his laws vigorously enforced in the Indies." Don

Nicolás finished his glass of wine, and after a nod from Tío Domingo, José hurried to refill it.

"To His Majesty!" said Tío Domingo, raising his glass.

"To our king," Don Nicolás replied.

Don Nicolás reapplied himself to the papers and to the Madeira. "Where are you taking this beef and these hides?" he demanded. "Surely Matanzas has plenty of its own."

"How true that is," smiled Tío Domingo as the light from the transom made the beads of sweat on his forehead glisten. "It is for that reason that I have this license to trade in Caracas." He pulled the paper from the sheaf on the table.

"It is all well and good to have a license for Caracas. It is still better to have a cargo that does not contain contraband goods." Don Nicolás drained his glass of wine, and a trickle ran out of the corner of his mouth. He shouted to his subordinate, "Pico, take the men below and inspect every *pulgada* of that hold. I want to know if there contraband. Tobacco, snuff..." He thought for a moment. "Perhaps timber from His Majesty's forests, anything not listed in these papers." He sat waving his empty glass, and José automatically filled it.

Tío Domingo, who for the first time in José's life did not seem in command of the situation, sat silently, watching his guest finish off the wine. Don Nicolás arose and went out on deck to confer with his subordinates. Tío Domingo told José to follow him and observe.

On deck, Pico had been joined by a slight, rat-faced *pardo* man whose eyes darted about the sloop. Those eyes took in Osorio, nervously pacing about the forecastle, his pockmarks vivid in his suddenly grey face, and Renzo, gazing over the side as if weighing his chances of swimming for shore.

Vicente stepped into the cabin to confer with Tío Domingo. After several minutes he reappeared.

"Why do you tarry?" Don Nicolás shouted at his men. "Go below and inspect their cargo. Examine very inch of the hold. If there is contraband, we must find it." He disappeared into the cabin again, no doubt remembering that the bottle remained unfinished.

"Follow me," said Vicente, and descended the companionway. The two *guarda costas* followed. There was a long silence, interrupted occasionally by a raised voice. José was sure that he heard the sound of wood against wood, indicating that they were moving the cargo about as they inspected it. He thought of the casks of snuff hiding behind the bales of hides and felt weak inside. The waiting on deck was unbearable. Osorio collapsed on the deck, his head between his knees. Renzo pulled out his Rosary and began fingering it.

At long last a banging arose from below. José crept over to the grating and looked through the hatch. Suddenly his nose was filled with the scent of cigars. He saw the three men, each holding a stave, each banging them in turn while they smoked cigars.

Pico expelled a rich cloud of smoke. "This tobacco is very fine, much like that grown by my father on his *vega*," he said in the unmistakable accent of a *criollo*.

"My father, too, was a *veguero*," responded Vicente, closing his eyes as he savored the cigar. The rat-faced man whacked a barrel with his stave.

"It is the humble farmer who makes this all possible. He sweats, he toils, and then the crown men come like locusts to devour it all," commented Pico.

"They consumed my father and all he had. How many times did I see his harvest sitting, unpurchased, in the shed because it had been passed over by the men from the *Factoría*?" Vicente's voice rose slightly. "Does the king grow the tobacco? Does he mill the snuff? Whenever the king sees a profitable business, he makes it a monopoly, whether it be tobacco or timber. He already has our taxes. If he wants to go into the tobacco business, let him set up his own *vega*." José had never seen Vicente so passionate.

Pico held up his hand to silence Vicente. "I will hear no words against our king. And I have no interest in harassing his loyal subjects. I would instead like to know where we can find the English smugglers who infest our coasts. They have goods worth the seizing, and taking their vessels is the duty of a servant of His Catholic Majesty."

"The English are pirates and should be driven from our shore," asserted Vicente.

"They are foul beasts. We once seized an English slave ship. A filthy business," agreed Pico. The rat-faced man nodded in agreement.

"I have heard that they have been frequenting Manzanillo because they believe that the *guarda costa* is seldom there," said Vicente.

"And they would be right," replied Pico, and then he smiled. "But not for much longer."

The men extinguished the butts of their cigars in the bilge water that had accumulated in the bottom of the hold since the morning and ascended the companionway, but not before Vicente had passed them each a small bag that clinked.

"All is in order," announced Pico when he at last stood upon the deck.

"You found nothing? No contraband? No goods not listed on the bills of lading? It seems that it requires the heart of a native Spaniard to perform the service owed to the crown, and not one tainted with the blood of a mongrel." José saw the rat-faced man stiffen at these words.

Don Nicolás turned awkwardly and began to descend the companionway, hesitating for a moment as each foot sought vainly for the next step. "Rojas, get down here! Do you not see I need assistance!" His voice rose from the hold. Rojas, the rat-faced man, proceeded with the greatest deliberation towards the hatch, first hiking up his pants, carefully tucking in his shirt, and spitting on his hands in order to carefully smooth down his coarse, unruly hair.

He saw Don Nicolás pry open a barrel of salt beef, and its pungent odor wafted up to him. Then, unsteadily, the man climbed atop another one, reaching up to tug at a bundle of hides behind which, José knew, stood the small casks of snuff that, rejected by purchasers from the royal monopoly, were travelling abroad in search of a more welcoming harbor. "Rojas, where are you?" shouted Don Nicolás and as if on cue, several rats seemed to fly from behind the hides, landing upon the shoulders of Don Nicolás and, after perching there for a long second, leapt down to the bottom of the hold. Don Nicolás waved his arms as he vainly tried to maintain his precarious balance. Just then General Scipio shot out from behind a barrel and landed on the head of Don Nicolás. He dug his claws into the captain's face for purchase, then leapt down after the rats, and Don Nicolás fell with a crash. The Spaniard slowly raised himself, several cuts across his cheeks already oozing blood.

Now at last Rojas found his way down into the hold. He assisted his captain up the companionway, as Pico called out to him, "These men tell me that there are rich English vessels sailing impudently in and out of Manzanillo. If we make all sail perhaps we can catch a few of them in the act."

"Yes," mumbled Don Nicolás in a dazed voice. "We must make haste and catch them before the French do. *Tempest fuga!*"[1] It was with difficulty that José avoided laughing.

Pico and Rojas eased the captain down the ladder and into the boat that still waited patiently alongside. They rowed smartly back to the *Potencia* as the crew of the *Orfeo* watched, anxious to see them depart. They heard a cheer rise from the men on deck, and in a flurry of action, its sails began to fill with wind, but not before they saw Pico draw back his great fist and deck the man José had previously seen mincing about the deck in imitation of his captain. The *Potencia* disappeared behind the cliff from whence it had emerged.

After a decent interval the *Orfeo* again stood out to sea, setting a course south-southeast for Jamaica, and the starboard watch hauled their bedding out on the deck for much needed sleep.

José paused for a minute to ask Tío Domingo, "How did such a man get a commission? He has had a poor education –he only pretends to know Latin." José might not yet know a buntline from a bowline, but here he was on *terra firma*.

"He may be of a noble family, but I doubt that he is more than an impoverished third cousin of the Vizconde," said Tío Domingo in reply. "He took me by surprise. I will need to speak to my naval friends about this incident and perhaps they will help him understand the situation."

Late that evening after they had consumed their much-delayed dinner at the change of the watch, Tío Domingo went into the cabin and came out with a handful of cigars. He distributed them among the crew.

"We have been lucky today," he continued. "We must celebrate."

José put his to his nose and sniffed deeply. His first cigar! How he would savor it, away from Papá's vigilant eyes. It was only one, and he need not know. He took long, satisfying draws upon his cigar. He felt like a man while smoking it, no longer made nauseous by its acrid smoke. Renzo, meanwhile, cast his fishing line into the waters and caught a blue marlin. He pulled out his knife and deboned it, placing the carcass respectfully before General Scipio. The cat sat on his haunches, accepting the tribute as his due, and began to consume his dinner in the slow, deliberate fashion of a conquering hero.

---

1. The weather flies.

18

ISLAND OF HERETICS

They saw no more of the *guarda costa*. Vicente made much of General Scipio, reserving the nicest bits of his dinner for the cat, who in return would rub against his leg and lie on his chest while he slept. The General reserved his attention for Vicente alone, despite Osorio's attempts to purchase his affections with small dainties. Renzo set himself to win the heart of Lucía, as he had named his new bird, and tried to entice her to trill her song again, for it had not been heard since she came aboard. She, however, sat listlessly in her cage and paid scant attention to the items Renzo poked into her cage to tempt her appetite. He tried cornmeal, bits of cassava bread, morsels of meat, raw and salted, but Lucía would only peck at a few scraps of vegetable. One morning Renzo woke to find her lifeless at the bottom of her cage. He held her in his two large hands, as if hoping for a resurrection, but none came. He tossed the bird and the cage over the side and did not speak for the rest of the day.

"Some birds were not meant to live in a cage," Osorio told him when he learned of it.

At first José resented caring for the goats in addition to the chickens, whose numbers had been replenished in Boca Guaurabo. They seemed always to be eyeing him when he passed, bleating demands for more hay from the bales stowed below. They butted him aggressively when he came up with the hay, seizing mouthfuls before he could put it down. He began talking to them as a means of distraction.

"Hey, you foolish thing, wait your turn. And you, don't be shy, get in there and eat your share or your friends will leave you with nothing." Soon each one had a name.

Osorio shook his head. "Do not become too fond of them. They are destined for a Jamaican stew pot."

All the more reason, José thought, why they should enjoy life while they might, as he slipped Calypso a yam peel.

José had grown more comfortable with the routine of life at sea. He could take his turn at the helm with the rest, and adjust the trim of the jib when so ordered, although he did not understand why the change was made. He enjoyed most of all the slow time in the evening, before he turned in, when Osorio played ballads on his guitar and sang, and the others asked him to relate more of the adventures of Odysseus's arduous journey home. Sometimes, too, Osorio would play a lively tune, and Renzo would perform dances from Naples. Once José attempted a dance from Andalusia he had half-learned from Abuelo, and they all laughed. At other times Tío Domingo regaled with tales, occasionally ribald, from his privateering days. Vicente seldom joined in, but gave every appearance of enjoyment. On one occasion he spoke of his late father.

"I worked by his side in the tobacco fields, from morning until evening, gently nursing each plant as if it were a child. And if I faltered in my duty, he would thrash me. He was the best of fathers!" He smiled mistily, looking off at the horizon and remembering the innocent days of his youth.

Sunday passed as they made their way to Jamaica, but his rosary remained at the bottom of his chest. Next Sunday, he promised himself, as he helped Renzo fish. The next Sunday it remained undisturbed. Instead he reserved Sundays for his new indulgence – a cigar. He borrowed from Osorio on the future profits from his venture and joined the others in puffing luxuriously on the quarterdeck after Sunday dinner.

As they approached Jamaica, José was often sent aloft to sit in the crosstrees and watch for the Jamaica coast. After ten days of beating their way southeast, he saw it, a sliver of lush green on the southern horizon. It was early afternoon on the 27th of April, and a bank of clouds was drifting over the mass of land ahead. José thought he could see a grey line of rain below it.

"Land ho!" he cried.

Osorio clambered aloft to take a look, for he knew the landmarks. They continued to beat along the coast through the afternoon watch, now taking care to remain just out of sight of the land. At dusk, they ventured closer, sailing on short boards until Osorio spotted lights off the starboard bow. It was all hands on deck now as they neared their destination. They stood in towards the land until, perhaps a mile off, they hove to. José noticed that they carried no lantern on the masthead, although the light had almost vanished from the sky.

Tío Domingo ordered José to change into his good breeches and the new felt hat his uncle had insisted that he bring. His uncle arrayed himself in his best green coat, adorned with silver buttons. The buttons and the polished buckles on his shoes glittered in the lantern light of the phosphorescent calabash. He assiduously combed his long red locks until they, too, shone, and then tied them up in black silk ribbon. He looked in the small glass he kept in the cabin and his face smiled back at him with satisfaction. Now suitably attired, he ordered the boat lowered. Four of them climbed aboard and made for shore, leaving only Vicente on the *Orfeo*.

The oars were muffled in sennit, the sockets lined with leather, and so the oars made little sound as Renzo and José rowed. Sharp gusts of wind raised waves that drove spray into the boat. They beached the boat on a sandy spit of land, and Tío Domingo motioned José to join him ashore. He ordered Renzo and Osorio back to the *Orfeo*.

"We will meet tomorrow in Mosquito Cove, at dusk," he said softly as he and José pushed the boat into the surf. It disappeared into the dark waves.

They picked their way up from the beach by the light of the half-moon and the stars that shone between scattered clouds, heading towards the lights of the town of Lucea. José clambered awkwardly over the ground, missing the motion of the deck coming up to meet him. The air was warm and humid from the rain earlier that day, and José slapped at swarms of mosquitos. He was disappointed, now that he had arrived on a foreign shore, to find it to be little different than his own home. Why leave at all, he wondered?

Tío Domingo led them down a street white with sand and crushed shells to a broad, two-storied wooden building. Stripes of light showed between the louvres of broad jalousie windows, and the shouts and laughter of men's voices seemed to call out to them to join them. Tío Domingo had scarcely entered before he was embraced by a raw-boned, red-haired woman, a woman who was no longer young but was far from being old. Her green dress seemed to flaunt rather than to hide her buxom figure.

"Ach, Donnie, 'tis ye i' the flesh!" she cried.

"Thou're as bonny as ever, Elspeth," Tío Domingo responded, introducing her to José as Mrs. Ainslee, the proprietress of the establishment. His freshly shaved cheeks glowed as he wore his brightest smile.

She ushered them to a battered deal table and brought them two tankards of a dark, foamy drink. "A guid stout, just i' frae Bristol. Weet the whistle and A'll be wi ye whan time allows. Archie will fesh mair whan ye want it," she added, indicating a boy of about twelve whom José concluded to be her son.

José took a sip of the beverage and grimaced. It was strong and bitter, but lacked the bite of *aguardiente*. He watched Tío Domingo take a long draft and eventually took another swallow himself, his thirst overcoming his distaste.

José looked about the tavern. These were the English heretics he had heard about all his life! In the corner a table of red-faced men roared out a song. The men's rough dress suggested that they were sailors, and he had seen the masts of a ship silhouetted against the sky as they entered. At another table José recognized, with discomfort, several British soldiers in frayed red coats. One carried on a persistent flirtation with a comely young *morena* slave woman. She returned his smiles, and her hips swayed slightly when she passed near him. The leers from the other tables she regarded with indifference. An assemblage of sun-browned, sharp-faced young *blanco* men shared a meal whose savory odors mingled with the tobacco smoke emanating from the pipes of two middle-aged men in the corner. Candlelight flickered on the older men's faces as they bent over a game of backgammon. Their rounded cheeks and silver buttons spoke of their prosperity.

Tío Domingo leaned over and spoke to José in a low tone. "Speak nae leed but English here. And i' Jamaica, mind yer name is McIntyre. And sae is mine ain. Donnie McIntyre, just Donnie McIntyre." He sat back and fell silent, observing the room.

José listened to the strange words that swirled about him, but understood only snatches. He felt his eyelids drooping from fatigue and the effects of the stout. He had rowed long that afternoon, and ordinarily he would now be asleep in his hammock. He marveled at the boldness of these heretics: laughing, singing, drinking, oblivious to the perilous state of their souls. Recalling the rumors of war, he wondered if the soldiers he saw would soon be facing Spanish arms. If so, they would fare poorly, as he watched two of them stagger out red-faced. The sound of retching came from outside the door.

He must have dozed off, for suddenly he awoke with a start to see Mrs. Ainslee sitting with Tío Domingo. The tavern had emptied of patrons, and Tío Domingo was presenting Mrs. Ainslee with a fine white handkerchief trimmed with delicate lace.

"Here's the bonny gift tae a bonny lass," murmured Tío Domingo, taking her hand. His long hair, carefully combed and queued before they left the *Orfeo* shone red in the candlelight. It was his smile, however, that lit up his handsome face.

"Stop wi' the flethers, A'm nae lass," Mrs. Ainslie laughed in return as she dabbed her nose genteelly with the new handkerchief.

She took him by the hand and led him to the stairs outside the building that led to the upper chambers, leaving José alone with her son and the serving woman. Over his shoulder Tío Domingo said, "Archie will tend tae thee."

José stood up, feeling decidedly uncomfortable. He was old enough to understand what took place in the low establishments in the neighborhood of Campeche in Havana. Nonetheless he was shocked to discover that his own uncle disported himself with women in foreign ports. He understood now his mother's warnings.

"You'll bed down on the floor outside the door where Captain McIntyre is sleeping. That's where the slaves sleep," announced Archie officiously.

José looked down upon the head of this insolent boy. Did this fellow think that he looked like a slave? And then he remembered his last glance at his reflection in Tío Domingo's looking glass. His skin had darkened noticeably in the sun, and his hair had grown unkempt, fighting to free itself from the ribbon he used to tie it at the nape of his neck, and sometimes winning. Moreover, his shirt was dingy, his breeches frayed, and one of his stockings sported a ladder from top to toe. It was true – he looked more like a wharf rat than a student from the *colegio*.

His anger bubbled to the surface. "Ach, thou muckle softie, A'm nae slave, but his nephew!" José snapped.

Archie's face broke into a broad smile. "Forgive me, I could tell as soon as you opened your mouth that you were a Scotsman. You've an odd accent, though."

Archie took a candle and led the way up the stairs. As he followed, José wondered at the mysterious way a few words had transformed him in an instant from slave to Scot, just as Don Nicolás's comic attempt at Latin had cost him respect. He wondered, too, at Archie's peculiar speech. Did they not speak proper English on Jamaica?

The hall proved to be a large front room, flanked by bedchambers. Louvered walls separated the chambers from the hall, and from one came loud snoring that José guessed must emanate from Mr. Ellis and Mr. Whittaker, the backgammon players, who had rented a room for the night. As Archie brought out a hammock for José to use, the slave woman came in and curled up in a blanket on the floor of the hall. They entered Archie's chamber through a door along the back wall of the hall, and Archie slung the hammock from hooks already affixed to the walls of his chamber, suggesting that he was accustomed to hosting visitors there.

They settled in for the night, but as soon as Archie blew out the candle and rolled over in his bed to sleep, they could hear the slave girl arise and creep out the door to the stairs.

"Congo Jenny is going to see her soldier boy," Archie said with a laugh. "She won't be back till the morning."

José lay in the hammock and felt his head swaying as if he were still on the *Orfeo*. Through the louvered wall of the other room at the end of the hall José could hear thumping sounds, accompanied by Tío Domingo's voice and the laughter of Mrs. Ainslee. He longed to be back on the sloop. He covered his ears with his hands and willed himself to sleep.

They were awakened the next morning by Mrs. Ainslee's scolding voice. "Whaur hae ye been, Jenny? A've been up thae twa hours and ye were naewhere to be found."

Jenny began to speak but Mrs. Ainslee cut her off. "Tell me nae mair of yer muckle lies and boil us a kettle o' tea," she snapped.

Jenny moved to do her bidding, albeit at a pace of her own choosing.

Mr. Ellis and Mr. Whittaker came down to breakfast, paid for their lodging, and departed. José stowed away a heaping plate of fried plantains and papaya. Mrs. Ainslee placed slices of a lumpy browned cake on their plates.

"Oat cakes, hot frae the oven, as guid as iver ye'll find i' Glasgow," she announced with pride.

"It may stay i' Glasgow for all o' me," grumbled Tío Domingo. "A'd as leif niver eat another oat in my life." José noticed, however, that he ate two of them.

Mrs. Ainslee poured them all steaming cups of a dark water that proved to be tea. José found it a sorry, weak drink, but much improved with the addition of milk and sugar, and he added generous amounts of both.

After breakfast they strolled down the main street of Lucea. It was an exotic place. Where Havana's brightly painted plaster walls flirted gaily for the attention of passers-by, Lucea's two-story buildings stood with dignified green doors and shuttered windows all open to the morning breeze. A few had glass sparkling in sashed frames. He saw also single and two-storied wooden shops splayed along the road, with broad double doors open to the public, and windows with covers that folded down like trays to display the shop's wares. Many buildings had second stories that extended out over the edge of the roadway, providing a shady passageway for passers-by.

Just as in Havana, however, the street was bustling with people taking advantage of the morning air that, if not cool, was at least not yet torrid. José was shocked to see even well-dressed *blanco* women walking down the street unaccompanied, and entering shops to negotiate directly with shopkeepers with nary a *volante* to be seen. The shoppers, however, were outnumbered by the *morenos* coming and going on errands for their masters, and José began to suspect that on this island a mere handful of *blancos* ruled over a vast mass of Africans. He saw a few *pardos*, too, higgling goods on the street or presiding over tiny shops.

They turned down a side street and Tío Domingo stopped before a solidly built wooden house. Through louvered windows José could see stacks of barrels and crates very like those in Señor Anselmo's warehouse. With an air of familiarity, Tío Domingo advanced up the stairs to the family quarters. They entered a long front hall that was sparsely but elegantly furnished. In the center stood a well-used mahogany table surrounded by Windsor chairs. All the louvers in the windows were opened wide to the morning air, and stripes of sunshine fell upon the individuals in the room. At the table sat a youth of José's age, reading, and along the inner wall, a woman with the first strands of grey appearing in her dark hair was knitting what gave every evidence of becoming a stocking. Next to her sat a girl, her dark wavy hair slipping out of her cap to fall upon the embroidery in her lap. A papaya-colored cat rubbed against her leg and earned a caress. At a desk in the corner a man in spectacles poured over an inky ledger. He turned at the sound of the door, removed his glasses, and hurried to welcome his guests.

The man reached out an ink-stained hand and seized Tío Domingo's in a clasp that soon became a warm embrace.

"*Mi amigo!*" he exclaimed in Spanish. "How good it is to see you!"

"And you, Samuel," replied Tío Domingo, in his warmest tone.

"And who is this young man?" asked the man called Samuel. "Could this be José?"

"The very same," replied Tío Domingo. "José, this is my good friend and business associate, Samuel Fernandez."

José was startled. Were there Spaniards, then, living among these heretics?

His astonishment must have shown in his face, for Tío Domingo said, "Do not be surprised to hear Mr. Fernandez speak Spanish. There have been Jews in Jamaica since the Spanish first arrived, well ahead of the Inquisition."

Mr. Fernandez added, "Old habits die hard. Our tongues still remember Spain, but our hearts are very much with King George." He went about the room, introducing the rest of the family.

José froze inside. Mauricio had regaled his friends with many stories about the heinous deeds of the Jews. They sacrificed Christian children to use their blood in their dark rituals and used it to bake their unleavened wafers. They lied and cozened unwary Christians out of their money and goods. They were descended from those who on Good Friday had called for Jesus to be crucified. Could these smiling, well-dressed people actually be the wily Jews about whom he had heard so much?

"Rebecca, have Miriam make us a pot of chocolate," Mr. Fernandez called to his wife, and she set aside her knitting and disappeared out the door and down the stairs.

Mr. Fernandez gestured to a chair, and took another for himself, pulling it up to the one of the windows. "We can creolize while we wait for our chocolate," said Mr. Fernandez, putting his feet up on the low window ledge. Tío Domingo followed suit. With trepidation, José took a seat at the table with Mr. Fernandez's son, Daniel.

"So, what news of the war?" asked Tío Domingo casually.

"It continues as if it may never end, at the cost of endless blood and treasure. Just two weeks ago the French made a raid near Martha Brae. They absconded with several slaves," Mr. Fernandez replied.

"Retaliation, no doubt, for the British seizure of Guadeloupe," replied Tío Domingo.

"That was a fine piece of work. If the war continues in this vein, we will eventually hold all the sugar islands," said Mr. Fernandez with satisfaction. José wondered if these piratical British longed to seize the Pearl of the Antilles, as well.

They were silent for a while, then Mr. Fernandez asked, "What do they say in Havana? Will King Charles come to the aid of his French cousin?"

"There are rumors, always rumors, but nothing certain. If he does there will be letters of marque available for any vessel that wishes to turn privateer," Tío Domingo replied.

Mr. Fernandez sighed. "Then we would be at war, you and I. I am loathe to see that happen, my friend."

"We two will never be at war," averred Tío Domingo, "although our sovereigns may."

"In that we are in agreement," confirmed Mr. Fernandez. "In the meantime, the whole island is in terror of these coastal raids. And they see a Jesuit spy behind every tree."

Tío Domingo burst into a long laugh. "The Jesuits are indeed a crafty lot," he affirmed, when he had gained sufficient control of himself. "But I do not think anyone will find one of those black-cassocked fellows hiding behind a banyan tree."

Mr. Fernandez joined in his laughter. "I fear it is our own Negroes who present the greater danger."

"I thought they had captured Tacky and his rebels and hung them from the nearest tree," replied Tío Domingo.

"Tacky himself, and his lieutenants, have suffered a far crueler fate than hanging," was the response of Mr. Fernandez, his voice grave. "But there have been incidents since then, and every time a few Negroes disappear into the woods, or assemble together in any number, the fear of rebellion arises anew. And with cause – there must be nine Negroes on this island for every white, and God in heaven knows many of them are treated most abominably. If ever they band together in force, God help us."

A *morena* woman appeared bearing a tray with an enameled chocolate set and placed it on the table. Mrs. Fernandez poured a cup for each of them and the two men continued their discussion, the talk now turning to business.

"Daniel," said Mr. Fernandez to his son, who resembled him closely, "why do you not show José our copy of Josephus? He has been studying theology at a Jesuit school and I am certain he would find the engravings in it most interesting."

Daniel took a heavy volume from a small bookshelf by his father's desk. Gilt letters on the spine read, *Antiquities of the Jews.* He placed it upon the table and opened it to a drawing of a soldier carrying off an enormous candelabra.

"The sacrilege of Antiochus," Daniel read in curt tones. "The rest you may find for yourself." He sat in cold silence, with narrowed eyes and thin lips.

José leafed through the book. The sentences meant nothing to him, despite his uncle's instruction. His study of Latin, however, suggested the meaning of some of the words, however. "Antiquities" must have something with past times. He looked with fascination at the pictures, and tried to break down the sentences like a puzzle.

In the background he heard bits of Tío Domingo's conversation with Mr. Fernandez, although the men spoke in low tones.

"The atmosphere here is very strained now..." he heard Mr. Fernandez say.

"It would be a great boon to me," from Tío Domingo.

"But can he play the part?"

"He is a clever boy..."

"Every mulatto now must wear a badge..."

"He is almost white..."

Meanwhile, he cast occasional sideways glances at Daniel and remembered Mauricio's lurid tales. How the boys had thrilled to them at the time! There was Mrs. Fernandez, humming softly to herself as she knit. Could she have baked Christian blood into wafers? Could Mr. Fernandez, now laughing at a jest of Tío Domingo's, have presided over dark religious rites? It seemed impossible. And yet he never would have thought that Renzo had once killed a man.

At last Tío Domingo and Mr. Fernandez concluded their business with a handshake and stood up. Tío Domingo clapped his hat on his head and José, too, stood up, having long been ready to leave.

Tío Domingo put up his hand to stop him. "Mr. Fernandez and I have reached an agreement. You will stay here with him and learn English until I return from Curaçao. In exchange, you will teach his son mathematics and geometry."

"You are abandoning me to these Jews!" José cried out in Gaelic.

Tío Domingo's face took on an angry cast. "I am entrusting you to my dear friend," he replied in the same language. "You will do all that you are told, and behave honorably. Do not shame me."

José balled up his fists and stood in angry silence. Tío Domingo was disposing of him like another piece of cargo, no better than a bale of tobacco. Across from him, Daniel's face, too, was stony and his back stiff.

Mr. Fernandez added his own warning. "Given the fears abroad on the island, we do not wish the authorities to know that we have a Spanish citizen as a guest. And while free people of color are required to wear a badge at this time, we do not wish to attract undue attention. During his stay, therefore, José will become Joseph Lopez, Mrs. Fernandez's distant cousin from Willemstad in Curaçao. He will hardly be the first cousin whom we have hosted in our home."

"Someone will bring your sea chest over from the *Orfeo*," said Tío Domingo. Then he added in Gaelic, "Be sure and take note of the British vessels that come and go in the harbor, just as we did at sea. It is good practice for you." And he was gone.

"Daniel, show your new cousin about the place," said Mr. Fernandez, now speaking in the same strange English spoken by Archie. Did no one on Jamaica know how to speak properly? "I am sure he would like to know where to find the necessary."

With wordless resentment, Daniel ushered José down the stairs and into the yard behind the house. "The necessary" proved to be a small wooden structure, built with the omnipresent louvered walls. Through the slats José could see a dark form in loose trousers. Suddenly the trousers dropped to the ground and he saw a black posterior plainly visible.

"How day, Kojo!" said Daniel, breezing past the building.

"How day, Massa Daniel!" was the cheery response, as if such exchanges were an everyday occurrence.

José was shocked at the lack of privacy. In Havana, his family performed these hygienic rituals behind thick walls, using chamber pots that were then emptied daily into the ditch that ran along the Calle Sumidoro into the harbor. This semi-public display struck him as vulgar and indecent, little better than the crude customs of sailors aboard ship.

The yard was not large, and was crowded with a small shed for cooking, a washhouse, and a sheltered pen for a cow and another for a flock of chickens. Daniel showed little enthusiasm as he pointed each one out. The he suddenly rounded on José.

"You are not my cousin, and you are not my friend. I do not want your arithmetic or your geometry." And with those words, he turned on his heels and returned to the house.

José followed awkwardly. Sarah soon took him in hand like a small child, officiously pointing to every item in turn and saying its name.

"There, now you say it," he heard at every turn. By dinner time José was exhausted and his head was bursting with strange new words.

Soon the sun was high in the sky, and Mrs. Fernandez began to shoo the family to the table for dinner in the airy hall. First, though, she had them line up before a washbasin and pitcher. Mr. Fernandez used the pitcher to pour water over first the right, then the left hand, and then rubbed his two hands together as he recited words in a guttural language that reminded José of Gaelic. He finished by drying his hands. Each member of the family followed suit. When it was José's turn, he poured the water over each hand and saw it run brown into the basin. He saw his hands for the first time in a while – brown, calloused, with a bit of tar under the nails from the caulking of the deck. He rubbed his hands together as Sarah helped him with the difficult words, and he watched the dirty water flow into the basin, the water now brown against the blue ceramic. As he dried his hands he left streaks upon the white cotton towel. Embarrassed, he began to apologize, but Sarah put her finger to her lips to silence him.

They sat at the table and Mr. Fernandez again spoke in the language José came to learn was Hebrew, and when he had finished, they all began to chatter as Mrs. Fernandez cut into a loaf of brown bread Miriam had placed upon the table.

"You can't speak before Father has said the blessing for the bread," announced Sarah.

"Forgie me. A wistna the haunts hereabout," José said apologetically, grateful now for his uncle's lessons in English.

He was baffled by the roar of laughter from the Fernandez family. Mr. Fernandez wiped the tears from his eyes with a cambric handkerchief and held up his hand to call a halt to further merriment at José's expense. José burned red with embarrassment and confusion.

Mr. Fernandez smiled upon him with sympathy and spoke slowly and clearly. "Your uncle and I always speak in Spanish, and it did not occur to me that he must speak Scots. Never you fear, it will give you a good leg up on English. You are halfway there already. And another language will never come amiss – just think, Spanish, Latin, Greek – Gaelic, as I recall, Scots, and soon English – you are becoming quite the polyglot."

José grasped only some of this, but he understood Mr. Fernandez's kindly tone. Miriam put an end to their conversation as she placed a pigeon pie on the table and served it onto blue china plates. Mr. Fernandez recited yet another prayer and poured them each a glass of well-watered wine.

"You must call us Uncle Samuel and Aunt Rebecca," said Mr. Fernandez as he speared a bit of the pie with his fork. "Never forget that I am taking a considerable risk in agreeing to this business. I would do it for few other men."

José enjoyed the meal. The rich pastry of the pie melted in his mouth, and they finished the meal with a bright red fruit called watermelon. It proved to be more water than melon, and full of troublesome black seeds, but it provided excellent refreshment on what was looking to become a day of scorching heat. Daniel and his sister Sarah began spitting the black seeds at one another until Aunt Rebecca stopped them with a sharp rebuke.

Mr. Fernandez then concluded the meal by reciting yet another blessing as José anxiously wondered what other rituals lay in wait to catch him out. Then the whole family joined in a song of prayer, in a language that at last he understood.

Bendigamos al Altísimo,
Al Señor que nos crió.
Démosle agradecimiento
Por los bienes que nos dió.

Let us bless the Most High,
The Lord who raised us.
Let us give thanks
For the good things which he gives.

The Spanish words and the pious sentiments reminded him of his own family, no doubt finishing their own dinner in the yellow house with the blue door. He looked about at the Fernandez family, with their dark-curly hair and Mediterranean complexions, so like his Abuelo, and the ache for home gnawed at his heart. He wished nothing more than to sit with his parents and sister, and even Augustín, and never again to set foot on a foreign shore. This prayer was not his prayer, this family not his family, this island not his island.

That night he fell asleep in a hammock slung in Daniel's chamber, alongside the boy who had made it clear that he did not belong. He hated his uncle for abandoning him in a strange land with an alien people, among heretics and Jews.

19

A JESUIT SPY

A t dusk that evening, Osorio appeared with José's sea chest. "De *Orfeo* drop de anchor in Mosquito Cove," he said in English, and winked at José. He neither sounded nor appeared English, but José knew that regardless of the vessel, a seaman might hail from almost any land. He wondered how Osorio would explain his presence if stopped.

The next day José and Daniel, along with Kojo, accompanied Uncle Samuel to Mosquito Cove. Mr. Fernandez rode his own horse, and borrowed two more for José and Daniel from his friend and neighbor, Mr. Aguilar. José eyed his mount nervously. He had never ridden on a horse before – in Havana, everything was within walking distance. The horse's wide brown flanks loomed above him.

"Don't worry, Joseph, Mr. Aguilar assures me that, despite his name, Picante is a docile creature. His frisky days are well past. He will take good care of you," Uncle Samuel said, stroking the animal's greying nose affectionately. José moved closer and followed suit. The horse shook its head, and a look in his eyes suggested that he had a few sparks in him yet. Uncle Samuel showed him how to put his foot in the stirrup and swing himself up into the saddle, and then led the group through the streets of Lucea to a road that meandered along the coast. It proved to be an hour's ride to the cove. The sun shone down upon them, but a stiff sea breeze kept the air cool and whipped the horses' manes into their eyes and threatened to rob the riders of their hats. Picante occasionally threw his head back and whinnied, to remind them that he was not yet ready for the knacker's yard, but did not prove Mr. Aguilar wrong. José quickly grew accustomed to the swinging motion as his mount docilely picked its way along the rutted road behind the others, but in time his backside began to grow sore and he longed to dismount and stretch his legs. Along the way, Uncle Samuel kept up a steady patter of conversation for José's benefit, speaking slowly and clearly over the sound of the horses' hooves and the cries of the birds in the bushes that lined the road. Daniel maintained a resolute silence, his face impassive, as if by ignoring José he could make him vanish from the island.

"We are going to Mosquito Cove to see to the discharge and purchase of the goods Captain McIntyre has brought on the *Orfeo*. I have a dock and a small warehouse there where I can store them until I arrange to move them to Lucea later today. Kojo will stay and protect them from thieves. He is a handy man with a gun."

Kojo patted the musket he carried along alongside his saddle. "Las time me deh, me shot two fellows. Dem ran fas' buh dem ne guh come back deh again." There was something in Kojo's erect stance and fierce features, as he scanned the distant tree line for possible foes that made José think that any man would be foolish to try his luck against him.

"I have given Kojo a ticket," continued Uncle Samuel. "It gives him my permission to travel alone. Slaves have always required such papers, and it is all the more necessary since the revolt. People around here are on tenterhooks and see a rebel in every Negro on the road. In truth, he cannot legally carry a gun, but everyone understands the need to allow trusted slaves to carry arms."

"I must also warn you to avoid imitating his creole English. Many whites," he continued, looking pointedly at his son, "have taken up the lazy habit of adopting the Negro style of speech. Do not follow their example."

There rode in silence for a time, then Uncle Samuel continued. "I have sent word to several of the plantation owners nearby apprising them that there is a vessel arrived to take their goods. I expect over the next several days to be able to supply the *Orfeo* with sugar, rum, some indigo, and perhaps ginger as well."

He continued with increasing enthusiasm. "I am what is called a factor, Joseph. I find purchasers for the goods that plantation owners bring me, and for the wares that are brought on ships by people like Captain McIntyre. I may live in a small town on an island at the fringe of the British Empire, but still the world finds its way to me here."

"Someday soon, you too will take your place in this network of commerce." José understood only snatches of Uncle Samuel's discourse, but he grasped that Uncle Samuel, like his real uncle, assumed that he would choose to follow Tío Domingo to the sea.

It took them an hour to reach the cove, where they found the *Orfeo* tied up at a small dock. José was much surprised to see the Union Jack flying on the *Orfeo*'s stern, and the name "Orpheus" glistening in fresh paint below, replacing the faded letters that had spelled out "Orfeo."

"We are a British vessel now, as long as we ride at anchor off a British island," said Tío Domingo, seeing the look on José's face.

To Uncle Samuel he added, "I wish the fort in Lucea were not so close. Our papers would not stand up to close scrutiny."

Uncle Samuel laughed. "That fort is scarcely more than decoration."

Osorio was chivying the goats down a ramp onto the dock. The animals bleated loudly, resisting direction, until Calypso, at the top of the ramp, put his nose in the air and picked up the scent of vegetation. He charged down onto the dock, followed by the others, Osorio close behind, bellowing at them to stay together. Tío Domingo was already standing on the dock, waiting, and gave his nephew a hearty clap on the back as they arrived. Then he and Uncle Samuel fell into deep conversation. Vicente disembarked and began to help Renzo round up the goats.

As they worked, Vicente gave a nod of recognition to José, and Osorio greeted him effusively. "Sabio, how are you? Perhaps Renzo and I will see you tonight in Lucea!"

"You will search for your true love again, Osorio?" asked Vicente, hauling back a goat that was attempting to escape through a gap in the bushes.

"Of course yes! Renzo goes in search of pleasure, and finds it, but I will not give up until I find a woman after my own heart," Osorio replied, narrowly avoiding being bowled over by a goat hurrying to join its fellows on the grass.

"How long, now, have you been searching for her?" asked Vicente, raising an eyebrow as he swatted a goat that had begun to nibble on his shirtsleeve.

"She is somewhere, I know it in my heart," Osorio insisted cheerfully, shoving a goat on the backside to direct it back towards the rest of the herd. "She must be," he mumbled softly to another goat as José began to lend a hand.

"Peter Nailor has already spoken for these goats. Daniel, you and Joseph will drive them to Gibeah. If you leave promptly, perhaps you can return within the day. If it grows late, however, Mr. Nailor will certainly offer you his hospitality."

Daniel's face took on a rigid look.

His father's face grew stern. "Those are my instructions, and you will follow them with a good grace. Mind you take the brace of pistols in my saddlebag, in case of trouble," said Uncle Samuel. Then, turning to José, "Bid farewell to Captain McIntyre, and then you two must be off."

Uncle Samuel then addressed Tío Domingo in Spanish.

"I have for you the customary list of goods sought by my purchasers in Lucea and beyond. It is unusually long – the French and their privateers are wreaking havoc with our trade. My cousin can help you obtain many of the goods, and I trust to your wit to seek out the others and negotiate a good price."

"The French will seize the *Orfeo*, too, if they catch her trading with a British colony. And once we change flags, the British navy may take an interest in us, as well," Tío Domingo replied. "May we be blessed with several moonless nights."

"I can assure you that my friends in the navy are far more interested in the activities of the French. At present the *Dragon* is pursuing two privateers recently seen off the coast of Saint-Domingue."

"Indeed?" Tío Domingo looked at Uncle Samuel intently. "When was this, precisely?"

"The middle of March. They took an English brig from Bristol and a brigantine from Plymouth and the Admiral is determined that they do no more harm."

"They might wish to look south of Trinidad as well. We saw a French frigate some 10 miles off the coast on the 25th of April," Tío Domingo offered.

"Thank you, my friend," said Mr. Fernandez softly. "My countrymen in the navy will find that most interesting. And remember me to them, should you by some accident be stopped."

"I will be sure to do so," replied Tío Domingo. Then he turned to José. "*Beannachd leat*," he said with unusual warmth, in the language he usually shunned. "*Adios*." He then turned away quickly to bark at Renzo. "Careful there! I want those bales on land and not swimming about the cove with the sharks or you will find yourself swimming with them!"

D aniel found a stick in the underbrush and began waving it at the goats, driving them towards a narrow path along a winding creek that opened into the cove. As he did, a long, wide canoe appeared around the bend, loaded with casks, rowed by two black men.

"How day!" Kojo cried out to the men in recognition.

"How day!" they replied, pulling up at the dock, and Kojo hurried to help them begin unloading their cargo.

"Lend a hand, why don't you!" Daniel shouted irritably at José. The goats were milling about, paying little attention to the other boy, and José moved in front of them on the path and they began to follow, hoping for a treat. They stopped occasionally to sample some especially tempting verdure, and Daniel then urged them along with his stick, encouraging, but never striking, the animals. They continued in this way for some time in complete silence, dappled by the stray rays of light that penetrated the dense foliage overhead, palms and a vast array of leafy trees unfamiliar to José. He was particularly struck by a tall tree covered with purple blossoms, its smooth branches spreading out in strange contortions. Flowering vines wound up the trees, desperately reaching for the light above. Never before had he been deep in the woods, and he felt the alien power of the trees closing in and trapping him in a strange landscape.

They walked in silence, and yet the air was full of sounds. José had heard people speak of the quiet of the countryside, but the forest was instead a cacophony of birdcalls, insect sounds, and the rustling and cries of unseen animals. He longed for the rattle of carts in the streets of Havana, the sound of things seen and understood. Above, a bird shook the leaves as it took flight, and a large insect dropped on José's neck. He flinched and hurriedly brushed it away. Daniel, in contrast, seemed at home in these woods, and walked with an air of calm confidence, ignoring José.

At last he could bear the silence no more. He turned and faced Daniel. "Why do you hate me so?" he asked in Spanish, no longer caring to speak the language of this hostile land and its people.

"Because you put my family in danger," he replied. And then he added, "And because I believe you to be a Jesuit spy."

José was gobsmacked. "Jesuit spy? Do you think I want to waste my time on some crafty Jew who eats bread made with Christian blood?" José shrieked back. The words sounded ridiculous as soon as he had uttered them. Nonetheless, they had been said, and with that, the two fell upon each other. Fists flew and found their mark, and blood mixed with the dirt of the path, staining their faces and shirts.

Weeks of frustration and anger had built up in José, and it all went into his fists. Daniel, too, landed more than a few blows. At last, all anger spent, they collapsed in the dust, their eyes looking upward at the branches of the tress through bruised eyelids. They were silent for a time, only the sound of their panting filling the air. José was exhausted, battered, and yet strangely elated. Here at last was someone whose insults he could return. He felt happy, as if he were back at the *colegio*.

Wearily he said, still panting, "I do not know how to spy. The Jesuit fathers taught me to be a good Catholic and, oh, so many verb conjugations. *Amo, amas, amat...*" He was silent for a long moment, then he had to ask the question that had been gnawing at him. "You do not actually eat Christian blood, do you?"

Daniel snorted. "Who thought up such a revolting idea? What sort of monster would do such a thing?" replied Daniel.

José realized the absurdity of Mauricio's fantastic tales and he laughed, and then Daniel laughed, and then they were both rolling about, roaring with laughter, clutching their aching stomachs, tears running out of their eyes.

Suddenly their laughter caught in their throats as they heard the sound of a shot coming from the direction of the creek. Daniel crept through the bushes to the bank and looked cautiously up and down the waterway, trying to find the source of the noise. He took one of the pistols and loaded it with powder and shot. At last they saw a canoe round a bend farther upstream, paddled by several blacks. At the head of the canoe sat a man brandishing a musket. He was adorned in a plumed hat and a bright blue broadcloth coat, and against the backdrop of the forest he reminded José of a tropical bird.

"That is Captain Quaco, of Trelawney Town," whispered Daniel, relief in his voice. "He is one of the leaders of the Maroons," he replied in response to José's puzzled look.

"They are the descendants of slaves who escaped long ago during the English invasion. The government finally granted them permission to keep their towns in the mountains in exchange for their help in hunting down escaped slaves. They may be in search for some now, or simply on their way to Lucea to trade."

Daniel stood up and waved a friendly greeting to Captain Quaco. The captain returned his wave, and his men rested their paddles for a moment to do the same and the canoe was carried along by the current. They then dipped their paddles into the water again and shot forward.

The goats had taken advantage of the bout of fisticuffs to wander far into the woods, and it took some time to round them up. It was well past the dinner hour when José shooed the final goat, bleating triumphantly, onto the path towards Gibeah.

At last the path led away from the creek to open fields. At a distance, on a hill, they could see a large two-story dwelling surrounded by a long piazza, overlooking a cluster of outbuildings.

"That's it – Gibeah plantation," said Daniel. "From henceforth you must say nothing. Even a word from you would excite suspicion. If you must speak, use Spanish. And if you need to take a piss, do so now."

José looked at Daniel quizzically. As he did so, Daniel undid his breeches and relieved himself into the bushes. José's amazement deepened as he saw the bare tip of Daniel's member, naked and vulnerable without its customary cap.

"Every Jewish male must be circumcised. It is a mark of our covenant with God," explained Daniel, buttoning his breeches.

"We have baptism to mark us for God," said José, as they herded the goats towards a field that lay ahead, where he could see bright figures moving.

"But no one can see your baptism," said Daniel smugly.

"Well, no one will see your covenant if you do not wave it at them," retorted José. "A Christian shows his baptism through his good works." He felt a sudden flush of gratitude that his years at the *colegio* had prepared him to defend his faith.

"Then judging by their works I think that very few of the whites in Jamaica have been baptized," was Daniel's reply.

"That is because they are heretics," explained José, demonstrating that he, too, could be smug.

"I did not realize that Papists were such prigs," said Daniel.

Papist. He had not heard that word before. "Why do you call me a Papist?" he asked, suspecting that this was some kind of insult.

"A Papist is a Catholic, one who puts the commands of the Pope above all things," explained Daniel.

José considered these words. "The Pope is the Vicar of Christ, the successor of St. Peter, and the head of the church. Of course we follow his direction." He was pleased to have learned a useful English word. He would be sure to work it into conversation as much as possible.

The goats bleated loudly as they passed through a grove of plantain trees and approached the field, and the figures there turned to examine the strangers, putting down their hoes to lean upon the handles. José had noticed the laborers as he and Daniel had approached, and saw their hoes rising and falling across the rows of the field. Children followed behind them, shoveling scoops of dung into each hole as it was dug. At the side of the field, in the shade of the plantain trees, an older woman sat minding several infants, and a young woman sat beside her, nursing a baby. The women were dressed in loose garments of coarse unbleached osnaburg that were now streaked with sweat and dirt, and the men wore shirts and pants of the same fabric, or went bare-chested. Many wore straw hats that provided but small relief from the intense sun of the open fields. Both men and women sported gaily colored kerchieves, adding a modicum of cheer to their drab apparel. There was not enough calico in the world however, to hide the dispirited slump of the black forms at work along the rows.

"Nuh stan deh lakka yuh have neva see a goat before," called out a black man whose erect stance and confident voice announced that he was the driver.

"An dat a fifth drinkz ah wata today, Amma," he added as a woman made her way towards the keg and dipper that stood under the plantains. "Me have me eye upon yuh."

"Well, whole heap a fellows have dem eye upon me," she said, with a toss of her head.

"Dem all a git to see yuh git a whipping if yuh keep up dat sass," he replied, but his eye held a note of admiration. The warmth in his voice suggested that this was an idle threat.

As Amma raised her shoulder, the sleeve of her loose-fitting dress slipped down and exposed her upper arm and a mark, perhaps an old burn, that resembled the letter "N." José looked about and saw the same mark on the shoulder of a shirtless man working in the next row, then on another. Yes, it was the letter "N." He began to look more closely at the men and women in the fields. Several of the men, and some women, too, had scars on their backs, largely hidden by their garments but still visible when garment ended and skin began. One or two had notches clipped from their ears, and one man a slit in his nostril. The hoes went up and down, up and down, as the sun beat down, each down stroke making a dull thud.

José had seen many slaves in Havana and Matanzas. They worked as servants and *caliseros*, they labored on wharves and in the shipyard, they worked as tailors, shoemakers, and carpenters. In time, they could earn their freedom through the *coartación*. He knew that slaves were sometimes taken to the Arsenal to be whipped by a sergeant, that sometimes they ran away, and that they lived in unenviable conditions. Never before, though, had he seen such an assembly of broken and dispirited people. This Peter Nailor must be a kind of ogre, he thought, and then remembered that Nailor was an Englishman and a heretic, and wondered no more.

The bleating of the goats had attracted a white man from beyond the plantain walk. "How day!" His friendly greeting reached them from across the rows.

"These maun be the goats Mr. Fernandez hae bought tae Mr. Nailor." José was relieved to hear Scots again. He had begun to understand some of Uncle Samuel's speech, but now he understood not a word that had been spoken by the slaves. This island was proving a veritable Babylon. How many languages did the people of Jamaica speak?

The man did a quick inspection of each goat, examining teeth and limbs, and gave a quick nod of approval. "Plymouth, drive these goats tae the pen ahint the boiling house."

A boy of about ten dropped his scoop of dung and began shouting at the goats, his face wreathed in smiles at the chance to escape the tedium of field work.

"Take heed ye dinna dawdle," the man called after him.

"Let me introduce my cousin, Joseph Lopez. He is visiting from Curaçao," said Daniel. "Joseph, this is..."

"Colin Christie. Ah'm verra pleased to meet ye," said the man, holding out his hand.

"Yes," replied José, remembering Daniel's warning but feeling the need to make some reply. He compensated for his taciturnity by pumping Mr. Christy's hand with exceptional vigor.

"Hae ye eaten?" asked Mr. Christie. "Mr. Nailor wouldna forgie me if I let ye gie without a wee something."

Both faces broke out in smiles. "We would be most grateful!" exclaimed Daniel. "We have not had a morsel since breakfast."

"Than let us haste tae the house," replied Mr. Christie. "Sally's pepperpot cowes all."

As they walked up towards the house on the hill, Mr. Christie described the plantation's features for José's benefit. On a distant hill, visible to the south, were the slaves' provision grounds, where they worked on Sundays to grow their own food. Also visible was a pasture for cattle and an indigo field. The large buildings below the house were the sugar works and a shed for storing tools and supplies. Scattered behind these buildings were a number of small, thatched houses of mud and wattle. José could see several chicken coops and pens for pigs. Daniel wrinkled his nose in disgust at the smell as they passed by and the sound of squeals reached their ears.

Mr. Christie led them up a broad set of steps onto the shady piazza of the house, and invited the boys to seat themselves in Windsor chairs that appeared to be waiting there for visitors. A few minutes later a well-dressed, tawny-complexioned man came out, followed by Mr. Christie, who introduced him as Peter Nailor, the owner of Gibeah.

Daniel introduced José again as "my cousin, Joseph Lopez."

Peter Nailor shook José's hand warmly.

"Yes," José replied again, feeling acutely the inadequacy of his response.

A woman of color came out, bearing a tray with glasses of lemonade.

Mr. Nailor turned to Daniel, "I must thank you for bringing the goats all this way. You have saved me sending someone myself. You must be wilting in this heat. Sally has made lemonade and she will consider it an affront if you do not stay and partake of her pepperpot. I would join you, but I am about to ride out to the Sorrell Hill to visit with Mr. Filton." His tone was light, and his smile charming, as he sat down to join them.

Mr. Christie finished his lemonade and began to descend the steps, then turned again. "Mr Nailor, afore I gae, I wissta report that Quashie hae broken three hoes this week past. I hae ordered ten lashes for him this even."

Mr. Nailor frowned. "You know I do not care for flogging."

"Aye, and they ken your easy nature and take advantage. A guid lashing for Quashie will do muckle tae forfend mair mischief," argued Mr. Christie.

"Very well, do as you see best." Permission granted, Mr. Christie returned to his duties in the field, whistling as he went.

Although Mr. Nailor had said that he was leaving, he lingered, putting his feet up on the railing to "creolize." The boys followed suit, and José found it a most comfortable pose. The proprietor shared gossip of the neighboring plantations, and regaled them with amusing anecdotes. José, despite his initial apprehensions, found him an utterly engaging host.

José had been studying Mr. Nailor in silence, surprised to realize that he was a man of color, most likely a quadroon. His rough brown hair, like José's, was soft enough to permit tying back in a queue. José worried for a moment that Mr. Nailor would notice this shared physiognomy and raise questions, but the man was preoccupied with his toilet. He smoothed back a few unruly tendrils of hair and placed a broad black hat on his head at a jaunty angle. The face under the brim of the hat had handsome features, fine-boned, but the soft curves of his African ancestry prevented them from appearing angular. His smooth, unblemished skin spoke of a life untroubled by heavy toil, but a slight fullness beginning to overtake his slender figure suggested that ease might have turned into dissipation.

At last Daniel said, "Mr. Nailor, my father was hoping that I might be able to collect the payment and thus save you a trip into Lucea."

"That was very kind of him, but I fear I do not have ready cash at the moment. I will be sure to settle my account with him when next I am in Lucea." Mr. Nailor seemed more interested in adjusting his neckcloth, whose snowy folds made a pleasing contrast to his blue satin waistcoat.

"I must be off," said Mr. Nailor, tipping his hat good-bye as a boy brought a tall chestnut horse to the steps and held it while Mr. Nailor mounted.

"Thank you, Jackie," he said, and, doffing his hat to the boys, rode off.

José and Daniel were left on the piazza. The lemonade, made with cool well water, had restored their spirits. Those spirits ascended to new heights as Sally came around from behind the house, bringing out two bowls of steaming hot pepperpot. At her heels followed a mulatto boy of perhaps two.

"You boy eat up. Eh a lang way back to Lucea. If eh gets late, Massa Nailor ne go mind if you spend di night." Her tone was full of kindness, and José could not help but notice her shapely form as she retreated behind the house again. The bright green calico of her dress enhanced the dark color of her skin. She made stark contrast to the figures in the field below in their coarse osnaburg.

José said a silent prayer and began instinctively to cross himself. Daniel slapped his hand down. Then the two dipped their spoons into the stew before them, no longer able to resist its tantalizing smell. There was a swirl of leaves that were strange to José, mixed with pieces of yam and plantain and tender goat. José thought guiltily of the flock that had trustingly followed him here to no doubt one day end up in Sally's kitchen, then lost himself in the satisfying richness of the dish. Its spiciness reminded him of Mamá's cooking, and he felt a pang of homesickness.

Sally made an occasional appearance to bring more lemonade and then some pineapple to finish the meal, as well as to fish for the compliments that Daniel ladled out as liberally as she did her stew.

"Me nubby did have pepperpot so good!" said Daniel, more than once. He chattered with Sally in the strange creole lingo.

At last, when they could eat no more, they rose to depart, and Daniel thanked their hostess once again. José, remembering that he was forbidden to speak, smiled his thanks, then seized her hand and kissed it, as he had seen Tío Domingo do. Sally smiled broadly and laughed.

The sun was making its way towards the tree line, and Sally sent Jackie to fetch a man named Falmouth from the fields to take them part of the way back in a canoe.

"Mind you come back quick. You ne have a pass an nowadays dem will tink any Negro wandering bout afta dark a raising a rebellion," Sally warned Falmouth. He fetched a musket from the house, and soon they were gliding down the river in the cool shade. José seized a paddle to help, grateful for something he could do without speaking.

"Thank you for your help, Falmouth," said Daniel, ever polite. He had switched to his father's English for José's benefit.

"Oh, Me ne mind. Mi would radda be upon di riva dan inna field." Indeed, he seemed ebullient, keeping up an enthusiastic commentary on the passing sights, noting the wharves belonging to neighboring plantations, and sharing gossip about their inhabitants, largely for José's benefit. José struggled to understand his creole English, but Daniel assisted with commentary in Spanish.

"Dis one a Pomfret. Miss Mary, Massa Peter's sistah live deh. Eh a fine place. She areddi have two fine boy dem. She take some addi Gibeah folks wid her wen she married. Me have a gal deh. Expec me wi her dis Satday night." He smiled, and his paddling slowed, as if he wished to linger a few minutes more in the neighborhood graced by his love.

Falmouth also pointed out notable examples of the flora and fauna to be found on the riverbank. That morning José had found the river an alien and discomfiting place. Now Falmouth's enthusiasm opened his eyes to a variety of natural wonders. He marveled, looking in fascination as Falmouth indicated each plant or animal.

Falmouth told him the name of the strange tree with purple blossoms he had seen earlier – lignum vitae, the source of a hard wood Papá sometimes used, and a medicinal concoction much favored by Señora Peña. The whole forest abounded with the gifts of nature. He imagined that the Garden of Eden must have been much like Jamaica.

"How did you come to know so much?" wondered Daniel.

"Me listen an me look," answered Falmouth. "No place me would radda be dan upon di riva."

Soon Falmouth delivered them to a low spot on the riverbank. "See there? Dat path take you right tuh Lucea. Alla di Negro folks use ih. You may come across a few."

José and Daniel thanked Falmouth again, and set off down the path he had indicated. The sun was barely visible through the branches of the trees, and long shadows darkened their way. A faint, acidic odor hung in the air from rotting vegetation. Knowing the names of some of the birds and animals that rustled in the brush did little to dampen the boys' growing unease. Daniel loaded the pistols and handed one to José, and they walked on, watching and listening at each sudden noise. José wished that he knew how to use the weapon.

"Daniel, will you teach me to shoot one day?" he asked, his voice sounding loud in the dusk.

"Gladly!" cried Daniel, as if his voice could crowd out their fears. He kept talking as they walked, and José hung on his every word, as if they could protect them from the gloom that was beginning to envelope them.

"I knew Peter Nailor would not pay us today. His debt to Father keeps growing. He is like so many of the planters – when times are good, they spend on luxuries and amusements, and when the harvest is poor, they borrow. Then when we try to collect the debts, they complain that Jews are greedy bloodsuckers."

"Mr. Nailor is a charming fellow, but mother says he is wasting away his substance. His father, John Nailor, never married, but he had two children by his mulatto mistress, and Peter inherited the plantation. His sister received a generous dowry and married well. She is now mistress of Pomfret, as you heard. Mother says John Nailor spoiled Peter, and now he drifts about, mooning over some white governess who refused him. Everyone knows he keeps Sally as his mistress, and that little boy is his son. Father says he should be a man, run his estate, pay his debts, and find some sensible girl of humble background who will take him in hand."

Daniel had much more to say about the neighboring plantation owners, with whom his father had frequent dealings. As they talked they forgot their surroundings until they suddenly found that the path had narrowed to a mere sliver between the bushes. Someone had once used a machete to hack this passage through the woods, but the broken branches were growing back, as if no one had passed this way in some time. The sky was darkening quickly, and José felt a drop of rain on his hand, and then another. In the distance there was a faint rumble that might have been thunder. Soon their pistols would be of no use.

"I fear we have taken a wrong turn," said Daniel. "We should find our way back to the main path."

"Maybe not," replied José. "Look, up ahead!" Just discernable through the bushes were glimpses of white, and a few patches of red and yellow, in an arrangement that appeared unnatural and suggested a human presence.

"Huzzah!" cried Daniel. "We must be nearing Lucea!"

Their feet sore but hearts elated, they pushed their way through the bushes and found themselves in a small clearing. The white patches that had caught their eyes, reflecting the last rays of daylight that slipped through the trees, lay arranged near the edge of the clearing. They approached slowly. José bent down and found, half-buried in the forest debris, fine bones, perhaps from an animal. Pushing aside a large fern leaf, he saw staring back at him a small skull, unmistakably human. He looked about and saw that the clearing contained the remains of several skeletons, a mix of bones that had once belonged to children and adults. The bright colors they had seen were scraps of clothing, kerchieves and rags of osnaburg. He wiped his hand in horror on his shirt, but was too terrified even to speak. It was Daniel who gave a terrified cry, pointing upwards at rotting nooses that hung from the branch of a large tree.

They ran. They ran through the narrow pathway, oblivious to the branches that tore at their clothes and scratched their skin. Daniel tripped and his pistol went off, and he and José dropped their weapons and ran faster. The sky opened up and rain poured down. Flashes of lightning illuminated the murk of the path and they ran still faster. They ran, in wordless terror until, panting and with aching sides, they found themselves within view of the lights of Lucea.

20

WINDS OF FREEDOM

Aunt Rebecca gasped when the boys entered the Fernandez house. "Good gracious, were you attacked? What has happened? Have you suffered any injury?" She rushed to examine them closely.

The boys could hardly answer for the torrent of words, until Uncle Samuel help up his hand to silence her. "Tell me everything," he said, as Aunt Rebecca called for Miriam to bring a basin of water and some balm for their scratches. She came, accompanied by Kojo.

Daniel told them of what they had found in the clearing, of the skeletons, the scraps of cloth, the nooses, and their terrified flight. He did not mention the earlier fight, and no one thought to ask about their black eyes and bruises. The family was silent, Sarah wide-eyed.

It was Kojo who broke the silence. "Me know dat place. People say eh haunted. Nobody guh deh now. Dem people deh from Nineveh. Dat mon Mingo, he join Tacky. Den when dem capture Tacky, he ran, take fit 'em woman, fit 'em chillen, he hid inna caves by di riva. Me guess he did tink he could take a boat and gwaana Santiago."

"And then they got caught…" Daniel interrupted.

"Nuh, nobody nebby ketch dem. Dey just did give up, give up and hung demselves. Dem get away inna end, me guess." Kojo shook his head.

"Let us speak no more of this," said Aunt Rebecca, seeing Sarah's horrified face. She hurried her to bed. Uncle Samuel followed. Daniel and José lingered, hoping to learn more details.

Kojo was eager to oblige. "Mingo did from Nineveh, di massa deh a devil. Di bookkeeper, he whips di people alla di time, sometime he pickles dem." He paused so Daniel could translate for José.

"Pickle?" José asked.

"Dem rub salt, lime, and peppa inna dem after dem whip dem," explained Kojo. "Sometime dem doh worse."

José listened with growing revulsion.

"Mingo was mad, mad bikause Massa Markman kept a take wit him woman. She did a good looking woman. Me expect dat did what make he joined Tacky. He couldn' take any more," Kojo continued.

José was overwhelmed by the horror of it. Suicide was a mortal sin. "Surely it couldna be worse if he is caught!" he exclaimed, fighting the tears in his eyes.

Kojo shook his head grimly. "Me hear say what dem did to Tacky and de mon wit him. Dem burned dem. Slowly while dem did still alive. Dem start at di feet and just burned dem until dem did dead. Dem hung others up inna cage inna market in Savannah la Mar and leff dem deh inna sun. No water, no food."

He shook his head again. "Falmouth did see dem and he say dem never cried out. Just sat deh and look lakka kings."

"It is true," said Daniel. "Mr. Tavares witnessed such punishments in Savannah-la-Mar. He was in awe of their courage, if not of their cause."

The night was late before José fell asleep. Kojo's strange words persisted in his mind. The words of a people set apart by color and by language, marked by cruelty and alone in their suffering. The English were a cruel people, living outside of the Catholic Church. He was proud to be from an island where such things did not happen. He stared at the moonlight slipping between the louvers of the window, marveled at how the eerie shadows it created distorted the appearance of everything in the room. He remembered how earlier he had thought the forests of Jamaica were like the Garden of Eden. He thought, too, of the slaves pickled and disfigured, of the rebels burned and hung, and of the remains in the clearing of a final act of despair. The serpent had surely slithered onto this island and set up his throne.

T he bright morning sunshine that poured through the windows made yesterday's events seem phantasmagoric. The family breakfasted on fish and
papaya, and conversed of mundane things. Daniel teased Sarah, Aunt Rebecca
remonstrated with her children, and Uncle Samuel gave instructions for the day's
work. Later, however, Uncle Samuel and Mr. Aguilar returned to the clearing
to say prayers over the bodies and give them a decent burial. Uncle Samuel also
succeeded in recovering the pistols, dropped by the boys in their terror.

Uncle Samuel first requested, then ordered, Kojo to accompany them, but
Kojo was adamant in his refusal.

"Dat place haunted," he said with set jaw. "Me would radda be beaten." José
silently shared his sentiments.

Uncle Samuel did not whip him, but set him to work hauling heavy casks of
tobacco to Mr. da Silva's shop. "What sort of man would I be to follow up such
a tragedy with a whipping?" he said.

A few days later Friday arrived, and with the setting of the sun, the Sabbath.
It proved a trial for José. As the light disappeared from the sky all labor had
to cease. No one could mend a shirt, empty a chamber pot, or light a candle.
Nor did Miriam or Kojo perform any work. Kojo disappeared, to join the slaves
from other Jewish households for some kind of merriment, according to Daniel.
Miriam observed the Sabbath in her own little house with her grown son. She left
a cold collation for the morrow's dinner, waiting for them in covered dishes in the
kitchen. That night they sat in the hall, conversing, but the evening came to an
abrupt end when a stiff wind from the sea came through the louvered windows
and blew out all the candles. They sat in the dark for a time, and then they all
went to their beds early.

José was still wide-awake. "Could we not light one candle?" he asked, before
saying good night. "Would God mind so very much?"

"God gave us the Sabbath as a gift and to dishonor it is to call into question his goodness and wisdom. And he who cannot be faithful in the small things will in time go on to greater sin," was Uncle Samuel's grave reply. José still wished for the candle.

Sabbath worship was also a further ordeal. They gathered for prayer the next day at the spacious home of Mr. Tavares. For three long hours they sat on benches in the increasing heat, listening to prayers offered up in the guttural language he had heard before. The men sat on one side, the women on the other, all with heads covered. José saw Miriam there, with her son, and several other blacks and free people of color who had converted. After the interminable service, they returned home for a dinner of pickled herring, bread, and fruit, and a brief nap, and then, to José's consternation, they went back to the Tavares residence for two more hours of prayer. He breathed a deep sigh of relief when it was all over and they went to the home of Mr. Aguilar to drink lemonade and creolize. He longed for the gaiety of Havana, where people might choose to work on Sunday, many shops were open, and they enjoyed Mamá's excellent cookery after Mass.

José was glad when Sunday arrived. While the other white residents of Lucea were in church, Daniel and José accompanied Mrs. Fernandez to the market, with Sarah in tow bearing a large market basket. In a central area of the town slaves from the plantations came to sell the products of their provision grounds, spreading them out on blankets. They were dressed in their finery, bright scarves and feathered hats, shawls and figured calico skirts, purchased with the income from their sales. They called out to passers-by, touting their wares, and flirted with slaves from other plantations. They were utterly transformed from the wretched scarecrows he had seen but a few days previous. This was their world, in which they, for a few hours, were their own masters, conducting commerce rather than being the objects of it, selling rather than being sold. Suddenly a familiar face was before José.

"Sabio! How goes your new life as a Jew? Have they circumcised you yet?" laughed Osorio.

"Shh!" whispered José. "I am cousin Joseph from Curaçao."

"None other!" replied Osorio cheerfully, now *sotto voce*.

"And what of you? Have you found your true love yet?" José asked, quite willing now to needle him.

"I have!" Osorio whispered ecstatically. "I have found her at last! And what a woman she is! I am on my way to see her now with a present. She is worthy of silks and velvets, but this will have to do," he said, waving a bright green ribbon in the air.

"I am glad to have found you. I sold your limes for you," Osorio continued, handing him a clutch of silver. He paused.

"There is an additional matter of business, repayment for the cigars I advanced you," he continued cheerily.

José counted out the payment for the cigars, one silver bit after another. All his profits from his venture were gone, gone up in smoke! He would even find it difficult to repay Señor Morejón for the money he had advanced him.

On Wednesday, his hold filled with cargo, Tío Domingo came by to complete his business with Mr. Fernandez and bid farewell to José. "Do not look so glum," he said. "There are few men I trust more than Samuel Fernandez. Trade is built on such trust. Never conduct business with a man of dishonest ways or a shifty countenance. In the meantime, you would do well to consult with him on your next venture."

José burned with embarrassment. He stood, shuffling his feet, and then confessed his folly.

Tío Domingo guffawed. "That Osorio is a sharp one! Well, you have learned at a young age what it takes many men their whole lives to learn – do not waste your money on frivolities. Save, and invest in commerce."

"But you smoke cigars!" José exclaimed.

"I can afford to. Your father thinks me irresponsible still, but I have saved and prospered. I said no to many a smoke and tavern tipple, and now I may permit myself the occasional cigar and a glass of Madeira. And do not let Osorio fool you – he is a canny trader and has squirreled away a tidy sum to build a house someday for his lady love."

"He says he has found her," interjected José.

Tío Domingo snorted. "He finds her every voyage, and after she accepts his gifts, she disappears."

And then, with a doff of his hat, he was gone, whistling as he made his way to Mrs. Ainslee's tavern for a final farewell.

With the *Orfeo*'s departure, the Fernandez family fell into a new routine. José instructed Daniel in mathematics and geometry. While he had sometimes struggled with those subjects in the past, he found that the concepts became clearer as he explained them, and his pupil's enthusiasm awakened his own.

"Papá says that mathematics reveals to us the perfection of God," he observed one morning.

"Your papá is a wise man," observed Uncle Samuel.

He also introduced the whole family to astronomy. They stood in the yard on a cloudless night, batting away the mosquitos, while José pointed out planets and constellations.

"I wonder," said Uncle Samuel, "that Christian civilization is so enamored of pagan myths."

"Christian civilization is built upon the inherited wisdom of the Greeks and Romans," replied José, dutifully reciting his teachers' explanation.

"And that is what I find discomfiting," was Uncle Samuel's response.

It was intended that Daniel teach José English, but it was Sarah who took that job upon herself. She chattered at him incessantly, and obliged him to answer questions and reel off all that he had learned.

"You must forget the Scots you have learned. Then we will make a proper Englishman of you," she commanded.

"I am the loyal subject of King Carlos, and am for always," he proclaimed stubbornly.

"King Charles," she said. "You must say King Charles."

He was surprised to learn that she, too, had her studies. Uncle Samuel instructed her in reading and writing, and some arithmetic as well.

"For what a girl need these things?" he snorted.

She stood defiantly and balled up her fists. "Every proper housewife should be able to keep a book of receipts. I have already collected fifty! And she must maintain the household accounts. My husband will have a well-run household."

"What makes you think that any man would wish to marry such a scold?" asked Daniel.

"I have already decided upon Joshua Tavares," she answered stubbornly.

"Does he know about this?" her father asked, raising an eyebrow.

"Not yet," she said, not in the least disconcerted.

"Never you fear," Uncle Samuel said. "I am sure that somewhere on this island you can find a man over whom you may tyrannize."

José and Daniel also helped Uncle Samuel with his business affairs, delivering goods to customers, collecting purchases, and handling payments. In time José confessed his foolishness to Uncle Samuel, who gave him additional tasks to earn enough for a new venture. José developed new muscles arranging and rearranging the wares in the ground floor storeroom.

Sometimes on a pleasant Sunday afternoon, Daniel took José into the woods to teach him to shoot. José thrilled to the sound of the musket's boom as they shot at wildfowl, and he almost burst with pride when he brought home a guinea fowl to Aunt Rebecca. They went bathing in a river or creek, stripping naked and splashing in the cool water. It was a delightful respite from the heat as well as a hygienic measure much encouraged by Aunt Rebecca. The Fernandez family often seemed to be engaged in some washing or bathing ritual. He found it peculiar at first, but came to enjoy the feeling of cleanliness. His rosary, meanwhile, continued to collect dust at the bottom of his chest.

In the evenings, after a light supper, the family sat together in the hall. Uncle Samuel went over his books, Aunt Rebecca took up her knitting, Sarah practiced her needlework, and the boys devoted themselves to edifying literature. Sarah set José to reading the newspaper, encouraging him to pick out the words he recognized. These were few, for the spelling of the English was as unorthodox as their theology. Uncle Samuel would often read the newspaper to the family. José was astounded at the information provided: news of ships coming and going, the progress of the war, the debates in distant Parliament, and the activities of the royal governor and his council. His father and Tío Domingo relied on hearsay from friends and tavern-goers for such items. Some of these interlocutors proved faithful reporters of fact; others, imaginative storytellers competing to outdo each other with ever more fantastic tales.

Often, however, light conversation turned into heated discussion. José was especially intrigued by the discussions of the political issues of the day. Politics were little mentioned at home. He knew only that King Carlos was good, that Bonny Prince Charlie should now be on the English throne instead of the German from Hanover, and that Scotland had long been oppressed by the wretched English. The Pope was good, and heretics were bad. All was clear and simple.

In the Fernandez household, every proposition was up for debate. They questioned it, took it apart, examined it from every angle, argued first in favor and then against. He could only listen in astonishment.

It was Daniel who often raised the most provocative topics. "Mr. Tomlinson says that if Jamaica broke its connection to Great Britain, we could manage our affairs much more to our satisfaction."

"Do not forget, son, that if it were up to the proprietors who govern Jamaica, the liberties of Jews would be even more constrained than they are at present. It is the crown that rejects petition after petition to strip us of our already limited rights," his father replied.

"The king provides a navy to protect us from the French and Spanish, and as part of the British empire we have access to a vast market of goods. How else would the goods of India find their way to these shores?" he continued.

Aunt Rebecca spoke up. "As long as we are upending our political establishment, why should not women have a voice in public affairs?" She bent her head down over her knitting to hide her smile.

"Petticoat government? Why, what would you ladies do if you were at the reins?" asked Uncle Samuel with bemusement.

"Well, to begin, I would have every man in Jamaica who fathered a child out of wedlock flogged, and flogged soundly," she said, with pursed lips, no longer in jest.

"I fear that Jamaica would run with blood under your rule, then," said Uncle Samuel, with raised eyebrows.

"Why, Father, I have often heard you decry the immorality of the men of Jamaica!" exclaimed Sarah.

"Sweet reason and persuasion are more likely to bring about a reform of morals here," he replied.

"Did not the men of our synagogue reason with Mr. Belisario, and yet he still has a Negro mistress and three children by her?" said Aunt Rebecca.

"Well," said Uncle Samuel, uncomfortably, "he lost his wife and was lonely."

Aunt Rebecca looked up from her knitting. "Then it seems to me he was lonely well before his wife died."

"I would pass a law against drunkenness, gambling, and all forms of dissipation!" cried Sarah.

"Huzzah!" said her mother. "Surely you can see now what good women might do if we were included in government?"

"Would women allow Jews to participate fully in political affairs?" asked Daniel, for this was a favorite theme of his.

"To be sure," his mother replied. "We would be beneficent to those who lead decent and orderly lives, and a terror to those who do not."

Now it was Sarah who cried, "Huzzah!"

"Then I very much favor petticoat government," said Daniel with a laugh.

"I thank God we shall never see it," said Uncle Samuel, with a sigh that indicated that he was weary of this subject.

"How then, Father, will Jews in Jamaica ever obtain equal consideration under the law?" asked Daniel in frustration.

"Never fear, son, it will come in time. There are winds of freedom sweeping through these islands, and they will find us one day. Every ship from England comes bringing some new idea or other," Uncle Samuel said with a calm air.

"Will those winds find the slaves as well?" asked Daniel.

Aunt Rebecca threw up her hands. "Heaven forfend! If not for the swift response of the militia, we might all have been slaughtered in our beds last year by Tacky and his men. I fear a world in which such men may prowl at will."

"Perhaps they would not have arisen were they not so barbarously treated!" replied Daniel. "Oh mother, you did not see those bones!"

Uncle Samuel spoke gravely. "And that is precisely why we cannot consider abolition. There are nine Negroes for every white on this island, people who have been most shamefully mistreated. Were they all to be suddenly freed, their vengeance might be insatiable."

Aunt Rebecca shuddered at this. Sarah looked up bright-eyed, hoping to hear more about bloody rampages.

"So you see no hope for them?" asked Daniel, in a saddened voice.

"I did not say that. I think an end to the slave trade would be a good beginning. Without constant replenishment, the number of Negroes would gradually decrease. And we might attract more whites, and a better breed of them. As it is, every fourth son of a Scotsman arrives hoping to make his fortune. He is willing to brutalize as many slaves as is necessary to do so, and either expires of disease or dissipation, or, should he make a fortune, he returns home with it. We need settlers, not slaves."

"I doubt very much you could find white men, even the most degraded of Scottish highlanders, to work on the sugar plantations," said Aunt Rebecca. "And everyone knows this island's wealth is built on sugar."

"If Parliament ended the slave trade, what then of the slaves who remained? It would do nothing to reduce their suffering," argued Sarah.

"A sensible government would see to their decent treatment. Slavery has existed from time immemorial. It is in the Torah. We must simply follow God's law and treat them decently," said Aunt Rebecca.

"A sound flogging for any who mistreat their slaves!" cried Sarah.

"That government would be chosen by the same slaveowners who govern today, and their wives, if ladies voted as well. Would they have their wives flogged?

Their brothers? Neighbors? As long as some men enjoy absolute power over others, they will misuse it," argued Daniel.

Aunt Rebecca looked doubtful. "But what would become of all those Negroes if they were freed? They could hardly take care of themselves. They are an ignorant and shiftless lot, as far as I can see."

Daniel became passionate. "They manage quite well, I imagine, in their home countries, and free people like Miriam succeed in keeping body and soul together. They might need some assistance at first, such as schooling."

"When I marry Joshua Tavares, I will set up a school for them!" pronounced Sarah.

"You will be very busy, then, for there are a good many slaves on Canaan. Perhaps you will allow Abraham Tavares some voice in how his plantation is run," her father smiled.

After a pause, Sarah asked, "If you oppose the slave trade, Father, why do you sometimes trade in slaves?"

The candle flame flickered in the breeze from the window, making the lines in Uncle Samuel's face suddenly seem deeper. His voice was soft as he said, "My clients require it, and I cannot afford to lose their custom. If I were a braver man, I would throw caution to the wind and refuse, but we belong to an unwanted people living on sufferance here, and dare not stand against the world." He sighed deeply.

Then he added, "I supposed that I am waiting for those winds of freedom to do what I will not. I only hope they do not prove winds of wrath."

It was a Saturday, the fourth day of July, and the Sabbath had ended hours ago, at sundown. José and the Fernandez family were all in their beds, hoping that the light sea breeze slipping in from the north would relieve the muggy heat enough to permit slumber. Voices from downstairs chased away all thought of sleep. There was a clatter of footsteps on the stairs, and Mr. Aguilar and Mr.

Tavares burst into the hall, to be greeted by the family in nightshirts and robes, hair loose and disheveled.

"They are mustering the militia," announced Mr. Aguilar in a grim voice.

"Tom Finton just rode into Lucea, wild-eyed, his horse half-dead, proclaiming that there is a slave uprising at Sorrell Hill. We're mustering at Ainslee's tavern," said Mr. Tavares, in a voice still grimmer.

"I will dress immediately," replied Uncle Samuel.

"May we come?" begged Daniel, eyes wide with excitement. "I'm a good shot, and Joseph a fair one."

"Bring the young men," said Mr. Tavares. "We need every man who knows how to handle a gun. Nailor has already sent word to Trelawney Town for Quaco and his men."

The boys dressed hurriedly, and, armed with muskets, hurried down the steps into the soft darkness. Kojo appeared out of nowhere, and Uncle Samuel handed him his pistols and ordered him to keep watch over Aunt Rebecca and Sarah. Kojo gave a quick nod, and disappeared again.

Uncle Samuel saddled his horse Reina, and Mr. Aguilar again lent the boys horses. Mr. Tomlinson at the livery stable made sure that every man had a mount. They stood outside the tavern, the horses whinnying softly. The sliver of a moon barely outlined the figures in the dark. José recognized Peter Nailor in the gathering, accompanied by a slightly older man he assumed to be his brother-in-law, Florentius Winn. Several men were accompanied by trusted slaves with muskets. A handful of soldiers from the fort joined them. José was surprised to see how few in number they were. As they waited, Mrs. Ainslee, Archie, and Congo Jenny hurried to supply the men with ale. The silver rattled in Mrs. Ainslee's apron pocket, and she had a smile and a greeting for every man. Archie gave José a broad wink upon seeing him standing with the Jewish men.

Tom Filton stood there, dressed in a purple silk dressing gown, his hair loose, gesticulating wildly as he described his mad flight in the dark. "I could hear drums coming from the woods, summoning the Negroes, and when I looked for my people, most of them were gone. Just a sick old woman, some small children, and those too frightened to speak." Someone went to fetch him more suitable attire.

Two men in black robes came out of the tavern. One held up his hand. "Some of you I have already met. I am Brother Wildey, of the Moravian Brethren. My companion, Brother Ettwein, and I would like your permission to ask a blessing for this assemblage."

"I can see no objection to that," replied Lt. Markman, who commanded the militia.

Brother Wildey began. "Lord, I ask thy protection for these men and for their families. Let them be guided by love rather than anger, mercy rather than hate. So too, let love and forgiveness animate the hearts of the slaves, so that they will place their trust in thee and not in works of wrath. We ask for peace, peace among men, and peace in the hearts of men. We ask this in the name of thy son, Jesus Christ, who sacrificed himself on the cross that all might have forgiveness and eternal life through him. Amen."

Several cries of "Amen!" arose from the assembled men. Uncle Samuel and the other Jewish men did not join in, but said a prayer of their own. José's hand itched to make the sign of the cross, but then he recalled that this prayer came from a heretic.

"We have not mustered to hold a prayer meeting, but to crush an uprising. And we do not need your kind coming to stir up our Negroes. They will gather to pray, and finish by raising up a Moses," said Lt. Markman curtly.

"Ve teach dem only de gospel, and the luff of Christ," said Brother Ettwein in a mild tone.

"Surely you would not deny them the joy and comfort of salvation," replied Brother Wildey. "Their burdens are great, and we come only to offer succor."

"Ve are pacifists!" protested Brother Ettwein. "Ve go only to make de mission at Beulah, mit de inffitation of Mr. Gordon. He has de most tender heart for dem."

"He is in Edinburgh, and knows little of their devilish tricks," snapped Lt. Markman in reply. "And he does not have to contend with the results of his folly." He turned to marshal the militia, then turned back to the missionaries.

"Set foot on Nineveh and I will shoot you for trespassing, black robes or no," he hissed in a voice heard only by a few.

They set off, riding through the dark streets of Lucea to a rutted road that would take them to Sorrell Hill. Fragments of conversation floated back to José as they trotted along. He tingled with excitement. He had been overcome with terror the last time he was in these woods, but now he felt secure, surrounded as he was by armed men.

"I cannot agree that the Moravians present a threat," said one voice. "I blame Jesuit spies. They are the Pope's hellhounds."

"I blame Finton. He needs to take a stronger hand," came another.

"In truth, Markman bears some of the blame," he heard later. "He drives his slaves beyond reason."

"I have taken Mrs. Winn and the boys to friends. Had I left them at Pomfret, I fear they would have been slaughtered in their beds, just as those others murdered in St. Mary's parish last year," he heard Florentius Winn say.

"They would be fortunate not to be ravished first," another commented.

"A host of them shamefully abused a mulatto woman last year," came the voice of Peter Nailor.

José listened to these scraps of conversation in silence, in inner turmoil. He did not like these alien Africans, with their strange speech and mistrustful eyes. He resented Agustín, occupying his own place at home. He detested these angry beings on the plantations who threatened the people around him. He had also, however, seen the broken people at Gibeah, and learned of the brutality with which so many were treated.

At last they reached Sorrell Hill. In the faint moonlight they could just see the long house on the hill, surrounded by outer buildings. All was quiet until, as they approached the buildings, a goat bleated. Then they heard the faint pounding of drums. A shout came from the woods, then another. They dismounted and tethered their horses, whispering hoarsely among themselves. Leaving a few men to guard the horses from the rebels, they took a moment to load their weapons, and then followed Tom Finton through the trees and brush. The damp ground muffled the sound of their footsteps, and only the occasional crack of a twig was heard against the increasing throb of the drums. More shouts were heard, and wild singing. José's heart beat faster and he felt a thrill run through him – his first fight. He clung tightly to his musket, which threatened to slip from his sweaty grip. He struggled to see through the branches and bodies ahead, and thought he saw a trace of smoke in the sky above.

Suddenly a shot rang out and the mass of men charged ahead. The sound of screams from both men and women were heard. José's heart raced. He froze with panic, then Daniel called to him and he raced after him. Soon they found themselves at the edge of a clearing. Torches fixed around the edges of the area revealed a scene of chaos. A few men were firing into a scattering crowd of Negroes, men, women, and children, who cried out and rushed for the tree line. Flashes of bright skirts disappeared into the murk. José tried to make sense of the scene.

On a bed of dying coals a large kettle lay on its side, empty now, its contents in the ashes and dirt. One of the soldiers was using the butt of his musket to batter in the heads of several abandoned drums, and Tom Finton was smashing a banjo over the head of a man who had not fled quickly enough. Lt. Markman was pursuing a fleeing woman, lashing out at her with his horse whip, occasionally making contact. She tripped and fell and he lashed her over and over as she curled up in ball. In the center of the melee lay the form of a woman, moaning, eyes to the stars, a dark substance oozing out from under her. Bent over her was a man whom José recognized as Falmouth.

"It did just a party for Nancy!" he sobbed. "Everybody want to say good-bye to dat good woman. It did jus a party!" He collapsed over the woman, clinging to her body as if by doing he could keep her soul from fleeing.

21

LIBERTÉ

Falmouth picked up the woman, cradling her in his arms. There was just enough moonlight to see that a dark stain was spreading across his shirt front. She fell limp, and he bent closer as he stroked her hair. Her head lolled listlessly under his caress, and he clutched her tightly to him, rocking back and forth as he held her.

Peter Nailor approached and stood over them. "When we get back to Gibeah I will decide how to deal with you," he said in a voice loud enough for the others to hear.

He added, in a gentler tone, "Help me get her body on a horse to take her back to Pomfret."

Florentius Winn joined them. "A damnable shame. She was a steady wench and gave me very little trouble."

Falmouth and another Negro silently carried the body of the woman and lay it across the back of a sturdy little brown horse. Her head hung down, lifeless, and blood dripped on the ground. One by one, the proprietors mounted their horses for the long ride back to their estates, taking their slaves with them. It was a quiet ride back to Lucea for the townsmen, no longer animated by fear and excitement. Occasional comments penetrated the fog of fatigue that enveloped José.

"They knew enough that all Negro gatherings were forbidden."

"That coxscomb Filton dragged us out of our beds, all for naught."

"The *obeah* men are behind this," came the voice of Mr. Tavares.

"Filton was too much of a poltroon to investigate for himself and now Florentius has lost a valuable girl."

"Captain Quaco will have a laugh when he hears of it."

"Filton has had three bookkeepers this year alone. 'Tis no wonder they do as they please."

As he listened to the chatter, José could not forget the image of Falmouth holding the body of the woman he loved. He wondered if the others thought of the dead woman, or if their thoughts were only for their own affairs. The men had rushed through the night to put down a slave rising, only to find themselves breaking up a wake for a much-loved woman. Did they regret that their precipitous actions had cost a woman's life, or did they see it as the inevitable toll for maintaining order?

He thought, too, about his own actions. He had been frightened at first, but he had stood his ground and not panicked. He felt a certain thrill when he looked back on the mad chase, the drums, the shots. The business had ended badly, but he was proud at least that he had proven himself. When they returned home, saddle-sore and tired to the bone, Uncle Samuel gave a brief account to Kojo and the relieved females, and then they all gave themselves up to sleep.

The 11th of July was proving an exceptionally humid day, and Aunt Rebecca was already fanning herself that morning as Mariam cleared the breakfast dishes. They were shaken from their languor, however, when Tío Domingo appeared in the Fernandez hall, exuding energy.

"Ach, José, hae they Englifeed ye while I wis awa?" he laughed, taking him by the shoulders and looking into his eyes as if he might find an Englishman lurking there.

José shook off the terrible thought. "Still I am the subject loyal of the king," replied José in his new English.

Tío Domingo smiled with delight. "I thocht nae different," he replied. "You hae been overlong here, I imagine Samuel and his family have grown weary of you. Time to hie ye back to the *Orfeo*."

"We have been blessed by his presence," said Uncle Samuel warmly. "Thanks to him, Daniel has become a master of mathematics, and we have all enjoyed gazing at the heavens together under Joseph's instruction."

After this polite exchange, Tío Domingo and Uncle Samuel became engrossed in a discussion of trade and José began his farewells to the rest of the family. Aunt Rebecca embraced him tightly and fetched a pair of socks out of her knitting basket for him.

"Thank you, Mrs. Fernandez," he said, painfully aware of the stiffness of his reply.

He felt at ease again as she replied, "Stop that! I will always be your Aunt Rebecca."

Sarah threw herself upon him. "If you stayed and became a Jew, you could marry me! I would take good care of you," she added, as she gave him a peck on the cheek.

"Do not forget yourself," chided Aunt Rebecca, pulling her back.

"Why, have you forgotten Joshua Tavares so easily?" asked her father, as the family laughed.

Sarah flushed with embarrassment, and José regretted that he had been the cause of her discomfiture. Recalling Tío Domingo's frequent gestures of gallantry with the ladies, he took her hand and kissed it, saying, "If I am ever a Jew, I marry you the first!" He was rewarded with a smile and a squeeze of the hand.

He and Daniel were left looking awkwardly at each other.

"I did not think I would ever become so fond of a Jesuit spy," said Daniel at last, with a clumsy slap on the back.

José's heart was full, and his English words seemed inadequate to the task. "I will write tae you a letter by Tío Domingo," was all he could muster, promising future words in place of the ones he could not find today.

"I would like that above all things!" said Daniel, shaking José's hand vigorously.

"I thank you again, my friend," said Tío Domingo, reverting to Spanish.

"He is welcome in this home anytime, as are you," replied Uncle Samuel. "It is not good to be alone."

"Do not fear," said Tío Domingo, turning to go. "I am seldom alone."

"No?" asked Uncle Samuel, raising an eyebrow. "Do you never wish to settle down, to sit under your vine and fig tree and fear no more?"

"I need neither vine nor fig tree," was Tío Domingo's brusque reply as he seized José by the hand and they clattered down the stairs of the Fernandez house into Lucea's main street.

José received an enthusiastic welcome back on the *Orfeo*, hidden once again in Mosquito Cove.

"We have missed you, Sabio!" grinned Osorio. "Now you can return to scrubbing the deck and caring for the chickens. I have grown weary of it."

"We wish to know more of Odysseus," interrupted Renzo. "Already it is time for him to kill the bastards who want to steal his wife and home!" Then, in a more amicable tone, he added, "And I still must teach you to catch the squid."

Vincente took his hands and examined them. "Grown soft, I see. We must harden them again." Soon José was helping discharge the cargo the *Orfeo* had brought from Curaçao designated for merchants in Lucea, the customers of Uncle Samuel. Other goods remained on board, reserved for buyers in Cuba. José saw two pairs of manacles lying on top of a cask.

"Those were for the two slaves we brought. They were delivered on arrival, so the manacles may go in the starboard locker," said Vincente in a matter-of-fact tone.

José stared silently at the manacles. How many times had Tío Domingo promised Papá that he did not deal in slaves? He wondered what other lies his uncle had told.

In the evening he collapsed into his hammock, his muscles protesting their return to heavy toil. Tío Domingo remained on shore, no doubt enjoying the hospitality of Mrs. Ainslee. Osorio and Renzo also spent their nights in Lucea, Osorio with his latest love, and Renzo in pursuit of strictly earthly pleasures.

Vicente remained on board. "If I wished to find a trollop I would not need to leave Matanzas," he remarked, puffing on an evening cigar as he watched the shore birds return to their nests in the fading light, the sound of frogs coming to them over the water.

The 16th arrived, and, its hold now filled, the *Orfeo* was to depart that night under cover of darkness, slipping out on the receding tide. She would be once again the *Orfeo*, her name to be repainted again at dusk. Osorio was frying fish for breakfast as the others shaved and prepared for a long day of rest before a night of toil. Tío Domingo sent Vicente below to ensure that the cargo was snugly stowed. José leaned over the bulwark, watching the occasional fish pass below in the pellucid waters of the cove. Suddenly they heard the shouts of Vicente and the scream of a woman. Osorio rushed to the companionway as a Negro woman emerged, almost pushed onto the deck by Vicente.

"Look what General Scipio found below, stowed away with the rats. Without doubt she has escaped her master and thinks to make her way to Cuba." Vicente pushed the woman towards Tío Domingo.

"*Mi tesoro!*" cried Osorio, pulling her towards him. "She is no stowaway, but my love, *mi reina*, my queen." He threw his arms about her, as if he could envelope and hide her from all harm.

José stared at the woman. She was no beauty, or it was better to say, was no longer beautiful. Only her well-proportioned form, clad in rough osnaburg, suggested a past allure. Her shoulders bore the familiar scars of the whip, and on each cheek the letter "M" was branded. A notch had been taken out of one ear and her nostrils, too, had been slit. She buried her disfigured face in Osorio's shoulder.

Tío Domingo stared Osorio in the face. "You put this vessel in danger by bringing her aboard, and I will not have it. You must take her ashore before she is discovered. Make your farewells and be done with her."

"We cannot leave her. Her master is a beast, and she will suffer cruelly if he finds her. See the marks of his savagery!" he begged. Osorio's eyes, pleading, were fixed upon Tío Domingo.

"You had thought to trick, to hide her away until we were far offshore. What would happen if we were stopped? You have endangered us all," said Tío Domingo, his face stony. "Ashore she goes."

Osorio's eyes again searched Tío Domingo's face and found no hope there. His shoulders slumped, and he held the woman tightly in his embrace, whispering something in her ear as tears ran down both of their faces. Then he led her gently to the side and guided her down the Jacob's ladder, again with a whisper in her ear. She looked up into his face, and began to make her way down. Osorio followed her, and they stood on the dock where he gave her one last embrace, caressed her face, and spoke softly to her. She turned and walked briskly towards the woods, turning back several times to look at him. Osorio did not make a move to return to the ship until her she had disappeared from sight.

José watched as her form disappeared into the underbrush. She had not made a sound as Osorio and Tío Domingo argued her fate, simply following the debate with her eyes, although she could not have understood the Spanish. He had heard it said that the eyes are the windows of the heart, but her eyes had been shuttered. Only Osorio knew what thoughts and feelings stirred behind that mask.

Osorio climbed back on to a lifeless vessel. The wind barely rippled the water of the cove, boding ill for their departure that night. General Scipio lay sleeping in a coil of rope, occasionally opening his eyes to cast a baleful eye upon the crew, only to close them again. Tío Domingo stood idly on deck, hands clasped behind him, staring at the vegetation on shore.

Osorio went about his duties listlessly, until Renzo said, in way of consolation, "She not love you, she only wanna make for clear of here."

Then Osorio turned on him like an alligator, and José thought they would see bloodshed, but Renzo backed away saying, "Maybe she not so bad, maybe you see her more."

José had not realized until then how much Osorio's cheerful spirit had eased the tedium of their work. Now every minute dragged. He longed for dark and the distracting bustle of departure.

Suddenly Tío Domingo turned to them. "I have some final paperwork to be concluded with Samuel Fernandez. José, you will accompany me. And Osorio, come with me. I need you to obtain some additional plantains for our provisions. They will last the longer if purchased fresh." He motioned Osorio into the cabin with him, and after a long while they came out again. Tío Domingo handed Osorio a heavy purse, which the latter placed carefully in the pocket of his jacket. Osorio seized his hat, and then followed Tío Domingo and José over the side. He gave them a wave as he headed off in a different direction, away from Lucea.

Tío Domingo spoke of many things on the walk to the town, but the name of Osorio never crossed his lips. José could think of nothing else. In Lucea he remained at Ainslee's tavern while Tío Domingo went to the Fernandez home. José had made his farewells once and could not bear to do so again. Tío Domingo soon returned and disappeared upstairs with Mrs. Ainslee, leaving José a silver bit to buy a pint of one of the unpleasant brews so favored by the English. He instead pocketed the money and stood under the shady overhang in front of the tavern, intrigued by the sight of the Moravian brethren attempting to collect passers-by for a worship service under a spreading lignum vitae tree.

When they had gathered a small group of Negroes and people of color, Brother Wildey began with an opening prayer. Several passing whites stopped to observe for a moment and then moved on. A few laughed. The motley congregation stirred restlessly and talked among themselves. José wondered if they were merely there out of curiosity or to rest in the shade. The brethren ended their prayer, "In the name of the Father, the Son, and the Holy Ghost." Suddenly José felt the sting of salt in his eyes and a tightening in his throat. How long had it been since he had heard those words, "*In nomine Patris et Filii et Spiritus Sancti.*" He wished with all of his heart to be at home with Mamá, Papá, and Magdalena, kneeling on the stone floor of the church of Santo Cristo del Buen Viaje. He was a son of the Colegio de San Ignacio, and he did not belong on this island of heretics. He wondered how much longer it would be before Tío Domingo finished his shameful business and they could return to the *Orfeo*.

The brethren began a hymn. A few of the seated spectators, but only a few, clapped their hands in rhythm. José shuffled his feet restlessly as Brother Wildey spoke to the assembly of sin and redemption, of suffering and of peace, and of the love of the Father for all of his creation. The crowd dwindled in number as, one by one, his listeners left to return to their duties. By the time Brother Wildey closed in prayer all but one had vanished. The prayer completed, that man rose up and approached the Moravian. José was surprised to see that it was Falmouth.

"Me wan' to know more o' di land weh dere is no mo' death an' no mo' crying," the man said earnestly.

"And you shall, dear fellow, you shall," replied Brother Wildey, taking him by the hands. "On most days you may find us at Beulah, but tell me where you live, and perhaps we can gain permission to visit you there."

Brother Ettwein appeared at José's elbow. "Vould you like me to pray vit you?" he asked.

"I am of the church Catholic," he was shocked to hear himself say, then thought reassuringly that within a few hours he would be gone from this place.

"De church is found vere ever se gospel is truly preached and de sacraments are truly administered," replied Brother Ettwein. "Perhaps se church is here."

"Come along, lad, steer clear of that rogue. I would swear to it that you are drawn to priests like a fly to honey. We have enough of these black-robed leeches in Havana. You need not seek them out here, as well." Tío Domingo seized José by the arm and soon they were on the road back to Mosquito Cove.

Back on board the *Orfeo*, they learned that Osorio had not yet returned. Tío Domingo seemed unconcerned. As they prepared for their departure, José would stop time and again to scan the shore for some sign of the missing man.

Night fell, and the sky filled with stars. Tío Domingo smiled to see ripples on the water in the cove. He gave the order to raise the gaff and the mainsail rose above them. José and Renzo loosed the fore staysail and Renzo raised it up upon its stay. Vicente, his eye on the telltales that showed the direction of the wind, hauled on the sheet till the sail was trimmed to his satisfaction and then sheeted it home. At each step José asked anxiously, "Are we to abandon Osorio?" but each man looked to his work as if he did not hear. The *Orfeo* slowly, oh so slowly, eased out of the cove, without Osorio. José threw one worried look over his shoulder at the shore, dimly lit in the moonlight, but Vincente's sharp voice told him to keep his eye on the waters ahead, where the curl of the wave might indicate a hazard below the surface. Renzo took soundings as they went, speaking only to call out the depths. At last they were in the deeper waters of the sea. José looked up at the stars and knew that somewhere below them, on the disappearing island behind, Osorio remained.

Tío Domingo stared at the sails with an air of disappointment as the slight breeze barely moved the canvas. He ordered the topsail and additional headsails set to catch every puff of breeze, and set a westerly course. Vicente raised his eyebrows.

"I have heard that the *guarda costa* is plying the waters between here and Cabo Cruz. We will hug the shore until we are farther west, then head northwest for Trinidad," Tío Domingo told Vicente. Then he and Renzo turned in.

José was left to stand watch alone with Vicente, and he suddenly realized that he would spend the rest of the voyage alone under the mate's critical eye.

And sure enough, there he was, at José's elbow. "Osorio has made his choice, Sabio. He is with his woman. May the Virgin protect them," he said.

"They will be caught. You cannot imagine the things they will do to him," replied José, his voice raw with anxiety.

"If he can obtain a boat, all will be well. It is but ninety miles from Jamaica to the coast of Cuba," said Vicente calmly.

"How will he manage it? He has nothing for the necessary supplies," José replied, his imagination filled with the most terrible scenes.

"He has the money for the plantains," was Vicente's response.

"So he has gone off with the *Orfeo*'s money!" José gasped, with a horror that brought credit to his teachers at the *colegio*.

"We have plantains enough to last three weeks," Vicente replied. "Are you so addlepated as to think we needed more?"

José began to understand. "Why, then, the ruse? Why did Tío Domingo not simply give him the money and tell him to be off?" José asked in bafflement.

"He does not wish to be accused should Osorio fail," Vicente said. He was quiet for a time, then added softly, "Nor does he wish to be thought of as a man of sentiment."

When morning dawned they were off the northwest coast of Jamaica at Orange Bay. The Spanish merchant flag flew prominently on the stern proclaiming the *Orfeo*'s status as a neutral vessel. Renzo tried his hand at breakfast, but the result was a corncake half-burnt in the skillet.

"I catch fish, we eat good," Renzo promised, washing down the last of his corncake with a large swallow of bitter coffee.

José was heading to the cabin to turn in when he saw Tío Domingo at the larboard side, using the glass to follow something in the distance. José followed his look and saw a slight movement offshore. He joined his uncle at the gunwale. The others soon joined them.

"It is canoe, maybe," said Renzo, squinting.

"Two people, I think," said Vicente, who now held the glass. With a grim look, he added, "A canoe is ill suited to the sea."

José felt a tingle of excitement. Could it be Osorio and his love?

The figures were more distinct now as the *Orfeo* neared the canoe's position. At first it seemed as though they must intersect, but the wind was beginning to pick up and soon it was clear that the canoe would never succeed in overtaking the *Orfeo*, should that be its intent. The wind was picking up and the canoe labored among the waves. As it grew closer the figures within, black against the eastern sun, paused a moment to wave their paddles in the air. One stood up and his faint shouts just reached them.

José could not contain his excitement. "Surely it must be Osorio! Will we not heave to?"

"They could never have traveled so far in such a short time," Vicente observed laconically. "Escaped slaves, no doubt, hoping to reach Cuba."

"Not today, I think," said Renzo. "That sail, it follow."

And sure enough, something small and whitish had appeared behind the canoe and was growing in size as it slowly overtook the escapees. Although the increasing wind slowed the canoe, the pursuers were sailing against the northwest wind and were forced to tack and tack again. Still, the men in the canoe were surely tiring. Figures were now visible in the tiny sloop. One stood and raised what might have been a musket. The faint sound of a shot reached them. The canoe faltered, then moved forward again, but more slowly this time. Beyond it, the figures in the small boat moved about.

"They have raised the jib. They will surely overtake them now," said Vicente.

They could see the men in the canoe clearly now, two *morenos*. Again they waved their paddles, and their cries were louder now. Behind them, the pursuers prepared to tack again. An unexpected gust caught the mainsail in its brief moment of freedom and whipped it to starboard, knocking one of the men, carelessly positioned, into the water. The other figure scrambled desperately, the boat hove to, and then gradually shrank from view. There were more cries from the canoe. Through it all, Tío Domingo had stood silent, watching the scene unfold before him.

José's heart beat fast as if in harmony with the men in the boat. "We could rescue them!" he cried.

"We press on," said Tío Domingo.

The canoe soon fell away off the *Orfeo*'s stern and it, too, disappeared from view, along with the last flicker of green on the Jamaican coast. The *Orfeo* was now alone at sea, accompanied only by the increasing wind on the sails and the slap of the waves on her side. The crew returned to work.

"Heave to!" Tío Domingo's voice rang out. All hands moved to obey. José looked at Renzo, who replied with a shrug. José thought he saw Vicente smile to himself, ever so slightly. Perhaps he imagined it.

The *Orfeo* lay motionless in the water, its sails backed and rattling vainly in the wind. Tío Domingo said nothing, but once again took up the glass and studied the horizon.

"There she is!" said Vicente.

Now they were all at the stern, watching as the canoe struggled against the waves. The men's paddles dipped into the water more slowly, but still she came on. Tío Domingo watched placidly. At last the canoe reached the *Orfeo*, and they could see that one of the men was wounded. Blood ran down his arm and stained his paddle. Tío Domingo ordered the Jacob's ladder lowered, and the men climbed up, one laborious step at a time, and collapsed on the deck. They lay there, panting, muscles quivering with fatigue, unable to move. The canoe was allowed to drift away, and the *Orfeo* made a course northwest, towards Cuba and home.

José was exhausted after the prolonged excitement of departure, and collapsed into his hammock soon after the rescue was accomplished. It was not until midwatch rolled around at midnight, therefore, that José felt fully rested. They had learned that the *morenos* were named Beaubroin and Christophe. Vincente used his smattering of French, accompanied by many gestures, to learn that they had been taken captive when the English took Guadalupe, and had been sold to a plantation owner in Jamaica. Beaubroin had faced fearful punishment for some infraction, and so Christophe had helped him escape. The two had been told that the King of Spain would grant freedom to any slave of the Catholic faith who reached his lands, and so they made for Cuba. More than once they crossed themselves, and repeated the word "*liberté*." That word José understood.

Vicente dressed Beaubroin's wound, which proved not to be serious. The grateful man, his injury still tender, repaid their attentions by taking over dinner preparations from Renzo and presenting them with a stew of chicken and plantains that was filling if unremarkable. Tío Domingo promptly appointed him cook. The new men took over José's duties as ship's boy, and Christophe was assigned to the larboard watch. José would teach him the Spanish he needed and the rudiments of seamanship. He was a real mariner, now, José thought. How proud Papá would be to learn of it.

The first watch had ended at midnight, yet Tío Domingo remained on deck, watching the stars. José, emboldened by his promotion, asked his uncle in Gaelic, "Why did you not stop for the *morenos*, when you might have spared them further agony and the danger of failure?"

Tío Domingo turned and looked him in the eye. "Life belongs not to the weak, but to the strong. Robbie believes that fortune favors the virtuous, but life has not rewarded him. It is the strong who prevail in the end. No one has given these men their liberty; they have seized it and they will treasure it all the more for that.

"A man must learn to master life, or he will be mastered by it," he added, warming to his theme. "A man must never be afraid to seize what he wants. Small dreams make a poor recipe for life," said José's uncle, gazing across the sea in the clear night.

José's anger made him reckless. "Is that why you fornicate with Mrs. Ainslee?" he asked, and then was aghast at his own effrontery.

Tío Domingo erupted in a roar of laughter. "Fornicate! What language you have learned in that school! Latin and Greek are all very well for acquiring a little polish and making the right connections, but I fear the priests have turned you into a carping old maid. Men and women are meant to enjoy one another's company. He is a fool who lets God or man blind him to that."

"We were created to love and obey God," said José, remembering his catechism. He was glad that the *colegio* had provided him with useful morsels of wisdom for difficult situations.

"I do not believe in a God who does not want his creatures to be happy. He wants us to love him, but he denies us love. Religion is a snare and a folly. It makes of men small and groveling things. There is a world out there," he said fiercely, gesturing to the sea before them, "full of riches, adventure, women, and you will never be free to seize these things if you choose to be a priest-ridden milksop."

José felt a rage build within him. Tío Domingo had disparaged the church. He had never wanted to be here on the *Orfeo*. He did not want to be a mariner. He wanted to be with Papá and it was Tío Domingo who prevented him.

"You speak of seizing the world, Tío Domingo, and yet you are alone." He stood, shocked at his own cruelty. He waited for the blow that would surely follow. He had seen Tío Domingo level Renzo with his fist for much less. He expected it, and knew that he deserved it.

Tío Domingo looked at him for a long hard minute. His fist clenched, and then unclenched. Then, with a voice that trembled with anger, he said simply, "Ask Robbie why I am alone."

A gust came up and rattled the stays. Then it was José who found himself standing alone.

The *Orfeo* made good time home. The prevailing winds, which had forced them to tack most of the time on the outward voyage, now allowed them to set a straight course, sailing mostly on a broad reach. Tío Domingo estimated that they would get home in a third of the time. Christophe and Beaubroin, informed that they were now paid members of the crew, threw themselves into their work. They presented a stark contrast to the slaves José remembered seeing at Gibeah, hacking numbly at the earth. Christophe was soon able to make simple conversation in Spanish and easily mastered every new task. During the tedious dark hours of the midwatch, he in turn taught José some rudimentary French. The tale-telling from *Odyssey* did not resume, for the mere mention of the book put Renzo into a black funk, for it reminded him of Osorio and his pursuit of his lady love.

Vicente, however, in one of those rare moments in which José was in his favor, inquired, "Well then, does Odysseus ever smite the men who seek to rob him of his wife and goods?"

José shrugged. "I think he will find justice in the end."

"I am not so sure," Vicente replied. "It often evades men in life. It would be good, however, if they could find it in stories."

They again made a visit to Boca Guaurabo, where they sold many hogsheads of North American flour, as well as some of the foreign manufactures acquired in Curaçao for more salt beef, artfully stowed so as to mask the contraband deeper in the hold. José had become skilled at helping Tío Domingo fiddle the books to make all seem legitimate. Thus he felt less trepidation than he might have when, upon leaving the Bay of Xagua, the *Orfeo* espied a frigate, the Bourbon flag of Spain prominent on its stern. Sightings of warships had become more frequent than ever. His stomach took a turn, however, when he saw the yards hauled about as the frigate changed course and stood towards for the *Orfeo*. As the frigate neared, a cry came over the water for the *Orfeo* to heave to, but Tío Domingo had already issued the order. The *Santa Bárbara* lowered a boat and the rowers delivered the captain, resplendent in blue and gilt, to the sloop. The men rowed with deliberate magnificence, confident of their tactical and moral superiority.

The former slaves had disappeared below decks, but José followed the lead of the others, who stood stiff with respect as the captain climbed the rope ladder. The officer swung himself agilely over the bulwark and stood before them, whereupon Tío Domingo doffed his hat and held it to his chest as they all bowed deeply. Tío Domingo greeted the officer effusively and made a point of introducing José.

"My nephew, José Albañez." José bowed deeply, and wished that there was less tar on his hands and his slops.

Tío Domingo ushered the captain, Don Julián, into the cabin and offered him a glass of Madeira. José expected that Tío Domingo would then present his cargo manifest, registration, and other papers for inspection, but instead he pulled out a heavily marked paper that had been hiding at the back of the log. He placed it before Don Julián. The captain pored over it, and began to quiz Tío Domingo about the many warships the *Orfeo* had spotted over the course of its journeys – nationality, name, guns, position, and heading, speaking in measured, erudite tones that hinted of Andalusia. Then Tío Domingo turned to José.

"José, tell Don Julián about the vessels you saw in the harbor of Lucea. And do not forget the troops stationed at the fort."

It was at that moment that José realized that Daniel Fernandez had been right all along. He was indeed a Jesuit spy.

22

RUNNING BEFORE THE WIND

José was confounded by Tío Domingo's shifting loyalties. He confronted his uncle about this one night before turning in.

"Tío Domingo, I have heard you profess your friendship for Uncle Samuel, yet you took the information I gathered while staying with him and gave it to our navy. How can you betray his friendship so?"

"Do you not think that Samuel Fernandez also shares what he learns with the British officials in Jamaica?" Tío Domingo asked.

"Intelligence that you have passed to him!" José realized in shock.

His uncle shrugged. "We are both men of the world, and do what is necessary to carry on our trade."

"Have you no loyalty to Spain?" José asked in horror.

"I am loyal to no country. They are the projects of greedy tyrants who use such loyalties to enslave their subjects. I am loyal to myself, and myself alone," Tío Domingo replied.

José was reminded of another grievance against his uncle. "And you promised Papá you would not trade in slaves, and yet you have done so!"

Tío Domingo laughed. "The economies of these islands are built on slavery. He is a fool who pretends otherwise. Remember, your own attendance at the priests' school was made possible by slavery."

José was stung into silence. It was true, the despised Agustín had bought his education at the price of his family and his country. He lay awake for a long time that night, thinking on this, and did not again castigate his uncle.

Although Christophe and Beaubroin had taken over many of José's duties, his workload had grown rather than diminished. Vicente was teaching him to splice. He enjoyed using the fid to do the fine work of joining one line to another or making a loop. At first Vicente, having examined his work with a critical eye, would make him undo it and begin again, but in time his handiwork earned an approving grunt. He was less fond of tarring the rigging. Tío Domingo had ordered that all the standing rigging must have a fresh coat of tar, both to protect it from sun and salt and to make a great show when they returned home.

"Every head will turn when we sail into Havana Harbor," he boasted. "They will say, 'There goes a fine vessel indeed.' And Policarpo and Gaspar will burn with jealousy."

Christophe was a hard worker, but Beaubroin, after his initial burst of enthusiasm, now was more often laughing or telling stories than tending to his duties. Renzo watched him diligently to make sure he completed every task.

"That Beaubroin, he make me work," Renzo complained, in a voice meant to be heard.

Christophe spoke to Beaubroin. "You work, work *le meilleur*. You no work for master now, work slave, you work free, work for Beaubroin." Still the laughing Beaubroin could be found idling when the bilge needed pumping or the chickens awaited their feed.

The *Orfeo* profited from steady winds and Tío Domingo was determined not to waste a puff of that air. "I do not wish to be caught in a late summer storm," he said, and during the day he ordered the topsail and jib set, and sometimes even the flying and outer jibs. The stays strained, the wood groaned, and they were often at the pump as the vessel's seams worked. José saw Vicente purse his lips as Tío Domingo ordered more sail, for Vicente was a cautious sailor, but he too was eager to avoid a hurricane. As dark fell they reduced sail, and José would find himself aloft tying the gaskets onto the topsail, or clambering onto the bowsprit to furl the headsails.

"Mind your footing, Sabio," Vicente would caution him. "There are more widows made on the bowsprit than on the yards."

During the night they kept well off Los Jardines, under mainsail alone, and José and Christophe kept an eye off the starboard bow for any sign of coral heads or the dark lines of the shore.

Sometimes, during these hours, he talked with Christophe. He learned that in Guadalupe he had been a driver on a sugar plantation. José noted his muscled frame and dignified bearing, and did not wonder at it.

Beaubroin, too, had been a slave on that plantation. "Christophe, he ze good man, *c'est vrai!*" he said, struggling to cobble together enough French, English, and Spanish to make himself understood. "Me go only wiz Christophe. No Christophe, me be zere on Jamaica still. In Igboland, his papa le *homme grande, très grande*. Him boy, man steal him, sell to ship. If him zer now, him be *le grand homme*."

One night Christophe told him of how he had been captured on Guadeloupe. "Man say, *les anglais* come, we run. Me say, '*Mais non*, what *les anglais* wan' wiz us? We stay, work ze plots, work for *les anglais*. Les angalis, les français, tous les mêmes.*"

He shook his head, and his voice became strained. "*Les anglais*, ze take us, *tout le monde*, me, *ma femme, mon enfant*, Beaubroin. *Femme, enfant*, gone somewhere. Gone." He shook his head again.

"Zat Osorio, ze say zat man go, free *sa femme*, he good man, best man. Me, no good man." Christophe fell into a silent gloom that lasted the rest of the watch.

Christophe repeated this lament the next day at supper, and Beaubroin flew at him like a gamecock.

"Eh, what you say? You free, you get rich, you find her, you buy her. You good man, best man," scolded Beaubroin.

"And you, Beaubroin, you have a woman?" asked Renzo, to turn the conversation away from Christophe, who stood looking sorrowfully over the gunwale towards the east.

"Eh, me, on Guadalupe me have *deux femmes*, two, on Jamaica just one. In Cuba maybe me have two again. Me never find *les femmes, les femmes*, zey fin' me," Beaubroin replied.

"These women, they are pretty?" asked Renzo.

"Eh, pretty, no, but zey go go, *comprende*?" laughed Beaubroin.

"We take your meaning very well," replied Vicente, ending the conversation.

More than once after that José saw Christophe look across the sea, towards Jamaica, and knew he was thinking of his *femme*.

On Wednesday, towards the end of his late-afternoon watch, the wind had increased somewhat, the sky was grey, and the waves sported white caps. Vicente was at the helm, his face taut, watching sea and sky with anxious eye. A line of black clouds appeared on the horizon, and he barked orders to Christophe to reef in the topsail and for José to haul down the outer and flying jibs. José was proud of how easily he could now make his way out on the bowsprit shrouds.

"Sabio! Do not moon about out there like a girl in love! I need you to douse the fire and stow the cooking gear," Vicente's voice came to him from the helm.

The *Orfeo* heeled in the wind and the spray left a salty film on deck and rigging, sails, and crew. Rain began to mix with the spray, and soon water was pouring over the deck and out of the scuppers. Although Christophe had no experience at sea, José found his steady presence reassuring. Tío Domingo appeared from the cabin, looked about, and roused Renzo and Beaubroin.

"I need all hands," he said, and José knew that his watch would not end until the storm did.

Tío Domingo ordered them on a southwest course, to take them farther out. "We do not want to find ourselves on a lee shore," he said, looking at the sky.

"We not reduce sail before, not sail well off. Now we see some trouble," José heard Renzo grumble. "That Domingo, he a madman."

All was now motion on deck. The wind fought to pull the awning from their hands as they took it down and stowed it in a locker. They moved the chickens into the cabin and lashed a tarpaulin tightly over the boat. José was sent below to check that the cargo was tight in the hold and would not shift. He saw General

Scipio perched atop the bales, ready to ride out the storm. When he came above, he saw they were rigging a lifeline across the main deck.

Tío Domingo, gesticulating, stood by Vicente at the tiller. As Vicente nodded in agreement, Tío Domingo gestured for the crew to join them.

"We will scud before the wind," he announced. Seeing the blank faces of José and the *morenos*, he continued, "We will change course again and sail with the wind directly aft, flying as if we would outrun the wind itself. It requires a skilled helmsman, and Vicente is one of the finest. I will spell him as necessary."

He stood on the quarterdeck, firing off orders. They would sail wing-on-wing, one sail to starboard, the other to larboard. Down came the jib, to be replaced with a storm trysail raised high up on the forestay. They raised the throat of the gaff, leaving the peak lower towards the boom, to form the great sail into a small triangle. The topsail was reefed and its yard lowered until it almost touched the yard below. Now was the time, as well, to batten down the hatches with tarpaulins, leaving only a small corner to the leeward to provide air. They eased the stays, to compensate for the tightening that occurred when they grew sodden. Through it all, Tío Domingo stood on the quarterdeck, surveying their work with an excited, almost manic gleam in his eye.

"Northwest," ordered Tío Domingo. "Keep the wind ever so slightly off the starboard quarter. Pray we do not find ourselves on Cabo San Antonio." The crew hastened to trim the sails accordingly. The *Orfeo* surged forward on the new course, heading further out to sea.

"If this storm, she last too long, maybe we see Mexico," said Renzo.

"Zey have *les femmes* zer, too!" said Beaubroin, but no one smiled at his jest.

Tío Domingo called to José. "Your task is to light the binnacle lantern, and keep it lit. Vicente must keep us true to our course, or we may find ourselves broached-to." From his tone José knew that this eventuality was much to be feared.

Night fell, and the wind roared as it tore at rigging and spars. Vicente stood at the helm, which had been rigged with relieving tackles to keep it steady. The mate took only occasional breaks as he was relieved by Tío Domingo, and the others took turns adding their strength to his to steady the helm. The crew pumped almost without ceasing. The night was black as pitch, and the crew felt its way about the *Orfeo*, clinging to the lifeline or the shrouds. They were long since soaked through, at one with the rain and the seawater. Exhaustion numbed José's limbs, fatigue dulled his brain. At one point he opened his eyes to realize that he had fallen asleep with his arm wrapped through the shrouds. More than once he heard, through the raging of the storm, Renzo reciting a Hail Mary. Only Tío Domingo never seemed to flag, growing more animated as the night wore on, striding the decks, giving orders, as if he had lived all his life for this moment.

Through the night José stumbled at intervals up the companionway to check the lantern in the binnacle. The candle burned resolutely, safe behind its glass. Near midnight the flame began to gutter at the bottom of the lantern, and José brought up a new one. As he lit it and carefully put it in place of the first, never allowing the light to go out, he ventured, shouting over the wind, to ask Vicente what might happen should the sloop broach-to.

"It would mean she veered of a sudden towards the wind. We might end up on beam-end, or the violent change of direction could leave us dismasted, especially in an old vessel like this one. There is less strain on the masts when the wind is aft," he shouted in return, his eye watching the sails, then checking the compass, his hand steady on the tiller.

"So we are safe so long as we scud before the wind?" José asked.

"So long as a following sea does not poop us and smash our rudder or batter in the stern," Vicente answered calmly. "That is why we must maintain our speed. The trysail and mainsail, one trimmed to starboard, the other to larboard, balance the force of the wind. The trysail lifts the bow up and it rises above the waves. The height of the trysail, aided by the topsail, ensure that we still catch the wind in a trough and do not lose steerageway."

Gradually the grey lines of the ship began to materialize in the light of dawn, but the gale raged on still more fiercely, and Tío Domingo ordered all sail hauled down. They would sail on bare poles until it abated. Christophe and Beaubroin began to lower the topsail yard. José heard, rather than saw, the topmast crack and blow forward, taking its yard with it. The full weight of the spars crashed down upon the bowsprit and jibboom. Mast, yard, and jibboom hung there to larboard, caught in the bowsprit shrouds which miraculously continued to cling to the bowsprit. The bowsprit itself had been sprung by the blow it had taken. The spars banged against the *Orfeo*'s hull as she continued to plow forward.

"Holy Mother and all the saints!" screamed Renzo, crossing himself. "We are lost!"

"Not yet," said Tío Domingo sharply. "We must cut the shrouds away or those spars will batter a hole in our hull."

The four crewman, hanging over the bow, began cutting away at the lines that fastened the shrouds to the hull. Renzo swung the axe madly and the lines began to fall away. Still a tangle of line that had been the outer jib stay remained caught in the broken wood at the end of the bowsprit, and the tangle of line and spars hung there, pounding the strakes of the hull.

"We chop away bowsprit!" cried Renzo.

"Too long! It will take too long!" Tío Domingo shouted after him.

"We cut ze stay!" José heard Christophe say, but José was nearest the bowsprit, and with a hard swallow, he pulled himself upon the bowsprit, squirmed past the knightheads and the forestay, and began to shimmy his way up the bowsprit to sever the stay. José began to saw at it with his knife, glad of the sharpness of the blade. How thick the line was! Strand by strand, he cut away, more by feel than by sight.

He had almost finished the work when the bowsprit cracked further. José, startled, dropped his knife. His grip faltered, and he felt himself falling. He reached desperately for the wood above, but grabbed instead the bobstay, close to where it met the bowsprit. He clung to it as the *Orfeo* plunged forward. He pursed his lips against the spray and his heart filled with silent prayer. How foolish he had been to think that he directed his own life. He felt his grip weakening, and he prayed for a miracle.

And then, through mist-filled eyes, he saw one. Christophe, above him on the bowsprit. He held a loop of thick rope.

"I drop ze line! We pull you up!" Christophe shouted over the wind. "Let go ze one hand! I drop ze line!"

José was paralyzed with fear. If he let go, even one hand, surely he would drop into the waves below.

"Let go! Must let go!" shouted Christophe, and José released his left hand.

Quickly Christophe dropped the loop of rope over his arm.

"Ozer arm!" Christophe called.

José relaxed the grip of his right hand and thrust it through the loop. He could feel the pull of the line under his armpits.

"Let go!" shouted Christophe.

José let go of the bobstay and screamed as he felt himself fall, his feet touching the water, then a fierce tug on the line began to pull him up, up, banging against the hull. Arms reached over the gunwale and pulled him in. He collapsed in the bow, bruised and bleeding, tears of terror mixing with the salt water on his face.

He heard Beaubroin shout something in French.

Christophe responded, "I cut ze line!"

Suddenly there was a great snap as the final strand of line gave way under Christophe's knife. There were screams all around him, and a splashing sound.

He stood and then boosted himself up on one of the pin rails to look over the bow. The mass of spars and rigging was racing away off the larboard bow. In the water below he could see Christophe just disappearing below the waves.

"Him no swim!" screamed Beaubroin.

Renzo seized a line and threw it out over the bow, but Christophe did not resurface. The *Orfeo* continued to race forward, the wind still pushing her on. They watched for a time, frantically searching the sea for any sign of him, but at last they realized that all hope was lost. He was gone.

"Ze line snap, it hit ze face, he go down. Him good man, ze best man. Now him gone!" Rain mixed with the tears that ran down Beaubroin's cheeks as he collapsed to the deck and covered his face with his arms.

Tío Domingo was haggard-looking, his face grey. He gripped José's arm till it hurt. "What would I have told your mother?"

But the wind still blew, and the rain lashed them without regard for their grief, and they returned to their duties. José felt hollow inside. If he had only kept his grip, cut the stay himself, Christophe would not have been out on the bowsprit.

Through it all Vicente had stood with a firm hand on the tiller, resisting the attempts of the wreckage to pull the *Orfeo* to larboard. José mounted to the quarterdeck in search of tasks that would allow him to shelter in Vicente's lee. As he did so, he looked back, and thought he saw a dark form on the crest of a wave, and then the wave came crashing down to sweep whatever it was east, in the direction of Jamaica.

"You have game, Sabio," said Vicente, in a voice that ached with exhaustion.

José was silent for a time, then burst out, "He was a good man! Why did God take him?"

"It is always the good men we lose," replied Vicente. "They take risks precisely because they are good."

Tío Domingo appeared in order to take the helm. "Take a rest, both of you. The wind has eased somewhat, and I think this storm will blow itself out by evening. And we will have much work ahead of us."

The larboard watch turned in, without Christophe.

Tío Domingo was right. By evening the winds had died down, and they turned into the wind, raised the mainsail and staysail, and hove-to for the night. They slept, watch on and watch off, like dead men.

In the morning, Beaubroin's corncakes and coffee restored their strength. José felt a guilty thrill at his survival. It was true, he was still fatigued, but he had been tested and not found wanting. He had hung on in the most desperate of circumstances. Vicente has said that he had game.

Renzo seemed more saturnine than usual. After breakfast, he caught José alone.

"You learn with the Jesuits. You think, man like me, God forgive him?" he asked, clenching José's arm.

"Yes," answered José, "if he is truly penitent." The pat words flowed easily over his tongue.

Renzo looked at him blankly.

"He has to ask for forgiveness, and want it," José explained.

"How many times a man need to ask?" mumbled Renzo, as he turned away.

José felt inadequate. How could he, a fifteen-year-old boy, counsel a man like Renzo about sin? He, whose sins had consisted largely of teasing his sister and fighting at school. Renzo, he thought, had probably broken most of the commandments. Then he remembered his own cruel words to Miguel. The shame of it still stung, although he had confessed it and received absolution.

He caught Renzo by the arm. "When we get to Havana, go to the chapel, Santa Casa de Loreto, on the Calle San Ignacio. Ask for Father Borrero. He can help you. I think God listens to him. And he listens to God."

Renzo stopped for a moment. "Maybe I see this priest."

Suddenly Beaubroin stood up, speaking loudly so everyone could hear.

"We say words for Christophe, him good man, ze best man, need words," he announced.

All nodded their ascent, and they gathered on the quarterdeck to give Christophe his final due. Tío Domingo, however, did not carry a missal aboard, and declined to offer a prayer himself, pleading ignorance of the proper form.

"Me say words," interjected Beaubroin. "Him is *mon ami*, me have ze good words for him."

Tío Domingo gestured to him to speak. Beaubroin collected himself, then began, "Christophe good man, ze best man. *Tout le monde*, zey love zat man." He hesitated, reaching among the jumble of languages that rattled about in his head for words in his new Spanish that would invoke his friend, and then a stream of passionate, incomprehensible French poured forth.

Tío Domingo stepped forward and began to translate, like a violinist reading a sheet of music, playing Beaubroin's song of the heart.

"Christophe was like a tree that sheltered us all. More than once he saved us from the whip. I know he saved me. I faced death, and he left Jamaica, where his wife and child remain, to save me. He was a loving father and husband, and the most loyal of friends. He showed us what it meant to be good and true, and we were all the better for having known him.

"He was born free, and freedom sat like a king in his heart. Though he was a slave, we saw freedom like a lantern burning in his heart and so we followed him, wanting that freedom for ourselves. I followed him to the sea, and I would have followed him to the gates of Hell itself for such was the spirit he inspired.

"Now I am left alone, without my sheltering tree, without my lantern of liberty to guide me. I was born with slavery in my heart, but he lit the lantern of liberty within me and I promise you I will follow Christophe with my heart. If I am but half the man he was, I will die a proud man."

José realized that they had not really known Christophe or Beaubroin until then. A wall of words had stood between them, an amalgam of half-understood French, English, and Spanish. No doubt Tío Domingo had polished Beaubroin's speech, but the man's passions rang out in his tones. And José, who had spent his young life in pursuit of language, suddenly found himself without words. So, too, did the others, and they stood there, crossing themselves, in silent homage to Christophe. They felt his loss all the more deeply because they realized only now the man they had lost.

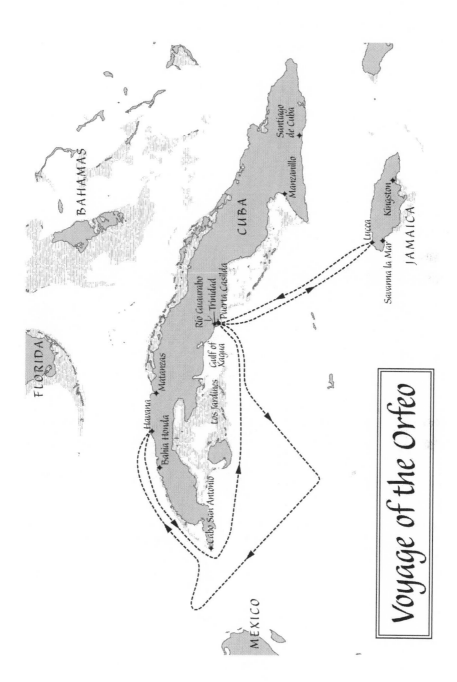

Voyage of the Orfeo

23

UNBEARABLE

Tío Domingo attempted to determine their new position and set a course for home. How many miles had they traveled while scudding before the storm? All of that time, they had been on a northwest heading, sailing south of the island. Had they already passed Cabo San Antonio? Tío Domingo showed José how to use the sextant to take readings of the sun and use his navigator's manual to estimate their latitude and, with much less certainty, their longitude. José's head ached as he attempted it. Tío Domingo calculated that they had already passed the Cabo, and, the wind now coming from the southeast, he set a course east, close-hauled on a starboard tack.

"If we sight land before noon tomorrow, we will have found Cuba. If not, should the weather permit, I will taking a reading of the sun at noon tomorrow and see if I can determine our exact position," he told Vicente as they poured over the chart in the great cabin. Vicente picked up the sextant, examined it, and placed it back on the table.

Much work faced them now that the storm had passed. The undamaged mainsail and forestaysail allowed them to continue homeward, albeit at a more moderate pace, while every waking moment was spent repairing what they could. Nothing could be done about the lost topmast until the *Orfeo* reached Matanzas. Tío Domingo also discovered that the bowsprit was sprung, a great split having opened up along its length.

"It will need to be fished," Tío Domingo said, maneuvering about the bow to look at the damage from every angle. "Yet another delay."

He gave orders to heave-to, and then to detach the forestay from the bowsprit, thus reducing the tension of the failing spar, and rig it instead to one of the knightheads. José listened in bafflement, as did Beaubroin.

"We must place two lengths of wood along the side of the bowsprit, then woold it around with line to secure it. That should keep us until we reach Matanzas," Vicente explained.

Now José understood why they kept an assortment of line, blocks, and sail-cloth on the sloop. So too, there were a few worn strakes, a broken studding sail boom from some other ship, and a spare top yard lashed inside the gunwales. It was from these they would jury-rig their fish for the bowsprit.

Vicente selected the studding-sail boom and a long strake while Renzo climbed out on the bowsprit and took measurements. While the mate marked the desired length, José fetched a saw from the impressively well-stocked tool locker on deck. He helped Vicente balance the boom over two of the lockers and then was sent to examine the coils of line Renzo had hauled on deck for a piece of suitable size and strength. He glanced over occasionally as Vicente began cutting into the boom with the saw. The deeper he cut, the more the saw would bind in the kerf. At last he could resist no longer.

"The saw will move more easily if you coat it with a bit of wax or tallow," he advised. He waited for the tongue-lashing.

"Fetch some, then," said Vicente, as the saw caught in the wood again.

When José returned with sample of the beeswax they had acquired in Boca Guaurabo, Vicente handed him the saw. "Do you think you can saw better?" he asked.

"My father is a joiner," replied José proudly, standing a little straighter.

"So he is," said Vicente. "We shall see if you favor him."

José cut into the wood with long, certain strokes. He thought of Papá, and felt a deep contentment. Soon he would be home again and work like this beside him.

"Here, hold the end!" he called to Renzo, and then with a few final strokes the end broke away from the main piece, leaving a clean end.

Vicente surveyed the work. "You do your father proud," he said. José basked in the praise. There was, then, one thing on this vessel he could do well, and Papá had taught it to him.

José then cut the strake to length, and Vicente put him to work making wedges from scrap pieces. These would be used to make the pieces tight to the curve of the bowsprit. José watched as Renzo climbed out onto the bowsprit to bind the wood on with the length of line, carefully straddling the great spar, no longer protected by the bowsprit shrouds that had formerly hung below. José's nerves were ragged until he saw Renzo climb back down onto the deck. He wondered if he would ever feel safe out there again.

The work completed, they once again rigged the forestay to the bowsprit, raised their sails and stood eastward. During each watch they kept a close eye to starboard, after night fell, looking for any sign of coastland.

"It is better that we find the land than that the land find us," said Vicente.

When José arose to stand watch at midnight, Renzo greeted him with a smile. "You smell it? Flowers, and all that is green. Always that is how you know the Cabo."

The *Orfeo* hove-to on Tío Domingo's orders, until they could see their way in the morning light past the vast rocky shoals north of the Cabo, and then beat their way home.

José felt a thrill of pride as the *Orfeo* entered the crowded Havana harbor. El Morro and La Punta seemed to salute them as they sailed past. The *Orfeo*'s lines were freshly tarred, her mainsail mended and taut in the wind, her jury-rigged forestaysail still steady. Tío Domingo stood resplendent in his blue coat, conveying orders to Vicente. The mate, in turn, barked commands loudly enough to ensure that every ship in the harbor would know that this vessel knew her business. A smile lit up Beaubroin's face as the harbor revealed itself, assuring him that he was now protected by the power of its warships. They were now in the finest harbor in the New World, and neither the English nor the French could touch them here.

It was a tedious business warping in the *Orfeo* in the scorching heat of late summer. How long till he could depart and walk up the Calle Obispo to the street of the avocado and walk through the blue door into the yellow house? He felt a surge of excitement as he leapt down onto the wharf to help tie up. It was too late in the day to begin discharging their cargo; tomorrow, just as the sun rose, they would begin and deliver their goods to Señor Morejón's warehouses. Tío Domingo had already paid a boy to take a message to him.

He finished coiling down the end of the line, wiped the sweat from his eyes, and turned to see Señor Morejón and beside him, Papá. His heart almost burst, and he wanted to throw himself into his father's arms, but he remembered that he was now a man, one who could work a ship alongside other men, and must comport himself accordingly.

Papá gazed upon him gravely. "I hope you have done nothing to disgrace the family," he said.

"His conduct has been satisfactory," commented Vicente, who had joined them. He added, "He has become a thorough seaman."

Papá's face eased, as if he were considering a smile. "I am most grateful to hear it."

Tío Domingo joined them. "We have done all that is possible for today. To-morrow, Anselmo, you will tell us how to dispose of our cargo. Beaubroin will remain aboard, so you may sleep on shore should you so desire, Vicente."

"I need no berth ashore," said Vicente. "I will save my pesos for my wife and children."

"You may stay with us," offered Papá. "We would be pleased to offer you a bed."

José's heart sank as he heard Vicente accept Papá's offer. How he had looked forward to escaping life under the eye of Vicente. Now the mate would dog his heels on land, too.

As soon as they entered the blue door of home, Mamá rushed out and held him close until he thought his bones would crack. She then stood back, took his face in her hands and looked deep in his eyes.

"Still my boy," she said softly.

"No," said Papá. "Not a man yet, but no longer a boy. I must teach you to shave that mustache."

José smiled and proudly fingered the faint growth that had begun to darken his upper lip.

"How tall you are!" cried Magdalena, stretching on tiptoes to give him a kiss.

It was true, José realized. He was more than shoulder-height to Papá. No wonder he had so often hit his head upon the door to the great cabin.

"Were the English heretics very terrible?" Magdalena asked.

"Tío Domingo left me with an English family for six weeks," replied José. "They were charming and kind. An English girl gave me a kiss before I left," he added, to provoke her.

Magdalena's eyes grew wide, and so too did Mamá's. He regretted the remark.

Agustín turned from his work at the bench and gave him a broad smile. "Welcome home, José," he said, waving a chisel at him. "You look very well." What a change a few months had made in his Spanish.

Mamá and Magdalena fussed over him during their simple supper that night, and paid Vicente many attentions as well. José washed carefully before eating, as had become his habit since living with the Fernandez family.

"Now you, too, have become a cat!" remarked Mamá.

José noticed how Magdalena had filled out in his absence, and realized that she was already thirteen, and no longer a child. She was learning to cook and had made the supper they were eating. Her eyes filled with pride as she watched José shovel down his rice and beans.

"Perhaps my son should eat more like a scholar and less like a deckhand," Mamá hinted.

Excited voices contended to tell him all the news he had missed. Magdalena related that Señora Peña next door had been ill, and Mamá had been nursing her.

Then Mamá gestured towards Agustín and told how he had been hauled into court for assaulting a *blanco*. It seems that Dionisia, the slave girl hired by the Morejón family, had been returning from the market when this man had put his hands on her in an indecent manner. Agustín witnessed the affront, and laid the man in the mud of the street with one blow. Agustín would have been whipped, but Señor Morejón and Papá testified to his good character. This might not have been enough, but Señor Espada also gave witness that this *blanco* was known throughout the neighborhood for his lewd behavior towards women, even *blancos*. Agustín was cautioned to guard his conduct, and the *blanco* man received a stern tongue-lashing. Mamá heard that he had since moved to another neighborhood, where he had already offended his neighbors.

Agustín sat in silence as Mamá told this story, but sat a little taller as Papá nodded his approval of his conduct. Mamá whispered later that Papá had given Father Borrero several pesos to put towards Agustín's *coartación* price.

After supper Papá poured a glass of Madeira for Vicente.

"Before I can be the master of a ship I must first be a master of navigation, at least if I wish to command more than a coasting vessel," Vicente remarked with a sigh. "Thus far, the mathematics of it have mastered me."

Papá leaned forward. "If you like, I might assist you with that. After all, I taught Domingo, why should I not teach you?"

Vicente raised his eyebrows.

"When I was young, I thought to study mathematics in Edinburgh," Papá continued. "I fancied I might find employment as an engineer one day." He bent over his glass and continued in a low voice, "Fate had other plans for me. My father died, and I was needed at home."

José sat stunned. Conversation swirled about him, but he no longer heard it. Papá had wanted to attend university and become an engineer? Never had he mentioned this. What else did he not know about his father? And why mention this casually, to a man he had only just met, and never to his son?

After that evening, Papá and Vicente sat up every night as Papá set the mate to doing problems. Sometimes they went out in the courtyard and studied the sky and the constellations. Papá gave José sums to work, as well.

When Papá spoke of mathematics, the lines seemed to fade from his face, the red in his hair outshone the grey, and his sagging shoulders lifted.

"Mathematics is the next thing to worship," he said in a rapt voice as he checked one of Vicente's problems and found it satisfactory. "It promises order in a disordered world."

Vicente nodded his understanding.

Afterwards, the two sat over *aguardiente* and talk until the bells signaled the closing of the city gates, and then on into the night. José felt alone then, and retreated to read the *Aeneid* until sleep closed his eyes.

The day after their return José slipped over to the Morejón house, hoping to see Rafael. To himself he admitted that he also wished to see Marianela. Rafael had been sent on an errand to the countryside, to deliver some goods commissioned by a wealthy customer, but Marianela was there, sitting over her sewing. Her hair was pulled back with combs, revealing smooth coffee skin and delicate cheekbones. José felt suddenly shy in her presence, although he had known her since she was an infant. She was fourteen now, and by far the prettiest girl of his acquaintance. She lowered her eyelashes demurely, but a slight smile suggested that she was not unaware of her attraction for him. He sat down beside her.

"Rafael has missed you, José," she said, raising her eyes to his and then dropping them again as she plied her needle.

"And did you miss me, too?" he asked, trying to sound as if it did not matter.

"We have all missed you," she replied. "Papá says you make the best chocolate," she added, almost laughing as she kept her eyes on her needlework.

"Does he not have you to make chocolate for him?" he teased, and soon they were laughing again, and the other Morejón children swarmed about him, until Señora Morejón gave them a look and they scattered.

"I have brought you something," José said, pulling a red satin ribbon from his pocket. Uncle Samuel had helped him choose it. Magdalena had told him that Marianela preferred red above all colors.

"It is beautiful, José," Marianela said, running her finger along the smooth length of the ribbon. "Thank you." She looked him full in the eyes and smiled, entirely justifying the dent the gift had made in the profits from his venture.

"Will you tie it in my hair?" she said softly. "I cannot easily reach."

With awkward fingers he tied the ribbon in a bow, where it shone brightly against the dark of her hair. He stepped back quickly as Señora Morejón descended upon them, and soon made his farewells. Marianela smiled at him as he left, then ducked her head down over her sewing.

The next day was Sunday, and in the evening Rafael appeared in the Albañez kitchen, accompanied by Sebastián. The boys whooped with glee and pounded José on the back, anything to avoid yielding to the temptation to throw their arms about him in an unmanly embrace.

"I would not have known you!" cried Rafael. "No one could mistake you for a *blanco* now. You look like a mahogany log!"

"So, tell us all! Did you outrun the *guarda costa*? Face down a storm? Fire a cannon?" Rafael asked, only half teasing.

"Do tell us that you did something that would discomfit the good fathers," Sebastián urged him.

So many memories crowded José's mind. What could he tell them? Of the long hours of tedious labor? His disgraceful conduct early in the voyage? His participation in the attack on the slave funeral in Jamaica? Or fleeing in terror from the skeletons in the woods? The loss of Osorio? Almost losing his life in the gale? Or, he thought, with a tightening of the throat, of the death of Christophe?

He shrugged. "We acquired a black cat in Trinidad and named him General Scipio Africanus."

His friends roared with laughter.

"We have come to take you to a dance," Rafael announced as the laughter died down. "Put on your Sunday best and follow us."

Mamá looked dubious. "He is only fifteen," she protested.

Papá said, "He has returned from the sea, none the worse for it, surely he can navigate the streets of Havana for an evening without meeting with misadventure."

They stepped out into the black of the city streets, lit only by the starlight that fell between the closely ordered buildings. Sebastián walked ahead with an ornate lantern. Imported from Spain, José thought.

"Tell me, in truth, what happened out there?" Rafael whispered, moving in close to José. "Don Domingo says he will not have you on the *Orfeo* again."

José's cheeks burned. So Vicente had only humored him when he pronounced his conduct "satisfactory."

"He says he would find it unbearable. His heart cannot take another such voyage. That he could not face your mother should you be lost," Rafael continued.

Ah! So that was it. He remembered Tío Domingo's grey face after the storm. He parceled out the whole story to Rafael. Sebastián fell back to listen.

The lamplight flickered in Rafael's eyes. "How I wish I had been there! Within a year, I will be. Papá has promised it. I have been clerking with him these two months since leaving the *colegio*, and have done all he has asked and more. At last he threw up his hands and said I deserved the chance." Rafael almost crowed.

"So you will become a ship's captain, some day, I think, and then you will marry Magdalena," said José.

"And you will marry Marianela, and we will be brothers twice over!" rejoiced Rafael.

Sebastián lowered the lantern, and their faces were lost in darkness.

"I, too, will go to sea!" interjected Sebastián suddenly.

"Truly?" José asked.

"He is going abroad," laughed Rafael. "Did you think his father would have him become a ship's boy?"

"My father is sending me to stay with relations in Salamanca. There I will continue my studies. He says my Castilian has lost its refinement due to the company I keep," Sebastián laughed. As he spoke, he left a number of consonants by the wayside as if in defiance of paternal authority.

"Then," he continued, gathering up his consonants again, "we will travel. He says that there are many interesting thinkers in Europe today, especially in France. He would like me to become more familiar with their ideas."

"I will name a ship in your memory after you expire of boredom from listening to the droning of the schoolmasters. Its sails will be filled by the windy utterances of a legion of tendentious talkers..." Rafael said in disgust.

"I fear your ship will founder on the rocks of some African coast, for you slept through too many geography lessons," was Sebastián's reply.

Their banter ended here, for sounds of voices and the faint strains of music reached their ears, and soon they found themselves in front of a respectable-looking house on Calle Tejadillo. José recognized it as the shop and home of a *pardo* tailor who purchased cloth from Albañez y Morejón. They pushed through the crowd gathered outside, and found the inside cleared for dancing. Perspiring couples swirled about to the sound of a band in the next room. A violin and oboe provided a lilting melody, accompanied by the beat of a drum. A tenor voice sang a haunting *décima* of lost love. Groups of young men and women lined the walls, awaiting their chance. Others gathered around a refreshment table, filling small plates with savories and sweets. Nearby stood punch bowls full of *agualoja*, lemonade, and sangria.

Presiding over it all sat an old *parda* woman, dressed all in black, smiling and nodding to admirers gathered around. José noticed the black lace trimming the sleeves and neckline to be of Dutch manufacture, and the dress itself was of the latest fashion, or at least the latest to have reached the shores of Cuba. Gold earrings sparkled in her ears.

"Congratulations on your saint's day, Señora Gavira," Rafael said, bowing to her, and the others followed suit.

"Thank you," she replied, beaming. "What a fine young man you have grown to be, Rafael."

At the refreshment table, José reached for a glass of *agualoja*, but Rafael pushed his hand away and ladled out sangria.

"Two of us are already sixteen," he said. "Why should we not drink a real punch?"

They joined the other young men along the wall, watching the dancers. The crowd consisted largely of *pardos*, but among them were also well-dressed *blanco* men. The prettiest *parda* girls buzzed about them like bees. Several *blancos* had found partners and were dancing the *guaracha*. José watched with unease as the dancers swayed their hips sensuously, drawing close to their partners and exchanging amorous glances. Most of the dancers were older than them, but scattered among the crowed were a few young girls more their own age. Suddenly he saw that Rafael and Sebastián were swaying about among the others, pretty girls in their arms. How confidently Rafael moved.

José waited for a more sedate *bolero*, and chose a young girl who did not look as if she might fall out of her bodice. He was grateful that his female cousins had obliged him to serve as their dance partner, for now he stepped comfortably across the floor. He began to enjoy himself. Later, a girl in a green dress seized his arms and pulled him onto the dance floor, where he found himself stepping through the *guaracha*. He felt his blood stir in response to the sangria and the beat of the drum. He was keenly aware of the charms of the girl turning gracefully in his arms, and could not but notice her pronounced décolletage. No wonder, he thought, that men yielded to temptation.

The air in the room began to feel oppressive, and José stopped to refresh himself, taking another glass of sangria. How many was it now? Rafael and Sebastián joined him against the wall.

"The girls here are very charming," said Rafael.

"Not so pretty as Marianela," observed Sebastián.

"I think many of them are here simply to meet *blanco* men," said José.

"Are you surprised? Half the *parda* women in Havana are in pursuit of the same thing. They all want to 'lighten the blood,'" Rafael said.

"It is indecent," groused José.

"I do not think they give much thought to decency. I have heard that some of them are quite ready to go with a man if he asks. I see one of them now, winking at me," laughed Rafael.

José also saw the girl, smirking and tossing her curls at Rafael. He saw Rafael wink back. He felt dizzy from the heat and the motion of the dancers. The sangria, and the ever-louder rhythm of the music, made his blood pound in his veins. He turned and put his face in that of Rafael.

"You wish to marry my sister. Do not even think of laying one finger on one of these trollops or I will lay you flat on the ground," he hissed, stabbing Rafael in the chest with his finger.

"Calm yourself, *amigo*! I have done nothing. *Dios mío*, I think the English have poisoned your mind." Rafael sounded shocked.

José, too, was shocked. Was he becoming Vicente? At the same time, it was somehow gratifying to see the older Rafael back away from him, intimidated.

A *volante* came to collect Sebastián. Rafael and José declined the offer of transportation home, and instead borrowed Sebastián's lantern to walk back together.

"We must be the best of friends and enjoy our time together before you leave home again," said Rafael in a conciliatory tone.

"Leave? You told me that Tío Domingo no longer wanted me on the *Orfeo*. I will work in the shop with Papá," José said. Why did the stars move about so?

"I apologize," said Rafael. "I omitted to add that he now wants you to sail with Señor Policarpo, on the *Alejandro* sloop."

Rafael held José's head as José felt himself collapse in the street and an evening's worth of sangria found its way into a large puddle.

24

THE MOUNTMEN

Although it had indeed been decided that José was to sail with Tío Policarpo, his uncle was still at sea, and so it was not until five months later, in February of 1762, that he actually joined the crew of the *Alejandro* sloop. Until then, José spent several peaceful months working by his father's side, continuing to learn the joiner's trade. Now more than tall enough to work at the bench, he measured and sawed, shaved and sanded. He began, under his father's watchful eye, to measure joints and gouge them out with a chisel.

It was quiet in the shop, for all there – Papá, Agustín, and José – preferred the sound of the tools and their own thoughts, only broken by rare fits of conversation or the occasional visitor. Papá worked more slowly than in the past, and his hair had more grey, although according to Mamá he was only forty-eight. At dinner, she quietly ensured that he always got the best bits, and fussed at him until he finished the last morsel on his plate. Agustín helped, as well, hurrying to pick up the heaviest pieces of wood to spare Papá. There was a grave look in Agustín's eyes as they followed Papá about the shop. José suspected that he worried about what might be his fate should anything happen to Don Roberto.

Agustín had an agreeable routine, working in the shop, attending his *cabildo*, and accompanying the family to Mass. In his free hours he worked on his own account or paid court to Dionisia. He smiled often, laughed at times, and only now and then did José witness a shadow pass across his face, usually when he encountered a man with a small boy.

One afternoon, as the rumble of thunder filled the shop, Agustín's voice burst out.

"I pray to the God of all, the Father says he sees my boy far away. How can God find my boy if he does not know and call to God?"

Papá went and put his hand on Agustín's shoulder. "I will pray for your son to learn the true faith." He sat down again, and added softly, as if speaking to himself, "God must be besieged with the cries of fathers praying for their lost sons."

"How do we know he hears us, then, with so many prayers in his ears?" asked Agustín.

"That is why they call it faith," replied Papá, and then a clap of thunder ended their conversation.

ele

The Albañez family spent Christmas again in Matanzas. José could not resist swaggering about a bit, hinting to his cousins about his adventures, until Jacinto smirked and said, "I heard that you fell overboard," and everyone laughed, except for Mamá. Later, Abuelo scolded him for his carelessness, and Abuelita kissed him.

Osorio had rejoined the *Orfeo* sloop, for he and his lady love had found their way back to Matanzas. Osorio had stolen a small boat during the night and spirited his love across the sea to Santiago, whence they had made their way overland to Matanzas.

"He has spent the money and married that woman. He calls her his queen and she now goes by Reina," Tío Gaspar told them. "There they were in the church, she arrayed like the Queen of Sheba, and he strutting about like a peacock. Now he has set her up in a little house. It seems he has been saving his silver all these years just so he might lavish it upon whatever woman would accept his homely mug."

"But is she a good woman?" Mamá asked.

"She is no cook, but she is a hard worker, thrifty, and does not flirt with other men while her husband is away," replied Tío Gaspar. "That is more than many men find."

"And Nicolaza says that it is enough that she makes Osorio smile," he added.

Mamá was pleased that José was now to be under the eye of Tío Policarpo. Tío Domingo was the favorite of the ladies, for he made much of them. The children loved Tío Gaspar, who had nicknames for all of them and made them laugh, although at times his jests could prick. Tío Policarpo, however, enjoyed the esteem of the men. He spoke little, but when he did, they stopped to listen. So, too, did Mamá.

"Policarpo will not take foolish risks," she said.

José joined the *Alejandro* in Havana, where they picked up several passengers. Then, in Matanzas, they loaded casks of snuff to join the salt beef in their hold. José was uncertain about the provenance of the snuff, which in theory belonged to the royal monopoly, but there were clandestine meetings with local *vegueros*, and some goods were loaded after sunset, in a small cove several miles away.

Tía Beatriz was rowed out to make her farewells in person. Tío Policarpo embraced her tenderly as she clung to him.

"*Mi cariño*," he whispered, as she cooed like a dove in his muscular arms.

She stooped to pat the deck before she disembarked. "Watch over my dear one, Alejandro!" she said, and then her plump form swayed down the Jacob's ladder.

José laughed, and Tío Policarpo rounded on him. "Do not think of mocking her. It is true, the spirit of Alejandro is in this vessel. He died here, on this very deck, and his heart's blood seeped into her. Wherever we go, now, he sails with us." He, too, knelt down and reverently touched the deck boards.

Tío Policarpo had set watches, leading the starboard watch himself, along with Cipriano and Tondo. Cipriano was a weathered *pardo* with a game leg that made José question why Tío Policarpo kept him aboard. There were traces of grey in his rough, curling hair, and tobacco had made his voice hoarse, but he approached his duties with the energy of a younger man and the wisdom of experience. Tondo was a youthful *moreno*. He was also, José learned, a slave, and had been leased out to Tío Policarpo for two years now by his master in Matanzas. He was already a competent seaman, with an open, friendly face.

The mate Calixto was in charge of the larboard watch, consisting of José and Beaubroin. When Osorio returned to the *Orfeo*, Beaubroin had transferred to the *Alejandro*, to take the place of Pío, a crew member who had died of a bloody flux.

Tío Policarpo ran a very different ship than Tío Domingo. He provided his men with ample and healthful provisions, but did not devote deck space to livestock, so José quickly grew accustomed to dinners of dried beef stewed with yam, prepared by Beaubroin's indifferent hand.

The difference was most noticeable on Sundays, when Tío Policarpo gathered the crew on the quarterdeck and together they said the Rosary. The first Sunday, Beaubroin was discovered to be without one, and Tío Policarpo entered the cabin and reappeared with a set of simple wooden beads.

"No sailor should be without," he said.

José wished that he was on the starboard watch under Tío Policarpo. His uncle commanded respect; when he appeared on deck, the men stood straighter, and their actions became brisker...and he gave orders easily, with the expectation that they would be obeyed promptly, and no further direction would be needed. Yet, José noticed his eye missed nothing, and he could correct a crewman with a mere look.

The mate Calixto was a short, wiry man of indeterminate years. A livid scar across his right cheek suggested that those years had not passed peaceably. His squinting eyes gazed malevolently on all before him, from the wind-whipped clouds to Beaubroin, still struggling to master basic seamanship. Calixto hounded the man unmercifully.

"You must watch over Beaubroin," Tío Policarpo told José. "Make sure he learns all that is necessary." He added, "I have put you on the larboard watch because I trust you."

As they beat their way east-southeast along Cuba's rocky north coast, opposed by both current and wind, José found himself rushing to assist Beaubroin before Calixto could discover his errors.

Beaubroin would work in flurries of enthusiasm, singing gayly as he swept the deck or worked the pump. At night, he fell into silence, and sometimes José found him simply staring eastward across the water.

Calixto would squint at him and mutter, "A miracle indeed! A goat who can both sing and sweep. Perhaps he will juggle next." Calixto had an inexhaustible supply of such quips, the only thing that ever put a smile on his face.

When Beaubroin made a mistake, Calixto always seemed to appear at his elbow. When he struggled to express himself in Spanish, Calixto would shout, "*Dios mío*! Speak in Christian!"

José began to correct Beaubroin's Spanish as well, in order that he might be less of a target for the mate's scorn, and was gratified to observe that his speech was becoming more intelligible.

Once, when Beaubroin was at the bow, watching for reefs, Calixto caught him gazing idly at the clouds and his angry cry must have reached the masthead. "Saints in heaven, I need an eagle and instead I am stuck with a pigeon. Do you not see that coral head?" José hauled the helm to leeward, and disaster was only just averted.

One day, when gusts of wind were rattling the sails, Calixto ordered Beaubroin aloft to scan for other vessels. The man stood there, unmoving, his eyes turned uneasily towards the bowsprit, and José remembered Christophe tumbling into the water to be swept away.

"Get up there, you foolish goat! Earn your beans!" Calixto cried.

Beaubroin began to make his way slowly up the shrouds. In an instant, José decided to follow.

"I did not order you aloft," José heard Calixto shout, but he was already well up the shrouds, and made no sign of hearing.

Aloft, Beaubroin clung desperately to the top yard as they stood balancing on the footropes.

"Remember – one hand for yourself and one for the vessel," said José reassuringly. "I have learned to love the silence. Vicente's voice could barely reach me here."

Beaubroin smiled understandingly. They hung companionably over the broad spar, taking in the expanse of blue below, in no hurry to descend.

"Everyone I have ever loved is there," Beaubroin said softly, pointing eastward with his chin. And José felt Beaubroin's loneliness – one man, alone between the blue layers of sky and sea, with no one to mourn him on shore should he be lost.

That night he asked Beaubroin to teach him some French. He knew that he would not learn from him a polished French, but perhaps it would provide the man with some sense of accomplishment. Every night after that, as their duties permitted, Beaubroin schooled José in his native tongue.

One morning Tío Policarpo heard José singing a song Beaubroin had taught him.

"I hope," he said, "that you do not understand the words to that ditty, and even more so, that your mother never does."

Tío Policarpo found an occasion, when the weather was mild, to exercise the guns. These consisted of a swivel gun fore and aft, and a four-pounder on each side. Tío Policarpo devoted some time to training José and Beaubroin in the motions of worming and sponging the muzzle, ramming home the ball and powder, and lighting the powder with the linstock. José was disappointed that it was all play-acting. Finally, Calixto, Cipriano, and Tondo joined them as they used actual powder in one of the swivel guns.

"I save my shot for the English," said Tío Policarpo, then Calixto used the linstock to light the powder and there was a satisfying boom.

"Bravo!" cried Beaubroin, waving the worm in victory. "*Les corsaires*, zey are sunk!"

"A mere pinprick," grumbled Calixto. "Of less annoyance than your clowning."

"It would let them know we were no easy prey," said Tío Policarpo. "While we crowd sail and escape."

"What if we cannot escape?" asked Tondo, as if the thought had occurred to him for the first time.

"Then you would find yourself sold to a new owner," said Calixto.

"But Señor Policarpo has papers that say I am free. My master signed them, as part of the lease. I am only a slave on land, but at sea I am a free man. Surely the English would respect a paper signed by a notary." Tondo's face shone with innocence.

"That is the law, and a prize court should honor your papers," said Cipriano.

"The English are without honor," said Calixto.

"And that is why we will not be captured," Tío Policarpo assured them. "God is with us, and so, too, is Alejandro."

Another day, after dinner, Policarpo gathered José, Beaubroin, and Tondo for pistol practice. They took turns cleaning, loading, and firing at pieces of driftwood that Tío Policarpo tossed over the side. Only José managed to splinter the wood with a ball.

"You are a born privateersman!" Cipriano congratulated him with a slap on the shoulder.

Tondo made several more attempts, and his last effort sent up a splash of water just beyond the driftwood.

"I intend to be ready when we enter the war," he said determinedly.

"The English have enjoyed many victories. The war may be over before Spain can enter," advised Cipriano.

"I hope you are wrong," said Tondo. "Think of the prize money! I could buy my freedom within the year. I cannot measure how many years it would take if I must earn the money trading my ventures."

"It would be a pity if the war ended before Spain could strike back at these English pirates. They have harried our ships long enough. Every year they become bolder," said Calixto, the scar on his check working furiously.

"We are a neutral country, and yet still they seize our ships," said Tío Policarpo. "If war comes, the *Alejandro* will refit as a privateer."

"Well, I will retire soon from the sea in any case. Gregorio, my eldest, will sail with you," laughed Cipriano.

Target practice having concluded, Tío Policarpo brought out a bottle of *aguardiente* which he kept locked in a small chest, and poured them each a dram. He hesitated a moment before dribbling the liquor into Calixto's cup.

"*Viva la guerre!*" cried Beaubroin.

"To freedom!" was Tondo's response.

"Consternation to the English!" shouted Calixto, draining his cup in one gulp. He might have been suspected of smiling.

"To family," said Cipriano, clinking his cup against Tondo's.

"To Havana, the Pearl of the Antilles!" cried José. He would have toasted Papá, but did not wish to appear a homesick child. Instead he named the place where Papá sat hunched over his workbench.

"Spoken like a true subject of the king," nodded Cipriano approvingly.

There was a silence, then Tío Policarpo raised his cup and said softly, "To Beatriz!" and downed the fiery liquid as if it were water.

José was standing by the door to the great cabin when Tío Policarpo ducked his long form in to return the bottle to its place. He saw him lock the chest, then place the key at the bottom of his sea chest. Seeing that José was watching, he put his finger to his lips.

Coming out of the cabin, he said in a low voice, "I, and I alone, dispense the *aguardiente*. Is that understood?"

José nodded. He stood for a moment, then asked, "Do you truly think we will go to war?"

Tío Policarpo looked at him steadily. "Does that frighten you?"

José imagined how glorious it would be to do battle with an English ship amid smoke and shouts, and see the enemy strike its colors to the cheers of Spanish sailors. He imagined returning home, laden with prize money and glory, to the admiration of his friends. He looked at the deck where Alejandro's lifeblood had seeped out and also knew he did not wish to end his life here. He thought of how Mamá would weep.

"Was Papá a good privateersman?" he asked.

Tío Policarpo weighed his words. "I think he had grown weary of war," he said at last. "But he always did his duty, and he was fierce in battle against the English because of his great hatred for them, and who can blame him?"

"Why does he hate the English so?" José asked.

"Has he not spoken of this to you?" said Tío Policarpo in surprise. "Then it is not for me to tell. I will say this. The English defeated the Scots in a great battle at a place called Culloden. Those they did not slaughter they sent away in ships to be sold as labor for their plantations. We captured one such ship, and Domingo recognized his brother and rescued him from bondage."

"Is that why Papá hates slavery so?" asked José.

"All men of heart hate slavery," replied Tío Policarpo.

"Vicente says that slaves in Cuba have the opportunity to better themselves," said José.

"You have seen Jamaica," said Tío Policarpo darkly. "Do you think the *ingenios* in Cuba are any better?"

José remembered the broken men and women he had seen in Lucea, and shuddered within. Still, Cuba was not a sugar island, and so had few *ingenios*. The slaves he knew in Cuba lived far better lives than those in Jamaica, and could earn their freedom. He did not say this, however.

"If slavery is so terrible, why does no one put a stop to it?" he asked.

Tío Policarpo shrugged and spread his hands. "Why do men sin? We can only live in the world we find."

Tío Policarpo could often be seen watching the sky and the movement of the clouds, and studying the waves.

"He fears a nor'easter," said Cipriano after dinner one day. "This is no place to find ourselves on a lee shore." They were two weeks out of Matanzas and had exhausted the supply of fresh vegetables, and now it was nothing but salt beef with yams every day. José was already weary of it.

"Had we delayed six weeks, we might have avoided the risk of northerlies," commented Calixto.

"And risked finding ourselves in the midst of a war?" replied Cipriano.

"That may happen yet," Calixto snarled.

"Is that why we are taking the northern route?" asked Tondo.

Cipriano smiled broadly. "You are learning. Yes, following the southern coast, and taking the Windward Passage to Monte Cristi is the safest course. But the British also frequent that route."

"They do not risk the Old Bahama Channel," said Calixto.

"No one knows those waters better than Capitán Policarpo," added Cipriano proudly.

All hands were on deck as they navigated the channel. During the daylight hours, they had many tasks; heaving the lead, watching off the bow for obstacles, and making frequent sail corrections. When they lost the last of their light, they hove-to, and resumed their passage with the break of day.

The dreaded nor'easter did not hit until after they made their way out of the channel. Tío Policarpo observed the dark clouds to the north, the shifting wind that brought lower temperatures and sharp gusts, and directed them to the Bay of Puerto Padre, navigating the entrance channel with care. There they rode out the storm.

That night, as José stood alone on deck and felt the chill wind that rattled the rigging, Calixto suddenly appeared.

"This cold can only be mended by *aguardiente*. You know where the key is, fetch it, then," the mate said, his voice raised to be heard over the wind.

José remembered Tío Policarpo's words. "Only I dispense the *aguardiente*." He stood there, wondering what he should do. Calixto was the mate, and he must obey him, it was true. But Tío Policarpo was the captain. He stood there, making no answer.

"You heard me, fetch the drink!" Calixto's face was in his, his scar livid. The mate seized him by the shirt collar and shoved him up against the bulkhead.

José stood there and forced himself to stare into Calixto's eyes. "I will do so only on the orders of Tío Policarpo," he said, and he thought he could hear the fear in his own voice. The mate seemed about to strike him.

Calixto stood there, then let go of José and watched with wary eyes while José hurried away to check their mooring.

The wind shifted again the next evening, and in the morning they slipped out of the bay. After two days in Baracoa, where they added bales of tobacco to their cargo of salt beef and snuff, and replenished their water and provisions, the *Alejandro* left the shore of Cuba heading for Hispaniola. Now Calixto proved his worth. Using the sextant, he took the noon readings, and consulting the navigation tables, plotted a course for Monte Cristi on the chart.

"Your father taught me to read and to cipher, but the mathematics of navigation remain beyond my reach," his uncle confessed to José.

Two days later, the green bulk of Hispaniola appeared off the starboard bow.

They were all on deck as they approached Monte Cristi Bay. Cipriano had sighted the first of the Seven Brothers, the small cays that marked the approach to the bay. Once past the Brothers, they saw before them a forest of masts, belonging to some one hundred and fifty vessels.

"Zis Monte Cristi, it is a city *trés grande*!" said Beaubroin in awe.

"It is a fishing village, no more," said Calixto.

"There before you is the Mount, a city unto itself, some six thousand men, living, working, and sleeping aboard vessels from both the new world and the old," proclaimed Cipriano.

"*Et les femmes? Non?*" said Beaubroin. "*Zut alors!*"

They entered the bay cautiously, dropping the lead frequently to avoid the reefs that ringed the bay, then dropped anchor near a schooner called the *Charming*

Sally. Figures on the *Sally*'s deck waved and hallooed. José thought he heard a few words of English. The men of the *Alejandro* waved back.

The next day they lowered the boat into the choppy waves of the bay, ruffled by a dry wind coming off the land, and rowed through the long curling waves to pull up onto the beach. Tío Policarpo brought José, as well as Cipriano, Tondo, and Beaubroin, leaving Calixto in charge of the *Alejandro*. José noticed that he had slipped the key to the chest containing the *aguardiente* into a pocket of his jacket before they departed.

On shore, they found a cluster of small homes. Several men were repairing a fishing boat. A few sutler shops were all the commerce the village had on offer. Tío Policarpo sent the others to obtain fresh provisions and water, while he and José began to walk the three miles inland to the town of San Fernando de Monte Cristi. The sweat dried salty on their faces as the sun rose high overhead, evaporating what little moisture could be found in the barren landscape of sand and brush.

The town arose before them out of the haze, a few streets of one-story houses of plastered mud and timber. They hurried to a building that rose to two stories, lording it over its homely neighbors. There Tío Policarpo paid an entry fee, presented a list of his cargo, and received permission to trade from an official in a dusty uniform with frayed cuffs who barely lifted his eyes from his papers. Behind them waited the captain of a Danish ship.

"Where is the customs house?" asked José. "Where are the warehouses?"

"This is a free trade port, where the king has chosen to rule with a light hand. There are no customs duties, no meddlesome officers of the crown. And as for trade? San Domingo produces nothing but mules, half-tamed horses, and despair by the cartload," Tío Policarpo said, and José was once again grateful to have been born on the green and fruitful island of Cuba.

The next day, while Calixto gave Tondo and Beaubroin lessons in sail-mending, José and Cipriano rowed Tío Policarpo around some of the neighboring vessels to negotiate the sale of their cargo. Tío Policarpo was dressed in a blue coat of the newest fashion, and his best shirt, lovingly sewn by Tía Beatriz, shone white in the sun, as did his stock. The pewter buttons on his coat were brightly polished. Tío Policarpo brushed down his coat, checked his stockings for ladders, and wiped his shoes clean with a rag before they departed. He fussed and preened over his toilet as if he were a fashionable belle about to attend a ball, José thought. His uncle gave similar attention to José's dress.

"We must make a good appearance before these foreigners," he said. "Some will be set against us as soon as they see our color.

"Listen, and learn all you can," he added. "Domingo wishes you to learn all you can of trade."

The bay was alive with small craft, shuttling between ships or making for the shore, some pulled up alongside larger vessels to receive or discharge cargo.

They tried the *Charming Sally* first, calling out to them, "Ahoy!" A man in a blue coat hung over the side.

"Snuff! Tobacco! Salt beef!" shouted Tío Policarpo, in several languages, reminding José of a Havana street vendor.

"*Merci non*, no thank you, *gracias, no*," the man shouted back.

Even when there was no sale to be made, they were often invited aboard, and offered a small tipple or a pipe of tobacco. Tío Policarpo and the captain would sit and exchange the news, using whatever language came most easily.

Captain Grimball of the *Speedwell* brig, out of Philadelphia, asked in French, "They say there is a French squadron off Le Cap preparing to join the Spanish in the Havana for an assault on Jamaica. Is it true, do you think?" His sharp grey eyes watched Tío Policarpo's face carefully.

"The talk of war is constant, but so far, just talk." Tío Policarpo shrugged, and took a draw on the clay pipe the captain had offered him.

Then he leaned forward. "I have heard that there are many English ships off Cap Nicolas. What is their purpose, do you think? To lie in wait for our shipping? To continue their assault on France's sugar islands?"

"I wish I knew," replied Captain Grimball. "They will not meddle with us, though. I have a document certifying that we are the *Nuestra Señora de Asunción* out of Vera Cruz. And I have a crew member who will pass as captain should we be stopped. Blast this tomfoolery!"

Mostly, though, they spoke of trade and prices. The Irish were flooding the market with salt beef, but the French navy was buying up a good deal of it, so prices had not suffered overly much. Saint-Domingue was finding it difficult to ship its sugar – the French had been forced to carry it home on naval vessels – so they were eager to find buyers. And too, they spoke of the weather, of the movement of fleets and privateers, and told stories of past voyages. The Mountmen gossiped like women in the marketplace.

Another time they pulled up alongside the *Seaflower* brigantine from the town of Charles.

"Ahoy!" cried Tío Policarpo. "The *Alejandro* from Matanzas. We sell salt beef, tobacco, and snuff!"

A dark-haired man looked over the side and laughed. "Your captain looks a little young. Do you not have men in Cuba?"

"I am Captain Marroto," replied Tío Policarpo, with dignity.

There was a silence, and the dark-haired man conferred with his fellows.

"We do not do business with Negroes," he replied curtly, and turned away. José heard laughter.

Tío Policarpo ordered them to row on.

"His behavior was insulting," said José, burning with anger.

Tío Policarpo shrugged. "These North Americans can be a peculiar lot. The Mount is full of men who put profit before prejudice. We will seek them out, and leave these men to their pigheadedness."

He laughed. "Our tobacco is grown, harvested, and handled by *morenos*, and now that it is in a hogshead, they are fastidious about what hands sign the contract."

Tondo often accompanied them. This was his third voyage on the *Alejandro*, and already he had taught himself some English. He was eager to practice his skills in conversation with foreign sailors.

"I met a Turk today," he informed them, after one such visit. "He had the face of a *blanco*, but the skin of a *pardo*. I think I should like to visit Turkey one day for myself. Is it very far?"

"They are worse than heretics there," said José. "They are Mussulmans."

A look of horror crossed Tondo's face, and then he said, "Still, I think I would like to see it, just once. I would be very careful and say my prayers."

"I spoke to two Swedes today," he related on another occasion. "They have hair as white as corn silk, and they told me that in their country the snow piles up as tall as a man."

Calixto roared with laughter. "They have taken you for a green fool!"

"That cannot be true," Cipriano said, nodding his head sagely. "They would all freeze to death."

"Perhaps one day I will see for myself," mused Tondo.

"An amusing sight you would make, a black bean in the land of snow and corn silk," commented Calixto.

One day they awoke to find that Tondo was gone. He had been on watch alone, for there was little to do aboard ship while in Monte Cristi. Upon looking, they found that his few things were gone, as well.

"He has jumped ship!" cried Calixto. "The ungrateful little bastard." He followed this with language even less flattering.

"Why would he leave the *Alejandro*? Where would he go? There is nothing here," José asked.

"Ze *Speedwell*. He gone to ze *Speedwell*," said Beaubroin. The others looked at him.

"Zey look for seamen, ze money, it is good. I see zey talk wi' him," he continued.

"We must fetch him back," said Tío Policarpo tensely. "He is the property of Señor Pagueros."

"They were to leave this morning, wind permitting," said Cipriano. "And the wind is favorable."

Calixto stood at the gunwale and looked out towards the sea. "There! That is the *Speedwell*! Almost at the Brothers."

They stood in silence watching the brig, with Tondo aboard, stand out to sea.

25

PROFIT IS KING

Their commercial prospects began to look up when they encountered the *Little Martha*, a snow out of Providence from an island called Rhodes. The snow's crew dropped a ladder down, and Cipriano threw a line up to secure them to the vessel. The three of them made their way up the ladder, Cipriano struggling a bit with his lame leg.

A tall, red-haired man in a dun coat waved them into the cabin. Cipriano chose to stay on deck, offering cigars to the crewmen standing about.

"Captain Leverett," the red-haired man introduced himself, extending a hand. He was joined by Mr. Hubbard, the supercargo, who offered them coffee. Its bitter scent filled the cabin, masking the odor of salt and men.

"Captain Policarpo Marroto," said José's uncle in English, "of ze *Alejandro* sloop of Matanzas. José Albañez," he added, indicating his nephew.

"I welcome you to the *Little Martha*," said Captain Leverett, in excellent Spanish.

He grinned delightedly at their reaction. "During the late war I was a guest of the Spanish navy in Havana. I improved the time by making a study of Spanish."

"I, too, was in the war," said Tío Policarpo, smiling. "Perhaps you were on one of our prizes."

"Perhaps," said Captain Leverett. "But now we trade in friendship."

Tío Policarpo brought out of his pocket two small boxes containing samples of snuff and of tobacco leaf. Captain Leverett and Mr. Hubbard both took pinches of the snuff. They fingered the tobacco leaf and inhaled its aroma, then stepped aside for quiet discussion between themselves.

The negotiations began. Offers were made and refused. Counteroffers were politely declined. Captain Leverett raised his eyebrows. Tío Policarpo shrugged and raised his hands. Mr. Hubbard poured more coffee. José slumped in his chair. Then Tío Policarpo winked at him. He was enjoying this, José realized. So, too, was the captain from Rhodes. They were eyeing each other like gamecocks, looking for advantage, flaunting their commercial prowess.

Captain Leverett again stepped aside to whisper with his supercargo, and Tío Policarpo excused himself and led José out on the deck for some fresh air. Cipriano joined them.

"They are eager to depart," Cipriano said, speaking in a low tone. "There is a privateer waiting to capture them, but they have not quite filled their hold. They will take your price."

"Do not look so surprised, José," said Tío Policarpo. "Captain Leverett may have been our guest in Havana, but Cipriano enjoyed the hospitality of the English in Jamaica during the war."

The bargaining resumed. Soon, Tío Policarpo stood up to go. "I think we are finished here," he said. "I am grateful for your hospitality." He planted his hat on his head.

"Wait! Perhaps we can still reach an agreement," said Captain Leverett. Soon they were shaking hands and making arrangements for the transfer of the snuff.

"I do not understand," José said to Tío Policarpo as they rowed back to the *Alejandro*. "Why do they wish to be taken by a French privateer? Should they not avoid them?"

"Ah, you see, the privateer that awaits is from North America, and it will pretend to capture the *Little Martha* and place a prize crew aboard. The British navy will let them pass if they believe that they have already been taken," Tío Policarpo responded.

The English have forbidden North American ships to sell foodstuffs to the French. Their navy seizes these ships –as well as neutral vessels – for provisioning the enemy. *C'est la guerre.*"

"The *Little Martha* just sold a cargo of salt fish and flour to Frenchmen from Saint-Domingue. Some of it may end up on the vessels of the French navy," added Cipriano.

"So they are traitors to their king?" asked José slowly.

Tío Policarpo shrugged. "Here, profit is king."

During the evenings, Tío Policarpo would sometimes take the boat over to other vessels to trade for supplies, or boats would pull up alongside the *Alejandro*. This, too, was how the crew arranged the sale of their ventures. José had brought a bag of limes again, and sold it to a sailor from a city called New London. He used the proceeds to buy some simple lace from an Irish seaman. He knew several shops that would buy all he could offer.

One evening, Tío Policarpo returned with a bag of shiny red fruits for which he had traded some onions.

"What I do wiz zeze?" cried Beaubroin. "For why you sell my onion? I sink zey not for ze stew so good."

"You eat them, like this," and Cipriano took one in his hand and bit into it. He tossed another to Beaubroin, who caught it deftly before it flew down the hatch.

Beaubroin examined it closely, sniffed it, then took one dainty bite. His eyes opened wide, and a smile spread across his face. "*C'est bon!*"

He cocked his head to one side for a moment, thinking, then asked, "What else zese foreign men sell?"

That day Beaubroin was reborn. He began to accompany Tío Policarpo on trading sorties, engaging his fellow cooks in discussions of recipes, arms waving, pointing, exchanging fragments of English, French, and Spanish, sometimes Dutch. First he sought to learn the secret of preparing the apple, for so the fruit was called, and served them to the crew raw, fried with onions, and baked in the ashes. Then he began to experiment – apples tossed in molasses and baked were a triumph. Not all his innovations proved popular, however.

"This tastes of devils!" snarled Calixto, after pulling a slice of apple from his fish stew, and began to move menacingly towards the cook. For a moment José feared the mate would toss Beaubroin over the side.

Then Beaubroin cast his net wider. He discovered a new fruit, the pear, with a delicate flavor. He learned that the Irish ships carried a variety of cheeses, which kept well in the deep cool of their hulls and he held long, broken discussions with Irishmen on the merits of various varieties.

He no longer looked longingly towards distant islands, but chattered about the future. "Zer is a fruit, *très sucré, très délicat*, zey call it ze peach. Someday I see zat land where it grow. Zen, maybe, I save ze money, I buy ze farm, I grow many fruit, many good tings. I sell to people who love ze good food."

Tío Policarpo would shake his head. "I fear he will jump ship and hire himself out as a pastry cook."

They were several days transferring the casks of snuff to the *Little Martha*, a laborious process that involved lowering them into the boat, a few at a time, and rowing them to the snow, where they were lifted aboard with a can hook and down into the hold.

Tío Policarpo then plied the bay to market the rest of the cargo. At last he reached an agreement for the tobacco with the captain of the *John and Mary*.

Tío Policarpo brought out cigars to celebrate the bargain.

"A week yet to fill my hold, and then it's off to New York," said Captain Silvernails as his mate refilled their glasses with wine. His supercargo translated.

"*Bon voyage!*" Tío Policarpo saluted them, raising his glass.

"You might better say, *bonne chance*, for I must evade both the French and the English on my return. Those Kingston privateers are rapacious scoundrels," he groused, adding language even less decorous.

"The danger raises the prices, and the profit, too, does it not?" asked Tío Policarpo philosophically.

"There is danger only for those from North America. And neutral nations, of course," he added politely. "The English and Irish may supply the French with impunity, but the Flour Act applies only to us. The Irish may stuff the holds of the French navy with their beef and butter, while our vessels are in constant danger from our own navy."

"The English king does not mind if the Irish supply his French enemies?" José asked in astonishment, forgetting his place.

"The Anglo-Irish nobility whisper in the king's ear, but the king is too far away to hear the voices of his American subjects." The captain was red-faced with alcohol now, and waved his cigar like a baton so that plumes of smoked swirled about them as he vented his spleen at a king too distant to hear or object.

Emboldened by the drink, Tío Policarpo asked, raising his eyebrow, "Perhaps your king does not wish his colonies to supply the enemy with ordnance and naval stores?"

"And what if we do? Do they expect our ships to remain idle for years on end? To rot in the harbor? This war has proved damned expensive, and someone must pay for it, so that George can pay to protect his beloved Hanover, while Indians despoil our frontier." Captain Silvernails's stout form quivered as he raged.

As they made their way down the ladder into the boat, José thought of Tío Domingo, even now on his way to Jamaica with Rafael as ship's boy. Kingdoms fare best, he thought, when the monarch does not know all that passes within them.

The *Charming Sally* had sold its cargo of wheat for an excellent price, and on Saturday, to mark the occasion, their captain invited the men of the *Seaflower*, out of Philadelphia, to an informal dance. As an afterthought, he extended an invitation to the *Alejandro*, for Beaubroin had made himself popular with their cook by trading some dried ginger for wheat bread.

"He say zey bake bread wiz ze ginger and ze molasses," Beaubroin enthused. "He tell me all."

"A pox on these foreign innovations," snarled Calixto, and Tío Policarpo looked forbiddingly upon Beaubroin, who did not again mention exotic baked goods.

They crowded into the boat and rowed over to the schooner, leaving Cipriano to watch over the *Alejandro*.

"I will enjoy the silence as I rest my aching leg, and together God and I will discuss the affairs of men and reach some agreement," he said, settling down upon a locker and resting his game leg upon a coil of line.

It was two weeks later, on a hazy day that promised a rare shower, when they heard a shout off the starboard bow.

"Ahoy! *Alejandro*, ahoy!" It was the voice of Tondo. They lowered the Jacob's ladder and he climbed aboard, and the boat of the *Speedwell* rowed away, its crew waving in farewell.

He stood there, head lowered, before Tío Policarpo. "They said I could be free. Then after we stood out, I realized that I could never return home, never see my mother." He stopped to wipe a tear from his eye. "So, when the *John and Mary* stopped at Fort-Dauphin to pick up a cargo of sugar, I left her and hired myself out on a sloop back to Monte Cristi." He suddenly looked very young, almost a boy.

He stood, shamefaced for a moment, then added, "I will be free, but I will buy my freedom papers, and my mother's, too."

Tío Policarpo looked at him in silence, then his fist shot out and sent Tondo sprawling on the deck.

"You fool, do you have a problem in your coconut? This is a disaster. Do you think your master will allow you to ship with me again if he hears of this? Will any other master trust their men with me? What of other slaves who wish to earn their freedom?"

Tondo's tears flowed more freely now, and mixed with blood and mucus from his nose, as he lifted himself up from the deck.

Tío Policarpo kept Tondo on the *Alejandro* after that, occupying him with innumerable chores. Never had the sloop looked better as Tondo scraped, painted, and tarred. Tío Policarpo also altered the log to remove all mention of the incident, and swore the rest of the crew to secrecy. Tondo was a quiet man after his great adventure.

"Still," he said, as he sat, picking at oakum, "I think I would have liked to have seen New York."

José accompanied Tío Domingo as they visited the *Seaflower*, where an agent for a New York trading company kept office. He occupied a small cabin where he received representatives from the vessels of many countries and colonies, as well as from Saint-Domingue, arranging commercial transactions for his firm. Tío Policarpo discussed with him the purchase of wheat flour, but no final agreement was reached.

"He asks a great deal," said Tío Policarpo as José and Cipriano rowed him back. "He thinks the Spanish swim in silver."

They had left Calixto in charge of transferring their final hogsheads of salt beef to a small sloop that would take them to a buyer in Le Cap. When they mounted to the deck, they found only Tondo and a pile of splintered wood that had once been the *Alejandro*'s buckets.

"One of the hogsheads slipped as we were raising it from the hold. It fell upon the buckets. We are fortunate it did not break open," explained Tondo.

"The sailors of the *Constance* were very careless in their handling," he added quickly, anxious that he not fall any further in Tío Policarpo's opinion.

"Where is Calixto?" asked Tío Policarpo, head swiveling. "Where was he when this carelessness took place?"

"There is a cooperage in San Fernando. The *Charming Sally*'s boat was going in, and Calixto and Beaubroin went with them," replied Tondo.

"Beaubroin, too?" asked Tío Policarpo. He was pacing the deck, now.

"He wished to obtain more achiote. You told him that it added a note of perfection to his chocolate. He used the last of it when you entertained Captain Deming of the *Betsey*," said Tondo.

Tío Policarpo rubbed his forehead. "I should watch my words when he is about. Surely this matter could have waited a day. What was Calixto thinking? Do not say it, I know what he was thinking."

He stopped. "Where did he get the pesos?"

"He said that he would use his own money for the time, and that you would pay him back when they returned," Tondo explained brightly. He was no doubt relieved that the captain's ire was now shifted to others.

There was thunder in the air all afternoon, but it did not come from the clear sky over Monte Cristi Bay. Tío Policarpo glanced frequently towards shore, and was unusually sharp with the crew.

At last they espied the *Charming Sally*'s boat in the distance. Some minutes later, Calixto, red-faced and bleary-eyed, came over the side. He placed a bucket upon the deck, its new wood bright against the aged grey deck boards. He stood before them slump-shouldered, and his clothes hung disordered upon them, as if they no longer remembered their purpose. He said nothing.

"Where is Beaubroin?" asked Tío Policarpo slowly. The thunder was in his voice, now.

"Kidnapped," rasped Calixto. "Two mule traders, on their way to sell their stock in Saint-Domingue. He went into a tavern for a drink, fell in with some sailors, and began regaling them with the story of his capture in Guadeloupe and his great escape from Jamaica. These men overheard and waylaid him as he left the place. No doubt they hope to get a reward for him from the French."

Horror filled José's heart. Horror, and anger, too. What right had these men to seize his friend? He had papers issued by the authority of His Catholic Majesty of Spain, declaring his freedom.

"Where are these men now?" roared Tío Policarpo.

"We learned that they had already set off with him for the Massacre River. Once across, they are outside of Spanish jurisdiction," replied Calixto. He stared at his feet and shuffled nervously.

A cloud crossed the sun, and the light faded, as if the sky, too, mourned this news. The air was still, without movement or hope.

"The people of San Fernando say they know these men, they often pass through here on their way to Fort-Dauphin. They do a regular trade in the market there." He pulled himself a little straighter, not without difficulty, and said in a low tone, "We could follow them. We could take him back."

Tío Policarpo began to pace again. "It cannot be done, they have half a day's lead on us. And who would go? How would they get there? One or two men, against all of Saint-Domingue? Drink has addled your brains."

"I could go. These men would not care to meet me in the dark. If I found a sloop going to Fort-Dauphin, I could be there before them and waylay them on the outside of the city." His scar burned scarlet and his eyes struggled to focus.

"This needs a sober man," said Tío Policarpo.

Calixto flinched, then stood a little taller and said in a loud, hoarse voice, "I can be that man."

Tío Policarpo considered this proposition for a moment, then said, "You think to go to a foreign city, kidnap a man single-handedly, and bring him back? I tell you it cannot be done."

"He would not need to kidnap him. Beaubroin has his declaration of manumission, signed by a Havana notary, from a friendly nation, a Catholic power. Why would the authorities in Fort-Dauphin not honor it?" José interjected.

Tío Policarpo laughed. "This is Saint-Domingue of which we speak, not a schoolroom. The designs of scholars come to dust in the world of men."

"We cannot abandon Beaubroin," Calixto said, clenching his hands. Then, more softly, "I cannot abandon him."

"So now you care about the goat?" asked Cipriano.

"He is our goat," said Calixto. "He is not their goat."

"And you allowed him to stray," murmured Cipriano.

"It is impossible," said Tío Policarpo again. "One man cannot do it. And who would go? I cannot – I would find myself like Beaubroin. So, too, might Tondo. We are left with a cripple, a schoolboy, and a drunk."

This harsh assessment set them all aback, all the more so because it was true.

"I have just turned sixteen," José heard himself say. "And I am tall for my age."

He shocked even himself with these words. But he thought of Beaubroin, alone in a strange country. He thought, too, of Christophe, who had risked so much to save his friend. And he remembered how Christophe had saved him, as well, and he spoke again.

"We could try my plan to go to the authorities and demand his release. Please let me try, uncle." His words were brave, but his heart trembled as he spoke them.

"And what would I tell your mother if something should happen to you? And what would I say to your papá?" Tío Policarpo stood in the bow, alone, with his back to them. José thought he heard him whisper, "But then, what would I say to Alejandro?"

At last, crossing himself, he turned to them. "We will attempt it. I think Alejandro will be with you."

"I must be mad," he heard Tío Policarpo say to himself as turned away and entered the cabin.

José and Calixto left aboard a French sloop with the ill-favored name of *Bacchus*, which was returning to Fort-Dauphin full of salt beef and pork, oats, cheese, and butter. The two were dressed in their going-ashore clothes, so that they would be taken for men of repute and not common ruffians.

Tío Policarpo gave José Beaubroin's certificate of manumission, and his own papers proving his free birth. "Does he need it?" asked Calixto. "He might pass as a *blanco* – why put him at any risk?"

"I have been mistaken for a *blanco* before," said José.

Tío Policarpo studied him at length. "Your hair has a hint of your father's red, but so, too, do many *pardos*. You have the sharp features of a *blanco*, but also something of your mother's softness. And the sun has browned you like a cowhide. Perhaps some might be fooled, but the keen eye will know. You will be safer if you carry it."

Tío Policarpo also entrusted José with the silver, and with private instructions. "Do not on any account allow Calixto near a tavern, or this endeavor will founder."

"How would I stop him?" asked José, now feeling his youth.

"Remind him of his promise to me. He is not without honor, or he would not be making this effort," replied Tío Policarpo.

"Why does he drink so?" José asked the question that had long gnawed at him.

"Some say he drinks because of a lost love. Others, that he lost his love because he drinks. In truth, I do not think even he remembers any longer," sighed Tío Policarpo.

As they prepared to depart, with embraces and good wishes from Cipriano and Tondo, Tío Policarpo handed each of them a pistol with a supply of cartridges.

"You must attempt to avoid trouble," he warned. "But you must also be prepared to face it."

They were soon aboard the *Bacchus*, which was already preparing to sail. José was all nerves as the wind did not co-operate, blowing south towards the land. At last, late in the afternoon, the wind backed, and a land breeze allowed them to sail carefully past the reefs at the mouth of the bay and pick their way around the Seven Brothers. He knew their caution was warranted, but his heart resented every moment of delay. At last they stood westward, well offshore to avoid the rocky coast. At night they hove-to, although José thought that if they stood out a little farther they could have sailed through the night. He clenched his fists and tried not to think about the time lost.

Nor did the weather care about Beaubroin's plight. The sails sagged in the light wind as the sloop crept towards Fort-Dauphin. Calixto paced the desk, his scar burning on his cheek, and the deckhands kept well clear of him.

At last Calixto said to the captain, "I wonder you do not set the outer jib."

The captain roared at him and he retreated. A half-hour later, however, the outer jib rose up on its stay, and their speed increased ever so slightly.

They entered the harbor through a narrow channel. The captain shouted orders as the mate carefully guided the tiller to keep them away from the coast. Off the larboard side, several batteries of artillery guarded the approach. The channel opened up into a broad harbor, sheltered from wind and hostile vessels. In the center of the harbor, the fort itself, a large, circular structure of heavy stone, stood on a peninsula that extended out from the town. No one could be seen through its embrasures. Only a few vessels, of small burden, rode at anchor in the harbor: a few fishing vessels, droghers, shallops, and sloops used in the coasting trade. None of them carried more than a few guns. More boats were tied up along the piers that extended into the harbor. On the shore José could see a sloop being careened, workers bustling about, scraping seaweed and barnacles from its side.

"I wonder that there is not a fleet anchored here," José remarked, thinking how much this harbor resembled that of Havana. Calixto translated for Julien, a nearby sailor who was preparing to drop anchor.

"It is a poor anchorage for defense," Julien replied. "Ships can only depart one by one, and so it is easily blockaded."

José heard this with unease.

It had taken the better part of a day to reach Fort-Dauphin, and they had arrived well into the afternoon. A boat rowed out bearing the harbor master, and the captain presented the *Bacchus* sloop's cargo manifest to the port authorities and obtained permission for its two passengers to disembark.

José paced nervously, anxious to depart. Calixto's narrowed eyes and livid scar betrayed his own impatience.

"What is your business here?" asked the port official.

"Trade," replied Calixto curtly.

A nod of consent, and they were over the side and into a lighter. They disembarked at the wharf, where longshoremen were loading hogsheads of sugar onto a small sloop. A few sailors could be seen strolling about in their going-ashore finery, and others were marketing their ventures from planks supported on casks. A stylishly dressed woman in blue Indian cotton trimmed with lace from Flanders was bargaining for a pair of shoes. Warehouses stood at the ends of the piers, and at a distance back from the wharf they could see impressive single-story houses of cut stone with galleries shading the street like those in Jamaica. It was a sedate scene compared to the bustle of Havana's port.

"We are too late to waylay those men before they enter the town. Had we arrived in time, I could have hired a pair of ready men from the wharves, and then we would have put a pike in Flanders indeed. Still, I think we will find these men at the market, selling their mules," said Calixto, and inquired of one of the *moreno* longshoremen for directions.

Following his pointing arm, they walked the Rue des Bourbons and in four blocks found themselves on the Rue Grand, a broad, tree-lined boulevard of homes and shops. It seemed a vast expanse for the light traffic of slaves, shoppers, and officials who sauntered by. Through the clouds of dust raised by passing carts and horsemen, they could see that the town consisted of but a few streets – already they could spy cane fields in the distance. It had become clear why there was no naval vessel in the harbor, no soldiers crowding the streets. There was little here to protect, nothing to attract the enemy.

In a few blocks, they were at the market, located in a broad square. Ship's captains were there with stalls selling ribbons and soap, hardware and hats, all imported from France. One had a monkey on a chain, and proclaimed to all who would listen that it was tame and would make an excellent pet. *Parda* women, with gold earrings and headdresses composed of a fantastic number of scarves of Indian cotton, and still more scarves about their necks, also had stalls for their wares. José could see confectionary, jellies, and a variety of goods that were almost certainly contraband. *Moreno* slaves from the countryside had spread out cloths on the ground to display produce from their provision grounds, carved calabashes, and straw hats. Men and women shouted out their wares in enticing tones. "Plantains! Very fresh!" "Onions, cheap, very cheap!" "My oranges want to kiss you!" cried one poetical miss. Chickens, goats, and piglets contributed to the cacophony, unknowingly marketing themselves. They did not, however, see any mule vendors.

They went from vendor to vendor, asking if they had seen the muleteers. Some shrugged their ignorance, a few said yes, the men had been there earlier, but had left. The hour was getting late, and many were beginning to pack up their goods and return home.

"It is hopeless," said José.

"A meal, a night's rest, and we begin again," asserted Calixto.

They made their way to the nearest tavern. They blended in among the tired workingmen of all colors who crowded around the tables in the dark and smoky room. Glasses clinked, tankards were raised, and a clutch of *moreno* militia men sang a spirited song in the back corner. The two said little as they applied themselves to a dish of beans and rice. José lifted a spoonful to his mouth and gasped at its peppery heat. Still, the food was plentiful, and the *pardo* owner genial.

His wife came to pour them both a tumbler of well-watered wine. José froze, then screwed up his courage and said, "Water, *s'il vous plaît, madame*," looking at her with his most charming smile.

Calixto was staring at him stony-faced when the proprietress returned with the two tumblers. She smiled generously as she placed them on the table. José was gratified to find that she had squeezed in some lemon juice and sugar, and the refreshing beverage calmed his nerves.

They sought out cheap lodgings in an area frequented by sailors, on the outskirts of town where the houses were shabbier, for, not knowing how long they might be there, they wished to spare their silver. For ten sols each, or one livre total, they rented a room from a heavy-set *parda* woman. Her long lashes and a bow-shaped mouth suggested that she had once been a beauty, and her flesh was still distributed to her advantage. She conducted them to a small room looking onto a courtyard. The last faint rays of sunlight slipping through the slats of the shutters made barely visible two narrow bedsteads canopied in stained bed curtains, a battered chair, and a deal table. The room reeked of a hundred unwashed men, and from under the bed came the sound of tiny nails clicking on tile. José's despair deepened.

Calixto threw open the shutters, and a breeze blew in woodsmoke from the kitchen behind the house. "But what of the mosquitos? And the putrid night airs?" cried José.

"To perdition with mosquitos, airs, and all the rest," replied Calixto as he collapsed into a bed. Almost immediately a great snore filled the room. José removed his shoes, draped his jacket and rucksack over the chair, and lay down gingerly on the crackling mattress. He pulled a dingy bedcover up to his chin. After some time exhaustion triumphed over worry, and he, too, sank into a deep sleep.

José awoke to sunlight pouring through the window and across the bed. He sat up, swatting a blood-gorged mosquito on his arm, and looked around him. He was alone. There was no sign of Calixto. Hurriedly he pulled on his jacket and shoes, then looked about for the rucksack with the silver. It, too, was gone. He sat down on the chair, stunned. He was alone in a foreign port, friendless and penniless.

26

THE LAWS OF WAR

What folly this was. Why had he ever volunteered to travel on such a hopeless venture with a man like Calixto? The man was now undoubtedly in some tavern, drinking away Tío Policarpo's money, or perhaps had taken a berth on a foreign vessel.

How would he now get back to Monte Cristi and the *Alejandro*? He would have to find work on one of the many boats that sailed there daily. How foolish he would look upon his return. And then he remembered Beaubroin. There was no hope, now, for him. He would be sold off to some French *ingenio*, to be beaten and worked to the limit, his blithe spirit crushed by despair.

Slowly José rose up and placed one foot before another. Perhaps he still might find Calixto, passed out in some grog-shop, some few coins remaining him. He wandered from one establishment to another, entering to scan the room, query the proprietors with his limited French, and then continue on. He found nothing but shrugs, blank faces, and occasionally, a baleful look. At last he gave up, and looked towards the wharves, where the possibility of work lay.

He heard a cry. "Sabio, where do you think you are going? How can I find you if you wander off like a mooncalf? What would Capitán Policarpo say if I should lose you?" It was Calixto, approaching serenely as if it had not been he who had abandoned José.

"I went out this morning again to look for these men. Between this," he pulled out the rucksack of silver and handed it to José, "and this," now he patted the knife on his belt, "I have learned where Beaubroin must be.

"Those mule drivers are a real pair of ruffians, and the people of the marketplace did not want to run afoul of them. I calmed their fears, however," he said, patting his knife again. "They told me that the men have gone into the countryside to sell the mules to some of the plantations.

"Before that, however, they visited the office of the *maréchaussée* to try to obtain the reward for capturing an escaped slave. They left in great anger, for the matter remains to be decided. Beaubroin must be there still," Calixto announced in triumph.

He looked fixedly at José. "Now, Sabio, it is up to you. You must wave that paper in front of their faces and persuade them to release the goat. It is time we find out what all that book-learning is worth."

José suddenly felt helpless. What effrontery to have thought that he, just a schoolboy a year ago, could command the obedience of magistrates in a foreign land? Still, he knew that he had the law on his side. Spanish law had granted Beaubroin his freedom, and a notary had attested to this. All civilized societies, from the Greeks and the Romans, to their heirs in Spain and France, were built on respect for the law.

Calixto had bought some bananas at the market, and they sated their hunger as they walked. Calixto explained that the *maréchaussée* was responsible for apprehending escaped slaves. Although officially a rural police force, they had an office in Fort-Dauphin near the courthouse.

They could hear the whinnying of horses from behind the building as they entered the *maréchaussée* headquarters. A blue-uniformed *moreno* with neatly trimmed hair and clean-shaven chin sat polishing a pistol that already gleamed. Alert eyes looked them up and down, and wrinkled in confusion. Neither José nor Calixto resembled men who were seeking lost human property or conducting official business.

Calixto explain their mission, struggling to express himself in sailor's French.

Archer Manigat's face lit up with understanding. "*Mais oui*, we are holding that man in our cells. This is not the simple case. The slave is from Guadalupe, now in the hands of the British. How should he be dealt with? Do we simply sell him here?"

Calixto translated, and José pulled out Beaubroin's liberty paper. They were written in an impressively official-looking hand, with the bold signature of the Havana notary at the bottom.

"This document is Spanish," replied Archer Manigat, waving it away. "What is it to do with us? French slaves are always escaping, and those villains in Santo Domingo refuse to return them or let us pursue them. The losses to the colony are very great. If, for once, Santo Domingo returns a slave, why should we complain?"

"But the Spanish King offers freedom to all slaves who escape Protestant lands," José explained through Calixto.

"But this man is from Guadeloupe. He admits to it. We Frenchmen are good Catholics – your king has no business with him." Archer Manigat began polishing his gun again, as if to signal that their business was now completed.

He looked up. "If you wish to argue the case more, Brigadier Pincemaille will be back from patrol after the dinner hour."

"Notaries, documents, Jesuits, book-learning – so much bilgewater," snarled Calixto, face drawn, as they entered the street. He pulled out a silver dollar that had mysteriously remained in his jacket pocket, and without another word walked straight towards a noisy tavern.

It was all a shambles.

As Calixto found succor in a tavern, José found his in an undistinguished wooden building marked with a cross that stood by the market square. Its humble interior lacked the soaring grandeur of the churches of Havana, but the familiar shape of the altar and the paintings of saints that lined the walls nonetheless made him feel at home.

He found a statue of the Virgin Mother in a corner and knelt before it, pouring out his woes in prayer. His words came in Latin, for all his prayers in school and in church had been in that language, and surely it was the one preferred by God, for was it not the tongue used by the Pope, the heir of St. Peter, the Vicar of Christ? He imagined that Latin prayers jostled to the head of the queue in Heaven, elbowing aside those in French and Spanish. Polish prayers might never reach Him, and He certainly did not listen to those of the English – if they prayed at all.

He filled God's ear with his confessions, of his arrogance in thinking he could best a foreign legal system, his foolishness in trusting Calixto, his weakness in permitting him to stray into that tavern, where already he must be half-sotted. To this he added his betrayal of Tío Policarpo's trust, his undoubted disappointment of Papá, and whatever language he had used in French that would distress Mamá. And too, the cruel words to Miguel, which still nagged at his conscience. The tears began to fall, and soon they became an unstoppable flood, and soon he was blubbering like a child.

He felt a hand on his shoulder.

"Forgive me for listening, but perhaps I may be of some help," said a voice in Latin. José looked up to see the familiar black garb of a Jesuit, topped by a face tanned and wrinkled by years in the Caribbean.

"Why don't you tell me everything, from the beginning," the priest said, in a soothing voice. He conducted him to his rectory and poured them both glasses of red wine.

As the drink restored his spirits, José related the story of Beaubroin's escape and kidnapping, stopping frequently to answer Father Robillard's questions. When he had finished, the priest closed his eyes, folded his hands as if in prayer, and sat silently for several minutes.

At last he spoke. "I think you have a good case, but you must approach this correctly. The *maréchaussée* profit greatly from the rewards for captured slaves, and they will not give this up easily. It is best that I accompany you when you meet with Brigadier Pincemaille. I know him well. He is a good man and a faithful churchgoer, and he understands how to reach an accommodation."

A bell rang the noon hour, and Father Robillard politely invited José to join him for dinner. As a *moreno* man served them a spicy soup rich with chicken and vegetables, Father Robillard kept up a patter of conversation.

"When I studied in Italy, it seemed there was a church wherever one looked. Here, they cannot even build a proper place of worship. Money for stone houses, for horses, for finery, *mais oui*, but for the house of God?" He poured José another glass of wine.

"Well, I suppose it is understandable. Some of them are Huguenots, and we have, too, a few Jews. And..." he hissed, "...there are even free-thinkers among us."

"It all comes from reading filthy and blasphemous works by the likes of Diderot and Rousseau," he complained, as he buttered a slice of bread. "You do not read these scoundrels, so you?"

"I do not know of these men," replied José, "but I promise to avoid them at all costs."

Father Robillard's promise of help boosted José's spirits, and the soup renewed his strength. They left the rectory and made their way to the tavern. The crowd fell silent as the priest entered and all eyes turned to him. José pointed out Calixto, and Father Robillard marched up to him.

"Come," he ordered. "We have business with the *maréchaussée*." Calixto followed him, meek as a child caught at mischief.

As they approached the solid stone building, a handsome man with café-au-lait skin trotted up on horseback. He pulled up short in front of the building, his horse dancing a bit to show its mettle, and Archer Manigot hurried out to take its reins. Sparkling silver buttons and a sword with an engraved silver hilt proclaimed that this was Brigadier Pincemaille. He looked down upon then with regal bearing.

"These men have come about the slave Beaubroin," explained Manigot.

"Indeed," said the captain, dismounting. "It is a difficult case. Do you represent the owner? *Mais non*," he said, surveying them, "you must be here on behalf of the Spanish muleteers."

They followed him into the office, while Manigot stabled the horse.

Father Robillard began. "These men are crew mates of the said Beaubroin. They bring a statement from a notary attesting to his free status."

"But, my dear Father, this Beaubroin has confessed all," the captain protested, waving the document away.

"If they wish to pursue the matter, however, they may bring it before the *sénéchaussée*, which meets in three weeks. They will need an affidavit. I can recommend a good notary – he will charge only 20 *livres*. There will also, of course, be the cost of his maintenance in the meantime."

José gasped. Twenty *livres* and more – Tío Policarpo had never anticipated such endless expenditures. What other costs might there be?

Calixto's scar grew livid. He began to speak, the words pouring out, awkward, simple language, words of the docks, of slaves, of men who grunted for every *sol* and *dernier*. Their case weakened with every syllable. Captain Pincemaille listened impassively.

Calixto was mercifully interrupted by the return of Manigot. "I have fed the prisoners," he said, wiping his mouth with his hand.

"It might be more accurate to say that the prisoner has fed you," commented the captain, arching his eyebrows.

"*C'est vrai*, that man is an excellent cook! He says the secret is to go easy on the hot peppers..."

"Such a good cook will fetch an exceptional price if he comes to auction. We must keep that in mind," said the captain.

Father Robillard had been in whispered conference with Calixto. Now José poked him. "If I speak in Latin, will you translate for me?"

"*Mais oui, mon cher*," Father Robillard replied, all smiles. He turned to the policemen. "This young man wishes to address you. He has been educated by the Jesuits, and so will speak in Latin. I will translate for him."

Brigadier Pincemaille nodded his assent.

Latin it must be, for thus far they must have appeared no better than the ruffians who had kidnapped Beaubroin, shabby sailors looking to enrich themselves, to gull the *maréchaussée*. They needed words that would show them to be men of honor, of substance, words that persuaded. José summoned up all he had learned in those many declamations he had delivered in school. He felt light-headed. Then there had been nothing more at stake than schoolboy rivalries, but now the life of a man hung in the balance – the life of a friend.

He stood, drew himself up, and looked Brigadier Pincemaille in the eye, as Father Navarette had taught him.

"I contend that the man Beaubroin is legally free and thus by right must be released. I admit that he was born a slave, a French slave. As the resident of a French colony, he of course became a baptized Catholic. He was, however, captured by the English Navy as part of the ongoing war with France, and was thus a legal prize of war. This is in accordance with the laws of war recognized by all civilized nations, by the French, the Spanish, and even the English."

As he spoke, he studied the captain's face, but could not judge his reaction. Meanwhile, Calixto and Manigot were whispering in the corner, gesticulating furiously with many grimaces and shakes of the head. To his relief, the two soon stepped outside.

"Then a slave of the heretic English, he escaped to the refuge of the Spanish King, His Catholic Majesty, Carlos III, who promises liberty to any who follow the true faith and escape bondage in a Protestant land. And so, according to the laws of Spain, he was granted his freedom, duly recognized in this document." Here he waved Beaubroin's freedom paper.

"Imagine his relief on finding himself again in a Catholic land, to know that once again he was under the aegis of the mother church, under the care of those who were concerned for his soul rather than his value in the fields. Safe from the heathenism of his fathers, grateful for the faith he had been taught in a French land, he rejoiced to gain his liberty. Surely he would not be denied that liberty by the servants of the French king, citizens of that very land that brought him to the one true faith?

"France and Spain are both Catholic nations, and friendly ones. Soon, in fact, it is rumored that we will be allies in this war against the heretic English. In the spirit of that friendship, and out of respect for the laws of war and of our two nations, I ask you to recognize Beaubroin's legal and moral right to liberty and thus release him."

Father Robillard gave José a reassuring pat on the shoulder as he sat down, resting both his case and his limbs. "Your teachers should be proud. Cicero himself could not have done better."

The captain's face remained inscrutable. Manigot and Calixto returned to the room and the archer whispered in Pincemaille's ear.

The captain smiled. "Thank you for your words. I think I see a resolution at hand. We will release this Beaubroin to you once you have settled all the details with Archer Manigot."

José felt jubilant. His scholarship had proved of worth, after all. They trooped outside, Calixto lagging behind with Manigot. Soon Calixto returned alone.

"So," José could not resist crowing, "book-learning is not without its uses."

"Of greater use," growled Calixto, "was an agreement to pay the reward to the *maréchaussée*."

José's face fell. "Is it true?" he asked Father Robillard, translating Calixto's remark.

The good Father patted his arm again. "I do think they were moved by your devotion to your friend, for they set the reward as a tenth of the value not of a skilled cook, but of an ordinary laborer."

"How much is that?" José asked, dread in his voice.

"200 *livres*," Calixto replied tersely. He could not meet José's eyes. "We have to pay for his keep, as well," Calixto said. "These *maréchaussée* are like eagles when they sense Spanish silver."

"Is there no one else to whom we could appeal?" José asked, turning to Father Robillard.

The priest shrugged. "There is the *prevôt*, but he is an avaricious fellow. Sometimes the pay of the *maréchaussée* disappears into his pockets. He will propose the same bargain, but he will set Beaubroin's price higher."

"But we have only some 50 *livres* in silver remaining to us! *Dios mío*, we are no better off than before," José worried.

"We will return to Monte Cristi, and then one of us will need to return with the silver," said Calixto stoutly, but doubt lurked in his eyes.

"Anything could happen by then. Those men may return and press their case. The *maréchaussée* may decide to sell Beaubroin. The *prevôt*, or another official, may intervene." José would not feel easy until Beaubroin was back in Spanish waters.

An idea began to form in his mind. It was audacious, but they were desperate. He had spied a sign near the wharves that suggested a possible solution.

"I will attempt a different tack," he said suddenly. "Wait for me by the church. I may be awhile." He hurried away, half running.

There was the sign, "Fonseca *et fils*." Before entering he pulled his jacket straight, wiped his face clean like a cat, and adjusted his queue. His back erect, he opened the door and went in. He found himself in a room stacked with crates filled with dry goods, hardware, and exotic goods of every variety. A faint smell of spice and sugar hung in the air. On the wall, engravings of scenes from Athens and Paris attempted to give the room some dignity. At the rear sat a young, dark-haired man at a polished desk, entering figures into a ledger. He wore a shirt of fine white cotton, with lace at the cuffs, and green silk lining peeked out of the black jacket hanging from a hook behind him.

"I wish to speak with M. Fonseca, father or son," he said in Spanish, in what he hoped was a firm voice.

The young man looked up. "I am the son, Moïse Fonseca. My father is in the country on business."

"My name is José Albañez Velázquez, of the trading house of Albañez y Morejón, of Havana," he introduced himself.

The young man motioned for him to sit on a daintily painted chair. "I have heard of that company," he said, and waited. He pulled a ledger from a shelf. "Yes, I recall correctly. Two years ago in March, an agent of ours sold indigo to a Captain Policarpo Marroto representing Albañez y Morejón."

Now it was time to crowd sail and stand on. "I wish to obtain a loan of 175 *livres* from Fonseca *et fils*. Our sloop *Alejandro*, under the command of Captain Marroto, is currently at Monte Cristi and we can pay you in Spanish silver when we pass Fort-Dauphin on our return to Havana. We are an honorable house, and can be trusted to repay the debt by the time set."

Fils put down his quill and stared in astonishment. "What you ask is absurd! We are a trading house, not a bank. Why does not Captain Marroto come himself? And how do I even know you are who you say? You are a mere pup, in any case. Do not waste my time."

José drew a deep breath and reached into his jacket pocket for the document attesting to his free birth. "I am the nephew and heir of Domingo Albañez. You do not know me, but you have ties to friends of mine, the Fernandez family of Jamaica and Curaçao. I have heard Samuel Fernandez mention your firm, and I have seen it in his books."

José looked earnestly at M. Fonseca. "I know that my request is most irregular, but I am in great difficulty and have no one else here to whom I may turn. And Mr. Fernandez spoke well of Fonseca *et fils*."

M. Fonseca's eyebrows shot up, but he took the document and scanned it carefully. His eyes drilled into José's. "Tell me, how does Samuel Fernandez?"

"Very well, despite the challenges presented by this war," José replied. "I spent the summer with his family in Lucea, learning English. I taught mathematics to his son Daniel, and his daughter Sarah in turn took charge of my English lessons.

"And I kept Shabbos with them," he added, "although in truth I am a Catholic."

"So," asked Fonseca *fils*, twirling his quill, "how is Daniel settling in with his new bride?"

José started, then understood. "He will not marry for several years yet, for he is my age. There is talk, however, of one day finding him a match in Port Royal."

Suddenly young Fonseca was all smiles. "My father knew Samuel Fernandez's uncle in Curaçao very well, they spent time together in Kingston in their youth."

He leaned forward. "It is a poor merchant who leaves port without his finances already in hand. What is this about?"

Now he must sail close to the wind indeed. José considered manufacturing some plausible explanation, to mask this as a legitimate business endeavor, but he knew that trade relationships were built on trust. Never should it be said that he had deceived friends of the Fernandez family. He poured out the story of Beaubroin's kidnapping.

M. Fonseca tapped his chin with his quill, deep in thought. "The *maréchaussée* are not only skilled at chasing down escaped slaves, but they pursue every *dernier* with equal diligence. You are in the right legally, of course, and you might well prevail in court, but at what cost? And if you did not? No, you did the right thing."

He stared hard at José and continued. "But, *mon cher*, where is the profit in this?"

José's heart fell.

M. Fonseca smiled. "You seek only the money to redeem this Beaubroin. You are in Fort-Dauphin, where goods move in and out from Le Cap and Monte Cristi. I would have thought that a representative of Albañez y Morejón would not allow such an opportunity to pass him by."

Now the negotiations truly began. M. Fonseca proposed that José should take 150 *livres* for the *maréchaussée*, and tomorrow, he should go to the Fonseca warehouse and purchase 100 *livres* worth of indigo from one of the company's clients. He would provide in return a letter of credit from Albañez y Morejón, to be payable within two months. José felt considerable trepidation. This was not his money to risk, nor had Tío Policarpo authorized him to borrow money or engage in trade. Nor, he knew, was it strictly legal, for he was only sixteen and not old enough to make legal commitments. He imagined the faces of Tío Domingo and Señor Morejón when they learned of his audacity. Well, "Small dreams and a timid heart make a poor recipe for life," Tío Domingo had said. He put out his hand and he and M. Fonseca shook to seal the agreement. A notary would finalize the paperwork on the morrow. They would not mention to him that José was not of age.

Moïse called to the back of the house, and a pretty young woman appeared with a bottle.

"Both my bride and my wine are from Bordeaux," smiled young Fonseca, pouring José a glass of claret.

"It is a very great pleasure, Madame," said José, kissing her hand as he had seen Tío Domingo do. She blushed her thanks.

M. Fonseca swirled his wine in his glass. "So, you are some kind of *sang-mêlé*, a *metis*, perhaps, or a *mamelouque*? I make a study of such things."

There were very many terms for people of color, for every possible admixture. José knew of 64. "I do not know the French word," he explained.

"Mmm...I see. Well, no matter. Money knows no color. To a long and fruitful relationship between Fonseca *et fils* and Albañez y Morejón. And to a victory for the French and Spanish alliance!" He raised his glass.

To José's startled look he replied, "Have you not heard? The news came from a recent visitor from Le Cap. Admiral Blenac's fleet escaped the blockade at Brest and brought the tidings. Great Britain has declared war upon Spain. We are allies."

José smiled and raised his glass in return, but his mind was filled with thoughts of war.

José rejoined Calixto, who was loitering impatiently in the vicinity of the church. He showed him the 150 *livres*, represented by a jumble of French, Portuguese, English, but mainly Spanish, coin. He explained how he had obtained it.

Calixto whistled and shook his head. "It is good to be the nephew of the owner."

He took the money, along with the silver that they had brought with them, and entered the office of the *maréchaussée*. He reappeared with Beaubroin, who thanked Archer Manigot for his kind attentions during his confinement, and then admonished him, "Remember well, let the pepper and onions prevail – the hot pepper, she is a treacherous mistress!"

Beaubroin embraced José joyfully, and would have done the same to Calixto, but a fierce look from the mate stopped him. Calixto returned the rucksack to José. It was much lighter now.

José dashed into the church to thank Father Robillard for all his efforts and pressed a contribution to the church into his hands.

He chose this moment to inform his shipmates of that the long-expected war had finally come.

"This requires a celebration – we must toast our new allies. And Beaubroin's freedom, of course," cried Calixto, drawing them into a tavern, and pulling out of his jacket pocket a peso that had somehow escaped the *maréchaussée*. José protested, but Beaubroin was already tossing back a glass of spirits, and Calixto feigned deafness. And in truth, it felt churlish to deny Beaubroin his celebration. He took a glass of wine.

The rescue of Beaubroin was almost forgotten now, for all their talk was of war. How soon could the *Alejandro* fit out as a privateer? Where might the best prizes be found? And what men might be good to add to the crew? They would need to exercise the guns, as well. They would need a great deal of practice, José thought, or they would find themselves a prize.

How much time had passed he did not know when the *pardo* tavern keeper whispered in his ear, "You should take your friend here home while he still has his legs."

The man said, to no one in particular, "These *petit blancs*! They come here with nothing but their appetites and a dream of getting rich on sugar and slaves, and see what becomes of them!"

"Your father is just such a man, Rasteau," laughed a plump man at the next table.

"And I make him proud," boasted the tavern keeper. "I own this place and three slaves, and he and my mother live comfortably. He has nothing to complain of."

José understood enough of this to know that Calixto had been insulted. "He is no *petit blanc*, he is a good man – when he is not drunk."

"Eh, but he is drunk now, is he not?" replied the tavern keeper, and this was met with unkind laughter from a group gambling at cards. Rasteau added something else unflattering, but his words were drowned out by a group of soldiers in the corner who had chosen that moment to begin a rousing song.

José and Beaubroin helped Calixto up and out of the door. Rasteau had waited too long with his warning, for Calixto clung to them for support as his feet wandered beneath him. Outside, darkness had fallen upon Fort-Dauphin. José and Beaubroin propped Calixto against the wall while they discussed how to get him to their lodgings, more than a few blocks away.

Calixto slid slowly down on to the ground. Beaubroin shrugged, but the bright moonlight revealed the worry in his eyes.

"I like not zis town. We go home soon, *c'est bon*." He began to whistle a brave tune to pass the time.

"Perhaps if we wait for a time, we will be able to move him," José said hopefully.

Behind him he heard someone shout in Spanish, "That is the slave! And those must be the men who cheated us!"

Before he could turn to see the source of the voices, a powerful body knocked him to the ground. He groaned, and looked up to see a tall, thin man swing at Beaubroin. The *moreno* danced out of range. Then the big man joined his companion and the two circled about Beaubroin, looking for a moment to lunge and seize him. From the wall a drunken groan came from Calixto.

"Grab him from behind, Carlos!" cried the big man.

José remembered the pistol in his belt, but there was not time to fetch out a cartridge and to load. He pulled himself up and leapt onto the big man's back, pounding at him. He could feel the man's muscles working to throw him off, and knew that his powerful arms, once free, could savage him. He held tight and the man staggered about. The two had backed Beaubroin against the wall now, next to Calixto. The mate was slumped over, one bleary eye open.

Carlos reached for his belt, and José saw the shine of a knife blade. The big man roared encouragement. Carlos's lithe figure crept closer to Beaubroin, shoulders hunched forward, head swaying back and forth like that of a snake, the knife clutched close. Beaubroin's eyes widened in terror. Suddenly Calixto's leg kicked up, striking the thin man's knee, and Carlos toppled forward as Beaubroin stepped to one side. He struck his head against the wall and fell prone, let out a great moan, and was still. The moonlight shone silver on a dark pool that began to spread out from under the prone figure. The big man, with a great cry, threw José from his back and fled. Calixto, too, gave a moan, toppled over, and began to snore.

Men began to emerge from the tavern. An individual in sailor's slops turned over the body of the thin man. He had fallen on his knife, and the hilt still protruded from his chest.

"He has been stabbed!" he cried.

All eyes turned upon José and his companions.

"This man and his friend fell upon us in the street," Beaubroin protested.

"He looks to have been a villain," said a man with an expensive-looking pistol showing in his belt, prodding the body with a well-shod foot.

"How do we know it was not these drunken Spaniards who attempted to rob *them*?" asked a grizzled old *pardo*.

The tavern keeper, Rasteau, pointed at José. "Look at him! He has the face of an altar boy. Does he look a ruffian to you?"

Several men nodded in agreement.

"Still, Fabien, it might be good to call for the militia. They can question these Spaniards," offered a man in a genteel but shabby coat.

"In the morning," said Rasteau.

"But they will be gone by then!" protested the shabby man.

"Yes," replied Rasteau. "So, too, will the gamblers. I do not have a license."

"Perhaps a priest?" suggested a slight man with ink-stained hands.

"There is no need to disturb Father Robillard at this hour," said Rasteau. "This fellow is beyond last rites. There will be time enough for prayer in the morning."

The crowd dispersed to their homes, leaving the thin man's body lying in the street.

Rasteau motioned them back into his tavern, and José and Beaubroin hoisted up Calixto by the arms and carried him in.

"Sleep here for the night," said Rasteau. "That other man may seek vengeance, and your friend is in no condition to defend himself."

They curled up in a corner, and Rasteau brought them some ragged coverlets to rest under. They slept deeply, despite the gasping snores of Calixto, and awakened sore and bruised.

27

ONLY LIBERTY OR DEATH

They were awakened that morning by the sound of banging on the tavern door, banging that continued until Rasteau, still tucking his shirt into his breeches, shuffled out to answer it.

"What do you know of this?" asked a *moreno* militiaman, a comrade at his side. He gestured to the body in the street, now a subject of interest to flies.

"He was not one of my patrons," replied the tavern keeper, speaking truthfully.

"How did he come to harm? Who did this?" the militiaman pressed him.

"I did not witness the incident. Perhaps he fell on his knife." Rasteau shrugged, still remaining within the bounds of truth.

The militiamen moved on, banging on more doors. José paid the tavern keeper for their night's lodging and some bread to take the edge off their hunger.

They met with M. Fonseca at the company warehouse where Calixto learned that there was a commercial component to José's arrangement with Fonseca *et fils*.

"So, the French Jew has gulled you into taking his company's wares, and will earn a tidy commission in the bargain. But what are we to do with so much indigo?" he protested. "There is little market for it in Havana."

"True," said José. "But there is great demand for it among the Dutch weavers."

"We are not Dutch," complained Calixto. "They offer manufactured goods, and we have been commissioned to bring back flour. The market for that is very good right now in Havana."

"It is the English of the North who have the flour, and they are seeking manufactured goods," said José.

Calixto's shook his head. "Truly, you are an Albañez."

It would be a day's work loading the shallop, the *Vénus*, and then they would sleep on board and depart at first light on the morrow. Moïse Fonseca beamed as he toted up the commission his house would earn on the transaction.

"Remember us when next you return to Monte Cristi. Let this be just the beginning of the trading relationship between us – and our friendship," said Moïse, and he kissed José on both cheeks. José was embarrassed by this odd French custom, but politely reciprocated. Calixto stepped back in alarm.

It took the better part of the day to make Monte Cristi, as they beat against the wind, but at last the *Vénus* anchored in the bay near the *Alejandro*. José could see the figure of Tondo on deck, but the youth did not notice this latest arrival among the countless boats that moved in and out of the bay. The *Vénus* lowered a boat and rowed them over.

"Ahoy, *Alejandro*!" cried Calixto, and Tondo's delighted face appeared over the side. He gave a shout, and then Tío Policarpo's face was next to his, followed by that of Cipriano. The *Alejandro* dropped a ladder and the three of them scrambled up, one eager hand over another.

Calixto was the first on deck, face impassive, as if such adventures were routine with him. He looked about. "I see there is much work to be done here."

José was next over the side. His uncle gripped his shoulder and whispered, "Well done!"

Then Beaubroin's face appeared. Tears began to stream from his eyes, and he fell at the feet of Tío Policarpo. "*Mea culpa, mea culpa, mea maxima culpa!*"

Tío Policarpo pulled him to his feet. "I should flog you soundly. Still, I am glad to have you back, Beaubroin."

"No more Beaubroin!" the man replied. "Now, you see Cristóbal. I done wiz ze French, all ze sings French, all ze words French. Never I speak ze French again! I learn ze Spanish till I speak like you, till zey say, zer goes Cristóbal, ze very man of Spain."

"How did you manage it?" asked Tío Policarpo. Calixto stepped back to allow José to claim the glory or the shame.

José hesitated, tugged at his jacket, removed his hat and then returned it to his head.

Tío Policarpo raised his eyebrows. He waved José into the cabin. "Tell me everything, leave nothing out."

Tío Policarpo listened, with only an occasional murmur of understanding, until he came to the letter of credit.

"*Dios mío*! On what authority did you do this? That is a great sum!" cried Tío Policarpo.

José hung his head. "Otherwise we would have lost Beaubroin."

"But the indigo!" Then he laughed, and the laugh became a roar. "Well, the splinter is indeed like the stick. If Domingo had been here, he would have done the same, but he would have issued a letter of credit for 300 livres and bought sugar, as well."

Tío Policarpo looked grave when told the war news. "I wish we had learned of this before we left Havana," he said. "I only pray we return safely."

The next several days were spent first shifting the indigo to the *Alejandro*, then rowing from vessel to vessel in search of a buyer. Tío Policarpo left it to José to conduct the negotiations, only translating and offering hints as needed. At last the Danish brigantine *Laerken* purchased the indigo in exchange for several crates of shoes and dishes. These in turn went to the schooner *Lively*, out of Baltimore, for barrels of wheat flour. With each exchange, they made a slight profit.

"Well, this has turned out better than expected," Tío Policarpo said as the last keg of flour was lowered into the *Alejandro*'s hold. "The money does not make up the cost of redeeming Beau...Cristóbal, but it softens the blow."

Cristóbal's rescue had indeed come at some cost, and Señor Morejón would frown when he entered the disappointing profits of this voyage into the books of Albañez y Morejón. José understood now why Tío Policarpo, despite his years as a captain in this profitable trade, remained a man of modest means. Profit might be king in Monte Cristi, but nobler sentiments were enthroned in the heart of Policarpo Marroto.

T hey left Monte Cristi in mid-April, their hold full of American wheat flour. The wind and current were with them now, and they were soon at the entrance to the harbor of Fort-Dauphin. Tío Policarpo was not willing even to moor in the bay, so they hailed an incoming vessel and José was sent aboard. Once on shore, he made his way to the office of Fonseca *et Fils* with the promised silver.

"Just as I promised," said José. "We are an honorable house."

"I never doubted it, *mon cher*," replied Moïse Fonseca. "I look forward to doing business with you again."

"I will not return," José admitted sadly. "I plan to join my father in his joiner's shop."

"*Quel dommage!* You have a gift for commerce," replied M. Fonseca, and again he bid farewell in the French manner.

José was back on the *Alejandro* within the day. They sailed peacefully past Fort-Dauphin, a northwest wind on their starboard quarter. Cristóbal stopped to look at the distant batteries, a grim set to his jaw.

"You are not paid to enjoy the scenery. The bilge must be pumped again and before me I see the goat who will do it," growled Calixto, but his voice lacked its old conviction.

Cristóbal smiled and set to work.

That night, as an exceptionally loud snore arose from Calixto's hammock, Cristóbal said softly, forgetting that he had set his face against French, "Sleep well, *mon cher*."

José gave him a quizzical look as he climbed into his own hammock, the moonlight from the grating above making eerie patterns in the cabin.

"Now I am free, zanks to him, but him, his slavery he can never escape, *pobrecito*."

They maintained a regular lookout during the daylight hours. Either Tondo or José would ascend the shrouds and scan the horizon for sails. Tío Policarpo and Calixto, while at the helm, often had the glass at their eye, looking for movement.

At night, they carried no lantern at the masthead so as not to attract unwanted attention. It was early in the morning when they passed Le Cap, sailing well off the coast. Tondo gave a shout, and the larboard watch was roused from their hammocks to join the rest on deck.

"Perhaps a trading schooner," José volunteered.

"Ship-rigged," shouted Tondo, and the vessel drew closer, till they could all see its faint outline.

Tío Policarpo ordered the *Alejandro* to stand a point closer to the wind, taking them farther from the coast. Calixto, now at the helm, swung the tiller to larboard, while José and Cristóbal sheeted out the sails until they were on a beam reach. The unidentified vessel fell from view.

"It is perhaps an English frigate on the blockade of Le Cap," said Tío Policarpo. "In any case, it seems she has lost interest in us."

After a time Tío Policarpo ordered a return to their original course, and at dinner they found that the excitement had whetted their appetite for Cristóbal's peppery beef stew, for his change of name had not diminished his passion for the cookpot.

Tío Policarpo did not let up his vigilance, however, for it was known that the English had ships off the naval base at Cap St-Nicholas. There they could not only bottle up any French naval vessels, but intercept merchantmen taking the Windward Passage to Jamaica or the southern coast of Cuba. The *Alejandro*, however, would return home by the less-frequented and poorly charted northern coast, just as she had on her outward voyage.

The *Alejandro* maintained its lookout. The next morning, in a grey drizzle of rain, it was José who was aloft and called out "Sail ho!" He watched, occasionally wiping rainwater from his eyes, as the vessel approached. She was on a northerly heading, close-hauled, on a starboard tack. On her current heading the *Alejandro* would, in time, cross close before her. Tío Policarpo, already awake in readiness for his watch, joined him at the masthead. He had the spyglass.

"A British frigate," he announced, and soon he was on deck shouting orders. Both watches were on deck and at the ready.

Tío Policarpo ordered a new course. He observed their progress, shouting corrections, and occasionally raising the glass to see if the frigate had come into view.

"She is changing course in pursuit," Tondo shouted down, for he had taken José's place aloft.

"We can sail closer to the wind than any ship," Tío Policarpo said, his hands behind his back as he studied the taut staysail.

The *Alejandro* heeled as they sailed briskly on, heading slightly away from Cuba now, the sloop's sharp bow cutting through the waves, for she had been built as a privateer, for speed. The winds came in gusts at times, and the sloop would attempt to head into the wind, and her sails would begin to luff until Calixto quickly pushed the tiller to windward until she fell off again. Tío Policarpo was on the quarterdeck, then on the main deck, watching the sails, calling for corrections at every shift of the wind. José and Cristóbal could not move quickly enough for him, and felt the rough edge of his tongue until, like Cipriano, they began to anticipate his orders. Tío Policarpo took his eyes off the sails only to turn them to the British frigate. Perhaps it was a trick of the wind and the rain, but she appeared slightly closer now, each sail now distinct in the grey light.

"She is not as weatherly, but she has a well-trained crew," Tío Policarpo said tersely. He ordered the inner jib set. They could feel the *Alejandro* respond, and Calixto tightened his grip on the tiller.

The British ship raced after them, but this was nothing like the footraces José had run at home, the urgent pressure of his competitor close at hand, the wind in his face, heart pumping hard, chest aching. This was a tortoise race, continuing for hours, the frigate closing the distance, then falling away, as the wind shifted. There were burst of activity as they trimmed the sails, then long, tense spells of inactivity as they stood, drenched, watching the distant ship.

During the lulls in activity they observed the frigate. There was no song on Cristóbal's lips now, and his face was tense. "Ze British, ze take me once, I not want zem to take me again. Never do I want to see ze *ingenio* again. I have only just learn how beautiful ze liberty is. I cannot lose it."

"I have heard too many tales of their horrors. May the Virgin and all the saints protect us!" Tondo prayed, crossing himself.

"To be a prisoner is not to be a slave," said José. "There are laws at sea as well as on land."

"Men, zey not always obey ze law, on ze land or on ze sea," replied Cristóbal.

Tío Policarpo paced the deck, discontented with their progress. He ordered the outer jib set. José was glad of the distraction from his crew mates' fears.

"If we are taken we must throw our papers overboard," Tío Policarpo said tersely.

Cristóbal smiled and nodded, "Over ze side. I swear – over ze side!" He went up to the quarterdeck to relieve Calixto at the helm.

José's eyes widened. "Will not the absence of papers tell its own story?"

Tío Policarpo looked at him. "I keep a second set, if needed. You know where to find them."

Cristóbal called out from the quarterdeck. "We remember. Over ze side!"

Calixto, joining them on the main deck, said quietly, "Already I feel the strain at the tiller. If the rudder should break..."

Tío Policarpo fixed him with a look, but sent Cipriano to join Cristóbal at the helm. Calixto returned to gnawing one of the cold sweet potatoes that Cristóbal had shared out to stave off their hunger. José nibbled at his, but he had little appetite.

Suddenly the rain stopped, and a beam of sunlight could be seen glancing off the distant sea. They could now see that as the frigate continued on her current course, while she might close the distance, her heading would take her away from the *Alejandro*. Tío Policarpo's face lightened now, as if it too were in sunshine. José wondered if it was too late for Cristóbal to bring out his cookpot.

"Sail ho! To the northwest!" cried Tondo, who had been sent to the masthead for a final look at the British ship. At once Tío Policarpo had his glass to his eye. A white patch against the grey sky began to take the form of a ship bearing down upon them. They could not evade both vessels on this course. Even if they turned to flee, they would soon find themselves off the rocky coast of Saint-Domingue.

"The British ships are schooling here like fish," said Tío Policarpo, and, unusually for him, following this remark with an oath.

"Maybe darkness will fall before they overhaul us," said Cipriano.

"*Vaya con Dios!*" ordered Tío Policarpo. They would change to a larboard tack and so hope to escape both their pursuers and the reefs of Hispaniola.

All sails trimmed to their new heading, José prepared himself for another tense race across the sea, but now Tío Policarpo called, "Run out the larboard gun! I want powder and shot, make all haste!"

"You cannot think to take on two British frigates," gasped Cipriano.

"Take the helm. Calixto, to the guns." Relieved by Cipriano, Calixto descended from the quarterdeck, his face grim. He took charge as Tondo, José, and Cristóbal fetched the required ordnance from the hold. He assigned them roles in the gun crew, but they hesitated over the equipment, trying to remember which was the wormz and which the sponge. Calixto barked obscenities to aid their memory and Cristóbal dropped the rammer.

"Only liberty or death," swore Tío Policarpo, standing in the bow, legs splayed to keep his balance, as he gazed upon the two frigates.

The gun crew attempted to appear resolute, but José struggled to calm the butterflies in his stomach. He could see beads of sweat on Tondo's forehead.

Tío Policarpo paced the deck, his face drawn. Only Calixto stood relaxed, whistling as he watched the two ships.

The second ship continued its course, as if unaware of the *Alejandro*. Two more ships became visible behind it, with the bulky lines of merchantmen.

"Surely she has seen us," said Tondo.

"She has better prey in mind than us, I think," replied Calixto.

They watched admiringly as the first frigate changed course, coming about until all the vessels were on a southwest heading, slowly disappearing over the horizon.

"I could almost swear they came from the Old Bahama Channel," said Tío Policarpo.

"Everyone knows the British always sail south of Cuba," Cipriano replied. "They are no doubt patrolling the Windward passage for prizes."

Tío Policarpo did not reply, but only stroked his chin and stood for a long time, staring off at the sea.

That night, as he stood watch in the dark, Tío Policarpo appeared on deck. "I cannot sleep after such excitement," he said, rubbing his forehead.

"Tío Policarpo, do you believe death is truly preferable to slavery?" José asked, remembering his uncle's words earlier.

Tío Policarpo stared out over the side, watching the glint of moonlight on the black waves. In time he answered, "You cannot imagine what I have seen, on that island we just left behind. The slave owners there know no constraints – they know neither God nor law."

He leaned over the gunwale, his face obscured now by shadow, and continued. "My mother begged me to escape, and I gambled all to flee. I was floating in a small boat, unconscious from hunger and thirst, my companions already dead, when a Spanish privateer pulled me aboard. I know it was God who led them to me, for how else could they have found me in all this?" he said, waving his arm at the expanse of sea.

"Some wished to treat me as a prize, to sell me in Havana, where I might have fetched a good price, but Alejandro said, 'Here, this stout fellow would make a good sailor. He must join us.' Men listened to Alejandro, and so, too, the captain, and from that day I was one of them, a free man. The very air tasted better in my mouth, the salt beef had new savor, and I no longer feared to wake."

Tío Policarpo spoke to him like one man to another, telling of times that had long been a mystery, and José wanted him to continue. "What was Alejandro like? Everyone still speaks of him."

Tío Policarpo threw back his head and laughed. "Oh, the stories I could tell you of him! When he entered a room, all eyes turned to him. And he was handsome, oh yes! The girls, every one, made eyes at him, and he could have easily taken advantage of that, but he did not, and they loved him the more for it, the mothers, too. Your grandfather placed all his hopes on him, his only son. Alejandro would take over the shop and be the head of the family one day."

He sighed. "That all ended here, on this deck, as we took this sloop from the English. It was a great victory, but a costly one."

"How did he die?" asked José, bursting with curiosity.

Tío Policarpo's voice was low now. "He was a brave man, always the first in a fight. Such men are also the first to die."

They both stared out at the dark waters, only the starlight sparkling on the waves, and for the first time Alejandro seemed real to José. He could see him there, on the deck, waving a cutlass, firing a pistol at an Englishman. Tall, handsome, smiling, there among his father and uncles, amid the smoke and thunder of battle.

Tío Policarpo shook his head. "It broke the heart of my poor Beatriz. They were twins, you see." He smiled now, and his voice grew soft. "They were lovely, the three Velázquez girls, like flowers raised tenderly in a private garden. Safe there, they grew up sweet and gentle..." His voice trailed off. José struggled to imagine Tía Nicolaza as a delicate flower in anyone's garden.

"It was then that I met her, sweet girl. When you have lived in slavery, you cannot imagine such a girl. Slavery warps women. Hard usage and rapacious men make them coarse and sharp-edged, but my Beatriz is as soft as down."

José heard Calixto calling him to take his turn at the helm, and he left his uncle there, staring at the waves.

Calixto brought out the sextant and calculated their new position. José was gratified that the mate took the time to show him how he did it. After Papá's instruction, it was clearer. I can master this in time, he thought, but then remembered that he would not need to. The *Alejandro* passed only one more

English ship, a frigate, seen disappearing behind a cay, heading west along the coast of Cuba. Its crew appeared preoccupied with taking soundings.

"What is her business?" asked Calixto. "She will find herself in the Old Bahama Straits. The English do not go there, for their pilots do not know it. She will find herself aground soon, I warrant it."

In late April the *Alejandro* finally entered the safety of Havana harbor with the dawn as the city lifted the great chain that blocked the entrance to the city during the night. The harbor was filled with ships – some twelve ships-of-the-line, plus other smaller naval vessels. Some one hundred merchant ships were moored there, as well, safe under the protection of the harbor's fortifications.

They were surprised to learn from Señor Morejón that no news had been received of a declaration of war.

"Commander Castellón assures me that these are merely rumors. Perhaps the French are attempting to provoke us into premature engagement. The Governor-General has received no news from Madrid or the Admiralty of such a proclamation. Surely they would have sent a dispatch by now. No, nothing but the usual rumors," Señor Morejón said, waving it away.

The *Alejandro* would discharge much of its cargo here, under Señor Morejón's direction, then carry the remainder of the flour, along with some passengers, to Matanzas, where they would scour her badly fouled bottom.

Walking home down the street of the Avocado, José forgot the overwhelming stench of the stockyards as he spotted the yellow house with the blue door and suddenly thought that his heart would burst. He would never leave home again. He had put in his year, and more, first on the *Orfeo*, then on the *Alejandro*. He had fulfilled the terms of Papá's bargain with Tío Domingo, and the choice was now his – to stay with Papá and become a joiner, or return to the sea.

He knew his decision already, had known before he first embarked with Tío Domingo. He would stay with Papá. And he was needed, he knew as he opened the door and saw Papá rise up from his workbench. He was greyer now, and seemed out of breath, his skin pale. They embraced and José entered the backroom to cries of delight from Mamá and Magdalena.

Later, Agustín pulled him aside. "We watch over Don Roberto now, you and me. The little boy left, and the man returned, and he will take care of his papá."

Agustín's affection for Papá was real, but José suspected that the man also feared that if Papá should die, the shop might close, and he could find himself sold to a master far less generous. Five years remained before he was eligible for the *coartación*.

They had a light supper that night, some rice and beans leftover from dinner, and José regaled them with his adventures – the rescue of Cristóbal and the flight from the English ships. Mamá frowned and Magdalena's eyes grew wide. Then Papá settled into his chair with his accustomed tumbler of *aguardiente*.

"A dram, lad?" he offered.

"I had thought to visit Rafael," José said. "Surely the *Orfeo* has already returned." The sloop had left Havana at the end of October and had only intended to visit Jamaica, as Tío Domingo judged that the risk from English ships had made a longer voyage too risky.

There was silence, and the shadows made by the final rays of sunlight through the shutters, closed against dusk's mosquitos, grew longer.

"The *Orfeo* sloop has not returned yet," said Papá.

Mamá scurried out to the courtyard with the dirty dishes, her face averted.

"She should have returned by now," said José, slowly. "Perhaps she encountered heavy weather, and took refuge in the Bay of Xagua – or is laid up there for repairs."

"Perhaps," said Papá. "Though it would be easy enough to send word overland. Ours is a narrow island, if long, and it is only a few days by mule or horseback. Men travel that way with some regularity."

"Do you think…" José did not wish to say the words. "…she has been taken by the English? They are everywhere." A great pain had seized his heart. He knew he should think first of his uncle, but his worry was all for his friend – daring, confident Rafael, who had worked so hard for this chance. He thought, too, of Vicente, of Osorio, and of Renzo. Would he never see them again? He hated the sea at that moment.

"That is what I fear," said Papá, almost spitting. "God help them if they are. They are the devil's spawn, the English."

José visited Señor Morejón's storehouse the next evening and found him entering the *Alejandro*'s transactions into his ledger.

"So, here he is, the notorious speculator of Monte Cristi," Señor Morejón said, setting down his quill.

José blushed. "I know I did wrong, but I could not abandon Beaubroin."

Señor Morejón rubbed his eyes. "No, and Domingo, in your place, would have..." He sighed.

"Surely they are only delayed," said José. "By the weather, perhaps, or repairs."

"He planned to visit Port Royal," said Señor Morejón. "He would feign the need for repairs. *Dios mío*, the English do it often enough. Commander Castellón asked him to make observations of the English fleet."

José gasped.

"The price we pay for official neglect of our trade," Señor Morejón said wearily. "I hope the price has not been too high."

He sat silently. "I wish Rafael had not gone with him. He pleaded so, and I was too weak to say no."

"The *Alejandro* had several close encounters on the voyage home," confessed José. "I am glad to be safely back in Havana."

"I would feel safer if the Captain-General put more energy into our defenses," said Señor Morejón. José had never seen him so out-of-sorts before. "You can see the labor crews, working aimlessly on this project or that, none of them anything that will make any real difference in our fortifications. Meanwhile he has spent the last year so tying up the tobacco trade in regulations that I fear nary a leaf will ever leave this island again." He sighed, and stared at his ledger unseeingly.

José left Señor Morejón in order to visit with the rest of the Morejón family, but when he entered the kitchen it was Marianela's eyes he sought.

Señora Morejón looked him up and down. "So, someone returns from the sea. But it is the wrong boy." And with those words, she left the room.

Marianela pulled him into a chair beside her and leaned her head close to his. "She has become unbearable," said Marianela. "We all feel her tongue."

"More unbearable," said Gabriel. "She says that Rafael is her jewel and heart's delight, that he is the best of us..."

"And more of that sort," interrupted Marianela. "She is worried he will not return."

"And she blames Papá for letting him go, and so he hides in his storehouse," added Gabriel. "All her life she has bent everyone to her will, but now she finds she cannot conquer the sea or the English," said Marianela, bending her head over her needlework.

"Or death," said Gabriel.

"Hush! It has hardly come to that. Many ships are slow to return to port. They will come home," Marianela said.

Her calm voice soothed his fears. Her needle, with its bright red thread, moved in and out of the white cotton as the shape of a hibiscus blossom began to take shape under her fingers. Surrounded by the noise of energetic brothers and an imperious mother, she had always been an island of calm. The smells and sounds of the household flowed around her, leaving her equanimity undisturbed. He studied her now, noting the way even her skirt fell in orderly folds, and her hair maintained its order, no strand or curl out of place, pulled back against her head by a comb.

"I did not have time to buy you a present," he said at last.

"It does not matter," she said, and she looked up and smiled, her lips slightly parted. His heart missed a beat.

"Sebastián will be happy to see you," she said.

"Have you seen him lately?" he asked, suddenly uneasy.

"He calls to look in on us," she said, tying off the thread with a knot.

He noticed now the ebony comb that held back her hair. She had not had it when he left. She touched it self-consciously, and later, the thought of that comb lingered in his memory as he fell asleep in his cot.

M ay wore on, and still no sign of the *Orfeo*. José worked alongside Papá and Agustín in the shop, sanding, measuring, shaving, sawing, amidst the sawdust and curls of wood. Soon he would attempt his first solo mortise and tenon joint. They worked long, peaceful hours, and José basked in Papá's presence, the occasional hand on his shoulder or approving glance. On occasion, a faint whiff of salt air found its way through the grated windows of the shop and his mind would turn again to the *Orfeo* and its fate.

One night Papá brought out the Madeira and poured a glass for José, and then one for himself.

"The *Orfeo* may not return," Papá offered in preface.

Mamá began to weep.

"Hush, Faustina, we have all known the risks he takes," said Papá, going to her and putting a tender hand upon her shoulder.

"I weep for my soul," she said, rubbing a fist in her eye. "I weep because I wished him ill. I did not want him to take my José away, to tempt him away from God."

"It is I who should weep, then," said Papá, and he sat down and took a deep draft of Madeira. "I have been a poor brother to him.

"Nay!" he said, holding up a hand as Mamá began to protest. "I was the eldest, my father's pride, and I delighted in it. I never thought how Donnie might take it, how it might batter his spirit over the years to always be second pickings. I could have bolstered him, encouraged him, helped him find his way, but I fear I merely ground him down further with my warnings and exhortations."

Another swallow of Madeira, and he added, "I could have said all these things to him, but I did not, and now perhaps I never can. What I would not give to clap him on the back now." He looked greyer than ever.

Magdalena leapt to her feet and cried, "You have all but buried Tío Domingo and Rafael, and they are not overdue even two months yet! Many a boat has been gone overlong and returned safely."

Mamá took her in her arms. "*Mi hija*, my sunshine, what would we do without you?"

It was true. Magdalena refused to believe that the *Orfeo* might be lost, and often her encouraging words lifted their spirits. She had taken over more and more of the household duties as a distracted Mamá let them slip from her grasp. She conspired with Agustín to ensure that Papá did not overtax himself.

"You are right, *mi hija*, we must not despair," said Papá. "But we must also prepare ourselves for the worst."

"You are your uncle's heir," he continued, turning to José and fixing his eyes upon him. "You have not yet reached your majority, but he has not returned and you must take up your duties in Albañez y Morejón."

José felt betrayed. Papá had promised. When his time at sea was finished, he could work in the shop. He did not want to go to sea again. Had it not devoured Tío Domingo and Rafael? It was not that he was unwilling to fight as a privateersman – there was a certain thrill just in the word. It was that he knew, once he took up that life, he could not go back. Papá could not run the shop alone, not for much longer, and he would be condemned forever after to a life at sea. Papá did not understand the dark lures of the sea – the bribes, lies, and deceitful practices necessary to pursue Tío Domingo's trade, the coarse language, the rough taverns, and shameless doxies found in every harbor town.

"No!" he cried, from the very depths of his heart. "That was not the bargain!"

"Anselmo cannot run the company alone, not forever," said Papá. "Can you not see how overwhelmed he is? He had thought to have Rafael to lean on, and now he is alone. And the loss of the *Orfeo* is a hard financial blow."

"Many men, and their families, rely upon this work," Papá continued. "Many people count upon the goods they bring – God knows, they cannot rely upon the register ships. You have a duty to them."

"I have a duty to you!" he protested. "You need me in the shop."

"I have Agustín," Papá said simply, as if he did not know how those words cut. "And I can find another man if I need more help."

"But I do not want to be elsewhere," he cried vainly.

"Those are the words of a boy," Papá replied, his face grim and wan. "You are a man, and must take up the duties of a man. Take yourself to bed and think on it." He stared long into his glass of *aguardiente*, then took a great swallow.

José lay in his cot that night, staring at the curtains that had sheltered him since childhood, and wished that he were still a boy.

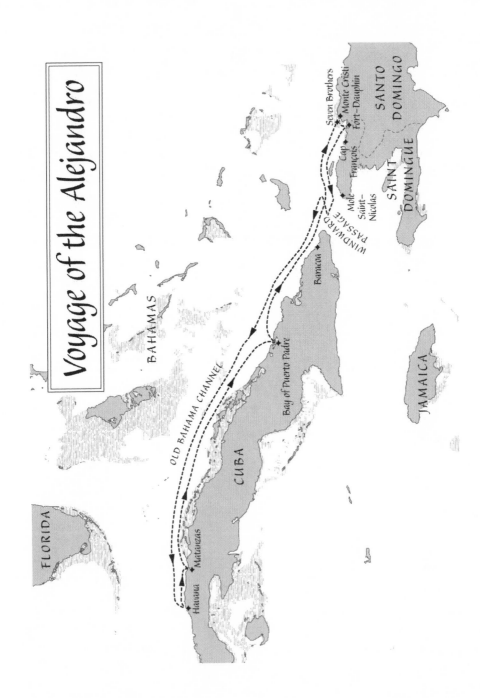

Voyage of the Alejandro

28

THE DAY OF THE MAMEYS

José made the most of his remaining time in Havana, enjoying the company of his schoolmates. They would meet in homes or in a comfortable tavern near the *colegio*. At their last gathering, before he left again with Tío Policarpo, they had raised a glass to Rafael.

"To absent friends," said Sebastián, raising his glass.

Diego crossed himself and said, "I say a prayer for him whenever I am at Mass."

"Then God's ears must be sore by now," said Mauricio. It was no secret that when Diego finished his studies, he wished to become a Jesuit.

"He is not dead," protested José. "He will return, and I will work in my father's shop again."

"God willing," said Diego, and crossed himself again. The others followed suit, all except Sebastián.

"My father says that Miguel is now a midshipman," said Mauricio. "He loves you so much that he has followed you to sea, José."

José had not seen Miguel since he had uttered those cruel words to him after the declamation. He felt the guilt slice through his gut like a cold sword and was silent. The noisy cries of men at the next table, celebrating a comrade's name day, diverted his friends' attention from his pained expression.

"Why are you not in the Navy, Mauricio?" asked Diego. "Your father could easily arrange it."

"He is already working on it. He is talking to the captains of the ships in the harbor, looking for one who will take on another young gentleman," replied Mauricio, raising his voice a bit to be heard over the revelry at the next table.

"If we go to war with the English, you might have a chance to fight and win prize money. This may prove a great chance for Miguel," said Sebastián.

"He may also have the chance to be killed. Perhaps that will be the fate of my stepfather," said Antonio, sweeping a stray lock of fine hair from his forehead. "I can pray that it will be so."

"God forgive you for such talk!" said Anastasio, echoing the thoughts of the others.

"He has tried to send me off to the army, but Father Borrero found me a position as a clerk at the Royal Shipyard. I will not leave my mother alone with him. If God does not take him and spare my poor mother, I will be obliged to do something," said Antonio, unrepentant. "When you become a priest like your father, you can pray for me."

"You know that bastards cannot enter the priesthood," replied Anastasio, unoffended.

"Then why are you in the university?" asked Mauricio.

"I like school," said Anastasio, struggling to be heard over the song that had begun at the next table. "I think I shall become a doctor."

"Speaking of the army, have you seen Tomás? He has been parading about the city in his new uniform like a peacock, and all the girls are swooning over him," said Mauricio. The tavern keeper appeared at his elbow with a bottle, and Mauricio nodded his assent.

"What of the rest of Catiline's followers? I have seen Pedro helping his father at his shop on the Calle de Mercaderes. He tried to cheat us on the payment for some Dutch teacups, but his father caught him and dragged him to the back by his ear," inquired José, who also permitted his glass to be refilled.

"I should like to have seen that!" laughed Mauricio. "I know that Francisco has gone to help run his father's estancia near Güines. I hear they will begin planting sugar if they can find the slaves."

"Vidal is a clerk at the Royal Shipyard, like me," said Antonio. He hesitated, then added, "He is pleasant enough when you get to know him. He invited me to attend a concert last week." He peered into his glass, but did not drink.

Sebastián swirled his wine in his glass and spoke. "That will last until he becomes your superior. Which will not be long, for his father will make certain of his promotion."

"I met Virgilio working in customs when we returned from Monte Cristi," José interjected.

"How can that be? *Pardos* cannot hold official positions," asked Diego. He was well into his second glass.

"When your father is as close to the Captain-General as Don Julio Altamarino, such laws no longer apply," said Mauricio.

"Sebastián, I thought you would be in university in Spain by now, learning to speak through your nose and look down upon mere colonials," said Anastasio. This elicited a laugh all around.

"The talk of war has put all our plans in abeyance for now," replied Sebastián. "In the meantime, my father has found me a French tutor. And he has encouraged me to find a better circle of acquaintance."

"Perhaps if we lithped we would prove suitable," said Mauricio, mocking a Castilian accent.

"Perhaps if you had read a book that was not assigned by the Fathers you would not be such a great ninny," said Sebastián, giving Mauricio a playful punch in the shoulder.

These were familiar discussions, and it was their very familiarity that José loved. Decades might pass, and they would still be here, in some comfortable tavern, sharing a bottle of wine, reminiscing over their youth. This was where he belonged, in one of the greatest cities in the world, his city, surrounded by friends, in the bosom of his family. And this was where he would always be.

He was returning from a visit with his friends when he encountered Father Borrero just leaving the house with the blue door.

"José, how good to see you safely home. Your father needs you now more than ever. The loss of his brother pains him deeply," Father Borrero said.

"If he needs me, why is he sending me off on the *Alejandro* again?" José burst out, regretting his angry words as he spoke them.

"You do not know how much it pains him," replied the priest. "This is but one more in a long litany of sacrifices he has made.

"And how do you fare?" Father Borrero continued. He looked José up and down, then looked into his eyes. "You are older now."

"I am sixteen," replied José proudly.

"I do not speak of chronology," smiled Father Borrero gently.

He continued, "How you must grieve Rafael! May our Lord be with him. And to lose your uncle as well."

José stood there, silent, as conflicting emotions tore at him. He remembered Tío Domingo standing boldly on the quarterdeck, a mad light in his eye as he guided them through the storm. He remembered his smile, his charms, the warmth and laughter he brought into a room. He remembered riding high above the world, when Tío Domingo swept him up on his shoulders. He also remembered his uncle's angry words for his father, his contempt for God and country, his sly dealings as he pursued his own advantage.

At last he spoke, his voice choking, "I had wished to be free of his influence, but I never..."

"Of course you did not," replied Father Borrero, placing a comforting hand on his shoulder. "You must light a candle for him, and for Rafael as well."

José doubted that there were candles enough in the world to redeem a heart so hardened against God.

Father Borrero turned to go.

José called after him, "Did you ever receive a visit from a man named Renzo?"

Father Borrero stopped, turned, and paused before he spoke. "He was on the *Orfeo*, yes?"

"Yes," replied José.

"He was a man with a deeply penitent heart," replied Father Borrero.

I n the time that remained before departure, José plotted with Agustín to save the shop should Papá become too ill to work. He prayed that the *Orfeo* would somehow appear at last, and he could return to the shop. Agustín was already a journeyman joiner, and he and José would run it together. They could find apprentices, and if necessary hire or purchase slaves. If the shop were sufficiently prosperous, he could in time free Agustín – if the *Orfeo* returned.

Señor Morejón was delighted to inform Tío Policarpo and Tío Gaspar that, thanks to the intervention of Commander Castellón, the Navy had decided to hire the *Alejandro* and the *Penélope* to transport wood from a small port east of Matanzas to the Royal Shipyard. On the outgoing leg of the voyage, the vessels would travel in ballast. For this reason Commander Castellón made a special request of them.

"We have many troops new to the island. Already they are dropping like flies from the yellow fever. Some of the officers brought wives and children. They are eager to escape the pestilence of the city. Perhaps you could carry some of them to Matanzas, where they could find lodgings in the hills, away from the miasmas of the towns," he suggested, and Señor Morejón agreed.

The yellow fever had indeed returned to Havana. Most Habaneros were un-afraid of the fever, for they had already had it as children. And *morenos* and *pardos* were little affected, in any case. It was the new arrivals, the *blancos*, who suffered, and some of the young children. A *blanco* child on their street had already died. The shop Zum-Zum was busy hammering together coffins, and almost every day funeral processions could be seen heading towards one of the city gates to the cemetery outside of the city.

They set sail on Monday, the 31st of May. Mamá had seized upon the idea that the Albañez family should also visit Matanzas. Abuelo and Abuelita were growing frailer, and she longed to spend more time with them. Papá, at the urging of Mamá, decided to travel with them. Mamá thought that the sea air and rest would have a restorative effect on his health. Agustín would stay behind and mind the shop, under the watchful eye of Señor Morejón.

Señora Morejón took it into her head to accompany them, along with Marianela, perhaps seeking to flee the reminders of her missing son. Señor Morejón saw her off with relief.

"Dionisia will take care of us," he reassured Señora Morejón as he bussed her on the cheek.

"Well, and who will see to Dionisia?" she fussed.

She was traveling on the *Penélope*, as she now avoided the company of José whenever possible, for he reminded her of the missing Rafael. José was sorry, for he would have liked Marianela to have seen him at work, handling sail and taking his turn at the helm. Magdalena wished to be with Marianela, so she and Mamá were also on the *Penélope*. Papá, however, chose to join José on the *Alejandro*. The two sloops were accompanied by the *Tetis*, a 22-gun frigate, the *Fénix*, an armed storeship, and the brig *Triunfo*, carrying 16 guns.

"Take care," said Mamá, kissing him on the cheek. "We will see you in a few days."

It would indeed be several days' sail to Matanzas, for they would be beating against the wind. José felt at home on the *Alejandro* now, and needed no instruction on his duties. He saw what needed to be done, and did it. Calixto saved his admonitions for Cristóbal, who accepted them with a smile.

They had a gaggle of naval wives and offspring with them, accompanied by maids, sleeping in the great cabin by night and resting themselves under the awning by day. Tío Policarpo and the crew slept on deck, or slung hammocks in the hold when it rained. Cristóbal had orders to procure the best of provisions for the trip, and brought on board a bevy of chickens, along with a veritable rainbow of ripe fruits and vegetables.

"Zey will never forget zeir dinners on ze *Alejandro*, zis I promise you," he said, kissing his fingers.

Calixto glowered at him. "That is what I fear. We shall become notorious for poisoning the wives of the Admiralty."

His fears proved unfounded, for the ladies exclaimed over his cooking.

"You must share your receipts with my cook," said Doña Ynés.

"There are families in Havana that would gladly offer you employment," added Doña Gertrudis. "Or perhaps your master might be willing to sell you, if you are a slave."

"He is a free man, and has employment already," intervened Calixto.

Cristóbal was gracious and solicitous, and the ladies were enchanted with him. He did not complain when the children climbed on his back or ran off with his onions. Only once did he forget himself and begin to sing, but was saved when Calixto fell upon him with a roar.

José, Tondo, and Cipriano also did their best to make their passengers comfortable, but the task began to fray their tempers, for the children seemed to be everywhere. Or, to be precise, the boys, for the girls sat demurely with their mothers, fanning themselves or attending to their needlework. Only one forward miss attempted to flirt with José, until her mamá pulled her aside and spoke to her in sharp tones, and the young lady looked back at José in shock.

The boys were of tender age, for their older brothers were back in Spain, receiving an education appropriate to their station. They viewed the trip as a grand holiday and more than once Tondo had to pull a young lad down from the shrouds.

"No matter," said Doña Gertrudis, his adoring mother and the wife of a frigate captain. "One day he will be at sea himself as a midshipman."

"Not if his brains are first splattered on the deck," growled Cipriano. To José he whispered, "If future admirals are to be lost, best it not be on the *Alejandro*."

The boys feared Calixto and fled as he approached, but they followed Tío Policarpo about like ducklings.

"Are you a pirate? I want to hold the tiller! Make it go faster! Will you fire the guns? Can I play with your pistol? How many men have you killed?"

At this last question, Tío Policarpo turned slowly about and stood, arms akimbo. "A better question might be, how many little boys have I slain?" and they scattered, squealing. He smiled as he watched it.

Tondo, too, was a favorite, for he allowed them to climb on the cannons and play with the swivel guns. He placed a bucket upside down so that they could stand on it and look out over the gunwale and he told them about the birds and the fish. When it was time to trim the sails, he let them place their tiny fists on the sheets and let them think they were easing the lines.

Cipriano, too, had his devotees, for at the dinner hour he sat upon a locker, his game leg upon the fife rail and told stories that made their eyes widen. It was possible that half of them were true.

One diminutive enthusiast of some six years of age, Alonso, had attached himself to José like a barnacle, dogging his heels and asking endless questions, most of which were "Why?" At night he would take his cover and lie down beside José in the dark.

"Señor Albañez, are you a pirate?" he asked on their second night out.

"No," a weary José replied. "But I was once engaged to marry a pirate princess."

There was a silence that spoke of astonishment.

"She jilted me for a French count," he continued. "They had a fine wedding on the island of Guadeloupe. His Catholic Majesty attended, as did His Holiness the Pope."

"I remember that wedding," whispered Cristóbal in the dark. "The whole island was there. They served gingerbread and every guest received a pear."

There was no reply to this, for Alonso had fallen fast asleep.

The next day Doña Ynés approached José. "What do you hear from your pirate princess?" she asked with arched eyebrows.

"Nothing for some time," replied José. "She was never a good correspondent."

The crew of the *Alejandro* relished the night watches, for they had the sloop to themselves. For José, there was time then to talk with Papá. Mamá had been right. He seemed more at ease, rested, and spent the day conversing with the ladies. He did not have to be urged to take a second helping of Cristóbal's cooking.

In the evenings he reminisced with Tío Policarpo on the quarterdeck while the captain took his turn at the helm.

"Do you remember when we retook that frigate? That day is seared in my memory. How we celebrated then!" he heard Tío Policarpo saying as he arrived to relieve him from watch.

"It is the comradeship I remembered," replied Papá. "The smoke and fear, the shouting and blood, all has faded away and I remember my friends."

"I remember that Alejandro died there, right in the bow," said Tío Policarpo, pointing.

"That day I shall never forget," said Papá with a deep sigh.

Papá slept near him on deck and, before they fell asleep, they gazed at the stars and talked in their secret language.

"You're a good sailor, José. I am proud of you. Policarpo has told me that he places great reliance upon you," Papá said.

"You need me in the shop," José said stubbornly.

Papá sighed. "We are done with that. Anselmo needs you, Policarpo and Gaspar need you. You think that you can shape life like a piece of wood. Life will have its way with us. It may seem, at times, to bring naught but disappointment and grief, but God, in the end, is not stingy with his blessings. They will find us when we least expect it."

José was not sure whether Papá was still talking about him. He stared at the stars, then fatigue overtook him, and he fell asleep.

The sun rose just before six on the morning of the 2nd of June. The sky was hazy, laden with moisture from the squalls that had beset them during the night and denied them rest. José could almost see the steam rise from the deck, still damp from the rain, but an ESE breeze cooled his cheek and promised good sailing. Tío Policarpo announced that they would change to a larboard tack in a few hours and head into Matanzas. José took a turn at the helm and then turned in below as the women and children began to stir, chatting cheerfully as they prepared to end their voyage. The charms of sea travel had faded and they would be happy to disembark, tired and bedraggled, in the city of the three rivers.

Sometime after ten he was dragged from the depths of slumber by Tondo. "The captain wants all hands on deck. He has seen more sails."

He was still numb with sleep as he mounted the companionway to the deck. Tío Policarpo and Calixto were at the starboard bow, staring at the horizon, Tío Policarpo occasionally putting the glass to his eye.

"I want to see," cried Alonso, tugging at José's slops.

"Is it the English? Will we fire our cannons at them?" came the voice of Gregorio.

Calixto turned on them, scar livid. "Return to your mothers or I will flog you all roundly, and then I will flog you again just for the joy of it."

They slunk under the awning to their mothers and sisters, like puppies that had been kicked. The women looked up in shock, but remained quiet. José saw Doña Ynés take her daughter's hand. Papá was sitting with them and murmured words of reassurance.

Cipriano had the helm, and the rest of the crew paced nervously, checking and rechecking the horizon, eyeing the sails to make sure that they were set to best advantage. They had a goodly breeze, and were under just the mainsail and staysail.

At last Tío Policarpo said, "It is the English. Two frigates. They are in pursuit of the *Tetis* and the *Fénix*. Our ships have changed course and are attempting to make Matanzas, I think."

"What of the *Penélope*?" José asked. "Can you see her?"

"No," said Tío Policarpo. "Nor the *Triunfo*. We must also attempt Matanzas, while those frigates are occupied with our warships. We can be but of little interest to them."

"The war has truly come now," said José, with a sense of unease.

"How did they manage the Old Bahama Channel?" asked Tondo. "I thought the English did not know it."

"They know it now," said Calixto grimly. "The devils."

"We must change to a larboard tack and then keep coming about another six points," Tío Policarpo explained. "Ready about!"

Calixto was at the helm, and Beaubroin and Calixto were ready by the mainsheet. Tondo stood ready to ease the larboard staysail sheet, and José was standing to starboard, ready to haul the larboard sheet when the time came. "Ready!" called out each in turn.

"*Vaya con Dios*!" cried Tío Policarpo, and on this signal Calixto began to ease down the helm, and the *Alejandro* slowly headed up into the wind. As José watched the staysail begin to luff as Tondo eased his sheet, he saw something on the horizon.

The sails were rattling in the wind now, but the *Alejandro*'s momentum maintained her headway. "Helms a-lee!" came Tío Policarpo's voice.

Tondo released his sheet. "Haul taut!" called out Tío Policarpo, the order for José to begin hauling on the starboard sheet. He had been watching the jot on the horizon take the shape of a sail and did not notice that Alonso had come up behind him. Suddenly the child was in front of him, grabbing at the sheet.

"Let me help, Señor Albañez! I can do it!" Alonso grabbed at the sheet and pulled it from José's hands, but it slipped away and was dancing in the breeze. José could not reach it for the child seemed to be everywhere, twisting and turning about, clutching at the sheet. Then Doña Ynés appeared, chasing him, and now she too was between José and the flailing sheet.

The staysail continued to flap about, and the *Alejandro* began to lose headway and fell off back on her previous tack, and Tondo again made fast his sheet.

"Sail ho!" cried Cipriano, for the outline of a ship was in clear view, on a course to intercept them.

Tío Policarpo erupted in language that José had never before heard him use. The passengers huddled under the awning, snatching fearful looks at the oncoming vessel.

They attempted to change tack again, and this time were successful, but much time had been lost. They could now see the outline of every sail on the pursuing frigate.

Tío Policarpo paced the deck, stopping at times to stare at the oncoming frigate through his glass.

"She is on a pace to overhaul us," said Tío Policarpo tersely.

José's stomach gave a lurch. Could they end up prisoners – or worse? He looked at Cipriano, and the lines on his weathered face seemed deeper. There was a glint of fear in Tondo's eyes, and Calixto's knuckles on the helm were white, and he glared at the oncoming frigate as if he might frighten it off. Cristóbal feigned hope, loudly whistling a gay tune, but his cheery tune seemed forced. José mastered his fear and stood tall, looking to Tío Policarpo for direction. His uncle gave him a brief nod of approbation.

Tío Policarpo ordered the jib set, then, half an hour later, the inner jib. It was the same agonizing tedium that they had experienced in their escape from the English frigate off Hispaniola, but this time, the frigate did not fall away, but stood on, its sails becoming more distinct as the morning advanced. By midafternoon the ship would overtake them.

At noon Cristóbal handed out stale cornbread for everyone. "Something to tide you over until we reach Matanzas," he said, attempting a cheerful mien, but no one was cheered, and they downed the meal with indifference. Only the children seemed able to forget their situation.

Still the frigate came on. "Loose the topsail!" Tío Policarpo cried. "José, Tondo!"

They loosened the gaskets and the topsail fell, to be pulled taut by Cipriano below. José looked out towards their pursuer. Two more sails could be seen beyond her, joining the chase.

The *Alejandro* was straining now under all its canvas, and Calixto's face was tense as he fought to keep the tiller steady against the pull of wind and current.

It was well past noon, and they heard the boom of distant cannon fire.

"A broadside," said Tío Policarpo. He continued to pace the quarterdeck.

"You must go below now," said Papá, ushering the women and children into the hold.

Alonso tried to resist, but his mother boxed his ears and pulled him along by his arm.

"It is for your protection," said Papá.

"We are naval wives – we know how to obey," said Doña Ynés, and disappeared into the hold.

Papá looked pale, and his forehead was damp with perspiration.

"You, too, should go below, Papá," said José.

"I will stay here. I may be of use," he replied, but his voice was weak.

The frigate was close now, and José could see that its gunports were open.

"Tondo, Cristóbal, powder and shot! Ready the guns!" Tío Policarpo bellowed, descending to the main deck.

"Are you mad?" Papá shouted. "There are women and children aboard!"

"This is war," said Tío Policarpo, his eye wild. "We must fight."

"That is a frigate," said Papá, voice hoarse with urgency. "She must have forty guns."

"Either liberty or death," replied Tío Policarpo. A mania had possessed him. "That is what we used to say, you and I."

"We were younger then, and manned a privateer. We have the care of families entrusted to us. Stop this madness. Strike your colors!" Papá said. His voice was firm, but his hand was clung to the gunwale, white-knuckled.

"You do not command this vessel, *mi amigo*," replied Tío Policarpo.

José and the others carried on, readying the powder and shot, rolling out the guns, hands slippery with sweat. They did not look at the frigate, closing the distance between them by the minute. It was on their larboard quarter now, just a half mile away. Only Calixto stood unshaken at the helm.

They heard the boom of a cannon, looked up to see a single puff of smoke from the frigate's bow chaser. Perhaps it had been meant as a shot across the bow. If so, it miscarried. Or perhaps it was intended to rend the mainsail and slow their progress. If so, it missed its mark. Instead, the ill-fated ball soared across the quarterdeck and instead found the helmsman. Calixto's headless body slumped over the tiller and soaked the quarterdeck with blood. They stared in mute horror.

The weight of Calixto's body shifted the tiller and the *Alejandro* headed further to larboard, towards the frigate. Tondo raced up the companionway to the quarterdeck to grab the tiller, but slipped in blood and fell to his knees. He got up, but then doubled over, retching. After a long moment he mastered himself and took the helm. The sloop slowly resumed its course, but the frigate was bearing down upon them. And beyond it, they could see more ships, coming by the dozens, perhaps a hundred or more, a veritable forest of masts.

"Strike, by all that is holy, strike!" cried Papá, but his voice was fainter now, and he lowered himself to sit upon a coil of line.

Tío Policarpo stood, surveying the deck, and looked at the frigate with its angry gunports.

"Strike the colors," he said at last, his voice dropping, his shoulders slumped. Then, standing straighter as if to prepare himself to face the worst, he said again, but more loudly, "Strike the colors." He stood, staring at the many-masted ship before them, as Cristóbal pushed past Tondo and grabbed the flag from the stern and took it in his arms. He clutched it to him as if it were a child.

"Heave-to!" ordered Tío Policarpo, and issued the familiar commands. José and Cipriano backed the topsail, then, joined by Tío Policarpo and Cristóbal, they hauled down the headsails. José's limbs felt like lead, and they moved slowly, deliberately. José thought he could feel the frigate bearing down upon them.

The frigate approached and it, too, hove-to. Her deck was a flurry of activity as they lowered a boat and prepared to claim their prize.

There was no more that José could do, and so he stooped down beside Papá. Roberto Albañez's breathing was shallow. He looked up at José without speaking.

"She is called the *Echo*," Tío Policarpo's voice came to them. "There are two more behind her. The *Belisle* – I cannot read the name. No, I see it now. The *Culloden*."

At the sound of that name Papá gave a moan and slumped over, his eyes closed. His breathing was barely perceptible now. His eyes opened slightly. José took his moist hand, but Papá looked past him.

"Papá!" José cried. "Papá!"

"Moire..." he mumbled in Gaelic. "Take care of our boy. I'll be with you by-and-by. Do not worry yourself." His breathing became ragged.

"Soon, Moire, soon," he said again.

José squeezed Papá's hand, but there was no response. "Papá!" he cried yet again. His father's eyes did not see him, and his head lolled to one side.

Doña Ynés had appeared by his side. She took Papá's hand and felt his pulse. "He is gone," she said softly, and closed his eyes.

He could hear the oars of the English boats splashing through the waves as if they were a thousand miles away. Time stopped. Now, as he knelt on the deck, there was only him, and Papá, and his father's mysterious words. Moire. Who was Moire? There was no sea, no sky, no cries of men or wails from children. There was only José, Papá, and that name. Moire. And "our boy."

There was another name, too. Culloden. It forced itself into José's consciousness. Tío Policarpo had said that name, the name of a battle. The Scots had lost, and so the English had taken everything from Papá. They had slaughtered women and children.

Suddenly the names, the places, the words all arranged themselves into a pattern. The English had taken everything. They had taken Moire, and the boy. Moire and Papá's boy. They were his everything.

All his life he had thought that he was Papá's everything, that he was his boy. But now, at the moment of death, the moment of truth, Moire and that long-dead boy had pushed him aside. It was they who filled his dying eyes, it was for them his failing heart beat, it was their names on his lips as he breathed his last.

The cries of the English had grown louder, but he no longer feared them. There was nothing they could take from him now. He had lost everything – he had lost Papá. Or, to put it more truthfully, he had learned that he had never had Papá.

With bitterness he imagined he knew why Papá had so readily handed him over to Tío Domingo. It is easy to give up something you did not value. He looked down at Papá's body lolling on the deck, his grey face, and thought that a stranger lay before him. He had never really known this man with his secret history, the family he kept treasured deep in his heart, far away from the people he shared his home with.

He was shocked back to reality when Tondo grabbed his arm. "What will happen to us now?" he asked. His voice was hoarse with fear.

He saw Cristóbal appear from the cabin and throw a packet over the gunwale, then he heard a splash. Cristóbal ducked into the cabin and came out again with the chest of papers, which followed the packet.

"Over ze side! Over ze side!" he cried triumphantly.

"You fool!" cried Tío Policarpo in a desperate, angry voice. "That chest contained our freedom papers!"

José could feel his stomach drop away, and saw the fear on all their faces, even the imperturbable Cipriano's.

The British boat was at the side now, and there were cries for a ladder. Cipriano heaved the Jacob's ladder down to them.

José watched all this as if in a dream.

He watched as a man in a blue naval uniform came over the side, followed by men in red.

The boys had escaped from the hatch. "They look like mameys!" cried the boys. The men did indeed wear coats as bright as the red fruit of the mamey.

Tío Policarpo stood before the men, tall and commanding, every inch the man who had helped take a frigate from the English in his youthful days of war. He pulled a pistol from his belt and aimed it at the Englishmen.

"Only liberty or..." but he fell, shot through the heart by a ball from one of the mameys before he could complete the phrase. He collapsed upon the deck amid the screams of women and children. Blood flowed from his wound, into the deck boards where so many years ago Alejandro had shed his own heart's blood.

"Quién is el capitán de eso barky?" asked the man in blue in execrable Spanish.

Tío Policarpo was dead, and so too, Calixto. Who now would take responsibility for the *Alejandro* and surrender her to the English?

There were many souls on the *Alejandro*, the frightened passengers, and the leaderless crew, now acutely aware of how much danger their skin color and lack of papers placed them in. José looked about. Cristóbal was bent over the body of Tío Policarpo. "*Mon Dieu!*" he said, and, crossing himself, began to pray. He saw Tondo looking at him with pleading eyes. Cipriano stood, grizzled and worn, and he, too, looked towards José.

Someone must take charge. They had no captain now, and no mate. Cipriano, in twenty years at sea, had never attempted to rise above ordinary seaman. Tondo was not even his own master. There was little left to be done, now. The English would give the orders, set a new course for the *Alejandro*, perhaps give her a new name. Only one task remained – to negotiate with these mameys for the proper treatment of their prisoners and hopefully, their freedom. That, at least, he could do. He would use his words, the skill he had cultivated for most of his youth. And he had what the others did not – the authority that came from being the heir of Tío Domingo.

His uncle had emerged victorious. He was now responsible for the *Alejandro*, the representative of Albañez y Morejón. He must do his duty, and he would.

Duty. That was Papá's word. Duty was not the thing one wanted to do, but the thing one must do, for others, and not for one's self. Papá had done his duty, as a soldier for the Stuart prince and to his lost family in distant Scotland. And, he suddenly realized, he had done his duty to his little family in Cuba, these many years. He had done his duty to him as a father, and raised him to be a man. Now he must prove that he was worthy to be the son of Robert McIntyre, and he too, must do his duty.

He turned to the man in blue and stood up straight.

"My name is José Albañez Velázquez, and I am owner and master of this vessel."

ACKNOWLEDGEMENTS

I would like to thank the many people who helped me with this novel. I am grateful to all my readers, Paula T. Weiss, Melissa Hecht, Randy Biddle, Julie Savell-McCandless and Brian McCandless for their helpful comments. I am especially appreciate of help from Jeremy Lawrence, former bosun of Tall Ship Providence, who caught my nautical errors, and Fausta Rodriguez Wertz, who provided advise on Hispanic nomenclature and culture in the Caribbean.

I learned a great deal from the opportunity to assist with maintenance on Tall Ship *Providence*, in Alexandria Virginia. I'm especially grateful to Captain Jonathan Fay for his patient instruction.

Suggestions from my structural editor, Edward Willis at the History Quill improved the narrative, and my copy-editor, Gareth Collinson cleaned up many errors.

I have to thank my family, as well; my husband, Blaine McCants, for barely raising an eyebrow as books on Cuba and seafaring flowed into the house, year after year; my daughter Mary, for providing comments on many chapters despite the lack of dragons; and my son Russell, for the many nights he has dealt with a dinner plan that consisted of "I don't know" and "See what you can find."

Any flaws or historical errors in the text are of course, my fault, and mine alone.

HISTORICAL NOTES

The characters in *Fearful Breakers* are entirely fictitious. Only two historical individuals are mentioned: Captain Quaco, the maroon leader from Trelawny Town in Jamaica; and Captain-General Cajigal de la Vega of Cuba.

I have taken a few liberties with the siege of Havana. The *Tetis* and *Fénix* were actual Spanish ships captured by the British. They were accompanied by an unnamed brig and two schooners, all on the way to gather wood for the Royal Shipyard. I have given the brig a name, and replaced the schooners with sloops under contract from Albañez y Morejón. The *Cullodon* was also in the fleet sailing to Havana, but in the rear. I have placed it in the vanguard. Although there were no families on board, it was not unusual at the time for those who could to flee the summer fevers of the city, since the filth and miasmas there were thought to produce disease, so I thought it reasonable that Naval officers might attempt to put their families out of reach of tropical pestilences.

The sloops in the novel are modeled on Tall Ship *Providence*. Built as the *Katy*, a trading sloop, she was later one of the first ships acquired for the new United States Navy during the American Revolution. Although square-riggers get more attention, sloops were the tractor-trailers of colonial commerce in the New World. Readers who wish to tour a real sloop, take a sail, or even, like José, haul on a halyard, can visit *Providence* in her home port of Alexandria, Virginia.

Interested readers can learn more about Caribbean history on the webpage for Antimacassar Books, and keep abreast of news about the next book in the Chart and Compass series, *Treacherous Shoal*.

Made in the USA
Middletown, DE
08 October 2023

40186467R00248